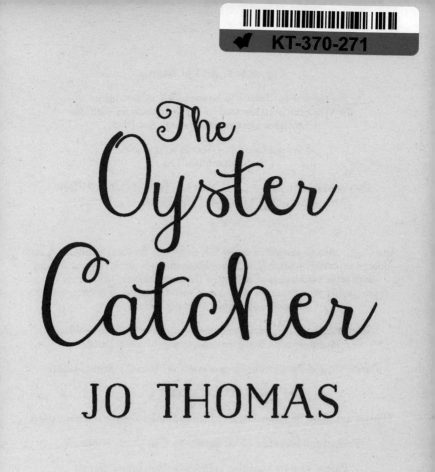

The Oyster Catcher

JO THOMAS

headline
review

First published in Great Britain in 2013
by Accent Press Ltd

First published in paperback in 2014 by HEADLINE REVIEW
An imprint of HEADLINE PUBLISHING GROUP

2

Cataloguing in Publication Data is available from the British Library

ISBN 978 1 4722 2368 5

Typeset in Caslon by Avon DataSet Ltd, Bidford-on-Avon, Warwickshire

Printed and bound in Great Britain by Clays Ltd, St Ives plc

Papers used by Headline are from well-managed forests
and other responsible sources.

HEADLINE PUBLISHING GROUP
An Hachette UK Company
338 Euston Road
London NW1 3BH

www.headline.co.uk
www.hachette.co.uk

To Mum,
for always being there and telling me to keep going

Chapter One

A bracing blast of sea air hits me head on. It's clean, fresh and smells of salt. I'm standing on the steps of the Garda station. Mind you, it's more of a shabby Portakabin than a police station, really. The wind blows my hair and I hold my face up to it, letting any tears that may have escaped mingle with the damp air. With my eyes shut and my face in the wind I realise two things. One, I'm in a place called Dooleybridge; and two, I am absolutely stranded wearing the only dress I have – the one I'd just got married in.

I open my eyes and shiver, pulling my arms tightly around me, trying to warm myself up and protect myself from the nightmare I'm in. Only forty-eight hours ago I was saying the words 'I do' and thought I had everything I wanted in life: a job, a home and a husband. It was all mapped out. Now I have no husband, not even a fiancé. I've left my job, my home and my life, in a stolen camper van that I'm apparently under caution for stealing, parking illegally and driving recklessly.

In a state of shock I walk back to where I'd last seen the camper. Well, where it'd come to a crunching halt after crashing into the harbour wall. Looking at the wall now, I don't know how I didn't see it. But I was very distracted at the time, to say the least. I remember the road getting bumpier and hitting some big pot holes. I could hardly see through the tears. I remember the final bend, not knowing whether to swing left or right. It all happened so fast. My heart was racing and suddenly the van was as out of control as the rest of my life. I couldn't stop. Today was supposed to be the first day of my married life. Now it couldn't be further from how I'd imagined.

I roll my shoulders back and rub my neck. A doctor visited me in the Garda station but said my injuries were nothing a hot bath and some TLC wouldn't cure. Maybe he's right, but I'm a long way from either of those things right now. A very long way indeed. And now the camper van has been reclaimed by the hire company and towed away, I have no idea what I'm going to do.

There are some scuff marks on the harbour wall and the remains of one of the headlights, but other than that I can't see any trace that the camper was there at all. I bend down to pick up the light and look around to see if anyone's watching me, but no one's there. Not like earlier when I had been escorted to the Garda station by a uniformed officer. With blue lights flashing we'd travelled all of 200 metres from the crashed camper to the station. You'd think he'd caught one of Ireland's most wanted criminals. I could feel eyes on me from everywhere – the doorway of the pub and the windows of the houses – as the sirens sang out and the lights lit up the buildings either side of the road. My cheeks had burned and my stomach twisted as I was escorted, in my wedding dress, from 'the scene of the crime'.

Oh, that's the other thing I realise as I look at the abandoned headlight in my hand: there's absolutely no way I can go home, no way at all.

I turn round and walk back towards the road; when I say walk, it's more of a hobble. My shoes are killing me and they're splashing water up the back of my feet and calves. But then it isn't really gold mule weather. It's cold and wet and I couldn't feel any more miserable than I already do. I head back up the hill, across the road just below the Garda station, and stand outside the pub. I pull a piece of paper from my pocket and look at my shaky handwriting. I must be mad even thinking about this. I'd jotted down the details of a job advertised in the paper I'd been looking through as I tried to distract myself from the wreckage of my life while the Garda filled in his report. I have no idea what made me copy it down. Maybe it's just my survival instinct kicking in, sink or swim.

I take a deep breath that hurts my chest and makes me cough. I look at the paper again. I have no other choice. I put my head down and step into a tiled doorway, touching the cold brass panel on the door, and with all the determination I can muster, I push it open.

The door crashes against the wall as I fall in, making me and everyone else jump. As I land I realise it's not the throng I was expecting but a handful of people. All eyes are on me. A hot rash travels up my chest and into my cheeks, making them burn, and inside I cringe. I feel as though I've walked on to the set of a spaghetti western and the piano player has stopped playing.

'Sorry,' I mouth, and shut the door very gently behind me. My stomach's churning like a washing machine on spin cycle. I look round the open-plan pub. At one end is a small fireplace and, despite it supposedly being summer, there's a fire in the grate giving out a brave, cheery, orange glow in contrast to the chilly atmosphere. There's an unfamiliar smell

3

in the air, earthy yet sweet. In the grate there are lumps of what look like burning earth. Back home I'd just flick on the central heating, but home is a very long way away right now. There's wood panelling all across the front of the bar, above it, below it and round the walls. When I say wood panelling, it's tongue and groove pine that's been stained dark. It's the sort of place you'd expect to be full of cigarette smoke but isn't. In the corner by the fire there's a small group of people, all of them as old as Betty from Betty's Buns. Or The Coffee House as it's now known.

Betty's my employer – or should that be my ex-employer? She refuses to take retirement and sits on a stall at the end of the counter, looking like Buddha. She's never been able to give up the reins on the till. She did once ask me to take over as manager but I turned it down. I'm not one for the limelight. I'm happy back in the kitchen. Kimberly, who works the counter, tried for the job, but Sandra from TGI Friday's got it and Kimberly took up jogging and eating fruit.

The group by the fire is still staring at me, just like Betty keeping her beady eye on her till. There are two drinkers at the bar, one in an old tweed cap and jacket with holes in the elbows, the other in a thin zip-up shell suit and a baseball cap. They've turned to stare at me too. With burning cheeks and the rash still creeping up my chest, I take a step forward and then another. It feels like a game of grandmother's footsteps as their eyes follow me too. The barmaid's wiping glasses and smiles at me. I feel ridiculously grateful to see a friendly face. It's not her short spiky hair that makes her stand out, nor her big plastic Dayglo earrings. It's the fact she's probably in her early twenties, I'd say, unlike any of her customers.

A couple of dogs come barking at me from behind the bar. I step back. One is black with stubby legs, a long body and a white stripe down its front. The other is fat and looks a bit like a husky crossed with a pot-bellied pig. I'm not what you'd call brave really. I've always thought it was better to try and skirt conflict rather than face it head on. I look for someone or something to hide behind but the barmaid steps in.

'Hey, settle down,' she snaps. She might be small but she's got a mighty bark. Unsurprisingly the dogs return behind the bar, tails between their legs. I think I'd've done the same if she'd told me to.

'Now then, what can I get you?' She wipes her hands on a tea towel and smiles again.

'Um . . .' I go to speak but nothing comes out. I clear my dry throat and try again. 'I'm looking for . . .' I look down at the piece of paper in my hand, the back of the parking ticket I was handed for parking a camper van illegally. It was the only paper I had. I still can't believe I'm even contemplating this, but I'm just not sure what else I can do. I look back at the barmaid, feeling as confused as she seems. '. . . Sean Thornton?' I say as firmly as I can. 'I'm looking for Sean Thornton.'

The barmaid cocks her head to one side and frowns. She reaches up on tip-toes and leans over the bar. Unashamedly her eyes travel upwards, taking in my shoes and the torn hem of my dress. I tug at it. Bits of hanging cotton, like tassels, catch round my fingers. Some come away and I shake my hand to flick them off. The rash starts to creep up my chest again.

Finally the barmaid nods over to the opposite side of the

bar from where everyone else is sitting. There's a man on his own. He looks up at me.

'Over there,' she nods again, keeping her eyes on me, as if I've got two heads which may start spinning in opposite directions at any minute.

'Thank you.' I turn to look at the man in the worn wax jacket. He looks terrifying. He's got a table to himself and I'm not surprised. He's scowling, tapping a pen on a notebook and making the white cup and saucer next to him rattle. He looks up at me and raises an eyebrow then beckons me with a single flick of the wrist. I'm rooted to the spot as he impatiently calls me over again. What I should do is leave very quickly. But my feet won't move. He does not look like the sort of person you'd pull up a chair with for a friendly chat.

'Oh, looks like someone's beaten you to it,' says the barmaid as we watch the younger of the two men from the bar, the one in the shell suit, go over and speak to Sean Thornton. 'Can I get you something while you wait?' she says a little more cheerily. I feel my spirits plummet even lower, and I hadn't thought that was remotely possible, as I look over at the man in the shell suit, sitting on a small green velour-covered stool opposite Sean Thornton.

'Do you do tea?' I sigh rather more loudly than I'd intended to. The group in the corner is still watching me.

'Tea? Sure.' The barmaid picks up a pen and pad. 'Anything to eat?'

I shake my head, thinking about the few euros I've got left after paying the damages at the Garda station. 'For reckless driving,' he'd said. He was probably right too. My stomach suddenly rumbles loudly, like a lion's roar. My hand shoots up to cover both it and my blushes at the same time.

'Soup and a sandwich,' the barmaid tells me rather than asks, with a raised eyebrow.

'Fine,' I quickly agree.

The barmaid flicks on the kettle with a flourish. I can't help but feel she's still keeping an eye on me. Now that she's moved to the back of the bar, I can see she's wearing purple leather-look shorts with tights underneath and a red T-shirt saying 'Drama Queen' in sparkles. In contrast I look down at my big grey sweatshirt and nude-coloured tatty dress.

'On holiday, are you?' she shouts over the noisy kettle, cutting into my thoughts.

'Um, well, not exactly. Well, sort of.' I can't answer this without going into a long explanation and that's the last thing I want to do right now. 'Excuse me,' I try and change the subject quickly. 'Could you tell me where the loo is?' To my surprise she put her hands on her hips and shakes her head. The kettle is still warming up noisily.

'Daloo?' She shakes her peroxide head again and then to my bigger surprise says, 'No, can't say I've ever heard of it.' She looks genuinely puzzled. For a moment I freeze and then the penny drops. OK, very funny. It's that Irish humour. I try and join in the joke and laugh good-naturedly.

'Hey, John Joe,' the barmaid calls over to the group huddled by the fire. Oh dear God, please don't tell me this is happening, that it's some sort of prank they pull on holiday-makers looking for the toilet.

'Any ideas where Daloo is?'

An elderly man in a holey jumper shakes his head.

'What about you, Evelyn? You've got kids living all over the place, any idea where Daloo is?'

Evelyn's in an oversized anorak. She turns down her mouth and shakes her head.

'Frank? Any ideas?'

Frank scratches the black spiral curls poking out from under his woollen hat.

'Grandad? What about you? If anyone knows about this place it's you.'

Someone nudges Grandad awake and he splutters.

'Daloo! She's looking for Daloo!' Evelyn shouts at him. He shakes his head and goes back to sleep, resting his elbows on the arms of his wheelchair and letting his head fall forwards.

If there really is a God, would he just let the floor open up now and let me fall through it? I look up to the ceiling and shut my eyes in hope. Nothing. Just like my mother, He's never been around when I've needed Him either.

'I think . . .' a voice pipes up next to me and makes me jump. My eyes ping open. Sean Thornton is standing beside me. The man in the shell suit is back at the bar, picking up his pint and shaking his head. 'I think,' he repeats slowly and quietly, 'that the lady is looking for the bathroom.' He puts down his cup and saucer on the bar. 'Through there to the left,' he points, and gratefully I put my head down and scuttle in that direction.

I grab hold of the porcelain sink and splash water over my face and then attempt to dry it with a stiff paper towel, which just inflicts pain. I look into the mottled mirror. The person staring back scares me. I hardly recognise myself. My eyes are swollen, my face blotchy and red, and I look as if I've aged ten years. A far cry from the blushing bride that left home yesterday.

'Sean told me to put your food over there,' the barmaid says a little sulkily as I return from the loo, like someone who's been told off. She goes back to polishing the glasses.

On a table tucked round the other side of the bar a bowl of steaming orange soup and a huge doorstep sandwich is waiting for me. My stomach roars again in expectation.

'Thought you might like to eat somewhere a little more private.' Sean Thornton nods to the group on the other side of the pub.

'Thank you,' I say and go to sit down.

'No problem. I'd like to say they mean well, but . . . I can't,' he says, throwing a look first at the locals on the other side of the bar and then at the two standing next to it. They pull down their hats and turn in towards each other. I realise I need to seize my opportunity.

'Actually, are you Sean Thornton?' I pick up the red paper napkin by my bowl and twist it in my hands. I try and smile but it probably looks more like a grimace.

'I am,' he says evenly and stares right back at me, making me feel nervous. There's no humour in his eyes.

'Good.' My throat is drying again. 'In that case,' I say really quickly, with what feels like a tennis ball in my throat, 'I've come about the job.'

Chapter Two

Just like the barmaid, he looks at me first in the face and then up and down, taking in the scuffed gold, kitten-heeled shoes, the dress with the newly fashioned, torn hemline, and the big baggy sweatshirt.

I flap my arms by my sides. 'Sorry, didn't have time to change.' I feel as ridiculous as I no doubt look. When he says nothing back, I cringe and my toes begin to curl. Then my stomach roars again.

'Sounds like your stomach thinks your throat's been cut. Tell you what, take a seat, eat your soup and then we'll chat,' and he goes back to looking at his notes.

I sit down self-consciously, pick up the spoon and sip the soup. It's warm and really tasty and I'm already feeling better. I look at the sandwich. I'm hungry but the knot in my guts won't let me eat it. Besides, it's hard to eat when you know you're being watched.

I'm just finishing the bowl of soup when the man with the mass of unbrushed spiral ringlets comes over and stands in front of Sean Thornton, spilling some of the pint he's carrying.

'How are ya, Frank?' Sean says politely, but there's a stiffness in his voice.

'Good, Sean, good. Now about this job. Evelyn says you

10

advertised in the *Galway Advertiser* for an assistant. And it's been on the Face Book, or was it Twatter? On the world wide web, anyways. Well, reckon I could fit the bill.' He has one hand in his pocket and is waving the pint around with the other, spilling a little more. 'I know my way around the farm and I'm local.'

'Ah, I wish I could offer it to you, Frank, but I'm looking for someone who can do some office work too, take phone messages, write them down, that kind of thing,' he says with an apologetic shrug. Frank nods and shrugs back. Then he turns to rejoin the group on the other side of the bar.

'Nice bloke but wants to fight the whole town with a drink inside him,' Sean says in a low voice. Surprised by this aside, I watch Frank as he reseats himself unsteadily on a high bar stool.

I dab the corners of my mouth nervously with the twisted paper napkin. Right, now it's my turn, I think, and take a deep breath, although I have no idea where or how to start. I put down the napkin and turn to Sean. Suddenly the woman I recognise as Evelyn, in her oversized anorak zipped up to her neck, marches quickly over and stands in front of Sean.

'I understand you're looking for someone up at the farm. I'm available,' she says curtly. My heart sinks. Sean looks thoughtful, even a little amused.

'Evelyn, you and John Joe have your own farm to worry about.' He tucks his reading glasses into his top pocket. 'This isn't for you,' he says, picking up a drinks mat and turning it over in his hands.

'Well, that's as may be, but the extra money wouldn't go amiss,' says Evelyn with a conciliatory sniff.

"Fraid it's more board and lodgings and pocket money,' he says with another apologetic shrug. Evelyn gives him a sharp nod and walks back quickly to her group. Now it's my turn. It has to be. I take another deep breath and go to stand when suddenly the barmaid appears with a pint of Guinness and puts it down in front of Sean. Don't tell me she's after the job as well, I think, flopping back down.

'Thought you looked as if you could do with this,' she says flirtatiously.

'Ah, Margaret, you're very good,' he smiles, accepting the pint.

'My horoscope said that an act of kindness would reap its rewards today.' She pulls out a damp cloth from her pocket and starts wiping his table. I get the impression she's keeping one eye on Sean and another on me.

'At least someone round here doesn't think I'm bad through and through,' he says, lifting the glass with its creamy top to his lips.

'They do not think that. Didn't three of them come and ask about the job?' She wipes down my table and scoops up my plate and bowl. 'Are you finished with that?' She looks miffed at the untouched sandwich.

'Yes, sorry.'

She turns her back on me and her attention onto Sean.

'That's only because they want to find out why I need an assistant,' Sean says, finally sipping the pint. It leaves creamy foam on his top lip that he sucks off.

'You're obviously looking for something quite specific . . .' and she sounds like she's fishing too. Either that or she's trying to put me off – which, in fact, she does.

I don't know what I'm doing here. It's a mad idea. I mean,

what do I know about farming? He's turned down three applicants already. Why put myself through even more humiliation? I'll have to think of something else. I stand up to leave, pick up my small carrier bag of belongings, pull down the disintegrating hem of my dress, lift my chin a little and make for the door.

'Hey!' He stops me in my tracks. 'I thought you'd come about the job?'

Not wanting to be made any more of a spectacle, I turn back.

'I just don't think . . .'

'Sit yourself down. We won't know until we've talked,' he says. My shoulders slump as I turn and sit on the little stool in front of him.

'Would you like something to drink?' he asks, gesturing to the barmaid.

'Could I possibly have a glass of tap water?' It might help my dry throat and the twisting, sick feeling in my stomach.

'Sure.' He looks up and catches the barmaid's eye. The barmaid gives me a look so icy it could freeze the sea and then goes back behind the bar.

'So, tell me, what's your name?' He slides his glasses back on and looks at me over them, making me feel like the new girl in school all over again, and, God knows, there'd been a lot of new schools.

'Fi—' I suddenly stop without finishing my full name. The last thing I need is for anyone to come looking for me. I don't want anyone to know who I am, just in case. And the best way I can do that is to change my name. I learnt very early on, when starting another new school, that the only way to get on was to keep your head down and become invisible. And that's what I need to do right now; I need to become invisible . . . again.

'Fi?' He looks up from writing it down. I can't think of a surname, my mind's gone blank.

'Hm, just Fi,' I nod, hoping I've carried it off.

'Surname?' he asks.

I'm stumped. 'Er . . .'

There's a silence which he finally fills. 'You're English, right?' He waves his pen at me.

'Sort of.' I don't want to tell him my name any more than I want to say where I've come from. I don't want anything to connect me to home. I mean, who knows, I could be trending on Twitter by now and another little piece of me dies with embarrassment. 'Moved around a lot,' I say through a dry mouth.

'English . . .' he writes down.

'That's right, Fi English.' I'm not great at thinking on my feet but that'll do. If my shambolic wedding becomes an internet sensation, no one here will be any the wiser.

He looks at me.

'Fi English,' he repeats slowly.

Tiredness is starting to get the better of me. I just need to get this over and done with and then I'll have to work out where I'm going to stay tonight.

'And what skills do you think you could bring to the table?' He's looking right at me over his glasses again. It feels as though he can see into my soul and knows everything about me. He has a long nose that looks like it could have been broken a few times. Maybe he's played a lot of sport. Or maybe he's got into one too many fights, I think guardedly.

He pushes back his long curly hair from his weather-beaten face while he waits for my answer.

'Well, I, um, I . . .' My mind has gone completely blank again. I'd be like this on *Who Wants to Be a Millionaire*. I hate pressure. It's all very well Brian and me shouting the answers at the telly from the comfort of the leather settee, but if I was actually there I doubt I'd even be able to get my favourite colour right. I'd probably answer brown instead of lilac. Lilac always reminds me of the garden of a foster home I stayed in once. But this isn't helping me think about my skills. Come on, brain!

'Tell you what, how about we start with proper introductions. I'm Sean Thornton and I've advertised for an assistant, a Girl Friday so to speak, to help me out on my farm. I've got . . . a lot on and I need extra help.' He looks over at the rubber-neckers in the corner. The barmaid returns and puts down the water in front of me.

'And this is Margaret,' he says with a little laugh as she puts her hands on her hips and cocks her head, 'our friendly barmaid.'

'Hey!' she flicks him playfully with a tea towel. I find a little smile tugging at the corner of my mouth, or maybe it's just the tension relaxing a little. I really need this job. I've got nowhere to stay and no money. There's a lot to feel tense about.

'Thank you,' I say, and sip the water.

'You're welcome,' she replies, and turns to go back to the bar.

'So, do you have any experience in the food production industry?' he asks as Margaret sashays away without him really noticing. He's looking right at me. Suddenly, I can answer this one.

'Oh yes! I've worked in a bakery since I was fifteen,' I say, slightly encouraged. 'And I work answering the phones at a local radio station at the weekends,' I add, remembering what he'd said earlier. Or should that be 'worked'?

'Any other skills, courses you've been on?'

'Well, I did a health and safety course at work,' I offer, and he writes it down and then when I can't think of anything else, I add, 'and a sailing course once too.' My mouth dries and I sip the water again.

'And you see yourself being here for a while?' He looks at me seriously. I'm not sure what to say, but I do know I need this job. I nod.

'No family here?' He's making notes on his pad. Under the table I feel for my wedding ring. It slides around my finger. I turn my engagement ring into my palm. It's harder to move as it's been on there a long time. I slide it up my finger and rub the dent it's left. I slide it back and shake my head.

'No, no family.'

'So you don't know the area very well?' he quizzes me.

I shake my head again. I have a feeling this is taking a downturn.

'And it's just the bakery work you're used to, no other food?'

Again, and feeling rather pathetic now, I shake my head. He looks at his notebook again, then starts to put it away. Now what am I going to do? I'll have to go back to the Garda in the Portakabin, if he hasn't clocked off, and tell him I'm stuck. If I thought today couldn't get any worse, it just did.

'Well,' I give a little cough. 'Thanks anyway.' I go to stand, feeling a little choked. Sean suddenly turns back to me with a huge smile on his face.

'Where are you going?'

'I take it I'm not what you're looking for,' I say, not needing to hear his reply.

'You've no experience and no knowledge of the area,' he states the obvious. 'You're exactly what I'm looking for! When can you start?' His eyes are wild and excited and his change of tack completely disarms me, like Willy Wonka in *Charlie and the Chocolate Factory* – you never really knew what he was going to say or do next.

'You're joking, right?' is all I can think of saying.

He shakes his head, still smiling.

There are so many questions I should be asking but I'm so grateful I just say, 'Thank you,' and, 'Right away, if that's OK?'

I should ask the questions, of course. But it's bed, board and crap pay; exactly what I need right now.

'Perfect!' He gathers up his belongings. 'Come on, let's get out of here.' He looks over at the group by the fire. 'Statler and Waldorf have got nothing on this lot.' He picks up his battered brown briefcase and does up his wax jacket.

'Who?'

He laughs.

'Let's get you settled in.' He looks around. 'No luggage?'

'Travelling light,' I reply quickly. Suddenly the memory of running down the cobbled path of the church as fast as my kitten heels would let me, holding my dress up to my knees as my flower tiara slipped from my head, comes crashing back, like something out of a film. Only it wasn't a film. I remember the horror I felt as everyone looked at me. I had to get away, and sprinted towards the waiting camper van minutes after we'd been pronounced man and wife.

Sean shrugs, seeming to accept my simple explanation, even though the reality is far from simple, and I follow him out of the pub and down to the harbour car park where any last links with my past life have all but disappeared. I stare for a moment at the space where the camper van had been, when I had been Mrs Brian Goodchild.

Now I'm Fi English.

Sean opens the door to a red Transit van and a large sandy-coloured Great Dane jumps out.

'This is Grace,' he says as she sniffs around my feet and nudges me with her big black nose. 'She used to be Gary, according to the tag on her collar, but I think Grace suits her much better.' He whistles and the dog jumps back in the van. I climb in next to her and stretch to pull the heavy door shut. As we drive away from the harbour I feel I'm leaving my past life behind. Like footprints in the sand, very soon there will be no trace Mrs Brian Goodchild ever existed at all.

Chapter Three

'How come she used to be Gary?' I ask, stroking the gentle dog's head.

'She was abandoned, down on the beach. Probably a summer surfing crowd, thought she looked cool. They hadn't even worked out what sex she was.' He pushes through the gears and we head off out of town along the coast. Grace lies down, her front legs over my lap, and I'm grateful for the distraction.

'So what kind of a farm is it?' I finally think of something sensible to ask.

'Sorry?' He looks at me and then back at the road. He indicates and we veer off up a single-track lane. The van sways from side to side, much like when I was in the camper van, only this time there's a Great Dane in the cab too. Her hair's whizzing round as the heaters blow warm air at us and it feels like I'm inside a Dyson vacuum cleaner.

'I mean, are you pigs, cows, arable . . . ?' All of which I know nothing about, but as it sounds like the job's going to be office-based, it doesn't much matter to me. I quite like the idea of looking out on fields of wheat or corn.

My new boss laughs, which is a little unnerving and actually a little irritating too. 'This is Galway, you know that much, right?' He looks from me to the road and back at me again. I nod. He grips the steering wheel and laughs some more. 'Look around you.' He waves towards the scenery. 'It's nothing but bog land.' He points to one side of the road. 'Not much good for anything.'

I'm confused. On the other side of the road there's nothing but the sea. He gives another little laugh, irritating me some more. His dark curls shake.

'I'm an oyster farmer. That's my farm out there.' He points to the vast expanse of sea. I wonder if he's joking, but he isn't, I can tell by his face.

Holy cow! I sink into my seat. Why on earth hadn't I asked before? What am I going to do now?

The single-track lane comes to an end. There's a 'no entry' sign and the lane turns into an overgrown track. If I thought the road before was rough, it was nothing in comparison to this. My soup feels like it's sloshing around in my stomach and for a moment I'm worried it's going to come back up again. Finally we come to a pair of gates to the right of the track and Sean pulls in. There's another 'no entry' sign.

He drives the van down a slope and then yanks on the handbrake, hard. There's a large green corrugated shed in front of us, behind that a small white cottage. To my right is the ruin of a house, or maybe a barn. It's an old white stone building with a russet-coloured corrugated roof. It may once have been thatched. Now it just looks tired and abandoned. The irony of that isn't lost on me. And beyond that . . . water, lots and lots of water, which is probably as bad as it gets for someone who's terrified of the stuff.

As I push open the heavy van door and step out, the smell hits me as quickly as the wind. Salt and seaweed scratch at a memory and give me goosebumps. The wind slaps me across the cheeks, even harder than before, stinging this time. It's like it's punishing me for being so stupid. Strands of my hair whip my eyeballs like an unruly mob on the rampage. Peeling them back I can see Sean picking his way up some higgledy-piggledy concrete steps to the cottage behind the big green shed. I cling to the door, using it as a shield against the weather. This is supposed to be June!

Grace pushes past me, nearly making my knees buckle as she catapults from the van over to the rocks, sniffing for messages. It's a bit like texting for dogs, I think. She stops and leaves her reply.

I stare out. There's a stream right in front of me, dodging and tumbling over rocks to the bay beyond it. The bay itself is surrounded by craggy, rugged hills, their tops shrouded in mist. There's a stillness and a quiet, apart from the wind and the lapping of the waves, that I'm not used to. I feel like I've fallen off the edge of the map.

There are two orange buoys, one each at the furthest points of the bay, like someone's marked out their patch. But apart from that there's really nothing to see. No sign of any kind of farming. No big fishing boats or pens. The only sign of any oyster activity is a huge pile of oyster shells just inside the gate, a mountain of them. Maybe Sean just likes to eat them, a lot. I can't believe anyone actually lives out here; there's no shops, no café, no pub, no . . . I look around, nothing. To say I feel like a fish out of water is a pretty accurate description. What do people do out here? How do they make a living?

A rough, rocky footpath leads down to the water and another snakes around the edge of the shore, away from the house where Grace is now slowly investigating more messages and sending more replies.

'You coming?' my new boss shouts from the front door of the cottage. The wind's blowing his hair around wildly. I shut the van door with effort. I wonder if I should leave there and then, say I'm not staying, that I'm terrified of water and that I might as well have landed on the moon, it's all so alien to me. But where would I go? I've got no money, no clothes, no transport. I pull out my phone from the front pocket of my hoodie. No phone signal either. Even if I wanted to call someone, I couldn't. But I don't want to. I turn the phone off and shove it back in my pocket. No phone, no Facebook, no emails.

I'll have to take my chances and stay, just for a while, until I can work out where to go next. I take a deep breath and make my way unsteadily across to the path leading to the cottage. The ground's uneven, on a slope with lots of tiny stones. I'm still wearing gold mules. I feel ridiculous, cold and very alone.

The cottage is small and white with a grey slate roof. The paint on the red front door is peeling. I take a good look at the place that's to be my home, maybe for the next few months. Home. I feel a twist of sickness in my stomach as I remember our flat: a modern, purpose-built block. Not like the room I'd had above Betty's when I first met Brian. The flat had all mod cons . . . not like this place, with its peeling paintwork and pebble-dashed walls. At home we were right in the town, everything was close by – shops, banks, restaurants and pubs. I look around me. There's nothing here. But at least something's finally working in my favour. No one's ever going to find me here, no one at all.

A noise like a fog horn makes me jump,

Eeee awwwww! Eeeeee awwwww! I look out to sea but

there's nothing. I turn back and look the other way, beyond the cottage to the fields behind it. Two small donkeys are standing by a stone wall. One has his head held high and is rolling back his lips, making him look like Mick Jagger. He's the source of the noise. I wonder if it's some kind of battle cry, like a guard dog. I grip the neck of my hoodie. Beyond the donkeys, or mules, or whatever they are, there's another field with some kind of wooden hut that's fenced in. Another noise shatters the silence. A huge bird is stretching its wings and joining the donkey in its chorus with a loud 'Honk! Honk!' The closest I've ever come to farm animals was a day trip to the city farm when I was a kid. Since then it's been a chicken wrapped in cellophane at Tesco's checkout. I hurry on to the cottage door, quickly glancing back at the sea and wondering how on earth I'm going to cope with the fear it fills me with.

I'm desperate to get in out of the wind and to meet Sean's wife and kids. Getting lost in a family could be just what I need right now. I force a smile, run my hands over my dress and step inside, bracing myself for the fuss that my arrival would inevitably create.

Inside, there's a dampness in the air. I give a little involuntary shiver. It's colder than I was expecting. And a lot more quiet.

Sean's gathering up what appears to be washing hanging on the backs of mismatched chairs. The kitchen table is pushed up against a big window looking out to sea.

'Sorry. I'm not used to guests.' He grabs a final T-shirt and adds it to the pile spilling over in his arms.

'Oops.' I catch a dark blue woollen jumper before it falls and put it on top of the unruly heap. He heads to a door at the far end of the room, leaving me to look round the kitchen-cum-dining-room-cum-living-room-cum-office, by the looks of the paper pile in the corner. To say it's not what I was expecting is an understatement. There's a small kitchen area, a red settee and a black pot-bellied stove. There's a pile of washing-up in the sink and dog food on the table next to a pile of thick rope. There's a guitar and a leaning tower of CDs beside the sofa. The window looks down the stream to the sea beyond, making it feel as though you're on board a ship. It's cold and unwelcoming.

'I'll get a fire going now and we'll be grand,' he says, busily gathering up sticks and matches and throwing open the doors on the stove. 'Like I say, I'm not used to guests.' He picks up some more sticks from the basket beside the fire and feeds them into the grate. He's still in his coat and pulls a lighter from his pocket. He makes a few attempts before it throws up a little flame and he holds it to the paper in the fire's belly. The paper catches and the fire suddenly erupts into life. He shuts the doors, letting the orange and yellow flames roar upwards inside. I'm still rooted to the spot, shell-shocked.

'I'll show you your room then I'll rustle up some supper,' he says, taking off his coat and hanging it on the heavily laden hooks by the front door. 'You're just through here,' he says, pointing to a room by the front door. 'Bathroom's to your left. I'm through there,' he points back through the living room to where he dumped the washing. 'And that's Grace's place.' There's a large box filled with blankets by the guitar. In the other corner, by the doorway to Sean's bedroom, is what I think is a desk, but it's hard to tell underneath the precarious piles of paper that are threatening to spill over. Some look as if they already have.

'Will your, um, wife be joining us?' I croak in a voice that doesn't sound like mine.

'My wife?' He shakes his head and laughs as he feeds turf on to the fire. 'No. No wife. It's just me and Grace here.' He straightens up and turns to me. At that moment Grace barges in through the door, letting in a huge rush of cold air. Sean rubs her head as he passes to shut the door. 'That's one of the reasons I need some help. I need someone to look after Grace when I'm not here. I've got some work, just summer work, but it helps pay the bills, so I need someone to be here for Grace.' He wipes his hands on a tea towel. 'And the other animals.'

My eyebrows shoot up. The closest I've ever had to a pet was a goldfish called Fred that I won at the fairground, and he died after three days.

'Other animals?' I try to swallow.

'Yes, there's the hens. They're laying pretty well so there's loads of eggs. And the geese, great guard dogs. And then of course there's Freddie and Mercury, the donkeys. I kinda inherited them from my uncle. They lived here before me. But apart from that it's just me.' He nods apologetically at the mess.

'It's just you,' I repeat. I'm slowly processing my situation. I'm miles away from anywhere, with a man I don't know, who's told me he's an oyster farmer. I swallow hard. The full stupidity of my situation is beginning to sink in.

'Do you want to see your room?' He puts out a hand to show the way. There's a single bed, an old dark wood wardrobe, a small dressing table that looks as if it was once someone's pride and joy, and a chair.

'Make yourself at home. I'll call you when supper's ready.'

He pulls the door to behind him. 'And don't mind Grace. Tell her to go to her bed if she comes calling,' he shouts back. I hear him in the kitchen; music goes on and he's singing. I sit on the bed, pull off my sweatshirt and then my ruined wedding dress. I hold it to my face, breathing in the smell of my former life, before folding it and putting it at the bottom of the wardrobe. Then I sit back on the bed and let the tears that have held off all day finally fall. Great big blobs of them. What on earth have I got myself into?

Later, after an erratic shower – hot, cold, dribble, full-force – I go back into my room to find some joggers and a T-shirt on my bed. I put them on and return to the living room feeling drained but clean. The smell coming from the little kitchen is surprisingly delicious. Sean looks up from his hot frying pan.

'I thought you might need some more suitable working clothes. Hope they're OK. They were the smallest things I could find. We can pop into town tomorrow if you need to pick up a few bits.'

'They're fine. Thank you. It's very kind of you.' I know it must seem odd that I have absolutely nothing else with me.

'I've got a spare toothbrush. Like I say, we can pick you up some more stuff when I go to work in Galway.' He goes over to the pot-bellied stove where a pan of cubed potatoes is frying on the flat top. He shakes them and releases another mouth-watering explosion of garlic, rosemary and olive oil to fill the little cottage.

'It's just omelettes,' he says, almost apologetically. 'Could you put the bread on the table?' He points to a large round loaf on the side. I pick up the board with the knife and the butter dish as well.

'What shall I do with . . . ?' I pick up the coil of rope and the bag of dog food.

'Oh, on the floor. Well, maybe not the dog food.' He takes that from me and puts it high on top of a cupboard. Then he puts two plates on the table with yellow omelettes on them, gets the potatoes from the stove and divides them between us and we sit down to eat. It's dark outside, which in a way helps. I can't see the sea. Sean slices bread and I find after 48 hours or more of living on Diet Cokes and Jammie Dodgers, my appetite has suddenly returned. It's delicious. I cut into the fluffy omelette and let the melted cheese stretch between my mouth and the plate.

After supper we clear away the plates, neither of us saying much, for which I'm grateful.

'Right, now off to bed,' he claps his hands. 'The spring tide starts tomorrow at around ten and we have work to do.'

'Fine,' I reply, suddenly feeling dead on my feet. Not only have I not eaten properly since I left the wedding, apart from the soup earlier, but I haven't slept properly either. I pulled out the bed in the camper van and hid there on the ferry, but I didn't actually sleep. With luck, everything will look better tomorrow after a good night's rest.

'Thank you for the meal.' I stand and tuck in my chair. I even manage a small smile. 'And thank you for . . .' What could I say – for the clothes, for the job, for not asking me why I'm here?

'No worries,' he says dismissively, standing up himself. 'Welcome on board. I'll show you everything you need to know in the morning and explain what I need you to do. Now get yourself to bed, get some rest.' He waves a hand to shoo me out good-naturedly. 'I'll be out with my hooker first thing if you want to join me. Don't decide now, let me know in the morning.'

The words hang in the air. I turn slowly and creep out of the room and into my bedroom. I shut the door firmly. Had I heard him right? I mouth the words to myself. 'His hooker? He's a pimp!'

I look around and then grab the chair, propping it under the door handle. I'm furious I've let myself be lulled into a false sense of security by a fluffy omelette and some homemade bread, even if it was delicious. Maybe it was poisoned, with that date drug stuff . . . I look out of my window to see if I can jump. It's pitch black, and I have no idea where I am. I can't go anywhere until it's light. I crawl into the bed and sit there with the covers up to my neck and my knees to my chest. There is no way I can let myself fall asleep.

Chapter Four

A noise catapults me from a deep sleep. My heart's racing. My cotton-wool-stuffed head shoots up from where it's been face down in the pillow. My vision is blurry. I haven't slept like that in weeks. Where am I? It's light. I quickly reach out for Brian, but he's not there.

I was dreaming. My pillow's wet from tears. I was back home, at work in The Coffee House. Everyone was pointing at me, laughing. I could hear my mother's voice telling me what a fool I'd been. Kimberly, my work mate, telling Betty that Brian was 'out of my league'. I could hear the laughter of the drivers when they came to take back the camper van. My husband had rung to say there'd been a change of plan. I could hear the laughter of everyone who'd been at my wedding.

There's a rattle at the door, the same noise as before. I twist round and sit bolt upright, suddenly remembering where I am. I'm in the middle of nowhere with a man who's gone out with his hooker and has brought me here to work too. I might have been dreaming earlier, but I'm awake now, and right in the middle of a nightmare. How could I have been so stupid? It's obvious now. He preys on vulnerable young women, bringing them here on false pretences of a job, board and lodgings, and then traffics them out to who knows where. Why else would he have been delighted that I'd come about the job? I had no qualifications, no family, didn't know where I was – I was ripe for the picking. He and the Garda must be in on it together. I should've seen it coming.

A sharp pain rips through my chest. I clutch it. My heart's thundering like a drum. My door rattles again. My pounding heart gathers pace. I hold my breath. I can hear heavy breathing outside my door. Oh my God! My eyes are glued to the door handle and the chair wedged under it. There's a scratching noise. Shit – they're here! Maybe I wasn't supposed to wake from that heavy sleep. They're obviously going to take me from here by boat. No one knows I'm here and no one will know that I've gone.

In panic I look around for something heavy to pick up. I'm up on my knees. I shouldn't have let my guard down, I berate myself. What was I thinking of, taking an offer of a room from a man I didn't know, in the middle of nowhere? I've moved around enough grotty hostels in my time to know that you trust no one. I need to get the hell out of here, right now. I spin round to look at the window as a means of escape. The door rattles again.

'Get away from the door!' I make a lunge for the lamp beside my bed, yank it out of the socket and hold it up high. The door stops rattling. There's a sniff.

'I'm warning you.' I stand up on the bed, still holding the lamp above my head. I'm wearing the T-shirt I put on last night, which comes right down to my thighs. I turn to look out the window again and see how big the drop to the ground is when suddenly the door gets an almighty thump. The chair flies away from it, falling with a clatter. I yell as the door flings open.

'Get away!' I shout, scaring both me and Grace, who has obviously launched herself at the door with both paws and is giving a great *woo-woo-woof*. She finishes her battle cry and stares at me on the bed. Her jowls are swinging to and fro. We stare at each other, her from the doorway and me from my standing position on the bed. I don't know who's more scared.

I jump off the bed, put down the lamp and go to her, rubbing her head and ears. 'Good girl, sorry if I scared you,' I say, feeling my heart slowing down.

Grace wags her tail and it thumps against the open door.

'It's all OK,' I tell her as gently as my wavering voice will let me. 'But I just need to get my stuff together and get out of here.' Talking to Grace seems to be calming me down. I pick up my Dunnes bag and my little bridal handbag with my passport and a few euros left in it. I slide my sore feet back into the gold shoes and wince. Then I pull on the joggers and hoodie, getting myself tangled in my panic to get out of there.

Grace lies down and puts her chin between her paws, watching me. For some unknown reason I make the bed. It's habit, when I leave somewhere. Then I look around for signs of Sean. I go to the bedroom door and listen. Nothing, which is eerie in itself. I'm not used to no sound at all. At least back home there'd be the odd siren going off, cars, car alarms, that kind of thing. I take a deep breath and decide to risk it. I give Grace one last rub on the head and then head for the front door. I glance briefly into the cottage's main room. The mess doesn't look any better than last night. In fact, in the cold light of day it looks worse. I chance a glance out of the window. I catch my breath. The sea seems so close. I take a step back, but not before I notice that the boat that'd been there yesterday is missing.

I need to get out of here now, take my chance, before I end up thousands of miles away with a pimp and a drug habit. I reach for the door with Grace following me, her head practically in the crook of my knee. It looks wet and grey out there. There's a jumble of waterproof jackets on the hooks beside the door. It wouldn't be stealing, I'd just borrow a coat. Perhaps I could send it back as soon as I'm settled elsewhere. Oh for goodness' sake, I tell myself, just take the coat! The guy's trying to sell you into the slave trade; it's the least he owes you.

I reach up and grab a yellow waterproof jacket, but as I yank and go to run, the whole rack of hooks and the shelf on top comes tumbling down in a heap right in front of the door, blocking my path and my escape.

Chapter Five

'Ah, for feck's sake! What have I done?' Sean looked up. He let the Atlantic blast beat his face, clearing his confused mind and making him feel alive.

His thick, curly hair blew across his face in a cross wind. He grabbed at it and pulled it back into the nape of his neck. Sean shut his eyes. He was tired, but being out here, where he was happiest, was the best rest he could get. It was where he always came to think through his problems. His mind flicked back to his latest dilemma. Had he made a terrible mistake?

He looked up at the deep red sails, the colour of a good red wine. The three sails worked together, scooping up the wind. They were full, deep and cupped like the shape of an oyster.

He knew nothing about this woman other than she'd done some sort of work in food production and a bit of work in the media . . . oh, and she was English. Other than that, nothing. He breathed in deeply, the fresh salty air giving him the head rush he needed to feel more relaxed, better than any drink he'd ever had.

What if she knew more than she was letting on, hoping to see his set up, find out how he was still making a living at this game? Or maybe she was working for someone else, someone after his land. His mind was whirring with possibilities. Why would a woman with no connections around here rock up out of the blue and want to be his assistant? It just didn't make sense.

The water lashed at the mahogany sides of the boat. The ropes slapped at the mast as he let out the sails, and his spirits lifted again as he felt the thrill of the boat moving even faster through the water.

She was either just what he was looking for – someone who had no idea about the people around here, him, or his oysters – or she was trying to play him for an idiot.

Sean heard the beating of wings and looked to his left to see his daily companion, a small silver and white heron, keeping pace beside him. His huge wings were moving up and down, carrying his large body as fast as they could. Seagulls dived effortlessly across him, but he kept going, steady and loyal.

Sean's mind turned to the villagers he'd seen yesterday. He'd watched their gossiping, wondering what he was up to, even having the nerve to ask for work. But let them talk; he'd put up with their gossip and their doubtful looks when he'd first arrived and moved in with his uncle all those years ago. It was the same when he finally took over the farm. Their silly chatter didn't bother him. He didn't want to give them anything to really talk about, though, which was why when he'd met Fi she'd seemed like the answer to all his problems. Now, though, he wasn't quite so sure.

He looked across at the little town and the coastline around it, bare, rural, rugged bog. It was in those waters that the real jewels lay. He looked towards the other side of the bay. Over there they had a reputation for having the best oysters just about anywhere in the world, just like Dooleybridge once had. But not any more. Oyster farmers had gone out of business. Families had packed up and moved away, gone to the city or abroad. Nothing had ever been the same since the rumours had started just before his uncle died. He swallowed hard. Over there they had everything that the community on this side of the water had lost.

A large wave hit the front of the boat. It dipped and rose, sending an arc of cold spray over him. He stood up and let out a tension-releasing roar. He teased and cajoled the sail ropes, urging the boat to go even faster. Still the grey and silver heron kept pace, despite its ungainly body.

The rain came and followed him all the way home, but he didn't mind. Rain was part of the deal out here. Besides, perhaps it was the rain that helped his oysters grow. One day he hoped everyone would know about his oysters, that they would be known as some of the best in the world, but first he had to get through his licence renewal in just a few weeks time. There was no way he could get the oysters ready for market, get the farm ready for the inspection and start his new job. This Fi was his only hope.

In the distance he could see his farm; his oyster beds would be starting to poke up through the water soon. He had to get a move on. He felt as he did every time he saw this place, like he was coming home, and he knew that he'd do whatever it took to save it.

As he reached the little wooden jetty the boat dipped and swayed. The heron landed on the gangplank and marched up and down, waiting for a treat to come his way. Sean pulled out his knife from his sleeve pocket, opened up an oyster from his red mesh bag, and tossed it to the heron. It clattered on the wet wood and the heron pecked greedily at it. 'You lucky beggar,' said Sean, and smiled.

There were lights on in the cottage, Sean noticed. The fire he'd stoked before he left was letting out little plumes of smoke from the metal pipe chimney. He might not know much about his new assistant, but she didn't know much about him either. Maybe he hadn't been mad to take her on; maybe it was just what he needed.

Having moored the boat, he picked up the red mesh bag. Let's see if this woman really did know about oysters; it was a risk, but one he needed to take. He slung the bag over his shoulder and lit a cigarette, then began to make his way up the shore towards the cottage. It had been a long time since he'd come home to lights on and a lit fire.

Chapter Six

'Damn it!' I start grabbing at the coats and boxes that are blocking my path.

When I think the coat rack looks much the same as before, I stand up, pull on a coat and grab my bag, ready to make a run for it. Well, a hobble anyway.

Suddenly Grace jumps up from lying on the wooden floor beside me and barks madly. I jump and then freeze. He's back.

The wooden door flies open.

'Woohoo!' He's rubbing his hair and smiling like all his Christmases have come at once. He's carrying a small red net bag over his shoulder. 'That's fresh out there. Do you not fancy a spin yourself, no?' He points towards the sea.

I shake my head vigorously. It's the very last place I plan to go. I'm on to him; he'll get me in the boat and then onwards to who knows where . . .

'No. No, thanks,' I say firmly. 'Actually . . .'

He's pulling off his coat and going to stoke the fire.

'Let me know if you fancy it.' He puts more turf from the basket into the fire and shuts its doors. This must be the subtle approach to getting me on to the boat. Wonder what happens when that fails? Well, I won't be here to find out.

'Now, let's have a coffee and sort out what needs doing

round here.' He turns to me, rubbing his hands, and then takes in the coat and my bag. My heart leaps into my mouth. I can practically see his good mood evaporating. I don't move or say anything. Finally he breaks the silence. 'Had enough already?' he says with the disappointment of a school teacher who had high hopes for his pupil.

'It's just . . .' I falter, then find my backbone and hold my head up. 'I'm not sure this is for me.' I don't know what's going to happen next. It's not like he's going to offer me a lift to the railway station and I can't run, not in these shoes. I have to persuade him just to let me leave.

'I see.' Sean turns away from me and back to the stove, opening it up and poking at the turf he's just put in there. He throws in some more and then pulls a red cast-iron kettle onto the hot plate. 'Well, it's certainly not everyone's cup of tea.' There's a hardness in his voice. It all feels a bit surreal, as if I'm turning down a perfectly normal job, not the chance to join his stable of prostitutes.

'I'm sorry,' I hear myself saying.

He sighs and shrugs.

I decide to take the bull by the horns. 'Look, if you could just take me back to the town. I'll never breathe a word of this, I promise.'

There's a long silence in which the kettle comes to a cheery boil and he picks it up and goes to the kitchen area, looking for mugs. 'Shame, I thought you were going to be the answer to my prayers.' He finds two. 'Then of course there's Grace. I need someone to look after her.' He looks at the dog and she wags her tail. Now that bit of the job I wouldn't have minded.

'Isn't there someone from the town who could help you?' I suggest helpfully.

'I like to keep my business to myself. You've seen them. Bunch of busybodies. They're only interested in passing on each other's news, mostly bad. I like to keep my business and my life away from the town.'

I know why, I think to myself. There's something unpredictable about his manner. I just want this to be over. I take a deep breath. 'Look, I don't know what's going on here or where you planned to take me, but I'm a bit long in the tooth to be some kind of sex slave. Really, you'd hardly get anything for me. I'd be a terrible prostitute. I don't even like holding hands in public. I'd be useless to you,' I blurt out.

He stops pouring the hot water and turns and stares at me, mouth open. 'What?' he says, his dark eyes flashing. I take a step back and eye up the poker by the fire. 'I haven't a feckin' clue what you're on about, but I think its best that you go,' he says angrily. He slams down the kettle. Then slowly turns back to me. His face begins to change, like he's processing the information. 'Oh my God, you think . . . you think . . .' he repeats, pointing a finger at me. I'm feeling uncomfortable. Then to my amazement he starts to smile and then lets out a small chuckle. I'm flabbergasted that he could find this so funny. The chuckle grows until he throws back his head and laughs out loud. See, definitely unpredictable.

I look away, waiting for his hysteria to subside.

'You thought I had a hooker, a prostitute.' He clutches his sides and I begin to shift from foot to foot with frustration and embarrassment. I have a strange feeling this is not going the way I was expecting it to.

'Well, that's what you told me!' I fold my arms across my body, indignant.

'It's a boat . . . s'called that.' He grips his sides and can barely breathe. Every time he looks at me he bursts into laughter all over again.

I've had enough of this. 'Wait a minute. Are you telling me your hooker is your boat?'

He nods wildly, brushing away the tears. When he's finally finished he straightens up. Every now and then a whimper of laughter escapes, but seeing my set face, he makes an effort to straighten his own.

'I'm sorry.' He holds up both his hands. 'It's my fault. I apologise. I should've explained.' The smile tugs at the corners of his mouth again.

I'm feeling really cross now. My arms are still tightly folded and I'm tapping my toe.

'Please, let me. Sit down.' He pulls out a chair for me. 'I'll make the coffee. I promise you I'm not trafficking sex slaves or setting up a brothel.' He's still holding out the chair. 'It's just me here, plus Grace and my boat. Please, sit down.' I take a step towards the chair. Not for the first time recently, I feel like I have 'sucker' written on my forehead. As I don't have many options right now, I sit down.

He puts a coffee pot on the table in front of me and motions to me to help myself.

'I'm a tea drinker,' I say, not meeting his eyes.

He sucks through his teeth teasingly. I look up. He's smiling at me this time, not laughing at me. He looks in the cupboards and manages to find a single abandoned tea bag. He throws it in a cup and pours on boiling water.

'So you really are an oyster farmer then?' I ask the question I should have asked yesterday.

'Yes, I really am an oyster farmer, and I really do need an assistant. Not a prostitute . . .' He quickly composes himself again. 'I really didn't mean to scare you,' he says more seriously, pouring himself hot coffee.

We establish that the boat is a hooker, a traditional Galway fishing boat that used to be his uncle's.

'Look, I've got my inspection coming up for my oyster farmer's licence. I've been here for three years and I need to pass it to keep my business. And it's June. I'll be starting work at the sailing school just outside Galway, teaching youngsters to sail at summer camps. It helps make ends meet. And . . .' He's suddenly very serious again, 'I can't be everywhere at once.'

'So what does the job actually entail?' I sip the tea and start to feel human again.

'I'll need you to help with the oysters themselves, bringing them in for grading and finishing them off ready to go to market. Then there's the other animals to look after, and we need to make sure everything is as clean as it can be before the inspection.'

'But I don't know about oysters.' I sip the tea again.

'You don't need to. You leave the actual growing bit to me. I'll tell you when I need your help, but like I say, mostly it's cleaning and house-sitting.'

It didn't sound like my ideal job, but at least I wasn't being sold as a sex slave.

'It's a precarious business, oyster farming,' he says. 'It's not like we can call in a vet if the stock gets sick. And we can't move them into shelter if the weather gets bad. But one of our biggest problems is theft. There's the oystercatchers for starters – they're a species of bird,' he explains at my puzzled look. 'They like to feed on my oysters. And then there's the oyster pirates. The people who think they can come in and help themselves to your stock just because it's in the sea. I'll need you to be here, keeping an eye on things.'

He stops talking and picks up the red mesh bag he's brought in with him. 'What do you think of these?' He empties the contents onto the kitchen table with a clatter, putting his arm round them to stop them falling off.

Even I can work this one out.

'They're oysters.'

'That's it?' He tilts his head slightly and I can see he's looking for more. But I can't think of anything else to say.

'Yes.'

He hesitates and then reaches for one. I lean back a bit. I don't mean to, it's an automatic reaction. He sits on the edge of the table, watching me with interest. He pulls out a knife from a pocket in the sleeve of his coat, pushes the knife into the hinge and twists it until it pops open. Then he slices along the top edge, pulls away the top shell, and shows me the slippery, slimy oyster inside.

'Want to try one?'

The back of my hand shoots up to cover my nose. I grimace and shake my head. I can't help it.

'No thanks, I don't like seafood,' I say, muffled because my hand is still over my nose and mouth.

He cocks his head again and a smile spreads across his face. 'Sure?' he asks, his smile broadening, irritating me.

'Sure,' I say firmly, still holding the back of my hand to my mouth.

He looks at it then tips it into his own mouth. 'Good,' he says, chewing and swallowing. 'Now all I have to do is leave them to it.' He smiles briefly and gathers up the rest of the oysters.

I decide to say something before he does. 'I take it that you don't want me to stay on, what with me not liking oysters?'

'On the contrary.' He wipes the back of his wrist across his mouth. 'The job's yours if you want it.' He brushes some bits of shell off the table. I'm confused and begin to say so, but just then Grace jumps up and starts barking. There's a car pulling in through the gates. Sean frowns, slides off the kitchen table and goes to investigate. He opens the door to let Grace out, whooping and howling. Sean groans. I stand and reach on tiptoe to see round him. Then it's my turn to groan.

'Morning, both.' The Garda from yesterday smiles as he climbs the haphazard steps. Grace's barking stops and she's sniffing at his shins now.

'What can we do for you, Eamon?' Sean practically growls as he grabs up the bag of oysters, puts them on the work surface and stands in front of them while the Garda steps into the cottage.

'Garda Eamon,' the man corrects, touching the brim of his hat. Sean ignores him, which makes me smile. The Garda is very full of himself, just as he was at the scene of the accident when he asked me if I was attempting to take part in the National Camper Van Diving Contest.

At the time I was still in shock. I'd just received a text from Kimberly at The Coffee House. Brian was back in work. Kimberly had served him and he'd changed his order. Brian never changed his order. Instead of his skinny latte and Caesar salad he'd had a bacon buttie and a cream horn. I felt like I didn't exist in that world any more. The tears had come thick and fast. I'd thrown the phone into the passenger seat and driven through the blurry vision. I hadn't seen the road come to an end, or the sea wall that I hit.

The Garda looks around the cottage, then back at me.

'Just keeping an eye on the defendant.' He gives me a stern look. I look from him to Sean.

'I'm not the defendant. You let me off, remember?'

'Still, it doesn't hurt to keep an eye,' the Garda says. The only reason I'm not in court is because he was at the end of his shift when I crashed and he didn't want the paperwork. He made me pay the camper van reps for the damage when they came to retrieve the 'stolen vehicle', and that was that. I'd used the very last of my money, which was why I was taking a job that in a careers interview would be at the very bottom of the list of suitable posts for me, given my fear of water, dislike of oysters and lack of experience with the countryside.

'So, I see you've taken responsibility for the defendant?' he says to Sean.

'I'm not the defendant!' I want to shout, but don't.

'Fi's considering working for me, yes.' Sean's leaning against the work surface with his arms folded. 'Isn't that right, English?' He puts the ball firmly back in my court and tucks the corner of the oyster bag behind him, as if he's trying to hide them.

'That's right,' I nod, a bit puzzled.

'Good,' the Garda says. I feel like I'm on probation, but I'm not – I paid for the damage!

Sean looks irritated too. It was the Garda who put me on to Sean and I was grateful at the time, but now I think it's just because he likes to know where his local 'criminals' are staying, to keep an eye on them. I can just imagine Betty and

Kimberly's faces if they heard I was considered to be a local crimewave. I put my hand over my mouth to make sure I'm not smiling. The Garda gives me a hard stare which makes me nervous and makes me want to laugh at the same time, so I try and frown and squeeze my cheeks with my thumb and forefinger. Sean catches my eye and gives me the swiftest of winks. He's smiling too, in the corner of his mouth.

'Hope you're not thinking of taking that boat out in weather like this,' the Garda says bossily.

'Garda Eamon, is there anything I can do for you? Or did you just come by to tell me when I can and can't sail my boat?' Sean unfolds his arms.

'No, like I say, just a friendly visit.' He takes off his hat and pulls out a chair. 'I've probably time for a quick coffee before I need to get back on duty.' He goes to sit down and my heart sinks.

Sean grabs his coat.

'We've no time for coffee drinking here. We've work to do, now if you don't mind . . . ?' Sean stands up straight but doesn't move. Garda Eamon looks taken aback. Then, with a slight nod of his head to Sean and another stare that tells me he's watching me, he leaves. Sean lets the door slam shut behind him and we both let out our smiles. The tension between us seems to have lifted.

'Don't mind him, ideas bigger than his station, literally,' says Sean, pulling on his wax jacket. We smile again and he grabs the bag of oysters.

'Must get these back in the water,' he says softly.

'Thank you,' I say, and stand up. Behind me another pile of paperwork spills over in the draught.

'So you'll stay?'

I nod, a lot more firmly than I mean to.

'How about we call it a month's trial? See how we like each other? We should have had the inspection by then. Then we'll both know where we stand. Deal?' He puts out his hand for me to shake.

'Deal,' I say. I shake his hand firmly. 'I'm a hard worker,' I feel the need to tell him. He holds on to my hand, as if making sure he's got my attention.

'I may live here on my own . . .' He stares straight at me with those dark eyes, as if the curtains were drawn on them a long time ago, '. . . and you may hear things about me in the village. Most of it will be untrue. But you have my word I'm only interested in having you here to help out with my workload. I am certainly not interested in you in any other way.'

My stomach nervously flips over. 'And to help with Grace, of course.' I give a little laugh, trying to find a way round my embarrassment.

'And Grace,' he smiles. 'I can assure you, there'll be no inappropriate advances from me. This is just business. The very last thing I'm looking for is . . .' He takes a deep breath. I think he's going to say 'love', but he doesn't. He stares at me as if trying to find the right word.

A shiver runs through my body. And then suddenly he lets go of my hand, leaving the sentence unfinished, and I swallow hard.

'So, no more secrets,' he says, and opens the door, flicking his head for me to follow.

Well, there is one more, but I don't seem to be able to find the words. 'I'm terrified of water' might put him off. I'm determined to show him I'm a hard worker and not afraid to get my hands dirty. I'll have to work around it somehow. I need this job.

'Let's get to work,' he says, handing me a large yellow waterproof jacket. He marches out, leading the way. The sea looks to be further back than earlier. See, things are looking better already. I follow him round to the sheds.

'The tide's going out and it's now that we can actually get to the oysters. This is a spring tide so we need to move quickly.'

'What's a spring tide?' I ask, hugging my coat around me tightly.

'It means the tide'll go back further than normal, so we can get to the oysters easier. It's when the sun, moon and earth form a line, so it happens twice a month, at the full moon and the new moon.' He's starting to get animated. I, on the other hand, can't really take it all in and feel myself glazing over, no matter how hard I try to concentrate.

'The neap tide, on the other hand, happens for the other two weeks in the month. The tide will hardly go back or come in. Makes it nearly impossible to do anything with the oysters.' He pulls back the doors to the shed with a clank and scrape and I'm hoping that's the end of the tidal lecture. I follow him into a room full of machinery and then into another room at the back. He turns to me. 'What size shoe are you?' He looks down at my feet, still in gold mules.

'Five,' I say, and he bends down and hands me a pair of green wellington boots.

'Six is the smallest I've got.'

Then he hands me some thick socks. I pull them on and then the wellies. I pick up the gold mules and give them a final stare. Then I go over to the dustbin in the corner of the room. I won't be wearing them again anytime soon.

Sean's watching me. 'Sure?' is all he says.

'Sure,' I say, and drop the shoes into the bin. I get the feeling me and these wellies are going to get to know each other really well over the next month.

Chapter Seven

I look like Mr Blobby as I emerge from the shed. I'm wearing yellow waterproof dungarees, wellies that are too big, and the extra-large waterproof jacket complete with sleeves that hang down over my fingers. I half think he's done this on purpose. Is that a smirk he's hiding from me? I bristle but am determined to show him I'm not afraid to get stuck in.

He hands me a pair of brick-coloured waterproof gloves and plonks a woolly hat on my head. I now feel as though every bit of dignity and femininity has been stripped from me.

'You'll need it out there!' He points to the sea where there are now poles in straight lines visibly sticking up out of the water.

I pull the hat down further so it covers my ears and hides my neat bob.

'Sorry, it's all I have,' he apologises again about the waterproofs.

'It's fine,' I say, and mean it. I feel completely detached from reality, numb. And feeling numb is much better than hurting. I just need to get this over and done with before my retreating resolve runs out on me.

'Where do you want me to start?' I look around at the untidy shed, but Sean is looking down the lane. A black

BMW is approaching. It pulls into the gates and stops. Grace starts up her impressive barking and Sean catches her collar and tries to quieten her. When Grace is firmly in Sean's grasp, the car door opens and a woman dressed in black jeans, a crisp white T-shirt and a leather flying jacket steps out. She pushes her sunglasses on to the top of her head, despite there being no sun. She looks like Sophia Loren.

'Who's that?' I look at Sean. He doesn't look back at me.

'Ah, that's Nancy. Nancy Dubois. My . . . partner.' He smiles and waves. Grace doesn't stop barking.

'Your partner? But I thought you said—'

'I said I wasn't married,' he cuts across me. 'It's different.' He looks directly at me. 'It's a good rule for life: never assume.' That look tells me there's an awful lot more to Sean Thornton than meets the eye.

I turn back to look at the stylish woman coming towards us in her shiny, black, expensive leather boots. Now I know why the idea of him being with a hooker, or having any designs on me, was so laughable. I shrink further into my waterproofs, actually grateful they're big enough to get lost in.

'Nancy has just taken over a new restaurant in Galway, The Pearl. It's her big passion at the moment, apart from me of course,' he jokes, and the slightly uncomfortable atmosphere disappears.

'Why can't you ever get mobile reception here?' Her accent is a strange mix of French with an Irish burr. She waggles her phone at him and skirts round Grace. 'I've being trying to ring. Don't tell me, out on the hooker.' She falls against him, one hand on his chest, one leg lifted slightly out behind her as she plants a kiss on his mouth. It's like a scene from a movie – perfection. I look away. Brian and I were more an awkward peck on the cheek type of couple, could never get the timing right; I would usually end up getting a kiss in the hair while I kissed his ear lobe. We probably didn't practise enough.

Nancy pulls away and spins round to look at me.

'Who's this?' She smiles widely.

'Nancy, this is Fi, my new assistant,' Sean says charmingly. He holds out his arm, inviting me to step forward. I do, but I can't shake her hand because of the waterproof gloves, so I wave instead, just like Mr Blobby.

'Nancy is my oyster broker. I grow them, she sells them.' His eyes wrinkle just under the corners.

Nancy holds up a well-manicured hand to say hello back. 'Brilliant! Finally he's taken my advice and got some help. You're very welcome. I'm delighted you're here. Now perhaps Sean can stop spending quite so much time out in this God-forsaken place and more time with me in town,' she says. She looks around as if monsters might jump on her from behind every rock and bush and I know how she feels.

But I'm sure Sean's smile has slipped, just a bit. He bangs his gloved hands together. 'Right, time and tide wait for no man! We need to get on,' he chivvies me along, reminding me I'm staff.

Nancy tuts. 'Just remember we're having dinner tonight. Chef has some recipes he wants to try out for me.' But Sean is on his way down to the shore and I feel I should follow. 'And iron a shirt!' she calls after him. He raises a hand in the air but his attention is focused on the sea in front of him.

'Sorry,' I say to Nancy, and pull my hat down further.

'That man is obsessed.' She rolls her eyes before pulling down her sunglasses.

I say nothing and follow him. I pull up my hood. With my hat firmly down, coat and dungarees on, stumbling over the rough stones, I feel hidden from the world. And being hidden from the world is exactly what I want right now. I'm invisible again.

Chapter Eight

'OK, I'll drive the tractor and trailer down to the oysters.' Sean points towards the sea which is creeping backwards like a scolded puppy. Poles dripping with seaweed are sticking up from the water, looking like creatures from the deep from a sci-fi movie. Despite the constant drizzle and damp in the air, I'm starting to feel hot.

'I have a big order that needs to go out at the end of the week; my share of the co-operative which Nancy runs. We'll grab some bags, bring them up, and I'll show you the sheds where we'll grade them. Then they'll all need cleaning and weighing and the bags they're in will need cleaning. When we've done that I can show you round the rest of the farm.' He pulls a set of keys from his jacket pocket, dangling from a hooker keyring.

'Let's go and grab some oysters! You follow the path round.' He points to the small worn footpath round the edge of the bay. I sigh with relief. I'm taking the dry land route. He climbs on to the blue tractor, swinging his leg effortlessly over the seat, and starts her up. The tractor roars into life, like a dozing understudy suddenly being called to take centre stage. 'Grace'll show you the way,' he shouts. He grins and pushes the gear stick forwards. The old tractor rumbles down into the shallow water, tossing its passenger this way and that. Sean holds the steering wheel firmly with one hand then turns back to look at the trailer. I watch him drive down the stream towards the sea, his curly hair being lifted by the wind, holding his face up to the sea air.

I put my head down and begin to pick my way along the uneven path. Grace follows me, sniffing all the way. The path is just a footstep wide, weaving its way round tufts of grass and rocks. What started out as drizzle on the shore seems much wetter the further I follow the path round the bay. Everything seems wetter. My feet begin to sink into the grey mud. Wading my way through it, a smell comes with it. I squelch on. I may well be a townie and feeling a bit useless and pathetic at the moment, but I'm not going to let Sean see that.

'Come on, English!' Sean's off the tractor and standing thigh-deep in the water. Oh dear God, I do hope he doesn't want me to go in that deep.

I'm level with him now. He's pulling two mesh bags behind him, one in each hand, towards the trailer. Slosh, slosh, slosh. Every time he takes a step my heartbeat gathers pace.

'Come on, the tide'll be turning if we don't get a move on,' he shouts over to me. A sharp blast of wind throws cold rain in my face and whips off my hood. I grapple for the hood while tentatively trying to dip a toe in the water. I misjudge the grassy edge and stumble forwards, landing with a splash. I freeze. Then I look down. At least I can see the bottom, see what's lying beneath the surface. I stand stock-still in the ankle-deep water. Sean lifts the two bags onto the back of the trailer and then starts to slosh his way over to me. I'm shivering.

'OK . . .' He rips off his gloves and wipes some of the rain from his face with his sleeve. 'These are the oyster beds.' He points to the rows of mesh bags, solid sacks with little holes in them, on trestle tables now just visible above the water. All I can think about is the fact I'm ankle deep in the Atlantic. I dab my top lip with the end of my flapping sleeve, trying not to let on how terrified I am.

'Right, fine.' I pull in my lips, trying to look like I'm in control and taking it all in, even though I'm not.

'These bags here are all ready to go to market, they've been graded and washed and are ready to go off for bed and breakfast at the co-operative before going to the super-markets.' He waves his hands, like he's talking about young ones flying the nest.

'Bed and breakfast?' I suddenly tune in.

He grins that same lopsided smile as he begins to explain with clear delight. His whole body language has changed from the uptight, scowling character I met in the pub. 'They go through a purification process at the co-operative plant before being sent on. I could put them through that process in the shed, but the co-operative takes care of all that. It's basically a water tank with ultraviolet lights. Makes sure they are as clean as can be before they get sent out. But as we're grade A waters it's a formality really. I'll show you later.' He's clearly in his element, sharing his world with me. He starts to lead the way further into the bay. I follow, concentrating as hard as I can on the shoreline and mountains on the other side. My arms are outstretched like I'm walking a tightrope, and that's a little how I feel – walking a tightrope without a safety net.

'These here,' he points to a row of bags on a trestle table, draped with brown, glistening seaweed, 'these with the yellow bands.' There's a coloured band threaded through the end of the bags to code them. 'These are the baby oysters, or spat. As they get bigger we change their band colour accordingly, green and then blue.' He points again to blue coded bags but I feel I'm barely taking anything in. I'm concentrating so hard on not turning and running back to dry land.

'We're going to take some of the spat up and grade it and hopefully, if they've grown, we'll move them up into bags with wider mesh, bigger holes in them. And we'll get some of the blue bags ready for market too. Later on in the week we'll check on the other bags, turn them, and make sure they're doing well. Happy?'

'Hmm, what? Sorry? Oh yes.' I nod overenthusiastically. Not happy, no, but I can't say that.

Suddenly Grace lets out one of her war cries and starts jumping around in the water, splashing around like a baby in the bath. The water showers me.

'Argh!'

Too late I realise I've grabbed his upper arm and am clinging to it. He looks at me with something close to despair and shakes his head. I'm not sure if it's aimed at me or Grace.

'Oystercatchers,' he gestures to a group of black and white birds with orange beaks which have just landed by the oyster beds. He peels my hand off his arm so I'm adrift again. 'Do you know they can get their beaks through some of the wider mesh bags and actually eat the oysters and leave an empty shell? You'll have to watch out for them. Send Grace out if you see any.'

I raise my eyebrows. 'Really?'

But Sean is already walking towards the tractor, like a

captain leading his battalion to war. I know I have to follow.

Breathe in, breathe out. And again. After several deep breaths he turns back to look at me. A hint of irritation flashes across his face. I can't afford to mess this up, and throw myself forward with great big sploshes. He's shouting something at me but I can't hear him.

I'm almost in front of him when I finally hear what he's been trying to say: 'Not so much movement or you'll get water over the top of your boots . . .' just as I feel the cold, wet trickle run over the top and all the way down into my socks.

'Wait there,' he commands. He marches off in search of the bags he wants. His shoulders are broad and he's swinging his arms to help him as he wades. I should be doing more but get the feeling I'd be more of a hindrance than a help at the moment. I stand, ankle deep in the water, looking past Sean who's scanning the tables. Beyond him there's just the sea. A huge bird lands with a flutter on a rock next to me. I jump but don't scream. It's incredible, the size of a small dog. I've never seen anything like it. It looks around in small, quick movements.

Sean's coming towards me, pulling bags through the water. I expect the bird to fly off, but it doesn't. Sean loads the bags.

'What is that?' I hiss, not taking my eyes off it.

Sean turns and looks.

'It's a heron,' he says, matter-of-factly. 'Never seen one?'

I shake my head in awe. He smiles.

'He's waiting for scraps.' Sean climbs on to the trailer, securing the bags.

'Scraps?'

Sean jumps down. Instead of flying off, the heron gives the merest flicker of its head.

'I'll grab a few more bags and we'll take them up to the shed,' Sean calls over his shoulder to me. He tosses something in the heron's direction. The heron swoops on it, drops of water from the sea rolling off his white and grey feathers as he surfaces, his sharp beak and long neck pointing upwards as he swallows his treat in one.

'Right, grab this,' I hear Sean shout, and see something flying towards me and it's not a bird. I put my hand up to catch it, not neatly but I don't miss it completely. It's an elasticated cord with a hook on the end.

'See if you can attach it.' Sean is securing the other side. I pull the rope over the bags of oysters, find a lip and secure it, finally feeling I'm being of some use. Then with a few more ropes in place he shouts, 'Hop up and we'll take them back to shore.'

I don't need telling twice. The water is now lapping above the welly line.

'Stand up on here.' Sean points to the crossbar of the trailer. I grab hold of the tractor seat and pull myself up. Water cascades off my legs and feet as I turn to lean against the wooden end of the trailer. Soon I'll be back on dry land. Thank God.

'You OK?' Sean swings into the tractor seat. I can't speak. Relief seems to have made me rather emotional, so I give him the thumbs up.

'Hold on,' he shouts over his shoulder and the tractor, trailer and I lurch forward. I do as I'm told and hold on tight. Then we begin to rock and dip our way back to shore. It can't come soon enough. Grace is running behind the trailer, regally lifting her long legs high out of the water, like a hound at the wheels of her master's coach.

I was completely useless out there. I know Sean must be thinking I was a complete waste of space. I have to show him differently. I can't let him think he's made a mistake.

Sean stared straight ahead. He knew he mustn't expect too much on the first day, but he'd hoped for a little more involvement, or even interest. She was hopeless. He looked around at his beds. If the licence went through he might be able to buy more spat and expand in the next few months. Maybe he'd try and get out on the boat and go round to the second bay before Nancy came back for him later that evening. But he had lots to do and an assistant with a severe case of first-day nerves wasn't helping. But, he thought with everything crossed, let's hope that's all it was, first-day nerves. Otherwise he'd never be ready for the inspection. He sighed and put his foot down.

The trailer seems to swing around even more as the tractor pulls on to the stony shore and up the steep bank. I cling on so hard that the tips of my fingers hurt. It would be crucifyingly embarrassing to actually fall off now. That really would confirm everything I'm sure Sean already thinks about me. The tractor and trailer swing round towards the gate and just for a scary second or two I don't think I'm going to be able to stay upright. But then I feel the tractor start to reverse.

'Head down,' Sean calls over his shoulder and I do exactly as I'm told. I crouch as low as I can so he can see over me as he reverses the trailer up to the shed doors.

Finally the engine shuts off and I stand up. By some

miracle I haven't made a complete prat of myself by falling off and suffering any serious injuries under the wheels.

'Let's get the spat done and then we can get into the sheds.' Sean jumps down from the tractor and looks up at the darkening sky. He opens the shed doors and reaches just inside for two big plastic crates. He puts them either side of the trailer and points for me to stand on one. It wobbles but I find my balance and wait for instructions. I go to pull off my gloves but he stops me.

'Leave those on, you'll need them. Cuts from shells can hurt, but if you get any under your nails then you'll really know about it.'

The drizzle turns to rain.

'We have three types of rain here,' Sean says as he pulls some of the bags off the trailer and drops them by my crate. 'It's raining, it's just stopped raining, and it's just starting to rain.' He smiles at his own joke, dropping another bag by me.

'Now then, empty this bag of baby oysters into this sieve here.' He picks up a large garden sieve and puts a big plastic bucket on the trailer. 'Anything that doesn't go through can move up into the next size bag; the other stuff can go back in the bags they came out of. Then we'll sit them in the water.' He nods to the shoreline that seems to be creeping closer. 'Tide's coming in so we'll take them back out to the tables in the morning.'

I put a foot on both sides of the crate to steady it and take the bag from him. The rain is getting heavier. Rivulets of water are running down my raincoat like molten silver. I reach up and pour the shells into the sieve, blinking back the rain. I keep my head down and keep going, focusing on the tiny oyster shells until I reach down and discover there are no more bags. I look over to Sean on the opposite side of the trailer where he's doing the same. I jump down and grab a couple more bags from his side and sieve them. It's absolutely lashing down by the time we've finished them all.

Then Sean finally says the two most welcome words: 'Coffee break.'

I put the last little oysters that haven't grown into their bag and look up. I catch my breath. The sea has crept up even further.

'Then we'll move into the sheds,' Sean shouts. 'This lot will have to stay back after school and learn to grow,' he smiles, pushing back his hood and looking at the baby oysters. Droplets of water run off his wet hair, which has sprung into spirals.

I hand him the bags and he lowers them gently into the shallow water. Waves are hitting his legs and I jump back with each one. He doesn't, of course. When the last one is in he points to the cottage.

Inside, the warmth from the little pot-bellied stove is lovely and welcoming. I stand and let the water roll off me. Sean has a coffee and I have hot water with a slice of lemon, having had the last tea bag that morning. We sit at the scrubbed pine table, me at the end so I don't have to look out to sea.

'With the inspection coming up we need to get everything scrubbed. By the end of the week the spring tide will be over. Then we'll start cleaning, every bit of equipment, everything. I'll be working in town in the day so I'll organise jobs for you to do and be back in the evenings, unless I'm in town with Nancy.' He tips back his mug and slugs his coffee. 'Right, to the sheds.' He stands up.

I finish my drink and stand up too, showing him I'm ready to work. He hands me my coat. It's wet and cold, as are my dungarees when I pull them back on. There are puddles of water all over the floor. I pull out my woollen hat from my pocket. It's cold and wet, much like I feel.

Chapter Nine

'You stand here and put one oyster in each of these little compartments on the belt.' He points to the conveyor belt in front of me. At least here, in the shed, it's not raining. Just wet, cold and dark.

'And this is where we wash and grade them.' He turns on a noisy generator and then a water pump at the bottom of a conveyor belt. More water!

'This machine will weigh them and sort them into size, ready for market, or if they're not big enough, they go back in the water. Look out for dead ones, open ones. We should hear a dead one coming through, they make a knocking noise, or you can smell them. But you'll learn all that in time. Ready?' He has his hand over a red button.

I nod, without a clue as to how I'm going to spot a dead one that makes a knocking noise, or smell one. It's all smelly to me. The conveyor belt suddenly judders into life. Outside the rain is getting even heavier, the day even darker, if possible. Sean presses the on switch of an old battered radio. Beside it there is a large blackboard on the wall with what looks like a plan of the trestle tables on it. The crackly sound of RTE 2 plays out. Then he picks up a bag of oysters. There's a rush of shells being tipped into the washer, and suddenly knobbly, seaweed-covered oysters begin to appear through the plastic flap at the end of the conveyor belt on their way to me. When the belt is full he stops it moving.

'Like this!' He shows me, picking up oysters, quickly checking to see if they're open, and putting them into the sections on the conveyor belt. I follow his lead, soon developing a two-handed technique. I'm moving through them swiftly and feeling confident when suddenly a fast-moving creature makes me jump back with my hands in the air.

'Just a crab. You'll see a lot of them. Just pick them up and put them in the bucket,' he shouts over the noise in the shed. I know it's a crab. I just don't think I've ever had to handle one up close and personal before. Sean scoops it up and drops it into a bucket beside me as if it's as easy as flicking away a fly. It scuttles round inside the bucket. I'm irritated at myself and at him. This is very different for someone who's grown up in the city. I'd like to see him negotiate the knock-down-price aisle in Morrison's at 5 p.m. or city-centre rush hour in a Ford Ka.

I go back to putting the oysters in their compartments as Sean loads on some more. I don't have to wait long for the next crab to come along. It's only small and I decide to just do it, but they're fast, wriggly, and hard to pick up when you're wearing big rubber gloves. It runs this way and that and I bite my bottom lip and grab it. I want to drop it straight away, but I don't. I plop it in the bucket and feel chuffed to bits with myself. I picked up a crab! I'm grinning like an idiot and turn to Sean, but he's deep in his own thoughts and I feel like he's popped my party balloon.

We stand side by side at the conveyor belt for what seems like hours. It probably has been hours in actual fact. Sean works hard and I'm determined to keep pace with him, no matter how much my back is aching.

'Last bag!' Sean finally shouts, and I look up to see him smiling as he tips the last bag of oysters into the washer and they begin to make their way up the conveyor belt.

When the noise from the machine finally stops it seems like I've taken root. My feet are like blocks of ice. 'Just going to put these back into the water, then we'll hose down and call it a day,' Sean says, picking up the bags and heading out of the shed. Relief floods through me. I'm exhausted, my hands are stiff, and I'm cold, really cold. Then a thought suddenly strikes me. For just those few hours, I haven't thought about Brian at all.

The final hosing down seems to be like pouring water onto water. Little runaway crabs that have found their way into the corners of the shed are caught, and then the generator, radio and lights are switched off and the doors pulled shut.

'OK, now for a tour of our other residences,' he says, pulling off his gloves as we step out into the wind and drizzle. We walk towards the fields behind the cottage.

'This is Fre— Ah, shite!' He throws down his gloves and puts his hands on his hips.

'What's the matter?' I ask. All I can see is a field surrounded by what looks like a precarious stone wall.

'That is where the donkeys, Freddie and Mercury, *usually* live,' Sean says with a sigh. 'Looks like they've gone again!' He turns back to the sheds and goes into the nearest one. He comes out carrying a bucket.

'Here, grab this and shake it.' He hands over a bucket of pony nuts, picks up two head collars and lead ropes and puts them over his shoulder. We head out on to the lane, him calling and me shaking.

'Freddie, he's always breaking out,' he tells me in between shakes of the bucket. I'm half-walking, half-running to keep up with his long strides. 'Think he's in love,' he says without a smile. 'Must've snuck past us when we were in the sheds. Ah, there they are.' We've gone a long way down the lane. Two donkeys are standing in the road. One, brown and black, has his head over a gate, nose to nose with a little white donkey. The other grey donkey is looking away, like a gooseberry. Sean strides up to them, slipping the two head collars off his shoulder. He begins to put one on the canoodling donkey and throws me the other.

'Here, stick this on Mercury.' I catch the head collar and try to work out which way up it should go. I keep looking over at Sean who's trying to stop Freddie slipping his clutches. Freddie is dodging left and right, trying to make a break for it. Mercury is standing there obligingly while I try and put a head collar on him upside down. He's nibbling at the pony nuts in my bucket. Finally I get it on; again I feel chuffed to bits by my achievement, but Sean is too busy in a tug of war with Freddie, trying to persuade him to leave his lady love.

'Shake the bucket, he might follow.' Sean nods up the lane and I turn Mercury and to my surprise he falls into step beside me. Behind me, Sean is pushing and pulling, cajoling and swearing as Freddie refuses to budge. He drops the lead rope in frustration.

'Shake the bucket!' he shouts. I'm walking backwards and give it a really good shake. Suddenly Freddie decides it's dinner time and chases up the road towards me. Sean's chasing Freddie and I'm running with Mercury and in no time at all we're back at the farm and Freddie and Mercury are back in their field. Sean secures the gate, really tightly this time. I hold my knees, trying to catch my breath. When I stand up Freddie has his head over the gate and Sean is rubbing him along his long ears. 'You have to watch for that. They're master escapologists. I've tried all sorts to keep them in, but nothing seems to work,' is all he says. I'm still catching my breath.

'And these are the girls,' he points towards the hen house in the next field and beyond that a gaggle of white geese. 'They have to be put away before the fox comes round looking for his dinner.' Sean vaults over the gate. The light is fading and the hens follow him to their shed, climbing up a ladder and into their bedroom where he shuts them in for the night. He does the same with the geese but they don't seem quite so obliging and he has to herd them, arms spread out to get them into their pen. An obliging donkey I may have been able to handle, but these look like a different kettle of fish altogether.

'You'll be OK to feed them in the morning?'

'Yes,' I say with more confidence than I'm feeling.

Just as Sean is switching off the lights in the feed shed, Nancy's BMW turns into the drive.

I give a little wave and Sean gives an apologetic shrug. She sticks her head out of the car window.

'You're not ready! Hurry up!' she calls, and the window whirrs shuts.

'Right . . .' He shuts the feed shed firmly and jogs round to the cottage steps, whereas I can hardly walk.

In my room I peel off my clothes. Despite the waterproofs, I'm wet through to my undies. I decide to brave the erratic shower to warm up. By the time I've finished and dressed in more clothes that Sean's found for me, the fire is cheerily flickering away, Grace is eating and Sean's in the bathroom. Nancy is pacing up and down the living room in her coat, her black high heels clipping across the floor. She shivers.

'So, you're English?' she enquires.

'Yes,' is all I can think of saying. I can't tell her I ended up living in Cardiff; too complicated.

'What brings you out to Galway?' She looks like this is the last place she wants to be.

'Oh, y'know. It was time for a change,' I say, not wanting to add that my new husband ran out on me and so I'm stuck here.

'Hmmm, you should've gone to France. The weather is so much better. Oh, where is he? Sean! I'm waiting in the car!' she shouts.

'Have a nice evening,' I say, as she heads out of the door. I turn to the kitchen and wonder what to do about supper.

'Don't turn round if you're easily offended,' Sean says. I can hear wet footsteps behind me and he's making his way through the living room to his bedroom. My God, is he actually naked? I fling open the refrigerator and stick my head in, looking for something to eat. I keep it there until I hear his door click shut. He really is too much. Nancy beeps her horn outside.

'I won't be back tonight,' Sean announces as he comes back into the living room, pulling on his battered wax jacket. He's wearing a crumpled cream shirt.

Nancy leans on the horn again. He ignores it. Sean Thornton is obviously not a man who likes taking orders.

'You shouldn't have any problems. I'll leave the tractor

keys just in case.' He puts a small set of keys on the table and heads for the door saying, 'Right, have fun,' over his shoulder.

I hear tyres spin and then the car roars off towards the road. And then there's . . . silence. I look around hopefully but there's no television, no computer, no nothing.

I sit down on the settee and eat bread and cheese. Every bone in my body is aching. My cheeks are burning with tiredness and exercise. I long to sit in front of the TV and tell Brian about the things I've done. For the first time that day I get a pang of homesickness. It's a physical longing and a sick feeling.

I decide to go to bed, but I can't sleep. The homesickness grows, like an aching in the pit of my stomach. The silence is terrifying. No people, no cars, no music. I get out of bed and switch on the lamp. Then I pull on my sweatshirt. It smells of Brian. I call Grace. She trots in and lies down by my bed. I pull the sweatshirt over my nose and finally fall asleep with the light on and Grace snoring by my side, trying to imagine I'm at home in my bed with Brian by my side.

Chapter Ten

I'm armed with a large stick and hen pellets. I don't know what I'm going to do with the stick but it's making me feel braver. I've managed to feed Freddie and Mercury by hanging over the gate to put buckets down with outstretched arms. The hens flew at me to get to their food and I ended up dropping most of it, but they seem happy pecking it off the ground. Now it's the turn of the geese.

I open the gate to their field. I can hear them stomping around, demanding to be let out. If I let them out they'll run at me. I remember their yellow staring eyes from yesterday. I have my arms wide, my hat pulled down, and I feel like I'm staking out the enemy. My heart is pounding. What if they all fly at me at once? They have huge wings and I remember reading somewhere they can break your arm with one beat. With a huge deep breath I pull back the latch. Out they rush. I drop the bucket and run. The gate is in reach but as soon as I stop to open it a goose is going to goose me. There's only one thing to do. I focus and then practically throw myself over the gate in a gymnastic move I wasn't able to master in my school days. I land in a heap. It makes my aching body cry out in pain, but I've cleared the gate. A goose is eyeballing me, strutting up and down in frustration. Its wings are still outstretched, its beak open, seeing me off.

I stand up stiffly and stare. It's not coming beyond the fence. I did it!

I turn back towards the cottage. My body hurts with every step I take, but on the plus side, it's stopped raining. I try not to look at the sea, as though I'm avoiding eye-contact with it. I find it helps.

As well as the house being empty, the cupboard's empty too. No tea. I can't function without tea. I have no idea when Sean will be back, and by the looks of it we can't start work with the oysters until the tide is out. I'm going to go and track down some tea.

'Grace!' I call, and she catapults back into the house, her legs flying in all directions. Her tail knocks over the stack of CDs and a leaning paper pile.

My shoulders, my feet and my back ache with every step. Grace gambols along behind me down the lane, then I put her on the lead and we follow the road, squeezing into the low stone walls when a car passes.

The petrol station is a surprise. Downstairs is a small supermarket and upstairs a range of cheap clothing and outdoor wear in amongst buckets, spades and pony nuts. I gather up some joggers, T-shirts, a hoodie, tennis socks and pants.

'It's promised rain,' says the big-busted woman behind the counter as she rings up my clothes, tea bags and milk.

'Sorry?' I ask, pulling out a note from my coat pocket.

'It's promised rain,' she repeats with a smile.

'Oh yes,' I reply, realising she's making polite weather chat.

'You on holiday?' She holds out her hand for the note.

'No, I'm, er, I'm working here.' I hand over the money.

'Oh, where?' She taps the money into the till and it opens.

'At the oyster farm, with Sean Thornton,' I reply. Her eyebrows shoot up and she cocks her head to one side.

'Well, welcome and good luck,' she says, handing me my change. But her eyebrows haven't come down to meet the rest of her face yet. 'I'm Rosie, by the way. Me and my sister Lily run this place. Give us a yell if there's anything you need. What's your name?'

'Fi,' I say, gathering up my tea and milk.

'Well, Fi, like I say, if there's anything you need . . .'

I look down at my change. The last of my money is going quickly. I skirt round the man in the queue behind me.

'Hello, Seamus, it's promised rain,' she says as she rings in his goods.

'Aye, it is.'

I know they're both looking at me.

I step out through the sliding doors and the promised rain hits me horizontally in the face. I grab Grace's lead and put my head down. I'm making my way back out of town when I practically fall over a sign in the road for The Tea Pot Café. There's an awning outside the little café that was once red and white. The need for tea gets the better of me. It's a long walk home and this way I can avoid a soaking at least once today. I tie up Grace under the awning and dive in for a quick cuppa while the worst of the rain passes.

The warm café is full of steam and the windows are misted up with condensation. The steam's coming from a big silver urn behind the counter. I feel like the Doctor stepping out of the TARDIS, waiting to discover if he's landed somewhere hostile or friendly. There's a ripple of gossip; it's practically tangible. The room's warm but the atmosphere is frosty. I shouldn't have come in, I should have headed straight back to the cottage. I thought it was going to be like The Coffee House back home. No one takes a blind bit of notice of each other in there.

'Is that her?' someone whispers. I turn to see a chubby woman in a delphinium blue crocheted hat with a large pink and blue flower on the side, a poncho and fingerless gloves, all in matching blue. She's knitting. I recognise the woman next to her as Evelyn from the pub. She has sharp, small features, like a ferret. She gives me a stern stare and leans into her friend as if I can't hear her.

'Yes, crashed a camper and is now living with Sean Thornton up at Tom's farm.'

There's a round of tutting. I'm not 'living with Sean Thornton'! I look around at the others shaking their heads. I recognise some of them from the pub. The one Sean referred to as Frank is there, tucking into a sorry-looking cooked breakfast. And there's one of the barflies, in the shell suit and baseball cap. He's drinking from a mug that looks like it's been sitting there some time, judging by the dried drips down the side. They both nod in my direction.

John Joe, Evelyn's husband, leans over and adjusts his hearing aid.

'Wassat, my love?' The hearing aid makes a high-pitched whistling noise.

'Shh,' Evelyn says in unison with the crocheted woman, who smiles at me and nods and carries on knitting, her eyes on me and her ears on Evelyn.

'It was never like that in my day,' John Joe says in a loud voice but with a look that says he thinks he's whispering. 'Families and communities stuck together. You didn't go bringing in outsiders to work for you. Typical of that young

Thornton,' he tuts. My cheeks begin to burn and my eyes start to smart. That familiar feeling of death by embarrassment is creeping round the back of my neck and into the pit of my stomach.

'In my day this place was the oyster capital of the world, the very best,' says a man in a wheelchair, waving his hands around expansively.

'Yes, yes, Grandad,' Evelyn silences him with flapping hands.

I look around the café. It's full of bits and pieces and they look to be for sale: 'a pair of slippers, worn, 50 cents', the little white label says; 'a make-up bag, very worn, 50 cents'. There's even a dressing gown, faded pink velour, hanging on the door into the toilets, 2 euro.

'Urn's been playing up.' A big man appears from behind the counter in a puff of steam and points a thick thumb behind him. He's got a Marilyn Monroe tattoo on his forearm and a triangular beard. 'What can I get you?' He rubs his hands together.

'Er, tea, to take away please,' I add, desperate to get out of there.

He turns to the steaming urn and over one shoulder says loudly, 'So, you're the new girl they're all talking about. How do you like things?'

Stunned that I'm the focus of so much unwanted attention, I don't know whether to nod or shake my head and sort of do both by rolling my head in a circle. I manage a quick glance over my shoulder to see all eyes staring back at me. I just need to get out of the gossip coliseum as quickly as possible without being rude.

Suddenly there's a thump.

'Ah, feckin' urn.' The café owner gives it another thump as it makes a whining, dying sound and the steam disappears. Looks like my quick exit has just become a slow and painful one. 'Won't be a tick. Just need to boil the kettle. Take a seat.' He points to the tables covered in wipe-down tablecloths.

I don't feel I can tell him I really don't want the tea any more. He's going to so much effort. There's a wall of interested faces looking at me as I turn and try to work out where to sit. Seats are shuffled and I'll have to share a table with someone. Then I spot a lifeline.

'Could I use the internet?' I point to the computer at a table in the corner.

'Help yourself. It's a euro for half an hour. It's all gobbledygook to me but work away, work away,' he says, dropping tea bags into a stainless steel pot.

'Thanks.' I put my head down and slide in behind the computer, which is now acting like a screen between me and the rest of the café. I skulk down as low as I can in the chair. I don't even know what I am going to do on it. It's not like I'm going to update my Facebook status with 'Having a crackin' time in Galway. Rain, rain, rain'. I'm avoiding Facebook and emails, I remind myself. I don't want anyone to know where I am.

I look up the weather forecast back home. Sunny with some cloud. Then I Google some jobs pages but don't know where to put as a location. My fingers hover over the keys. I can't help myself. I type in my password and find my fingers instinctively leading me to Brian's Facebook page, just to see how he's doing.

I look over the top of the computer. The interrogation

committee are still waiting. I take a deep breath and click on Brian's profile.

Everything seems as it always did. He still likes Status Quo and The Coffee House. He's still in Cardiff. He still works at Western Radio FM. Then I spot it. My eyeballs start to burn with humiliation and anger. I feel faint, light-headed. The words swirl on the page in front of me.

'In a relationship with . . .'

Hot angry tears feel like acid rain as they slide down my face. I feel like writing on his wall, 'I'm so glad you're happy! You've ruined my life!' But I won't. I'm too ashamed. He has it all and I have nothing, absolutely nothing. Not for the first time in my life my mooring has been cut and the rope is flapping around and I'm drifting directionless.

I read it and reread it.

'In a relationship with . . . Adrian Polsey!' it says.

Our best man! a voice shouts in my head as I bite the corner of my sleeve. I think we can safely say Brian has moved on.

Chapter Eleven

'Here's your tea, sorry for the wait.'

I jump like I've been caught red-handed. The café owner is standing beside me, tea in hand. I quickly minimise Brian's page, promising not look at Facebook again, ever. I brush away the wetness from my boiling cheeks with the palm of my hand and sniff, hoping he thinks it's a cold, and try not to look directly at him.

'Good on that, are you?' He uses the hand holding the tea to gesture at the computer. 'I haven't a clue about the world wide web. It's all passed me by.' He shakes his head. 'Now then, a scone to go with your tea?' He puts his free hand on his waist and his belly, covered in a big white wrap-around apron, sticks out even more.

I shake my head. He's being kind but I can't trust myself to speak without my voice cracking and making a total fool of myself . . . again. It wasn't long ago I was standing on the steps of the Garda station in nothing but a cut-down wedding dress. Blubbing now would really give the waiting audience something to talk about. In fact I feel like a guest waiting in the wings to go on *The Jeremy Kyle Show*.

'That's two euro then, for the tea,' he says, putting my tea on the corner of the table and turning towards the till. I stand up, rummage in the pocket of my waterproof jacket and take out my last note. I could try and draw some cash from our joint bank account but that would be a sure-fire way of Brian tracking me down.

I follow the café owner to the till, carrying my hot take-out tea. All eyes follow me and I find it hard to swallow or breathe. I stand at the counter and focus on a plastic plant that appears to be for sale for 20 cents, while the man looks for change for a fifty.

'Won't be a mo',' he says cheerily and goes off into the back room. Oh no, not again! How hard can it be to get a tea and leave? I focus hard on the photos on the walls. They're of the café owner with a woman, neither of them smiling. My eyes are stinging but looking up at the pictures stops more tears from falling. Finally the café owner reappears, just like Mr Benn. I take my change without looking at it and pour it into my pocket, only my blurred vision makes my aim a bit off and some of the coins fall to the floor. I bob down quickly, chasing them as they spin round. As I'm peeling the last one off the floor a shadow falls over me and someone hands me a coin.

'Here,' says a young woman's voice.

I look up. It's the barmaid from the pub.

'Thanks.' I take the coin, straighten up and dust myself down. The barmaid is staring boldly at me with an interested smile. Grace peers round the open door. There's a shaft of sunlight pushing though the watery path left by the rain on the pavement outside. I put my head down and attempt to side-step her, hoping she doesn't want to make small talk.

'Grandad, I've been looking everywhere for you,' she says, and I breathe a sigh of relief. I've been let off the small talk.

'So you're the joy-rider they're all talking about?' she says as boldly as she's looking at me.

The café goes silent.

Slowly I turn to look at her. The joy-rider! Wasn't it bad enough the camper van company representative had referred to me as 'the jilted bride' when he'd turned up to reclaim the van shortly before I was taken to the Garda station. The Garda said I'd stolen the camper van, but I thought it was still rented to me. I didn't know Brian had called the company to tell them of 'a change of plan'. Typical Brian, always organised. So now I'm the jilted bride and a joy-rider. I just want to be left alone.

'I'm not a joy-rider. It was a misunderstanding,' I say quietly.

There's a murmur around the café.

'She says she's not a joy-rider, it was a misunderstanding!' Evelyn shouts into John Joe's whistling hearing aid.

'And is it true you've moved in with Sean Thornton?' Margaret folds her arms like the bully in the schoolyard.

I take a deep breath. I'm shaking. I can't bear being the centre of attention, singled out.

'Yes,' I say quietly again, hoping this will clear everything up. 'I'm working for him. Now if you'll excuse me please.' I try to get round her. Again she shifts in front of me.

'So, you're not living with him as in "living with him" then?' she continues.

I want to say, 'Who I stay with and where is none of your business.' But I don't. That's not my style. Head-on conflict was never my thing.

'Two-timer!' Grandad pipes up.

'No, that's not his girlfriend in the car, it's his dealer,' Frank corrects him.

'Is it? A dealer? In the black BMW?' Evelyn reels off the number plate.

I go to make a quick escape. She side-steps me again, moving Grandad's wheelchair a tad so I'm wrong-footed. Only this time I'm so determined to make it that I crash straight into her and my tea plunges to the floor, soaking me and forming a great big puddle around me.

'Lift, Maire,' Evelyn instructs, and she and her friend lift their feet with precision timing looking like two inquisitive meerkats. I notice Maire is wearing floral wellies. Tepid tea drips from my hands and down my front. The barmaid's hands fly to her mouth and in all fairness she looks horrified by her actions.

'Oh God! I'm so sorry,' she says, grabbing a cloth from the café owner's waistband. He's arrived with a mop and bucket and starts swilling the tea around. The barmaid is trying to mop me down. My eyes may have shown a rare flash of fury.

'I really am sorry,' she says. 'Let me get you another. Here, sit down.' She points to a chair. The café begins to empty as the café owner cleans up. The smell of bleach is too much for some.

'No, really, I'm fine.' I brush away the barmaid's dabbing hands in my attempt to leave.

'No, you can't go, not like that. Here, Gerald, get another tea there and a bun,' she instructs.

'I'm fine,' I repeat, but no one seems to be listening to me.

'But not one of Evelyn's scones,' she calls to Gerald, and then, checking that Evelyn has actually left, says more quietly to me, 'They taste of fish,' and smiles. I look at her for a moment and wonder if I've heard her right. And then I can't help it, I laugh. Maybe it's some kind of nervous reaction, an emotional release, but Evelyn's fishy scones make me laugh.

The barmaid joins in too, her confrontational stance disappearing like the rain.

'That's better,' she smiles, showing her neat white teeth. 'Now, bring the tea over, Gerald. I'm sooooo sorry,' she repeats in her husky voice, like she's been smoking roll-up cigarettes all her life.

She guides me to a seat and I realise resistance is futile. Apart from anything, I still haven't had a cup of tea this morning. I look at the clock. I have to be back soon. Sean will be home and the tide will be out. Strange, I think, how quickly my life is being led by the tides. The barmaid sidles in opposite me.

'Sorry,' she repeats again, only this time I don't think she's talking about the tea. 'I didn't mean to come on so strong there. It's just not often we get blow-ins, and young ones at that.'

'Don't worry, love, I was the last blow-in, came from Dublin twenty years ago,' Gerald joins in with a whoosh from the urn. 'They still think I'm the newcomer.' He comes over and sets down the tea. 'They'll find something new to interest them soon enough. Just tell them your name and where you've come from and how long you're planning to stay and they'll leave you alone after that.' He gives the table a swift wipe and adjusts a pair of reading glasses on the shelf next to me. 'Now then, scone?' he asks, and I look at the barmaid and we both laugh. I shake my head and he wanders back behind the counter looking puzzled.

'Jeez, Gerald. We keep telling you, they taste of fish!' the girl shouts after him playfully.

Gerald picks up a scone and sniffs it. 'It's you! It's your tastebuds!' he bats back.

I smile at the banter and take a sip of the tea. It's fabulous. Not like the tea at home, which is usually just wet and warm. This actually tastes of tea.

'You look like you needed that. I'm Margaret, remember? We met in the pub.' She sticks out a hand; her nails are painted bright blue. I think about what Gerald just said: tell them your name, where you're from and how long you're staying, and then they'll leave you alone.

'I'm Fi, Fi English. I'm from the UK. Just staying for a month or so,' I say, hoping that will be enough.

'And you and Sean, you're not . . . ?'

I shake my head.

'Great!' she says. 'Just like to know the competition, if you know what I mean.' She's grinning broadly, clearly besotted with my prickly boss.

I knock back the rest of my tea feeling surprisingly revived. 'Thanks for the tea.' I start to stand up. 'And the scone advice,' I smile, and Gerald gives us a mock scowl.

'Working with Sean then?' Margaret persists.

'That's right.' Grace is whining impatiently now.

'Oyster farmer, are you?' She stirs her tea with a plastic spoon.

'No, I'm more of a Girl Friday. Doing a bit of everything.' Having given the locals all they wanted I do up my coat. Now I can go back to the farm and get on with my work.

'What's your star sign?' she asks cheerily.

I shrug. 'I'm not sure.'

She sighs good-naturedly.

'Well, when's your birthday?'

'August twenty-first.' This is a bit more than my name and where I'm from.

'Leo! Brilliant!' Margaret bangs the table. 'Just what we need around here. A leader. Someone who can take charge. You can be on our committee,' she beams at me.

'Com . . . committee? What committee?'

'The Dooleybridge Events Committee. This used to be a popular holiday stop. Couldn't move for traffic in the summer. Now the traffic's all one way, out of here. We want to put Dooleybridge back on the map. Something to bring the crowds, like the Volvo Yacht Race or Band Aid. Only trouble is, we haven't actually come up with any events yet. But we will,' she beams again.

'Oh no, I don't think so,' I stutter. 'I'm not really the committee type. Besides, I really won't be here that long.'

'Oh, just come along. We're a friendly bunch and we meet every week. Come to the pub, next Monday, seven o'clock. Bring some ideas. You might as well be there while they talk about you, instead of them doing it behind your back.' She sips her tea with a smile. I hurry for the door. 'I'll let the others know,' Margaret calls after me.

Chapter Twelve

Sean's waiting for me and he's not happy.

'Come on, tides won't wait, y'know,' he barks, and I run to get my boots with Grace following close behind.

'Thought you'd run out on me again,' he says as we march towards the water. He gives me a sideways glance from under his scowling eyebrows, like he doesn't trust me.

'Just went to the café for tea.' I try and keep up. 'Got the third degree.'

'Ah.' He rolls back his head, understanding.

We reach the tractor.

'Don't take any notice of the nosy beggars. Don't tell them anything either,' he says, his eyebrows lifting a little. He tosses the keys in the air and catches them. 'Suppose they wanted to know your life story?'

I think about Margaret. It wasn't so much my life story she was after, but more his. She's obviously in love with him. She actually seemed quite harmless in the end. And she really wants to do something for her town, which doesn't seem like such a bad thing to want to do. I've never been in one place long enough to feel strongly about its future. I quite like that about her. She's obviously a girl who wears her heart on her sleeve, not tucked in the back of the wardrobe like me.

'Actually they asked me to join their committee,' I say, defending Margaret.

'A committee? What kind of a committee?' Sean is doing up his waterproof jacket.

'The Dooleybridge Events Committee,' I say, suddenly wishing I hadn't.

'An events committee? Here in Dooleybridge?' Sean throws back his head and laughs. 'I've heard it all now. That's like saying we need a committee to deal with our drought conditions!' He looks up at the drizzling sky and then starts up the tractor, the noise of the engine seeming to join in his loud laughter. He gestures for me to get on the back of the trailer. 'You're not going to, are you?' he shouts over the engine noise.

'Not sure,' I say evasively. Of course I'm not going to go. I'm sure I couldn't think of any ideas. But, in a funny way, it felt good to be asked. And I don't like being told what to do. Sean Thornton might be my boss, but he's not my keeper.

'Good. I find it better to keep my personal life away from the town, you might find that too. Hold on!' Sean tells me.

If I want to go to the committee meeting, I will, I think firmly.

For the following week I'm a slave to the pattern of the tides. Some nights Sean is there, others he isn't. But it's the same every morning: I get up, feed the donkeys, open the hen house, and try to put the food in the feeder before they tip it over, and each morning I try to out-run Brenda the goose who's desperate to have a piece of my backside. I'm now clearing the gate in one swift movement. Oh, and I've named her Brenda after Brian's mother, who was also beady-eyed and vicious.

The only variety comes in the different ways in which it rains: sideways, straight down, drizzle, wispy flecks, icy pellets, and whooshing down and up again. Or those mornings when Freddie has broken out of the field and I have to run down the lane to get him back with a bucket of pony nuts. Sometimes Mercury is with him, sometimes he stays in the field. But Freddie's always gone to the same place, to be with his lady love.

After sorting the animals we either work in the sheds, cleaning mesh bags and equipment, or in the yard, fitting in the chores around the pattern of the tide. Everything must be spotless for the inspector's visit. Sean's cutting the grass with a big old petrol lawnmower and mending fences; I'm painting the window sills and door of the old barn, and we're ruthlessly clearing any trace of debris.

Then, every day I stand ankle deep in the water while Sean puts back the bags we've graded on trestle tables. The area with oysters ready to go to the co-operative is getting fuller by the day. They'll be collected just after the inspection, at the end of my month's trial. Once Sean's put the bags back in the water, he collects more. I stand around trying to look useful, but really I'm barely keeping the panic attacks at bay. Then I travel back on the tractor and work my socks off washing and grading. It's cold, wet, and makes me ache and I hate every minute of it.

It's Monday morning and Sean is dressed, drinking coffee and reading the tide times from a chart laid out on the kitchen table.

I've just out-run Brenda the goose and am puffing for breath. He gives me a puzzled look but doesn't ask.

'It's the neap tide,' he tells me. 'We won't get to the oysters this week; the tide won't go out far enough. I'm at the sailing school. The last lesson finishes at five, so I'll be home after that, but there's not much we can do when the tide's like this. Just keep an eye on things. We don't want anything going wrong with the inspection just round the corner, so make sure no one comes near the place.'

I slide the kettle onto the stove, nodding and rubbing my hands together to warm them up. The front door closes, the empty coffee cup is on the table, and I'm all alone. I put the radio on. It's Hector. I'm starting to like Hector's cheery voice.

I throw some more turf on the fire and wonder what to do next. I could walk into town and go to the café. It's stopped raining and it's just windy out there. I saw Sean sailing this morning before he went to work; flying along he was.

Just then Grace pushes open the door and with her comes a huge gust of wind and the paper piles on the desk swirl up like the hurricane in *The Wizard of Oz*. I spin around trying to catch them. They dance round me as I run to the door and slam it shut. The papers flutter to the ground and all over Grace, standing in the middle of the mess. There's only one thing for it. I clear the table of tide charts, spare rope and old newspapers. I put the newspapers by the fire in the basket and the rope outside the front door, ready to take to the shed. I'm a bit worried about touching the charts. I look around for something useful to keep them in. When I first moved into my bedsit above Betty's Buns, I had to make do for everything. But I was used to it. Moving was a regular thing for us. I'm not sure I ever spent Christmas in the same place two years running. I wasn't always sure why we moved. It usually followed a lot of shouting. I'd hide in my room, and then we'd leave and within a few weeks I'd have a new uncle. I hated moving. But I hated having new uncles more. I wished it could have just been me and my mum and that I could've looked forward to Christmas in the same place.

Whenever we moved anywhere new I always had to make what I could from the packing boxes. I'd put them on top of each other to create a chest of drawers and use a crate with a towel over it for a bedside table. Then of course I moved into our show-home flat with Brian where everything was new. In a funny way, although I didn't miss having cardboard boxes as a chest of drawers, I did miss not being able to make the flat into my home.

After a bit of rummaging around in the kitchen I've made a little organiser out of a cereal box and a milk carton. I roll the charts into it and put the whole thing on the window sill. The table is clear. Grace is watching me with a look of interest and puzzlement. I rub my hands together with satisfaction and then turn my attention to the papers scattered all over the floor, some with large muddy paw prints on them.

I gather them up on the table. Hector has handed over to Ryan Tubridy on the radio and I find I'm smiling at the banter and chat, as though they have become my friends, only I don't have to explain anything about my life to them. With all the papers from the floor picked up I look at the desk. I might as well have a go at it all, so I carry the precarious piles over to the kitchen table as well. I push back the sleeves on my baggy sweatshirt and set about putting them in some kind of order.

I create piles all over the kitchen table. Occasionally I look up, out to sea. The heron is there, as usual, on its rock. It's such an ungainly bird and yet it seems like part of the landscape now, not out of place as I'd first thought. The rain changes in its ferocity against the window pane and every now and again the sun attempts to push through, until the clouds outnumber it, bullying it away.

I think this job might take up the morning, but I'm nowhere near finished as the sun has one final go at pushing through the clouds then starts to sink in the sky. I'm beginning to get a good idea of how Sean's business is looking. There's more red ink on these bills than black. There's income tax and levies, animal feed, and generator repairs. There are papers all over the table, the settee, the chairs; some are sorted, some not. I stand up straight and stretch out my stiff back. Sean and I may not have much in common, or even particularly like each other, but for now anyway it looks as if we both need each other.

I go out and feed Freddie and Mercury and I'm delighted to find they're actually in their field. It's just a small thing but it puts a spring in my step. I give them an extra handful of pony nuts for good behaviour. Perhaps Freddie is finally starting to give up on his lady love.

The chickens have taken themselves off to bed and I slide down their wooden door. Just the geese to go. I grab my stick, keeping my eye on Brenda; she in turn is keeping her yellow eyes on me.

I crouch down and slowly herd the geese towards their old stone shed, my stick in one hand. I feel like the bird man, hoping to take off at any minute. I've just about got them to the shed when Grace lets out a huge joyous bark and runs towards the lane. There's a beep of the horn and I turn to see Sean's red van pulling in through the front gates. As I do, Brenda takes her opportunity to launch herself at me, pecking at my shins. I drop my stick and run to the gate, mistiming my leap and throwing myself painfully against its bars. I look up to see Sean and Nancy watching me. Sean is shaking his head in disbelief and Nancy looks thoroughly amused. I clutch my bruised ribs. I can't decide which is worse, staying out here and trying to get Brenda into her shed, or going into the cottage where Nancy and Sean will no doubt be laughing at my goosing. Then I remember the paperwork and, clutching my sides, I run to the cottage, hoping I can get there before Sean does.

Chapter Thirteen

'What the hell has been going on here?' I hear Sean roaring before I'm even at the cottage.

'I can explain!' I say, throwing myself in through the door. Nancy is blocking my path. I wonder if I should start with 'You have to crack a few eggs to make an omelette', but I don't think he's in a listening mood. But then Sean doesn't listen, he just roars.

'I pay you to work on my farm, not to go through my personal things. You're here to help with the oysters, get ready for the inspection, and look after the animals, although by the looks of it, you're not doing a very good job of that.'

Incensed, I start trying to tell him that I'm doing a perfectly good job, thank you very much, but my tongue ties itself in knots and my mouth just opens and closes. In fact, I'm so furious, I'm speechless.

'Well, we can't stay here tonight,' says Nancy. 'We'll have to go back to mine.' There is a tight smile in the corner of her mouth that tells me she's relieved. Sean tuts loudly and goes to make a fuss of Grace. Then he turns back to the paperwork.

'I thought I might be able to put it into your computer for you,' I finally manage to spit out.

'Computer?' he says with a scoff. 'Never used one. Never needed one and I've managed perfectly well until now.'

I'd love to beg to differ.

Nancy just looks amused and folds her arms. 'I think you're doing a great job of sorting things out,' she says. I feel a little of my tension ease. At least someone can see what I'm trying to do, even if Sean can't.

'Now we can go to O'Grady's tonight,' Nancy links her arm through his. He doesn't budge and looks at the piles of papers and then at me again. He is simmering under his big black cloud.

'Sean, we can't stay here and it looks like your assistant has got it all in hand.' She tugs gently at him.

'I wanted to get out in the boat,' he says to Nancy without looking at her, narrowing his eyes at some of the paperwork. I hold my breath. The last thing I want is him standing over me while I finish putting all these into some kind of order.

'Sean, will you just get back in the van? You can go out on the boat anytime. Besides, you've been out on boats all day!'

He looks around anxiously.

'Where are my charts?'

'On the window sill.' I point to their new container and he relaxes slightly.

'See, all in hand,' Nancy tells him.

There's an uncomfortable silence before he finally says, 'Just make sure it's all back where it was by the morning,' and turns and stalks out.

'Don't mind him. He's not used to help,' says Nancy. 'I think you're doing a great job.' She smiles; well, her face does but it doesn't reach her eyes. The van engine is already running. Nancy throws her head back so her long, shiny dark hair swings and her hand trails elegantly behind her as she sweeps out, leaving the door open. The papers fly up all over again. I sigh deeply. It's going to be a long night. Or, I think, still furious, I could just leave it all. Like he says, I'm not paid to look after his paperwork. I look around with a sinking heart. The thought of starting over again now is thoroughly depressing. So, I grab my waterproof instead, find another two sticks and this time get the geese into bed.

'That's one-all, Brenda!' I call to her as I march off, swinging my arms, towards the town.

I stand outside the pub, wondering whether to go in. I mean, I know Margaret said for me to come, but I'm sure they wouldn't miss me if I didn't. It's not like I could really help them with their committee meeting. Margaret'll have forgotten she even invited me. I've had my walk and calmed down. I could just go, walk back to the cottage. But the thought of another long night with only Sean's paperwork and my own thoughts for company makes me push open the door. Then I do what I always do, put my head down, say nothing, and hope no one notices I'm there.

Margaret's by the bar and spots me straightaway.

'I knew you'd come,' she beams. She's changed her hair. It's smoothed to one side tonight, and her Dayglo earrings are purple. 'It's great to see you. I got a bottle,' she leans over the bar and grabs a glass, pours me a white wine, and hands it to me. I'm usually a vodka and Coke girl, but it's very kind of her and I take the drink.

'Here, Grandad, there's a pint for you.' She puts a pint of Guinness down in front of Grandad, who's in his wheelchair next to the fire.

'Come and sit down and see who you haven't met,' she

calls for me to follow her. So much for keeping my head down. But Margaret makes me smile. She's the sort of person who takes life by the horns, it seems. She puts her drink on the table and bounces along the bench seat, making room for me by the fire. In my heart I know I've only come to spite Sean because I'm cross with him. It's probably best if I just have the one drink, tell them my name, where I'm from, how long I'm planning to stay, and then leave. I've made my point. Just because I'm working for Sean, it doesn't give him the right to be so uptight.

'Great, so we're all here,' Margaret says with great authority as the ladies from the petrol station arrive.

'Rosie, this is Fi. This is Rosie and her sister Lily,' Margaret says. 'Fi's working for Sean Thornton.' Her voice is loaded with excitement.

'Yes, we've met. And how long are you here?' Rosie says, pulling up a stool, as does Lily. Their large chests take up more than two seats and we all shuffle round a bit.

'Just until after . . .' I check myself. Best not mention the inspection. I don't know why but I don't want to do anything else to get on the wrong side of Sean. We still have to work together after all. 'Just for another couple of weeks,' I say, thinking the end of my trial period can't come soon enough, even if I haven't worked out where I'm going to go next.

'Shame. Good to have some fresh blood here.' Rosie sips her pint of cider. 'Some new ideas is what we need,' she says, and her sister agrees, taking a big swig of hers.

'Fi is an all-rounder, a multi-tasker, isn't that right, Fi?' Margaret announces to everyone.

'Oh, well, um . . .'

'Is that right?' Rosie asks. 'What do you do back home?'

'Well, I, um . . .' I take a sip of my drink as my mouth goes dry. 'I work in a coffee shop and at a local radio station.' I'm suddenly feeling in the spotlight and under pressure again.

'Really, oh, that's fab. You're just what we need,' says the woman in the crocheted blue hat. I recognise her from the café.

'That's Maire, Maire runs The Artbox. She's an artist and runs painting lessons if you're interested.' Margaret says it so firmly that I almost feel I should take up painting. But I smile and shake my head. I can just about manage a stick man.

'Haven't had a single student all summer,' says Maire, picking up her knitting.

For a moment they lose interest in me, and Rosie and Maire discuss the lack of holiday-makers and tourists. I have to say, it's not your ideal holiday destination. The whole town could do with a facelift. I look around the pub. I hadn't really taken it in when I was in there before. There are pictures on the walls, a lot of them in black and white. Men in aprons are holding cups, standing in front of tables covered in white tablecloths with bunting above them. Before I have a chance to look closer I get a dig on the arm. It's Grandad. No one's told me his real name, just 'Grandad'.

'When I was young you couldn't move in this pub on a Monday night. Monday night was always music night,' he tells me, reaching for his pint with shaking hands. I lean forward to pass it to him. He takes it with a nod and sips. 'All the lads would be in here after a day on the oyster beds.' He's talking to me but his eyes are seeing scenes from days gone by. Everyone else is talking to each other and I sit quietly and listen, still looking at the photos. 'Families stayed together. They had glue. Now there's nothing for them,' he says. 'All that's left is the memories.' He turns back to look at me. 'So you have to make them good ones,' he chuckles into his shaking pint.

'What are the pictures of?' I ask.

'Ah, those were the days, the Dooleybridge oyster festival. People came from miles away . . .'

'Right!' Margaret bangs the table with her glass and makes me jump.

Grandad is still enjoying the memories as Margaret silences the group. 'Couldn't hear yerself think in here in those days.'

Margaret goes round the group for my benefit. There's Rosie and her sister Lily, Maire from The Artbox, Evelyn and John Joe, Margaret, Patsy the landlord and his wife Sínead, Grandad, Tina from the hairdresser's, David the postman, Gerald from the café, Darragh who owns the souvenir shop and is landlord to Maire, Tina and Gerald.

'Thanks for coming,' says Margaret. 'This meeting has been called because . . . well, look around you. What do you see?' Everyone, including Margaret and me, looks around. Patsy the barman is standing with us, a tea towel over his shoulder. No one is waiting for drinks. The two barflies Padraig and Seamus are nursing pints, but other than that it's just them and us.

'Nothing,' Rosie keeps looking, 'what am I looking for?'

'Nothing. That's exactly it, Rosie.' Margaret slaps her clipboard on the table.

There's a communal intake of breath.

'It's June. The older kids have been off school for nearly a month. In a couple of weeks the national schools will be off for the summer too. And no one is coming here.'

'Might as well shut up shop.' Maire shakes her head while knitting.

'We need something to bring in the crowds. Show them what we've got. I grew up here, I don't want to leave like everyone else. I want people to come and see what a brilliant place Dooleybridge is,' Margaret says passionately.

'What have we got?' asks Tina through her long fringe.

'Well, there's—'

'This place for starters,' Patsy cuts across Margaret. 'If I don't get some good summer trade now I'll be forced to shut my doors.' He looks around at the few drinks he's sold. 'It costs me more to run the place.'

'Ah, no, don't say that.' Rosie takes a big slug of her cider and Patsy's wife Sínead puts an arm around him.

'That's how it is,' Patsy shrugs, and pats Sínead's hand.

'There's this place!' Margaret says, trying to inject some enthusiasm into proceedings.

'And mine!' Gerald joins in with a smile, holding his pint on his belly.

'And there's the beach,' Evelyn joins in. 'My kids spent hours on the beach when they were little. Rain or . . . whatever the weather.'

'Yes, but kids want more than that these days.' Rosie speaks as the voice of authority on the matter and everyone listens. 'They want funfairs, water parks, Wi-Fi everywhere they go . . .'

Maire puts her knitting into her lap thoughtfully.

'I've got the world wide web . . .' Gerald looks like he's watching a deflating balloon.

'We need ideas to bring the holiday-makers back. That's why we're here,' Margaret pushes on valiantly.

Grandad leans towards me. 'In my day you couldn't get on the beach for holiday-makers.'

'Yes, Grandad,' they all chorus.

Margaret rolls her eyes and lets her blank clipboard and pen fall heavily to her side, as though she's fighting a losing battle. I wish I could help but I don't really know the area and I certainly wouldn't have any ideas. I just made cakes when I worked at Betty's, that's all I've ever done. Now I scrub oysters.

'I fancy a night at the dogs,' Rosie nudges her sister, who smiles in agreement.

'Oh yes, a night at the dogs always goes down well. A family night, like,' says Evelyn.

'It's supposed to be something to bring the punters here, not a night out in Galway,' Margaret looks exasperated.

'We could do a table quiz,' says Rosie, getting excited.

'Oh yes, I'm great on geography questions,' says Maire, picking up her knitting again.

'And you could do celebrity ones, Lily,' Rosie nudges her sister.

'Oh yes, and I could do cookery questions,' Evelyn joins in, and everyone looks down at their drinks.

'Only trouble is, we need other teams to take part,' Patsy says, and spirits dip again.

'What about a good old music night,' Grandad suddenly pipes up. 'When I were a lad you couldn't move in here on a Monday night, all the boys from the oyster beds would come in,' he was pointing to the pub and the town beyond. 'On oyster festival weekends, this place was jam-packed.'

'Yes, Grandad,' everyone choruses.

'What about you, Fi? You're the expert in media, what do you think we should do?'

'I think . . .' Everyone turns to look at me. I struggle to think of anything, anything at all. My mind goes totally blank and I blush bright red. I wish I could help Margaret, I really do. She's waiting. I have to say something.

'I . . . I . . . I think Grandad's right. If you want this place jumping again, why not just bring back the oyster festival,' I say. At least I've offered something and now perhaps Margaret will ignore me and they can all go back to what they were talking about before. The pub falls silent and they all stare at me and I have no idea why.

After that the group starts to break up. Patsy goes back behind the bar and Frank and John Joe get out the draughts. Margaret tops up our drinks from the bottle.

'It's complicated,' she tells me. 'It's not just the memories it would bring back, opening old wounds. There's no one here to take part any more. It just wouldn't work.'

'No, it's a shame. They were the days all right . . .' Maire says.

'But it wouldn't work,' Evelyn does up her coat.

'No, no.' Rosie shakes her head. 'It would never work. Not unless we had someone who knew about the media and things like that. Someone to run the festival.' They all look at me.

'Oh, sorry, I just won't be here to help out. I'd love to but I'm not staying around.' I have no intention of opening up any old wounds. Besides, my only media experience is answering the phones on a Saturday afternoon radio show. I pull on my waterproof, do it up to the neck so I'm hiding in it, make my excuses and leave.

'See you next week,' Margaret calls after me. But I won't be coming back to put my foot in it all over again; from now on I'll keep my head down.

Chapter Fourteen

It isn't just the permanent rain that's making the atmosphere in the cottage frosty. All the papers were tidied away by the time Sean got back the following day, and I've even created a filing system of sorts from boxes that I found in Rosie's shop. But Sean's still marching around complaining he can't find anything and I'm silently fuming that he hasn't even said thank you.

This next week promises a spring tide and Sean's back working on the farm. There's just two weeks until the inspection; until I can take what little money I've earned and leave.

We work practically in silence, only speaking when we need to. There's no idle chit-chat, though Sean didn't really do chit-chat in the first place. I still can't bring myself to be much use in the water, but I do work like stink when it comes to washing and grading the oysters. I'm also a demon with the hosepipe, washing down the sheds. The harder I work in the day, the easier it is to sleep at night. And the harder I work, the more distance I seem to be putting between me and Brian. Physical exhaustion numbs the pain.

It's the end of my fourth week on the farm and the night before the inspection.

I feel like I've scrubbed everything in sight and that I've

had a hosepipe permanently welded to my right hand. I ache from the very top of my head to the tips of my toes. Even my earlobes ache from the cold. I'm wet and my cheeks are red from the wind and rain. I have never been so happy to see the inside of the cottage. I peel off my waterproofs and Sean does the same. We don't speak. There is a strange solidarity in our weariness though.

'Let's eat,' Sean says, hanging his waterproofs by the door. He puts a bag of oysters on the table with a clatter and then heads to the kitchen. 'You did well today, English,' he says with his head inside the fridge, so I nearly miss it. He surprises me and I smile. At least we're going to part on friendly terms by the sounds of it. 'You take the bathroom first if you like, I'll get some food on the go.' He pulls out some carrots, celery, an onion and a large white chipped pie dish.

I'd like to be polite and offer him first go in the bathroom or suggest I cook, but my freezing joints won't let me. If it was left to me tonight it would be a couple of slices of toast and bed.

'We need an early night. Big day tomorrow,' he says with the tiniest of winks, and I get the most stupid flush of embarrassment. He puts his hand in the red sack of oysters, pulls one out, taps it, then puts his knife in and opens it.

'Quality control,' he says with a smile, holding it to his nose. He sniffs, puts the shell to his lips and tips his head back.

'Whoa,' he says, looking like an addict who's just had his fix. He offers one to me. 'Sure?' But I shake my head. I just can't see the pleasure.

'I'm going to grab that shower if you don't mind.' I'm still holding up my hand to refuse the oyster. I shan't be sorry if I never see another oyster again after this month.

'You go ahead. I'll rustle up some food. Like I say, you've done well, English.' He opens another oyster and tips his head back again. A silly shiver of excitement runs through me.

'Hey, English,' he calls me back as I'm heading to the bathroom. 'I'm, er . . . I'm sorry about . . . before. I've been meaning to say, y'know, the other week, with the desk. I shouldn't have shouted. You did a great job. I'm just not used to, y'know, sharing my private stuff.'

A smile tugs at the corners of my mouth. So it wasn't all a waste of time then. I feel like a peacock, proudly puffing myself up. Then I have no idea what makes me boldly ask, 'Does Nancy know?' I'm talking about his money problems, of course, but I don't need to spell it out.

He stops opening oysters for a moment. I tense up, wishing I hadn't asked. I want the words to go back where they came from. But when he simply shakes his head I find myself breathing again.

'I just need to get through tomorrow. That lot waiting to go to market,' he nods in the direction of the bagged and prepared oysters, 'will pay the licence and get me some more spat. Then I can start sorting out some of the other bills.' He smiles and grabs a tin of Guinness from the fridge and cracks it open. 'Once tomorrow's out the way I can start moving forward. It'll be fine. You go and shower.'

I don't need telling twice and disappear to the bathroom. I turn the shower on full whack and wait for it to heat up.

Suddenly there's music playing loudly on the kitchen radio. I can hear Sean singing along. He obviously feels life is on the up. I step tentatively into the shower. Maybe it's time things got better for both of us. I smile. There's warm water for starters.

When I'm warm and clean I switch off the shower and step out onto the wooden bath mat on the floor. There are lots of towels spilling over the towel rail. I do something I've wanted to do since I got here and pull them all off. Then I fold and straighten them with a little feeling of satisfaction. You never know, the inspector might need to come in here too.

I can still hear Sean's music blaring out and realise I'm nodding along to it myself. The water drips off me. It feels like tomorrow is going to be a new start for both of us. Outside the rain has stopped. The sun is attempting to finally show me how pretty it can be, throwing a yellow pathway down to the sea, a bit like Dorothy's yellow brick road. If only I had a pair of ruby slippers! A soft, blurry rainbow reaches across the bay. I take watery steps towards my towel on the tidy rail and then hold it to my face. It smells of washing powder and peat smoke. But not like my washing powder at home. It smells soapier and not so floral. Brian liked the one with ylang-ylang in it.

I walk to the sink, naked, and look in the mirror. A lot has changed in four weeks. The way I look for starters. Thinner. More tired. But there's colour in my cheeks. In fact my face looks quite healthy. My neat bob is curling at the ends. I stand on tiptoes to see more of myself. I'm still hippy but I've lost weight off my chest. Brian and I didn't spend much time naked. We took it in turns in the bathroom and sex was a lights-off, under-the-covers affair. I look at myself again and I wonder if he ever really loved me. Or was I always just a decoy, throwing people off the scent? I don't expect I'll ever know now. But at least that explains him never wanting to see me naked.

I start to dry myself. My rings slip around my fingers. I slide them off for the first time since I said 'I do' and Brian said 'Sorry, I can't' after signing the register. I hold them in my hand. It's time to move on. And these rings are my ticket out of here. I turn them over in my hand and then clench them tightly. It's the end of my trial period. Tomorrow Sean will be through his inspection. I'm going to sell them and move on, even if it's just to my mother's lumpy sofa in Malta. Although I'm not sure her current boyfriend will be too happy to see me and I definitely won't be calling him Uncle. Especially when I gather we're very close in age. Just thinking about it makes me feel like I've stepped in cold custard. But I don't know where else to go. I may not like my mother or the way my teenage years panned out, but she is the only relative I have. All I have to do now is tell Sean. I know we'll never keep in touch, but he wasn't so bad. I can say that now I won't have to work for him again. Like I say, with luck we'll part as friends.

The floor's cold and my bones still ache. At least it should be hot in Malta. I turn back to the sink to do my teeth and just as I'm reaching for the Colgate on the window sill, a dark shadow falls across my hand. I freeze.

Chapter Fifteen

He's standing in front of the window, a man in a baseball cap, blocking out the sunset. He's turning slowly, holding a smartphone horizontally at arm's length, panning across the oyster beds. Only now he's slowly turning . . . towards me.

I snatch up the towel and just manage to throw it around me, clutching it to my chest before he turns and looks straight through his fingers at me. I don't know who's more shocked, but finally I manage to shriek and then so does he, dropping his hands, his sunglasses falling from his forehead to his face. Clutching both his hands on top of his head, he runs.

Shit! No way is all our hard work going to be jeopardised now. I throw back the bathroom door with a bang.

'Sean, Sean!' I run into the kitchen. 'Sean!' I yell again at the top of my voice, above his music and his singing. Even Grace takes a while to notice me from her place in front of the fire. The room's full of the most amazing smells: caramelised meat, red wine, herbs, roasting potatoes, coming from the oven.

Sean's standing with his back to me at the kitchen work surface. There's a lamp plugged in on the side throwing light on to the chopping board he's wiping down.

'*Sean!*'

He finally spins round. Grace jumps up and barks.

Clutching the towel, I lunge forward and press the off button on the CD player.

'Oh, good God!' he says, suddenly making me very aware that I'm standing in his kitchen with just a towel wrapped round me.

'Never mind good God! This is urgent! There's a man, in a hat, with a camera. Filming. Outside the window . . .' I garble and point. What if it's one of those pirates, oyster thingies he told me about? I couldn't bear it if they were stolen now, not when we've worked so hard. Sean doesn't need any more explanation. He throws down his kitchen knife and is at the door in two strides, calling Grace behind him. She jumps into action, letting out her war cry. Sean throws back the door and, stepping into his wellington boots, runs outside behind Grace who's already giving chase. I follow to see the man in the hat jumping into a black 4x4 and departing at speed, showering gravel in his wake as he drives away.

Grace barks for all she's worth, but the black 4x4 is already disappearing down the lane. Sean's shaking his head, having given up running after it. He's bent over, holding his knees. I'm still on the steps, anxiously wondering what damage they've done. Slowly Sean stands up and begins walking back towards me, still shaking his head.

'I didn't recognise the car,' he frowns. 'Could be from out of town.' He calls Grace to him and makes a fuss of her.

The yard itself still looks immaculate. A far cry from when I first arrived. Broken fencing has been fixed. Wetsuits and wellies have been tidied, and even the little bit of grass on the bank is trimmed. The front door of the old barn has been painted and I even planted up a few wall flowers I bought in

Rosie's petrol station in some old lobster pots and put them either side of the old barn door.

'I'm going to check the sheds and the stock,' Sean calls over his shoulder. 'Keep an eye on the dinner,' and he stalks away.

'No, wait, I can help.' I start to follow. He turns, puts his hands on his hips and raises an eyebrow.

'I don't think so,' he says, like a school teacher dealing with a challenging pupil. I bristle. He obviously still thinks I'm the wet-behind-the-ears girl from the city. I go to put my hands on my hips and remind him who's done most of the tidying round here, when the towel slips a little and I remember it's all I'm wearing. A black cloud of insects suddenly gathers over my head.

A tiny smile tugs at the corners of Sean's mouth; at least I think it's a smile. And now that the immediate panic is over, I'm suddenly feeling very awkward. The dark cloud lowers over me and begins to sting my skin. A gang of mosquitoes is obviously settling in for a full-on feast. I run inside, straight back to the bathroom, where I let the towel drop, rub my hair madly and then jump straight back into the shower.

When I re-emerge fully dressed into the kitchen, which still smells divine, Sean's back inside and the living room's had a change round. He's moved the table and pushed the settee away in order to be able to look out of the window at the oyster beds. He's peering at them through big, heavy binoculars. I straighten a box of fallen paperwork.

'You keep an eye out while I serve up.' He hands me the binoculars. 'The last thing we want is for the bastards to come back tonight.'

The binoculars are heavier than I expected. I step forward and take over where he's been standing. It's awkward negotiating the newly positioned settee and table. Nothing else has been moved to make space for them, and as I step forward, so does he. Just for a moment we're chest to chest and I try to tilt myself back so as not to be touching but nearly topple backwards. He catches my elbow. I catch my breath. Just for a moment we hold each other's stare and my insides unexpectedly leap. I look away quickly. It's not good to be this close and intimate with your employer, I scold myself, even if it is only for one more day.

He's wearing his blue knitted jacket with the hood. Its toggles press into me, emphasising how close we are. Just for a second or two I realise I've stopped breathing, and when I start again my chest rises up and down even more than before. I practically fall onto the settee, snatching the binoculars from him as I go.

'Heavy, aren't they?' I chirp, trying to forget the closeness we've just encountered. For a moment I felt like my whole body had been kick-started from a hundred-year sleep.

'They were my uncle's. There was many a night I sat here with him watching for oyster pirates.' He looks out to sea as if enjoying a cherished painting.

'You love it here, don't you?' I say, seeing his face soften.

'I do.' He looks back at me as if I wasn't just the hired help any more, but someone who understood what he was trying to say. It was like seeing through a tiny chink in the armour. 'Which is why I have to pass the inspection tomorrow.' Then he turns quickly towards the kitchen and I look out to sea with the binoculars. It's like wearing 3D glasses to the cinema, designed to exaggerate your worst nightmares. It's a small step, but there's no way I could have done this four weeks ago.

'Food's up!' Sean hands me a loaded plate. It's piled high with steaming mashed potato, golden, crumbly pastry, chunks of beef, and dark brown, rich gravy. 'Hope you like pie.' He hands me a fork and then steps over my legs to sit down next to me. 'I know you won't eat oysters, but I thought you might be all right with this.'

I look down at my plate as his jean-clad thighs reach over me. I move up the settee as far as I can. Honestly, you'd think I'd never been near a man before, instead of living with one for five years before marrying him; but then, I never really got to know him, did I?

'Right, eat up and then I'm going to stay up and keep watch. You can go to bed if you like.' He starts tucking into his plate of hot potato and pie. I dig in too. It's so good it's like being wrapped up in a goose-down duvet. Behind us the fire cheerily warms the room. I fork the beef into my mouth. Then I put my fork into something I don't recognise. I pick it up and look at it, sniff it and look at it again. Sean is mid-mouthful but can't help but laugh.

'OK, you got me.' He holds up a hand and is fully enjoying his own joke. I look at him accusingly. 'You wouldn't eat them raw so I thought I'd try them cooked.'

'Oysters? In the pie?' I'm actually enjoying the joke too.

'Just try one.' He hands me the ketchup from beside him on the floor. 'Try it with ketchup. Beef and oyster pie; it's a classic combination.'

'Really?' I look at it again and then stick my tongue out and try to taste it by licking a little bit of sauce from it. 'I'm sorry, I can't.' I still can't explain my bad relationship with the sea. 'What if it was a bad one, what if I got sick?' I say wildly, hoping he'll be fooled.

'You've pulled it from the sea yourself. It couldn't be fresher!'

I know he's right, but I just can't handle it. I shake my head and put the forkful down on my plate and he scoops it up and eats it. I pick out the rest of the oysters to the sound of his gentle laughter beside me, but finish the rest of the pie and scrape the plate clean.

'Thank you, that was delicious. Be even nicer without the oysters,' I joke, and take his plate.

'You don't know what's good for you, English!' he shouts after me as I head to the kitchen.

'I'll wash up,' I say, and he moves into my place and picks up the binoculars. Things have definitely thawed in our working relationship. I'll almost be sorry to go if we carry on getting on like this. Grace follows me, ever hopeful of a few scraps. I can't even say how much I'm going to miss Grace. Once I'm settled I'm going to get a dog of my own, I decide. No more living in flats with no-pet policies. I wash up and am drying my hands with the tea towel when I realise how important tomorrow is to me too.

'I'll stay up too,' I say.

He looks up from his binoculars as if pleasantly surprised.

'You don't have to.'

'I do. I'd hate it if anything happened now, before I went,' I add. There's a moment's silence.

'You've decided then, you're moving on?'

I fold the tea towel more times than it needs folding. 'Yes,' I say quietly, unfolding it again and putting it on the work surface. 'It's been great, but I don't think I'm ever going to make it as an oyster farmer.'

He tries to keep a straight face, but can't, and we both laugh.

'I'll advertise, after the inspection,' he says with gentle resignation.

'Make sure it's someone who doesn't mind the wet,' I tell him, putting on the kettle. 'And who wears size six wellington boots.'

'And someone who eats oysters,' he joins in, going back to his binoculars. 'I never did get you out on the hooker,' he says, as if he genuinely thinks I've missed out on one of life's greatest pleasures. I pull out mugs to make a tea and coffee.

'Well, the hooker and me didn't get off to a great start, did we?'

His face breaks into another rare smile behind the binoculars.

'And make sure it's someone who's good with geese,' I add, realising that he really isn't quite so bad after all; even quite fanciable in a grumpy kind of way.

Chapter Sixteen

'We can take it in turns to sleep and keep watch.' Sean looks up as I hand him his coffee. This time I have to step over his legs to get onto the settee. Not easy with a boiling hot cup of tea. Grace once more fills the gap between our feet and the wall and I pull my feet up underneath me, wrapping my hands around my cup. We slip back into silence and our own thoughts.

I look out to sea. It seems fairly flat tonight, apart from the waves crashing against the rocks in the distance. Sean too sits staring out at the bay. I try to think of something to talk about, but my mind is blank. Part of me is wishing I'd taken the offer of going to bed, but that wouldn't have been fair. I'd worked hard for the inspection and I didn't want it sabotaged by some measly oyster pirate. The silence goes on but for the occasional lapping of the water, the wind whistling through the poorly fitted window frames, the fire occasionally fizzing, and Grace's snoring. This could be a long night.

'I'd put some music on,' Sean's obviously feeling my awkwardness, 'but it's best we listen out for that car coming back.'

'Of course, yes,' I say. He doesn't take his eyes away from the binoculars. I try playing I-spy with myself but it doesn't work. Then counting seagulls – anything to stop my mind wandering back to home and what Brian and Adrian would be doing now. Hours pass. The sun finally sets and darkness draws in.

'Tell you what, how about a drink? Just something to sharpen us up,' Sean says, standing up. The tiredness is coming in waves. 'Call it a leaving drink,' he smiles.

'OK,' I say, grateful for the distraction.

'You hold these.' He hands me the binoculars like a baton in a relay. I hold them up to my eyes. There's just the odd light on the other side of the bay. He takes a large step over Grace and me. I lean back against the settee as far as I can. Perhaps a cup of tea is just what I need. Suddenly the lights in the room go out. My eyes take time adjusting. I turn and can just about see Sean by the light switch.

'Thought it would help us see out.'

'Oh yes, of course.' I look back at the dark outside. The moon is throwing a dim light on the ripples. It makes me shiver. I can't imagine what it would be like to be out on the water tonight. Whoever he is, the oyster pirate, he must be a madman, wild, impetuous. I look at Sean's reflection in the window, lit up by the lamp on the work surface. I'm thinking about the oyster pirate I remind myself, not Sean!

He comes back and hands me a glass with a small amount of golden liquid in the bottom: whiskey. I take it in surprise. The smell alone makes my eyes smart. I don't think I've ever drunk whiskey. I know it sounds daft, but I really don't think I have. Sean reaches over me again and sits down, taking the binoculars back.

'At least now we should be able to see any lights,' he nods out to the dark sea. He turns to me, raises his glass. '*Slàinte*,' he says, and sips.

'Do you speak Irish?' I hold the glass near my mouth. My eyes are still burning from the fumes.

Sean takes another sip and shakes his head. 'This area hasn't been Irish-speaking for years. Besides which I'm a blow-in. My uncle was born and bred here. But he was married to my aunt, my mother's sister. I grew up in Dublin, in a manner of speaking.' He takes another sip of his drink and I put the family tree together in my head. He doesn't elaborate any more.

I blink a lot as I hold the glass to my lips. It would be rude not to try it. I take my first burning sip. I can feel Sean watching me as the liquid fire slides all the way down. I blink even more and then try to speak. It comes out like a croak.

'So did you always want to be an oyster farmer?' I cough.

He sips from his glass then shakes his head, ignoring the croak.

'Not really. I mean, I always loved this place, but I didn't have any big plans, not really.' He doesn't look as if he's going to expand. But then he takes another sip and says, 'I loved coming here when I was younger. Then, when I was travelling, I spent some time in France, with Nancy's family, working for her dad. My uncle and her dad go way back, competing in shucking competitions together.'

I look at him blankly and he gives a little laugh.

'Opening oysters,' he explains. 'It's an art form and a sport all in one. There are competitions all over the world. You use a little knife to open them and the winner is the person who can do it the fastest and the neatest.'

'Ah,' I say, understanding, sort of. 'So you and Nancy have known each other a long time?'

'Since we were teenagers.' He takes another sip. 'I was

there just before my uncle got sick. All the other cousins had either moved abroad or had jobs in other areas. I came back to live here with him, and so the farm came to me.' He sips and so do I. It burns just the same. I grimace just the same and Sean smiles, just the same. 'It came at the right time for me. What about you?' Sean picks up the binoculars and looks out before resting them in his lap and looking back at me.

'No.' I twist the glass. I tuck my legs up further, as if curling myself into a sort of ball. 'I never had any big plans, other than . . .'

'What?' He looks at me with interest.

A tiny little dream bubble pops up and then disappears. I look back into the drink.

'Just to get through it, I suppose.'

'That's a bit pathetic,' Sean tuts. 'You must have wanted to do something when you were younger.'

'No, not really. I liked cooking for people. I liked how it made people feel better.' Ever since my mum left me weeks before my sixteenth birthday and went to Malta on holiday with her much younger boyfriend and ended up staying, I'd been at Betty's coffee shop. I was happy there, I think, tucked away in the kitchen, seeing the empty plates that came back.

'Did your mum ever cook, or your dad?' Sean asks, and I shake my head as the hole from the missing piece of jigsaw inside me opens up.

'Mum didn't cook. I don't know if my dad did. I never knew him,' I surprise myself by saying.

'Never?'

I shake my head.

'Did you ever want to find him?' he asks, interested.

I shake my head again. 'Wouldn't know where to start.

She can't remember anything about it. Not even a Christian name. Though,' I start to say, 'I do wonder. I wonder what life would have been like, you know, wonder who I am.' I stop suddenly. 'I think not knowing where you came from can make it harder to understand where you're going, to know who you are,' I finish.

'Sometimes I think it's better just to worry about where you're going,' he says, looking straight at me, and I feel my throat tighten and tears prickle my eyes. I give a little cough to clear it.

'What about you then?' I change the subject quickly. 'What were your big plans?'

'To play Wembley Arena, obviously!' He nods to the guitar, making me laugh too. I suddenly feel very relaxed, like I'm spending the evening with a friend, and a good-looking one at that. Not that I'm ever going down that route again. I don't need a man in my life, but being friends is nice. I just wish the excitement in my tummy would settle down.

'So what happened?' I take a smaller sip this time and it burns less.

He turns with a wicked gleam in his eye. 'Life.' He raises an eyebrow. 'And oysters.'

'I can see that,' I smile. The whiskey is loosening my tongue. 'Do you know, when you talk about oysters your whole face lights up. It's like you can't help yourself. I don't get it, they're just knobbly shells full of slime really. I don't get the excitement.' One small whiskey and I'm playing amateur psychologist with my boss. But all the time I'm asking him about his life, he isn't pushing me to talk about mine.

'Knobbly shells full of slime!' he says, outraged but still

smiling. 'I'll have you know oysters are the food of the gods! In Roman times they paid for them by their weight in gold.'

He nearly knocks the binoculars from his lap. I grab a cushion from between us and hold it against me as I turn to him, interested.

'Really?' I'm surprised. 'I don't get it. What's with the whole aphrodisiac thing then?' My tiredness ebbs away.

'Well, Aphrodite, Greek goddess of love, is supposed to have sprung forth from the sea in an oyster shell and straight away gave birth to Eros. That's the mythology behind it. And then of course Casanova was supposed to have eaten twelve dozen oysters at the start of each meal.' He stands up, still talking, and goes to fetch the whiskey bottle from the kitchen. He tops up both glasses. I think about saying no, but I don't. The burning sensation is less painful now, more numbing. Almost pleasant. And I realise I'm enjoying myself. It feels nice just to listen.

'But the real reason is that oysters are high in zinc, which increases a man's testosterone, making him fertile.' He sips his drink and so do I, to cover my blushes. But my mouth seems to have taken on a life of its own.

'You don't have any children then?' I ask.

'No. You?' he bats back.

'No,' I shake my head.

'What happened?' he finally asks, as if giving me the opportunity to tell him how I ended up there.

'Life,' I reply flatly. No matter how much whiskey I've had, that piece of my life is still firmly locked away. 'And a dislike of oysters,' and we both laugh.

'Life can be like that.'

I really hope he's not going to ask me anything else. We

lapse into silence again before Sean pipes up, 'Did you know that oysters have two hearts?' Steering us both into safer waters. 'And they change sex every year.' He leans back and kicks off his boots, waking Grace, who lifts her head just for a second before flopping contentedly back to sleep. 'The native oysters reproduce during the summer months and change sex every time they do so.'

'Really?' I find myself screwing up my nose.

'Yup,' he confirms and stretches out his legs, putting his feet on the window sill. 'They can be father and mother to two separate litters in the same year.'

'Ewww!' I can't help but grimace again and he gives a friendly laugh back.

'Good job you're off then and I'm not relying on you to sell my oysters.' He sips. This is the most relaxed I've seen him on dry land. He intermittently picks up the binoculars from his lap and looks out.

'So what will happen when I go? You'll need help still. Will Nancy move here eventually?'

Sean splutters into his drink, coughing and laughing. When he clears his airways he says, 'No, Nancy will never come and live here. Nancy hates it here. Nancy and I have . . .' He thinks about things for a while, '. . . a good partnership. I grow oysters, she sells oysters, and in the meantime we . . . enjoy each other's company. It works for both of us.'

'Oh, I thought—'

'Like I say, it works for both of us. It's a working partnership and not half as painful as true love. We're friends, our families are friends, we get each other.' He looks straight out to sea and that tells me all I need to know. It's funny, now I'm about to leave I start to realise Sean is almost human.

The sea is pitch black now. The living room is only lit by the flickering glow from the fire behind us. The moon has come up silver, big and bright, casting a light across the water. It suddenly looks very beautiful and calm. Stars appear all around the moon. They are brilliantly bright, twinkling, and make the sky seem deeper than I've ever seen; a blanket of stars that I want to travel through, get lost in.

'Now you see why I love this place so much,' Sean says softly next to me, and I nod, not taking my eyes off the sky, feeling like a child enjoying the turning on of the town's Christmas lights.

'See that, that's the Great Bear,' he points, and I see him hesitate, wondering if I know this stuff. But I don't. I look at the pattern of stars he's pointing at. 'And there, the Little Bear.' I keep looking where he's pointing.

'There!' he suddenly shouts excitedly, making me spill some of my drink, as a burst of stars arc across the sky.

'Was that . . .'

He nods, his eyes wide with excitement.

'I've never seen a shooting star!'

'You have now . . . make a wish,' he says. I dry my hands on my trousers and do as he says, not feeling ridiculous. I close my eyes and wish that life could always be like this, uncomplicated.

He tops up the glasses again and we both sit back, our feet on the window sill, making up our own silly shapes in the stars. The cushions that were between us have fallen on the floor and Grace is using them as a pillow.

'That one's a unicorn,' I say, pointing, 'with a wand.'

'A unicorn, more like a set of drums,' he argues, and points again. I lean in to look where he's pointing.

'I can't see it,' I say, right up against his arm.

'There,' he points again and laughs and turns to me. Our faces are up close and for a moment the laughter stops, time seems to stand still and our eyes lock together. I can feel his breath and my stomach flips over and back again. Grace nudges my legs and I fall back to my side of the settee and stare straight out at the stars. Did I just imagine it or could we have kissed if I'd wanted to?

'I have never seen anything so beautiful,' I say, focusing my attention back on the night sky. 'I didn't get it before. All that rain and no real green fields. But I think I get it now.'

'Get what?' He takes a sip of whiskey.

'Why people talk about Galway Bay. Write songs about it, you know. I won't forget this . . .'

We carry on, lost in our thoughts and pointing out silly star patterns, eventually leaning shoulder to shoulder, without realising it, as the early hours of the morning set in and sleep finally comes to both of us.

Chapter Seventeen

Whooof, whooooof, whoooof, whoooof! Grace's battle cry catapults me from my deep sleep. I try to move but a sharp pain shoots up through my neck, crippling me. I clutch my hand to it and lift my head stiffly from its resting place: a shoulder and a denim shirt that I don't recognise.

'Where the . . . ?' My mouth is dry, my head fuzzy. A blast of cold air freezes me as a door opens behind me. Grace jumps up, throwing my legs into the air. I go to spin round and a sharp pain shoots up my neck again. I am suddenly fully aware of whose shoulder I've been sleeping on. I force myself to sit bolt upright, despite it hurting. Beside me, Sean's stretching out slowly and yawning loudly. I daren't look round, I just can't make eye-contact. Falling asleep on your boss is about as embarrassing as it gets.

'Well, well, well,' a French voice with an Irish lilt says behind me. 'What's this?'

I'm half standing. The colour drains from my face. I don't need to spin round to know that Nancy is standing in the doorway. I feel like I've been caught with my hands in the biscuit tin.

Sean's up off the settee, swinging his legs over the arm.

'Hey, Nance.' He's over and beside her in a flash, picking up the empty whiskey glasses as he goes. I can't tell if he's as

122

embarrassed as me or delighted to see her, having had to spend an evening with me. Probably the latter. I hear him kiss her. I rearrange the cushions on the sofa, hoping my blushes will subside. Although why I'm blushing I have no idea. I've nothing to hide. I've done nothing wrong, but can't work out why it feels like I have.

'Oyster pirates,' Sean's explaining, matter-of-factly. But why wouldn't he be matter of fact? Nothing happened. It's all in my head. It was the whiskey, the stars, the moonlight, letting down my guard a bit, knowing I'm leaving. Except that in the moonlight and with a couple of whiskeys inside me, either one of us could've leant in and taken a kiss if we thought the other one had wanted it too. Thank God he hadn't. I rearrange the cushions all over again.

'Tried to take our stock last night,' he's explaining from the bathroom. 'We've been taking it in turns to stay on watch.'

I can't help but notice he's told a little white lie. Why? A little jolt passes through me. He can't be feeling the same as me. He's probably just trying to save my embarrassment, which is really kind. My mind flits back to his warm breath on my face. Was it me? Or was it him? I can't remember. I push it aside.

'Who were they?'

'Huh?' I catch my breath and spin round to Nancy, cushion still in hand.

'The pirates, who were they?' She's looking at me for a straightforward answer and I'm staring blankly back.

'You were watching for oyster pirates. Then what happened?' she prompts me again, then sighs and turns back to Sean in the bathroom. She must think I'm really stupid.

Yet how could I explain that the stars had put on some kind of private extravaganza for my benefit, and how beautiful it had been? How could I explain that I'd listened and learnt about oysters and that I saw Sean in a whole new light? I think about his face, how it lit up, how he came alive. So different from the grumpy farmer I'd first met. This is a man who cares, very, very much, and that can't make him a bad person. In fact, I rather liked the Sean I got to know last night. I liked him a lot.

'Sean, what happened?' Nancy's shouting through the bathroom door. But the sound of taps running drowns her out.

The oyster pirates hadn't come back, or at least I don't think they had. I go to the kitchen and put last night's glasses in the sink. Nancy is looking at them and then back at me. I'm feeling uncomfortable, but I don't know why, because nothing happened. I repeat this in my head. Maybe the problem is that I wish it had. The thought surprises me so much that a glass slips from my hand into the sink I'm filling with hot water and washing up liquid, splashing me with soapy suds.

I turn from the sink, clutching my neck, which is still locked into a slightly tilted position. 'I'll go and check outside.' I want to get out of there. Nancy's saying nothing, but I can feel her looking at me as I pass. Her arms are folded, her bright red painted fingernails, vibrant against the black of her smart fitted dress, are tapping.

Then Grace gives out another round of *whoooof, whoooooof*s. Sean sticks his head out of the bathroom door. 'Who's that?' He cranes his neck to look down the lane.

'Just thought I'd come by to wish you luck before the

inspector got here. Looks like I'm too late.' Nancy raises an eyebrow.

'What?' Sean and I say together.

'Looks like the inspector.' Nancy nods her head towards the drive.

'It can't be, he's not due until . . .' Sean looks up at the clock above the stove.

'Shit!' we say together.

Sean's pulling on his wellies and I grab my hat and waterproof coat.

'Oh, and by the way,' Nancy adds, 'I saw two donkeys making their way across the drive just as I was pulling in.'

'You get the donkeys, I'll see the inspector.' Sean flings open the door just as a short, fat man wearing an ill-fitting suit and wellies and carrying a clipboard gets out of his little white van. Grace is barking at him and he tries shooing her away with his clipboard, making her bark even more. Sean runs over to him and puts his hand on Grace's head. The man holds his clipboard in front of him like a shield.

'I'll do the water's edge, you do the lane,' I tell Nancy as I go to run outside. But Nancy doesn't move. I turn back.

'Nancy?'

'Uh?' She looks as if I've asked her to fly to the moon.

'The donkeys. We need to find them.'

'Oh, I'm not really a donkey person.' She waves her painted nails in my direction.

'This is Sean's inspection,' I say slowly but with a growing disbelief. 'We need to do this . . . now.' I surprise myself.

She stares as if she's about to challenge me.

I stare right back, feeling fury surging up inside me. 'Sean loves this place,' I hiss.

'And maybe you love Sean.' Her eyes darken. She turns her mouth down at the corners in disgust. I'm so enraged I can't speak. Instead I storm off, cheeks burning with indignation, in search of two runaway donkeys. I'm going to do whatever it takes for Sean to pass today.

The hens start up an almighty row, wanting to be let out of their run and fed. Sean is talking to the inspector, pointing to the boundaries of the farm. He looks nervously over his shoulder at me, then says something to the inspector and politely excuses himself.

He runs over to me and slings his arm around me, pulling me close and talking quietly into my ear. My body is on high alert, buzzing at his closeness.

'Any sign of them?'

I shake my head tightly.

'If they go anywhere near the oysters it could cost us the licence.' Sean is acting nonchalantly but his voice is full of panic.

'I'll find them,' I say, smiling at the inspector, acting as if there's no problem at all. But we both know there is, a massive one. I can't believe that this could fail him, after all the hard work we've put in.

Just then, two donkeys' heads appear from behind the shell pile, just by the inspector, heading for the water's edge.

'Get them away,' Sean hisses and gives my shoulder a hard squeeze. I don't need telling twice. All I have to do now is work out how to get two wayward donkeys back into their field without the usual game of grandmother's footsteps and without the inspector noticing.

Like a Tom and Jerry cartoon I grab my bucket of pony nuts and creep round the back of the inspector who Sean is showing around. I shake the bucket. The inspector looks round briefly but quickly turns back to his clipboard. The donkeys stand staring at me. I don't want to chase them as that'll only make them run right into the path of the inspector. I shake the bucket again. Mercury takes one step forward but Freddie isn't budging. I throw some nuts down in front of them but it just makes Mercury flinch, turn and take two steps back. I look back at the cottage. Nancy is watching me with an amused look on her face. I put the bucket down low to try and show them what's in it. Mercury looks interested. I can't shake it again without attracting attention, so I lie on the floor and start to crawl towards them on the stony ground. Sean is directing the inspector towards the path around the bay. He looks back at me, his face turning to horror, probably imagining all his hopes and dreams disappearing thanks to my ham-fisted attempt to round up two tame donkeys.

I begin to crawl and the donkeys look as if they're about to take flight, spooked by the rustling of my coat. I slip out of it and begin moving forwards on my elbows. They settle again. When I left home on my wedding day a month ago, I could never have imagined I would end up lying on the ground, clutching a bucket, underneath two donkeys.

Mercury looks at the bucket suspiciously. I give it a little rattle. He jumps but doesn't run. Freddie is determined to ignore me. Mercury sniffs at the bucket. I push it further towards him, pulling on my stomach muscles. I can hear Freddie's hooves. He's starting to move backwards. If they make a run for it now there's no way I'm going to be able to stop them. They'll charge right across in front of the inspector. And I'm not going to let that happen. I push the bucket towards Mercury, who finally sticks his head in and starts to eat. In one swift movement I stand up and sling the lead rope round his neck. Now all I have to do is hope Freddie will follow. I begin to walk towards the field, as if I've been out for a morning stroll with my pet donkey. I can't turn back and look in case the inspector is looking my way. I just have to keep walking and hope that Freddie is following. If he isn't, all is lost.

I pull back the gate and let Mercury go, putting down the bucket of feed. I take a deep breath and turn. I even have my eyes squeezed tight a little. I look out to the oyster beds but my heart lurches with love and gratitude to see Freddie standing right behind me, nudging me for nuts. Just call me the donkey whisperer! I look up at Sean and I know I'm grinning from ear to ear. Sean's grinning right back at me. He raises his hand in the tiniest of waves. I can see him relax and settle into the inspection. Nancy, on the other hand, looks like she's sucking on a lemon.

Chapter Eighteen

'We passed!' Sean shouts. He's holding up a piece of paper. The white van disappears off up the lane, listing this way and that on the uneven ground. Sean looks relieved and he's grinning like a daft schoolboy.

'That's brilliant!' I say, hands on hips, still a little out of breath from being chased by Brenda the goose.

'So that's it, the place is yours!' I can't help but smile with him because I can leave now knowing the place he loves, his livelihood, his passion, is safe.

'For the next ten years at least, providing there's no problems with the waters in the meantime. I'm in business!' He lets out a whoop and suddenly grabs me, picks me up and swings me round. I grab hold of my hat with one hand and his shoulder with the other. I shriek as he spins me round, just as Nancy decides to join us. Sean puts me down but doesn't let his smile drop.

'We did it!' He hugs and kisses Nancy. I'm still fuming at her lack of effort.

'I knew you would,' she smiles, giving me the merest sideways glance before cupping his face in both hands and kissing him long and hard. I look away, feeling like a big fat gooseberry. But Nancy manages to catch my eye when she comes up for air, giving me another pointed look, making sure I've got the message.

'So where do you want to go to celebrate?' Nancy rubs away traces of her bright red lipstick from his mouth as she stands with her arm around his back, practically entwined.

'You choose, I'm not bothered,' he says, bending down to rub Grace's head in celebratory mood. Nancy moves her leg away as Grace snakes around in front of Sean. Nancy and I may have crossed swords earlier but I hope this meal will mean we can put any misunderstandings behind us, along with any talk of Sean leaving the farm and going to work in her restaurant.

'Oh, I've got something for you.' Sean pulls out a brown envelope from his back pocket and hands it to me. 'It's not much, I'm afraid, but it's what I owe you and just a bit extra. I know how hard you've worked.'

I take the envelope of notes and smile. It was hard-earned money and it's going to have to last me until I find more work.

'Right, dinner tonight. Where's it to be?' Sean says to Nancy. I tap the envelope and smile some more.

'Sure you don't mind, Fi?' Nancy smiles sweetly at me.

'Mind?' I'm confused.

'You'll be OK here on your own, won't you,' she tells me rather than asks.

Sean looks up from rubbing Grace's ears. 'Oh, but I thought . . .'

'I mean, what if the oyster pirates were to return?' Nancy says. 'I'm worried sick about them coming back.' She looks at Sean.

I swallow and nod. 'Of course. I'll be fine.' My little celebratory bubble bursts.

'You sure you don't mind, English? I could go into town, get something and cook. We could all eat together this evening.'

'No, don't be daft,' I say, at the same time Nancy says, 'No, she's fine.'

I bite my lip.

'If you're sure . . .' Sean double checks with me and I nod. 'I'll grab a shower and we'll be off then. Nothing much more we can do now. Take the rest of the day off.' Sean grins, then runs into the cottage, obviously keen to get his night of celebrations underway. Nancy's smile drops and she throws me another warning look, then turns and swings her long dark hair and sashays up the uneven steps to the cottage with amazing steadiness.

'Looks like two's a party, three's a crowd,' I say to Grace, rubbing her ears. I breathe in deeply.

The air seems to have a calming effect. It smells salty and fresh. I'd like to try and remember that smell. The wind flicks at the ends of my hair poking out from under my hat. I need to get down to the café before it shuts and get on the internet to book a flight. I shut my eyes and let the freshness fill my head and lungs. At least I feel I'm leaving here a little more sorted in myself, compared to when I'd arrived. I might even miss it a bit. I watch as Grace sniffs at the rocks, up and down. I'll miss Freddie and Mercury too. But not Brenda the goose, or Nancy for that matter.

'I'm walking into town,' I call to Sean and Nancy as I grab Grace's lead from just inside the door on the coat pegs. But there's no reply and the bedroom door is shut. Together Grace and I set off down the lane.

* * *

Sean felt bad about not taking Fi to dinner with them. But Nancy was right, they couldn't risk leaving the place empty, just in case whoever had been there returned that night. Nancy was wrapped around him, kissing his neck, but he wasn't really in the mood. He was sorry that Fi was leaving. She'd worked hard, a bit erratic, but she'd been a star at cleaning, weighing and grading the oysters, and Grace loved her. It had been good to know someone was here. Now he'd have to advertise again. He couldn't risk losing his stock now he was on the up.

He'd miss Fi. His mind flitted back to the night before. Had he imagined it or had they nearly kissed? Thank God they hadn't. He had promised her he wouldn't overstep the mark. He put it down to a moment of madness, but he couldn't help but think how much he'd enjoyed himself last night. It'd been a long time since he'd really relaxed in someone's company. He hoped he hadn't bored her telling her about the oysters. She'd seemed keen to listen, as keen as he had been to tell her.

I unclip Grace's lead at the top of the stone steps and follow her down on to the sandy beach. Grace catapults across it, scattering the oystercatchers in all directions. She is running in huge circles, leaving footprints in the virgin sand. I walk down to the water's edge where waves are gently rolling in and over and then sliding back. I look out across the rocks, then as far as my eye can see. Next stop America. I stop and stare and wonder. That's the sort of place I could really get lost in. I turn to follow Grace along the beach.

'Hello there.' The voice makes me jump. It's Maire from

the art shop, bending down and picking something up. In the other hand a plastic bag is blowing like a flag in the wind.

'Hi,' I say, peeling back the hair that's flying across my eyes. 'What are you looking for?'

'Shells, any shells.' She's scouring the beach. 'Thought I'd have a go at some picture frames. Not going to get very far with this little lot though.' She holds up a bag with her few finds. I turn around, looking where I'm standing, and see a small shell in a little rock pool. I put my hand into the cold water and hand it to her. She holds open the flapping bag for me to drop it in.

'Thank you.' She smiles and we fall into step together, scouring the shoreline.

'So you're moving on then,' Maire says, bending for another shell.

'Yes.' I skirt a large rock.

Maire picks something up and holds it out to me. 'Looks like that one's got lost,' she says. It's a starfish. It feels weird on my skin, cold, wet and rough. 'Put it into one of the pools.' She points to a large rock with little pools around it. I look at it again and then slide it back into the water, feeling like I've helped it come in from the wilderness.

'So, you going anywhere nice?' Maire opens her bag for me to drop another small shell into.

'Not really. Probably go on and stay with my mother for a bit. She's in Malta. Unless another job comes up before then, preferably somewhere hot and not near water,' I laugh gently, and so does Maire.

'Doing the ski chalets is a nice job, but that's not for another few months. Or there's grape harvest in France,' she offers.

'You sound like you've travelled yourself.' Grace is now in the water, splashing around.

'Yes, but nothing beats coming home. It may not be the town it used to be, but it's home.' She stops, having found a patch of tiny shells, and I help collect them. 'Probably seems pretty dead to someone from the city,' she puffs a little.

'Well,' I shrug, not wanting to be rude, 'it is pretty quiet.'

'No one comes any more. They used to. This place was heaving. Businesses thrived, it was fabulous. Especially at the oyster festival. There were stalls, bunting, Tom Thornton even brought the donkeys down and the kids rode them on the beach. Brilliant days, they were.'

'So why did it stop?' I decide to ask. I'd like to know before I leave.

She sighs. 'It was Tom, Sean Thornton's uncle. There'd been a lot of rumours. The waters weren't coming up to standard. Everyone was pointing the finger at everyone else. Farmers were going out of business. Everyone was finding it hard. Tom blamed the Murphy brothers for their building work just down from his farm. Anyway, one night over the oyster festival they got into a row. Sean had just arrived. Rumours were rife . . .' She stops and stands up straight. 'People round here didn't wait to ask,' Maire carries on. 'The waters were bad and everyone was looking for someone to blame. Tom was ill. There was an argument the night of the shell-shucking contest. The Murphys said that Sean should be disqualified for being a blow-in, said it was for local people only. Well, everything got out of hand. There was a scuffle and Tom . . . Tom had a heart attack and died there and then, God rest his soul.' Neither of us said anything for a moment. The sky got a little darker.

'Sean took over the farm, causing mutterings amongst the other locals who said he wasn't really Tom's blood relative and didn't deserve it.'

'But his other cousins weren't interested. He was the only one.' I don't know why I feel I should defend him, but I do. 'They'd all moved abroad.'

Maire shrugs and we walk on, searching for shells. When we reach the end of the beach we turn and walk back the other way, letting the wind fill the silences between us.

'I thought you coming here might've changed all that,' Maire suddenly says sadly.

'Me? How could I change things?' We reach the end of the beach and I look up at the stone steps.

'Sometimes it takes someone from outside to . . . see things from a new perspective. No one ever mentions the oyster festival, until the other night.'

'I didn't realise—'

'Oh, it wasn't your fault, dear. It's this lot. It's time they all learnt to forgive and forget, to move on and leave the past behind. For just a minute I saw a glimmer of hope,' she smiles. 'What this town needs is someone to put it back on the map.' She rummages in her bag and pulls out a large shell.

'Here, a souvenir,' she says. I'm touched.

'Thank you.' I take the curled cream shell and look at it. 'I'm sorry it couldn't be me,' I say apologetically.

'Don't worry, dear. Hope you find what you're looking for.' We walk up the steps together with Grace following behind.

'I hope so too,' I say into the wind.

* * *

I head for the petrol station, still looking at the shell in my hand.

'It's promised rain,' Rosie says scanning my bottle of white wine and large bag of Doritos into the till.

'Yes,' I look out of the window. 'I think you're right, Rosie.'

'Coming to the meeting this week, Fi?' She holds out her chubby hand for the money.

'No, 'fraid not, Rosie. In fact, I'm not going to be coming to any more meetings. I'm leaving. Just off to look up flights on the internet.' I take my change.

'Ah no, what a shame. We were just getting used to you,' she says, shutting the till, and I half laugh, not sure if she's joking or not.

'D'you hear that, Margaret?' I turn to see Margaret, with her newly painted blue nails with silver lightning strikes, coming into the shop.

'What?'

'Fi's leaving us.'

'Ah, no way. I'll be the only young one in town again!' Margaret grabs a bottle of white wine and some Pringles.

'You two should have a party,' Rosie laughs, pointing to our wine.

'That's not a bad idea,' Margaret turns to me hopefully.

'Oh, I can't. I have to get back to the farm.'

'Hey, Seamus, d'you hear that, Fi's leaving us.' Rosie is passing on the news to the pub's regulars. 'Isn't it a shame, Padraig?'

'Aye. Going anywhere nice?'

I shrug. 'Maybe Malta, to see my mother.' I cringe at the thought. But staying here isn't an option any more, especially after I nearly made a fool of myself last night. I go to leave the shop and Margaret falls into step beside me.

'How's Sean?'

'Good,' I say, and smile.

'His horoscope says he's moving into a lucky phase.'

I smile again as I make my way back to the café.

'Thought I might pop in and see him. See if he fancies a drink. I've got the evening off.' Margaret holds up her bottle.

'I wouldn't if I were you.' I think I should tell her straight.

'But I thought you said that you and he weren't . . .' She looks crestfallen.

'We're not!' I interrupt her, almost too keenly. 'He's with his partner.'

'His partner?' She stops me in my tracks.

'Nancy. She's French. She's his oyster broker – you know, sells his oysters on for him. They go way back.'

'Yes, yes, I know what an oyster broker is. It's her, in the black BMW?' She flops down onto a bench looking out to sea. She looks up at me and I confirm it apologetically.

'I've seen her around. Heard rumours, y'know?'

'I'm beginning to understand.' I smile, thinking how much I've realised this place runs on rumour. I turn to look at the café. The door is shut and there's a sign but I'm too far away to read it.

'Ah, no. The café's shut.' I flap my hands against my thighs.

'Gone to Dublin to pick up a new urn.'

I turn back to see Margaret with the cap off her bottle of wine, swigging from it.

'Here,' she offers it up to me.

'No, really, I can't. I had to do something in the café and

then I have to get back.' I point with my thumb over my shoulder.

'Well, the café's shut. This is the only place you'll get a drink now.' Margaret takes another swig.

Oh, what harm could it do? The least I could do is sit with her for a while; it was me that delivered the bad news in the first place after all.

'You and Sean. Were you . . . ?'

'I wish,' Margaret says, taking big swigs. 'But it will happen,' she says confidently.

'Really? How do you know?' I wish I could be that confident about my life falling into place.

'It's in my stars,' she says with a dreamy look on her face.

'And how long have you thought you two were . . . fated to be together?' I ask, taking the bottle and sitting down beside her. Grace lies down at my feet. I take a swig from the bottle. It's warm but somehow hits the spot after the day I've had.

'For ever, I think,' Margaret replies flatly. 'I remember the day he turned up here, out of the blue, after he'd been . . . y'know.'

'Hello again, ladies.' Seamus and Padraig stop beside us. The squeaking on the bike Seamus is pushing stops. He touches the brim of his hat. I try to hide the bottle behind my leg but don't think I manage it.

'Making a night of it, are we?' Padraig laughs.

Just then a black BMW drives past with a blast of its horn.

'It's him, isn't it, going out with her? Staying in town, no doubt at some swanky hotel.' Margaret grabs the bottle and swigs deeply.

'Her place.' I've given her all the facts now.

Seamus touches his hat again. 'Should be a nice night.' He

nods at the reddening sky. 'Enjoy your evening.' The bike starts up its squeak again. Padraig walks beside him, talking in a low voice.

'Where will you go?' Margaret asks while staring straight out to sea.

'Probably to my mum's in Malta.'

'You don't sound keen.'

'I'm not. She left me to my own devices just before I turned sixteen, and hasn't really bothered with me since. I can't see her welcoming me with open arms. And to be honest, I don't think I can take all the "I told you so" looks.'

'I told you so? What about?'

I sigh, and instead of drinking from the bottle rest it down on the bench and open the Doritos instead. I take one out and bite it so the pieces shatter everywhere. I sigh again.

'She told me my marriage wouldn't last. I'd never make him happy.' It's my turn to look out to sea.

'And did it?' Margaret sticks her hand into the big bag and grabs a handful, tossing them into her mouth.

'No. The ink wasn't even dry on the register when he left me.'

Margaret's crunching faster and faster, her eyes fixed on me. I'll probably be the talk of the town by this evening, but what does it matter now – I'll be gone tomorrow.

'We said "I do", then he realised he couldn't.'

'Not one of the bridesmaids?' Margaret's still throwing Doritos at her mouth at superfast speed.

'The best man,' I say flatly.

Margaret nearly chokes.

'I thought it was the belly-dancing outfit he'd found in my going away bag at first.'

'Belly-dancing outfit!' Margaret bursts out, spraying Doritos. And, taking me quite by surprise, I find I laugh too.

'Don't!' I say, waving my hand around, enjoying the sense of freedom the laughter's giving me. 'Betty and Kimberly's idea of a honeymoon present!' I say through gasps for air. The thought of Brian's face if I'd actually put it on is making me laugh even more. 'Something to spice up our sex life,' they said. 'Well, after years of doing it in the dark on a Saturday night I thought it might actually help. But now I think about it . . .' Laughter washes over me again and I don't know if I should feel bad for laughing or just realise how ridiculous it all was.

'So the sex was shite then?' Margaret throws more crisps at her mouth, barely chewing them. I've hardly had anything to drink but my tongue seems to have taken on a life of its own.

'His idea of foreplay was separate showers. He found the outfit just before the wedding, when we were packing. I saw the colour drain from his face. I wasn't really going to wear it. It was just a bit of fun. But it wasn't that. Now I think about it, I can remember exactly when the lights went out in his eyes.'

'What?'

'Well, when I first met Brian I was doing the sandwich round from Betty's Buns, as it was then. I had to deliver the sandwiches to the radio station next door. Brian's studio was my last stop. When I got there his assistant had let him down, the girl who did the phones. It was a Saturday afternoon sports phone-in. Well, I helped out. I could answer phones. His assistant never came back and I helped out every Saturday after working in Betty's. By way of a thank you he took me to the staff Christmas party. It was fancy dress. I wasn't keen but he convinced me. He went as Becks and I went as Posh in a pair of sunglasses and some of Kimberly's high heels. D'you know, for the first time in my life I actually felt like I was somebody.' I sipped at the wine bottle. 'After that we just slipped into being a couple. I'd always hated all that dating malarkey, far too shy. This just became habit. I went out with him to work dos and in time he moved into my flat above Betty's because it was closer to the radio station, and he, well, he planned our lives. We saved for the next two years for a deposit for a flat, a new one, the show-home. And two years later, planned to get married. And the following year . . .' I swallow, 'we'd start a family,' I say quietly, suddenly feeling the need to blink quite a lot. Margaret grabs the bottle and swigs before handing it back.

'So what went wrong?'

'By the looks of it he was just hiding from who he really was, using me. It was all for convenience . . . a bit like the flat,' I laugh, but it's hollow. 'Then when I suggested we throw the life plan out of the window and start trying for children straight away, well, I guess that's when he realised he couldn't do it any more.'

'So where did the best man come from?'

'We went on holiday to Greece a few years ago, a sailing holiday. My idea, a bad one. Anyway, to cut a long story short we met up with some other people our age. There was one particular friend, Adrian. He and Brian got on really well. We stayed in touch for a while but lost contact when everyone started getting married and having kids. But when we finally got engaged, Brian went Facebook mad and got back in touch. Looks like he couldn't hide from his real feelings any more.'

'God, no wonder you went loopy.' Margaret slugged again.

'I didn't go loopy! I just remember seeing all those faces staring at me and I couldn't bear it. So I just ran. The camper van had been delivered for us to leave the reception and go on honeymoon in, so I just jumped in it and drove. I don't know what I was thinking. I just followed what the satnav told me to do but I went wrong. Ended up here. And the camper van company thought I'd stolen it.'

'Jeez, makes my shit look like a breeze,' Margaret says, holding the empty Doritos bag. I feel chilly. 'Are you good for money then?'

I push my hand into my pocket.

'I've got this.' I show her the diamond engagement ring.

'For feck's sake, that's not a stone, it's a rock!' Margaret takes the ring from me and holds it up. But it doesn't shine. Maybe it's because I've been wearing it so long, or maybe it's a reflection of life – it's lost its shine.

'Time I was off.' I stand up. 'Thanks for the laughs.' Tomorrow's going to be a new beginning. I feel ready to move on. I mustn't beat myself up about this any more.

'I'm sorry you're going,' she smiles up at me. 'We could've had fun.'

'By the way, Margaret, what did you mean earlier, when you said about Sean, when he first came here, after he'd been . . . ?'

'Released. From prison. Didn't you know?' Looks like Margaret thought I should have all the facts too.

Chapter Nineteen

Back at the farm it's all quiet. The hens and geese have taken themselves off to bed and all I have to do is close their doors for one last time. Freddie and Mercury are safely locked in their field. I rub their muzzles and foreheads and give them an extra handful of pony nuts each.

'Be good for your master, boys,' I tell them. 'Freddie, as much as you love her, you can't have her, she belongs to someone else,' I say, referring to the little white donkey down the road. Why then do I suddenly think about Sean? I push the thought aside. 'Mercury, keep an eye on him for me.' I rub his forehead and long ears then turn back to the cottage with Grace gambolling at my side.

The water's like a mill pond tonight. The drizzle has stopped and there's another rainbow across the bay as the sun attempts to wave goodbye, even though we were barely acquainted. I've hardly stood still when a gang of midges get me in their sights and set me as their new destination. I wave at them madly and run into the cottage, rubbing my hair. I shan't miss them.

I throw turf onto the fire and pull out some bread and cheese. I need to think about tomorrow. It's not like I've got a lot to pack, but I need to get into Galway, find a pawn shop, sell the rings, and then find an internet café. Once I've got the money from the rings I can buy a ticket anywhere. It doesn't have to be Malta. So where do I fancy?

I go through Sean's CDs, which are now all in alphabetical order. I put on some music, pour a glass of wine, and find a pad and pen from the now tidy desk. The old whiskey bottle has become a candle holder on the table. I light it. The room's heating up nicely. Grace is in her bed by the fire. The cottage has come to feel like home, far more than the modern flat that Brian and I shared. I put the pad and pen on the table and sit down. I chew the end of my pen, sip my wine, eat my bread and cheese. Still my pad is empty. With the world as my oyster I have no idea where to go.

I'm still staring into the distance as it gets dark. The moonlight is throwing its long, silver path down the bay. I blow out the candle and decide to have an early night. I'm sure the answers will come to me after a good night's sleep.

The darkness is looking in at me from outside as I clean my teeth and wash my face. Grace follows me into the bedroom and lies down on the little mat beside my bed.

'Good night, Grace. Thank you for being such a good friend.'

I feel a lump in my throat and turn out the light and pull the covers round me, breathing in the smell of turf smoke and washing powder for the last time.

Buzz. I can't believe it! I did everything to make sure no midges followed me in. I pull the covers over my head in the hope it will just leave me alone.

Buzzzz. It seems to be getting louder and is now keeping me awake. I'm going to have to get out of bed and swat it.

Buzzzzzzz. Either there's a house party of midges in my

room or . . . I listen more carefully. Grace is snoring gently, making occasional little yelps of joy. I listen again.

BUZZZZZZZZZ. That's not a midge, it's a boat!

I fling back the covers. Grace lumbers from her sleep, but no sooner is she on her feet than she's alert. I run into the dark living room wearing nothing but a T-shirt and press my face against the cold, damp glass of the window.

There's a light. No, two lights. They're back! My heart starts thumping so loudly it's banging my eardrums as well. My breathing quickens. What can I do? I rummage for my phone, but there's no mobile reception, not even for emergency calls. I can't phone Sean, and I can't phone the Garda either. I pull on my big yellow coat, grab the keys from the hook, but I have no idea how they'll help. Grace is now dancing around, tail wagging, hoping for a midnight walk. I step into my boots, grab a torch, take the biggest breath I have ever taken and open the door, really gently.

Grace pushes her way out with her nose, still dancing round my feet, and I'm hoping that she doesn't knock anything over. I don't turn on the torch. I have to get closer to see what's going on. The boat's engine suddenly cuts out and I stop. I crouch down, as if that's going to help. I wonder if they've seen me. If not, perhaps they can hear my heart thundering in my chest because it's deafening me. But they don't seem to have.

I smooth Grace's head. I can hear faint voices. I take quiet footsteps towards the tractor and hold on to the back of it. I can hear the water very gently lapping at the wheels.

Splish, splosh, splish, splosh.

I try and listen to the murmur of their voices. They're wearing head torches but I can't see their faces. The torches bob around like dancing fireflies. I can make out the outline of a boat, and then I see it. They're lifting a dripping sack of oysters from the water with a long stick. I have to stop them . . .

'Hey! Put that back!' Fear has been replaced by pure fury. 'Put it back!' I shout. Grace suddenly starts barking and jumping around in the shallow water, getting me wet. They don't seem to be moving. Grace stops jumping and I listen. I can hear the faint sound of laughter and then, unbelievably, see another bag being lifted.

'*Put it back!*' I scream, pointing with my finger. '*Put it back!*'

But they're not moving. They're lifting more sacks. Still I can't see their faces, they're both wearing baseball caps pulled down.

'Grr!' I grit my teeth in frustration.

I look around for something to help me, anything!

I grab a stone and throw it as hard as I can. It lands with a splash only feet away from me, but Grace thinks this is a great game and chases after it. I pick up and throw another and another, shouting all the time. But more and more bags are being lifted.

'*Leave them alone!*'

Splash! I launch another stone.

'*Go away!*'

Splash! Nothing is shifting them.

If only Sean were here he'd go out in the boat. I can't even get further than my knees.

'Grrrrr!' I'm so frustrated.

Perhaps if I can get higher. I gather up more stones and shove them into my pockets, then climb up into the seat of the tractor.

'*Clear off!*' I yell, and launch more of my missiles. They plop just in front of the tractor.

They're not moving because I'm not. They know I can't get to them. If only I could sail the boat . . . But I can't. I can't go any deeper. I'm frozen by fear.

But maybe if they thought I was going to get closer . . . I grapple in my pocket for the keys. I know they're here somewhere. I fumble with them, trying to find the right key and get it in the keyhole while holding the torch. Finally it goes in. I check the gear stick is in neutral. I'm not going to actually drive it, just roll it forward a bit.

'Go away! I know who you are! The Garda's coming!' Then I turn the key and the engine erupts into farting, spluttering life. 'I mean it! I'm coming! And so are the Garda!' But still they don't move, and more and more bags are being lifted from the water into their boat. I push down the tractor's clutch and push it into first. It clunks into place. I slowly release the clutch and gently push down on the accelerator. It begins to roll forward.

'*I'm coming!*' And by some miracle the boat engine starts up. I can still hear laughter but they're leaving. The boat spins round, closely missing the trestle tables loaded with oysters ready to go to the co-operative and shoots off out of the bay, outboard motor screaming with exertion, churning up the waters and leaving ripples of waves in its wake. I put my foot on the clutch and brake.

'Yessss!' I pull in a clenched fist. Adrenalin is pumping through my body. I did it! They're going. I can still hear the faint sound of laughter as the boat buzzes off out of the bay.

I sit back. 'Yesssssssss!' I punch the air and my foot slips off the clutch and the tractor rockets forward into the water.

'Nooooo!' I try to get my slippery foot back on the pedal. I can't see where we're going. The tractor tips from side to side and the torch flies from my hand. I can't get my balance. I try and grab the steering wheel, eventually get a grip and yank as hard as I can, then the tractor hits something underwater, knocking me off balance again. The accelerator is stuck. I'm slipping and sliding trying to get control of the runaway vehicle, but the water's getting deeper and I panic and before I can think about it, I bail out into the knee-high water. The tractor is heading further in, bumping and rolling its way towards the oyster beds.

I can only hold my hands over my mouth and watch as it lumbers like a hungry bear towards the trestle tables with what's left of the oysters ready to be collected the next day.

There's a bang, a clank, a crunch, a squeal, the sound of metal being mashed and oysters being crushed.

And the tractor gives a final dying sigh before sinking into a watery grave. I feel sick, physically sick.

'Shit! Shit! Shit!' Me and my bloody fear of bloody water. Terrified of the unknown. Terrified of my own shadow, more like. But not half as terrified as I'm going to be when Sean gets back tomorrow. 'Shit!'

Chapter Twenty

'Hang on, so let me get this right . . .' He takes a very deep breath. 'You're telling me I've lost most of my oyster stock because . . . why exactly?' Sean asks so quietly, it's almost a whisper. He's standing on the edge of the shore, staring out at the devastation in front of him. I've spent the morning trying to salvage what I could but it was hopeless, especially on a neap tide. Nancy's beside him, her mouth wide open. Part of me thought about running out in the night. But I've had that dilemma before, nowhere to go, no transport. I had to stay and try and explain. With a dry mouth and a shake in my voice, I start.

'It was last night. I wanted to stop them but . . . I tried throwing rocks and I couldn't call anyone. They had a boat. I shouted at them to stop but they wouldn't. The boat nearly knocked over the trestles. I tried to scare them off by starting up the tractor, then the accelerator got stuck and I had to jump off and the oyster sacks all fell into the water, but I couldn't go in after them . . .'

'It's not very deep, didn't you think to just wade in? Or why didn't you just get in the boat? I thought you'd been on a sailing course.'

'Because . . .' My mouth dries up.

'Yes?' He's looking at me intensely, coldness in his eyes. I lick my lips, trying to create some moisture in my mouth.

'Because I'm, I'm, I'm . . .' Oh, what did it matter now? 'Because I'm scared of water.' There, I've said it. 'I couldn't do anything about it because I'm scared of water.'

For a moment there's silence. He bites his bottom lip and then says slowly and quietly, 'And you never thought to mention this fact? Hmm? What with me being your employer,' his voice getting gradually louder, 'on an oyster farm!'

It's fair to say he has a point. I stop fiddling with the loose stitching on the sleeve of my jacket. I lift my chin and look at him.

'I needed the job and somewhere to live. And I don't think I've done a bad job for you. I might not have told you about my fear of water but I've worked hard and helped you get this place ready for the inspection.'

Nancy rolls her eyes incredulously.

'You've ruined his livelihood.'

Guilt is gnawing away inside me.

'I'll pay you back, every penny, I promise.' I'm wringing my hands over and over.

'Let's hope so,' Nancy cuts in again.

'How?' he says flatly.

Looking out, broken trestle tables litter the water, oyster sacks are ripped and floating. The oystercatchers, seagulls and that heron are having a feast. Sean's right: 'how' is the question.

He pulls the collar of his coat around his ears and marches towards the jetty, muttering, 'Feckin' incompetent!'

He's right again and it hurts.

'Sean, where are you going? We need to talk about this.

Customers will have to know. The truck will be on its way . . .' Nancy calls after him. 'Sean!' But Sean just keeps walking down the jetty to the hooker. 'What shall I tell them?' she calls again. 'Those oysters were going to France tomorrow.'

'I'm out on my boat. I have things to do,' he finally replies, zipping up his wax jacket, untying the ropes, and then jumping down into the boat as it sways this way and that. The heron suddenly lands on the jetty next to the boat and marches up and down as if waiting impatiently for it to leave.

'I can't help but notice you're still here,' Nancy says to me while trying to get a signal on her iPhone without success. She waves it around in the air. 'Bloody place! At least I won't have to come out to this God-forsaken farm any more. But I do need more oyster suppliers.' She's scrolling through her contacts.

'He loves this place. He won't leave.' My eyes sting.

'I know I wanted him to spend more time with me, but I didn't want you to ruin our businesses,' she says with a spiked laugh. 'Now, if you'll excuse me, I've got customers to speak to and oyster farmers to find.'

Nancy tosses her hair over her shoulder like she's in a shampoo advert, goes back to her car, and drives off at speed. Then there's silence; just the sloshing of the water and the fallen trestle tables in front of me. On the water Sean has the sails up, all three of them full and deep. He's urging the boat on as if his life depends on it. The heron's keeping up with him like a horseman loyally following its master's carriage. There's nothing more I can do out here.

I go to my room and sit down on the little bed. It creaks like I knew it would. I'm suddenly very tired. I didn't sleep much last night and when I did drop off, just before dawn, I dreamt about donkeys running amok though my wedding, ruining everything.

I start putting my few belongings into a plastic bag. I open the little drawer in the bedside cabinet and take out my rings. I hold the engagement ring up in front of my face. I remember when we bought it.

Brian had been away on a walking holiday, not long after we'd been sailing. I had to drop out. The new manageress had walked out and Betty was due in hospital for a hip replacement. She wanted me to cover and keep the place running, but Kimberly thought she should do it. I stuck to doing extra shifts in the kitchen and sorting out the mess Kimberly had made of the till at night. Brian and Adrian went on the walking holiday instead. When Brian came back he seemed different somehow, more interested in me. He took me out for lunch – well, sandwiches in Costa Coffee, which was a bit of a busman's holiday – and then said we were going to choose a ring; it was time we got engaged now we'd been together for three years. He didn't actually ask me, just sort of let me know. But that was as close as it got to romance with Brian. He was a very practical man, had life mapped out. Which is why I think he surprised himself as much as anyone when he ran out on our wedding day. He wasn't a man for impulsive actions.

We went and chose a ring and I went back to work. He picked it up two days later and brought it into The Coffee House – Betty's Buns had now become a faceless franchise. Kimberly nearly died when she saw the ring and decided the Atkins diet was the only way forward for her. Betty eyed it and told Brian it should've been bigger, what with him being a minor celebrity in the area. But I knew his minor celebrity wages wouldn't have been much more than mine. The radio station where Brian worked announced his engagement on air. He took the congratulations while I went back to baking a batch of blueberry muffins for the after-school rush.

I never really felt comfortable wearing the ring, though. Mostly I had it on a chain around my neck and Brian had to remind me to put it on after work. I was too worried about losing it in a French fancy or custard slice. I thought it was too expensive, but Brian assured me he had it covered.

I turn it over. It doesn't sparkle or make me smile, but it might just help me out. I stand up and Brian's sweatshirt, the one I have worn every night since I arrived here, falls to the floor. I pick it up, leave it on the bed and then walk out, shutting the door behind me.

Sean is coming into the kitchen at the same time as me. His hair is tossed all over the place and his face is pale and drawn, a far cry from the man who'd been so happy yesterday.

My heart does a quick double beat, then feels like someone's squeezing it tightly. I swallow hard and clear my throat. 'It can be repaired, right?' I say, feeling stupid. He looks at me and sighs. He goes to the cupboard and gets out two cups, one for coffee, one for tea, and then reaches down and pulls out a new bottle of whiskey.

'You won't sell up, will you? You won't leave?' I have to know.

He pours water into the cups and then bangs down the kettle, making me jump. 'What part of this are you struggling with? I'm an oyster farmer without any oysters to sell. Without oysters I can't pay for my licence, nor can I buy in any new spat to fatten up and sell.' He pours a slug of whiskey into his coffee.

He hates me, and why wouldn't he? I've ruined his business.

'Anyway, why does it matter to you? You're leaving,' he says coldly. He swallows his coffee, even though it's so hot it must have burnt his mouth, and marches out. He obviously can't stand to be in the same room as me.

'Sean, wait!' I run out after him with my bag of belongings. 'Where are you going?'

'Galway. See if I can find someone to help salvage what's left of my business.' He's pulling on his wax jacket as he stalks across to the van.

'Wait, I'm coming with you.'

He looks at me and then back out at the damaged oyster beds, and then gets into the van saying nothing.

We travel along the coast road in silence. Sean is gently simmering. Eventually, an hour or so later I summon up the courage to speak. I turn to look at him.

'Just tell me you're not going to sell up.'

He's looking straight ahead.

'Not if I can help it, but I'm not sure what options I have,' he replies. Then he turns to me. 'And now I don't even have an assistant.'

I look down at my bag of belongings. It's my turn to tut.

'I didn't think you'd want me to stay, not after what I've done. Or couldn't do.'

'What do you mean?'

'Well, not being able to get in the water.'

'Actually,' he says, 'I think what you did was quite brave, considering you're terrified of water. I did wonder why you never moved when we were turning the oyster sacks.' And to my surprise he laughed, just a little one, and despite myself I can't help but laugh too.

'So, how long have you been this scared of water?' Sean concentrates on the road. Somehow it's easier to talk when you're not looking each other in the eye.

'Ever since Brian, my . . . ex,' is the best way I can think of describing him. I don't know if he's my ex-boyfriend, my ex-fiancé or my ex-husband. 'We went on a sailing holiday. Greek islands. Thought it might be, y'know, exciting. I've never been that good around water, not since I got swept under a wave on a beach in Folkestone when I was a kid. Some woman dragged me from the water. I just remember the white foam all around me and then gasping for air. The woman took me back to my mum. I was so relieved, but she was just cross. She was always cross with me. She was with some new fella and told me off for spoiling her afternoon.' My throat tightens up and I have to swallow hard. Sean doesn't say anything. I still remember the white foam swallowing me up.

'Anyway, Brian was booking our holiday. It was always the same. Usually in the UK. He'd spend weeks planning a route, various walks we could do, historical sights, and pub grub in the evening. This one year, I thought we should try and do something different. So I booked the sailing holiday. We had two days of tuition and on the third day they told us to travel, as a group, to this next destination round the island.' I sigh.

'The long and short of it is, a storm got up. Brian was terrified and sat down in the galley. I tried to take down the sail but it jammed stuck and I couldn't get it down. We were being blown further and further out to sea. Eventually a couple of guys from our group came to rescue us. They got us to shore and poured us large brandies. We decided to stay shore-bound from then on.'

I remember telling Brian afterwards, in a mad moment, that I thought we should give up the five-year plan, buy the flat, get engaged, get married and try for a family. I thought we should just go for what we wanted. Life was too short, anything could have happened. I remember how he looked at me, the lights going out in his eyes. I decided to play it safe from there on in. But things were never the same after that holiday.

'We stuck to walking and pub grub after that.'

'What about the guys who rescued you? Did you ever see them again?'

'Oh yes,' I say matter-of-factly. 'One of them was our best man . . .'

We fall into silence. Finally he says, 'Have you been into the city before?' A line of traffic in front of us stops us by a harbour of small boats. I shake my head. There are swans being fed by parents with children. On the other side of the harbour is a row of brightly coloured cottages. They look like something out of a children's programme.

'Where do you need to go?' He sees a parking space and pulls in.

'I need a pawn shop.' I reach into my pocket and pull out my ring. 'My back-up plan,' I say with a tight smile.

'That's very sensible. Why haven't you used it before?' He reverses and straightens the van.

'Because I wasn't ready to.' I put it back in my pocket.

'And you are now?' He pulls on the handbrake with a crunch.

I just nod.

'Well, I have to go and talk to the bank, it's on Shop Street. Then I'll take you somewhere to sell it.'

'How come you don't go to the bank in Dooleybridge?' I ask as we get out of the van.

'I like to keep my business affairs private.'

He shoves his hands into his pockets and begins to walk towards a bridge over a fast-flowing river. I follow him. We fall into step side by side.

'Y'know, English . . .' He seems calmer now. 'We're all allowed to make one mistake.'

'Is that when you made yours, when you went to prison?'

He throws his head back and laughs. 'So the gossips have been at work.' He pushes his hands further into his pockets.

'I just heard you were in prison.'

'I was. In America. For working without a visa.'

'Is that all?'

'I was working in an oyster bar. The owner didn't want to pay me what he owed me and called the cops on me.'

'How come they don't know that, in the town?'

'Because,' he lights up a cigarette and blows out the smoke, 'they never asked.'

We carry on over the bridge and then cross the road. In front of me is a cobbled street. It's busy and there's bunting strung across it from shop to shop. Sean heads up the middle in between the bars and cafés on either side.

'Spanish arch,' he says, pointing to an old stone archway on the other side of the road as if he feels obliged to play tourist guide. 'And here we are.'

There are musicians playing in the street. Everyone seems

to have a spring in their step and there's chatter and music everywhere. People are outside the pubs and cafés, smoking and drinking. I'm almost getting caught up in the Shop Street atmosphere, forgetting everything that has happened, when Sean stops halfway up the street and says, 'I won't be long,' and heads into the big grey stone building of a bank without me.

A young girl is on the opposite side of the street playing the fiddle. She's not very good, hitting wrong notes, but she keeps going and every now and then someone throws money into her case on the ground. I realise her mother is standing beside me, keeping a watchful eye.

'She's very brave,' I say.

'Well, she's giving it a lash,' says the mother, one foot against the wall. 'It's all yer can do, isn't it, give it a go?'

The girl stops and smiles at her mum.

'Keep going, love, you're doing grand,' her mum calls back. 'Ya have to crack a few eggs to make an omelette.'

I remember nearly saying something similar myself. I think about the mess I've made of Sean's farm. That was more than a few cracked eggs. Mortification burns my cheeks and I wonder whether to just disappear into the crowds. Leave without a trace.

I look up and down the street. There's a jeweller's on the other side of the road.

'Have yer any change?' A woman shakes a pot at me. She's wearing gold sling-backs and red fingerless gloves, and smoking a cigarette with a long length of ash hanging off the end of it. She looks about eighty. Her thin dyed black hair hangs either side of her face. 'I can tell yer fortune,' she says, rattling her pot again. I shake my head. She nods and drags on the cigarette, the ash falls onto her knee and she brushes it away. 'Be lucky anyway,' she says.

Sean comes out of the bank much quicker than I was expecting. The young girl is still crashing her way through her play list. I look at him. He sucks in his top lip and then shakes his head.

'They won't lend me any more money.' He begins to walk and flicks a coin into the girl's violin case. 'In fact . . . they want some of what they've already lent me back. They want me to start repaying the overdraft.' He lights another cigarette. 'Anyway, like I say, not your problem any more. Let's get you sorted out.'

He heads off down Shop Street. My head is spinning. Do I go or stay? Would he want me to? Did he mean it when he said everyone was allowed one mistake? Besides, I seem to keep making mistakes. First the camper van, then not mentioning about me being scared of water, and now this.

'Oh God,' I say, following him. I made this mess, I have to help put it right in whatever way I can. I have to keep trying. 'Wait!' He's striding out and I have to break into a run. 'Sean, wait!' I shout. And he stops and turns to me. I take a deep breath and rummage in my pocket.

'Come on or you'll miss the shop.' He's back to being his irritable self.

I open my hand and hold out the ring. 'Here, take it. It should cover the cost of the damage, maybe get some new spat as well. I hope. Maybe it'll be luckier for you than it was for me,' I try and joke.

He frowns. People are passing on either side of us. Young men in hoodies, smoking, are holding up signs pointing to restaurants and tattoo parlours. There's a woman playing the tin whistle to a backtrack on CD. Beside her there's a man on a chair all dressed in silver, as if he were a statue, waiting for someone to put money in his pot before he'll move.

'But that's your . . .' Sean looks gobsmacked.

'Yes, I know, just take it.'

'I can't,' he says, looking at me and frowning.

'You can and you have to. I made the mess. Now I'm going to pay for the damage,' I say firmly.

'Are you sure?' He looks from me to the ring. I take hold of his hand and put it there and close his fist.

'Why? Why would you do this for me?' he says quietly.

'Because I need to put this right. Because . . .' I say, trailing off. Because I care, I realise, and not just about the oysters and what I've done. I care about him. I turn him towards the jeweller's. 'Just make sure you get a good price for them.'

He turns back to me, his head bent over his fist.

'Thank you.' He quickly and briefly kisses my cheek and without thinking my fingers fly up to touch it where it landed.

Chapter Twenty-one

'I need a drink,' I say as we come out of the jeweller's.

'Me too.' We stand side by side on the busy street. Sean puts his hand on my shoulder and guides me into the crowded street. Five minutes later I'm in a noisy pub with music playing and a large white wine in front of me. Sean has a pint of the black stuff. We both take a large sip and say nothing. Then another and finally I speak first.

'Fakes?' I look into my wine.

'I'm sorry. That can't have been easy to hear.' Sean turns his cold pint glass.

I shake my head slowly.

'Do you know, I don't think I even care any more. I should be angry, but in a way I'm not surprised.' I take another gulp of the wine. 'But that's it. I have nothing now.'

'You're in shock.'

'I never doubted they were real. Brian had everything planned – when we should buy the ring, buy the flat. He wanted everything to be right. I trusted him.'

'Love is a risky business, a bit like oyster farming.'

'But you keep going at it?'

'Some things are worth the risk.'

'Like your oyster farm,' I manage to smile and he smiles back.

'Exactly.'

We slip into silence, neither of us knowing what to do next. Then Sean puts down his pint and leans forwards towards me. He looks straight at me, his face very serious. It makes me nervous when he does that. I feel he can read my every thought and I don't want him to read that I'm finding him more and more attractive. Because the last thing I want is to ever risk my heart again.

'It meant a lot that you gave me that ring,' he says.

'What? The one worth two pounds fifty?' I'm twisting my glass now.

'You were prepared to give me everything you had.' He puts his hand over mine to stop me twisting the glass.

'Look, I was responsible for wrecking the place you love,' I say. 'I couldn't run away from that.'

'You're a very honest person. You're a good person. And I'm sorry about what I said. I didn't mean it about you being incompetent. Anyone who can work like you did when they're terrified of water has got to be pretty brave in my book.' He lets go of my hand and takes another sip. The creamy foam sticks to his top lip and he sucks at it.

'So, Brian . . . he was your . . . ? I mean . . .' He seems embarrassed to ask, but as Margaret has the whole story, there can't be any harm in telling Sean.

'I was married. Well, sort of married. He couldn't go through with it. Problem was, he realised that just *after* we signed the register and before the photos. I thought I had everything, the real deal, and it was all fake, just like the ring. That's it. For me, it's over now.' And it is. I shrug and am surprised at how comfortable I feel saying those words. No tears now, the anger diffusing. 'I may not forget it, but I would like to forgive him.'

There's a lull while we both consider the desperate place we're in.

'Can I come back and work for you?' I ask.

He sits up straight. 'Really?'

'I made the mess. I want to try and help put it right.'

'I'm not sure I'll have the money to do that, or to pay you.' He slumps again.

'It doesn't matter. Let me try and think of a way,' I say, desperate to make it up to him still.

'Look, I'm not very good at . . .' He clears his throat, '. . . trusting people.' He clears it again. 'Had my heart broken when I came out of prison. The girl I thought I'd marry . . . Anyway. I came here to look after my uncle.'

'Oh God, I'm so sorry.'

'But I think I could trust you. So, maybe there is a way still . . . if you really do want to stay and help?'

'I do.' I hold my glass tightly.

'Drink up then. Let's get this over and done with.'

I'm confused but feel a little shiver of excitement.

Outside the pub he lights a cigarette, takes a long drag, and then pulls out his phone. He smokes while he's talking.

'Yes, I heard about you through Nancy Dubois . . . she's my partner. You've helped out other farmers like me.'

He listens, turning away from me.

'No, no, no need to come to me. I'm in town. I'll meet you.'

He listens again. His cheek twitches as his jaws grind against each other.

'I'll be there in fifteen minutes,' and he slaps the phone cover shut.

I feel nervous for some reason.

Back in the van we leave the lively streets of the city centre and head out of town. I don't know where we are, and soon it looks as if we could be in any other out of town estate, much like the ones I grew up on.

Sean pulled up in a lay-by and looked both ways before getting out of the van.

'Wait here,' he told Fi. The less she knew about what he was about to do, the better. He didn't want to do this but he had no choice. The bank had blown him out. This was his only hope.

Nancy had mentioned this guy before. Everyone out Dooleybridge way knew his name. He was a loan shark. He helped out other farmers Nancy knew, oyster farmers she'd done business with. When times had got tough and the waters had become polluted, just before Sean's uncle died, a lot of farmers had needed help. That's when Jimmy Power stepped in, offering loans to tide farmers over until the waters came good and they could sell their stock and earn a living again. Some farmers made it and paid back what they owed, as well as the horrendous interest rates. If they couldn't, Jimmy Power claimed the land for himself. But that wasn't going to happen to Sean; he was going into this with his eyes wide open.

He pulled his coat around him against the damp drizzle and opened up the passenger door of the cream Mercedes parked in front of him in the lay-by. It looked out of place, unlike his old Transit van, the red paintwork dull and peeled due to the salty air.

Inside the Mercedes the cream colour ran on with the

leather seats. The car was full of the smell of cigars and strong air freshener.

'So, you are . . . ?' the wide-mouthed man, who looked like a toad, stuck out a hand dripping with gold jewellery.

'Sean, Sean Thornton.' Sean shook the hand briefly but didn't want to look him in the eye.

'Jimmy, Jimmy Power.' He shook Sean's hand firmly, as if making a statement.

'So, you're looking for a loan.' The man pulled out a cigar from the passenger glove box and lit it. He took a few puffs before finally opening the window. It was all Sean could do not to cough and splutter on the smoke. As the open window finally sucked the smoke away, Sean found he could breathe again.

'I'm an oyster farmer. Out in Connemara. My crop just got stolen and what they didn't take got trashed in the raid. I just need to pay my licence and get back on my feet.'

The toad sucked on his cigar and blew the smoke into the car.

'Risky business, oyster farming,' he sucked again. 'Lot of farmers out your way gone out of business. It's good building land out there. People'll pay a lot for a water-side plot, even in this climate.'

'I'm not having my farm turned into a building plot. That's where the trouble started. Everyone wanted to build bigger and better houses, borrow more money, but they drove out the real industry in the area. The water purity levels dropped when the developers moved in. If it hadn't been for that, Dooleybridge would still be as well known as Clarenbridge for its oysters. But now the waters are clean again, I can prove it.' Sean felt the wind go out of his sails as he finished his speech. What was the point? This guy wasn't going to help him. He went to get out of the car.

'I knew your uncle. He was the stubborn type too. He'd've done well to accept my offer and sell me that farm.'

Sean stopped and turned. Jimmy Power was sucking on his cigar.

'Can't make much money, a small farm like that.'

'It makes enough,' Sean snapped back.

'Clearly not, or you wouldn't be coming to me for a loan.'

'Ah, forget it. Some things are more important than a pocket full of cash!' Sean turned away angrily. He'd blown it. He shoved the door open.

'So how do I know I'll get my money back?' Jimmy Power said, as he sucked and studied the wet end of his cigar.

Sean took a deep breath. If there was a chance of getting the money to carry on, he had to take it.

'You'll get it,' Sean said, turning back to Jimmy. He hated dealing like this, but what other choice did he have? His uncle would be spinning in his grave if he knew what he was doing. But he couldn't just walk away from the farm, not when he was so close. His mouth was dry and he ran the back of his hand across it. 'I just need to keep going until September.' Sean bit his tongue, worrying he'd said too much, given too much away. It was this or nothing. His head began to ache with the throbbing in his temples. Jimmy Power looked at him sideways with a small smile. His earring looked ridiculous, thought Sean, glad he'd given up his own gold hoop some years ago.

'Tell you what then, I'll lend you the money you're looking for, and you pay it back in September, with interest. I'll text you the terms, give me your number.' He handed Sean the latest iPhone. Sean typed his number in and handed it back.

'Of course, if you don't manage to "get sorted" I'll be looking to be compensated. I've always fancied myself as an oyster farmer,' he laughed, a sound like a car engine refusing to start on a cold morning. 'My lad'll come with you to sort out the money.' He pointed to 'the lad' waiting outside the car. He was a younger version of the toad with a shaved head, and must have been in his thirties. The lad was getting into the Transit van beside Fi, and Sean felt a stirring of fury as he openly looked her up and down. He should've come alone. He nodded to the toad, got out of the Mercedes and opened the Transit's door.

'I'll take it from here, thanks.'

'Suit yourself.' The 'lad' took two envelopes from each inside pocket of his leather jacket and slowly counted the money into Sean's hand.

When he was done, Sean shoved the money into the glove compartment and started the engine. The lad took the hint and, with a leer, said, 'See you in September,' then jumped down.

The sooner he was out of there, the sooner he could get on with getting his business back on track. Because if everything went to plan, he'd be able to off this loan, no problem. And right now, he wanted to check that everything was indeed going to plan.

'Sorry,' Sean says as we get to the roundabout and head out of the estate. 'I didn't mean for you to be involved.' He's swinging the van as fast as possible round the roundabout and heading for the coast.

My mind is whirring. He's got the money but how on earth is he going to repay it? And what on earth did he have to do to get it? Sean looks very pale and his face is set with tension. I'm sure I can actually see his temples throbbing. He's obviously taking a big risk here, and it's not like the money's even going to go that far. By the time he's paid for the licence he'll only be able to buy baby spat and that will take at least three years to grow. This is my fault, I keep thinking, over and over again.

We drive the rest of the way back to Dooleybridge in silence. When we pass the town I have this strange feeling of familiarity, and I like it. It's probably that I'm just glad to be away from that estate. We pass Frank and John Joe going into the bookies. The café sign has blown over in the wind and rain. Margaret is pushing Grandad along the prom in a plastic cape. She waves cheerily, despite the rain and the fact she's not wearing a coat. I wave back. Sean doesn't. His face is set. He's thinking hard, but I can't tell what about.

Finally I ask the question. 'I don't get it.' I look out of the window at the ocean, feeling like we're racing the white horses home. 'How on earth are you going to be able to repay that amount of money in three months? Either you're crazier than I thought or there's something you're not telling me.'

We turn off the main road, and I'm thrown from side to side as we head down Sean's track. I can see him visibly relaxing. His cheeks aren't twitching and there's a tiny smile in the corner of his mouth. He pulls on the handbrake with a crunch and turns to me.

'I really hope you have a plan,' I say, because I don't want to be around when Jimmy Power comes to call in the debt. And I hope for Sean's sake it doesn't come to that.

'Of course I've got a plan,' he says with his usual gruffness.

'Well, what is it?'

'Trust me, I know what I'm doing,' he says, this time looking straight at me. A shiver runs up and down my spine.

'Why do I get the feeling there's something you're not telling me?' I give him a sideways glance.

He looks out to sea and for a moment says nothing.

'I told you. I know what I'm doing.' He taps the dashboard impatiently.

'You're mad! There's nothing else here that can make you any money. Not unless you're planning to sell up.'

'I'm not!'

'Well, what then?'

This time it's his turn to give me a sideways glance, and then he suddenly breaks into a broad grin, a slightly crazy one.

'I'll show you.'

He's out of the van and marching over to the sheds. Grace is greeting her master like he's been away for a month. He comes back out of the shed carrying two lifejackets, and hands me one.

'Put this on,' he instructs.

I stare at it and then back at him in horror. 'I can't!'

'Just put it on.' He holds it out further towards me. 'And then follow me.'

I put the lifejacket over my head. 'There's no way I'm going out on that boat.'

'Do you want to help get me out of this mess or don't you?'

I sort of waggle my head from side to side.

'You'll be fine, I promise. I'm a sailing instructor, for feck's sake!'

'Is there any other way?' I ask pathetically.

'No. Now get in the boat!'

Right now I'm not sure what or who I'm more scared of, the water or Sean.

Chapter Twenty-two

'Come on,' he beckons. But I can't. I'm rooted to the spot, shivering. I shake my head. He rolls his eyes and shrugs his shoulders in exasperation.

'You can single-handedly take on hairy-arsed oyster pirates but you're scared of a bit of water?'

'Yes, and look where that got me,' I say, referring to the oyster pirates.

'I said you took them on. I didn't say you took them on and won,' he says with surprisingly good humour.

I look down at the decking along the jetty and can see the water under it, moving around, making my head swim.

'And that's not a bit of water, it's a lot of water.' I feel like a petulant child. 'I can't, I'm sorry. Ask Nancy. I'm not your woman,' I say, walking away feeling stupid and pathetic.

'Oh yes you are,' I hear from behind me, and before I have a chance to answer, my feet are swept up from under me and Sean has me in his arms walking back up the jetty.

'You can't do this! Put me down!' I demand.

'Yes I can,' he says, matter-of-factly.

'Put me down!' I want to hit him, push him away, but find myself clinging to him for dear life as he walks down the jetty towards the boat. What if the jetty gives way? What if we fall in? What's down there? He marches on.

'There's nothing to be scared of,' he says evenly. 'You just need to trust me.'

'Trust is a very overrated emotion,' I squeak, tucking my head into his neck, my eyes shut. He smells so good and I wish he didn't. I wish I didn't want to stay hiding away with my eyes shut and my head in his neck for a very long time.

He puts me down and I open my eyes. I'm right on the edge of the jetty. I cling to him to stop myself falling in. I'm so terrified that I follow his every instruction and get in the boat. Every now and again as the boat sways I let out a little squeak, like a young child, or maybe a pig.

I clutch the sides tightly while taking the seat he points to. I sit absolutely stock still, barely breathing. My knuckles are white from holding on so tight. I take a quick look at the dark water to one side and wish I hadn't. Sean is working away with ropes, nimbly moving around the boat. My lifejacket is rubbing at my jaw and cheeks and pushing up my ears. I feel like a tortoise ready to retreat into its shell. I check out the location of the lifebuoy and fix my eyes on it.

Sean gets into position by the rudder and gently starts to move the boat away from the jetty. I stop breathing altogether. He's looking up at the sail and back at me alternately. I just don't move and wonder how long this dreadful ordeal is going to last. I feel like a contestant on *I'm a Celebrity . . . Get Me Out of Here!* Only I'm not a celebrity, I'm a nobody.

We are now nearly in the middle of the bay and I'm reminding myself to breathe intermittently. I am completely surrounded by water. My worst nightmare. The sails are flapping and thankfully we're not moving too fast. I keep my eyes fixed on the rocks on the other side of the bay. I can see where we're going, which I'm happier about. When you grow up with a crazy parent you like to know where you're going. That's why I think I was happy with Brian. He'd mapped out our lives for us. Then he cut me adrift, just like I feel now.

'Look, those are the oysters I showed you on the first day, you didn't know what they were,' Sean says above the breeze. I nod. It's all I can do. 'I said it wasn't important.' I nod again. 'Well, they are important. It was a test.' He looks back at me.

'What? What kind of a test?' I feel suddenly affronted. We're out of the bay now and making our way around a headland of rocks.

'Shh!' he suddenly says. And I feel even more affronted. He's the one who's brought me out here and is asking me the questions, and now he wants me to shush.

'But—'

'Shhhh!' he says again with his finger to his lips. 'Seals.' I follow where he's pointing. At first I have no idea what I'm looking for. And then I see it. A dark brown, shiny head popping up from the water. I catch my breath and cling tighter to the sides of the boat. It's both fascinating and confirming of all my fears. Anything could be swimming below us and tip us up. Then another head pops up. On the rocks beyond, there are two others lying out. One rolls over, stretches and slides into the water.

I'm entranced and terrified at the same time. They're behind us now and we've moved into a second bay, beyond the path I walked on the first day.

Sean loosens the sails and we slow to a stop.

'Look below you,' he instructs. 'Look on the sea bed,' he nods over the side of the boat.

'I can't,' I shake my head firmly. I feel sick.

He lets go of the rudder and comes over to me. I try not to

squeal out loud, but don't know if I manage it as the boat rocks from side to side.

'It's OK. I'm here and nothing's going to happen. What you need is a day at my sailing school.'

'It's the last thing I need,' I answer quickly.

He says nothing but puts his hand over mine. 'Just do it. What's the worst that can happen?'

'Oh, I could be catapulted out of the boat, find myself drowning in black waters, being dragged down by who knows what . . . nothing bad, really,' I say, hating the sound of my own sarcasm. I sound like my mother.

'You won't be dragged down into black waters because you can see the bottom. I promise.' He's kneeling in front of me, staring right at me, and I feel a flutter of excitement in my stomach. I want to trust him but . . .

'Just look for yourself if you don't believe me,' he continues, and he's probably right. I'll only believe it if I see it for myself. I slowly take my eyes off him and look to where he's pointing. The boat leans and I cling tighter, but still I look. The water is clear and I can see the bottom and all over the bottom are rocks of some sort.

I look back at him.

'What are they?'

His face breaks into the biggest smile, so different from his set and angry face when we left the city.

'They're oysters . . . wild oysters, native oysters,' he says. 'My uncle discovered them years ago. It proves the waters here are clean. Only I know about them.'

'So they'll replace the oysters that were lost?' I'm suddenly excited.

He shakes his head. 'No, they can't replace those. They

were farmed oysters, Pacific ones. If I can sell these they'll make far more money than all my other oyster stock. I'll be able to pay off the loan no problem, and keep the farm going.'

'But that's brilliant,' I say, still confused. 'Why haven't you said anything before?'

'These are native oysters, growing wild. They're more . . . fragile. They need tender loving care,' he laughs, and ridiculously I blush. 'Anything could happen. Too much water and they will fatten and open, and then of course there are the thieves. This is why I don't want anyone on my land,' he says firmly.

'I understand.' I feel privileged to have been let in on the secret. 'So this is where you come in your boat?'

He nods.

'It's why I wanted someone who knew nothing about oysters. I didn't want you to know what I was trying to do here. But now . . . now this is the only thing that will save me. I don't want Nancy to know about them until I'm sure they're going to make it. I don't want her lining up buyers before they're ready, just in case. Otherwise that will be her and my reputation down the pan for good. I can't let her or the customers down again.'

'Why can't you let Nancy have them now, sell them, and pay back Jimmy Power?'

'They're spawning; it's mating season. You can tell because the flesh is milky. They won't finish until the end of August, and then they'll need a rest from their parenting duties,' he smiles. 'But after that they'll be ready to sell. Then I'll need to get the best price I can for them.'

He suddenly peels off his waterproof top to reveal his

wetsuit underneath, clinging tightly to his chest and arms. He must've put it on in the sheds earlier. Then he peels off his waterproof trousers and is standing in front of me, the wetsuit clinging to his thighs and calves. I try to look away but my eyes keep darting back to him, taking in his big shoulders, his flat stomach. He moves to the side of the boat and then, very quickly, drops over the edge into the water. The boat sways violently to and fro and I'm too scared to scream. But then he's back in the boat with oysters in his hand. He pulls out a knife from a pocket on his bicep and puts it into the hinge of the oyster.

'They're different from the Pacific oysters you've been dealing with. They're rounder, flatter and harder to open,' he says, screwing up his face as he twists the knife to pop off the top shell. 'See, they're spawning. This is why Pacific oysters are better for farmers. They don't spawn in our cold waters. See the milkiness I was telling you about? That's why you only eat native oysters when there's an "r" in the month, when the waters are cold.'

'What's spawning again?' I'm trying to take it all in.

'Making love . . . they're breeding,' he says, and tips up the oyster into his mouth then dives under again.

'Why is no one else doing this round here?' I ask when he comes up again.

'The conditions have to be right. That stream, the mix of fresh water and sea water is what does it. It's magic. And the most important thing . . .' he holds one up to the sky. 'These oysters mean the waters are clean in Dooleybridge, and that means everything.'

He shakes out his wet curls, splashing me, but I don't squeal this time. I'm fascinated. Something catches my eye and I realise the seals are following us. Sean opens another oyster.

'Hey,' he says, and pulls something small and round from the shell and holds it up.

'A pearl!' I shout. 'Is it valuable?' My spirits suddenly start to climb. This could be the answer to our problems.

He laughs and shakes his head. 'Worthless,' he holds it out to show me. 'These aren't pearl oysters.'

'Shame,' I say, and my spirits start to dip again. 'Pretty, though.' I look at the little misshapen pearl, shiny and iridescent.

We head back round the bay as the rain really starts to set in. It's getting greyer and darker.

Sean helps me off the boat and with wobbling knees we walk back to the barn where we hose down the waterproofs and lifejackets. The radio is playing and Sean turns up the volume while we finish up in the shed. He's in buoyant mood, as am I. I clean down the blackboard. On the new spring tide we'll have to grade all the bags that are left and start charting their progress again. I dust the chalk off my hand. Time to do the animals and then a hot shower, supper and bed. I switch off the radio and put away the broom.

'So when exactly will they be ready to sell?' I ask, still thinking about the carpet of oysters Sean's shown me.

'September. I just have to make sure they make it to September. If they don't, it's all over. No one must know.'

'Fine by me,' I say, and go to turn off the light and pull shut the shed doors.

'No one must know what?' says Nancy, standing with her car keys in hand.

Chapter Twenty-three

'No one must know what?' Nancy repeats.

'Just talking tide times,' Sean says, shoving his hands in his pockets like a boy just caught stealing sweets from a shop.

Nancy folds her arms and taps a black booted foot. Sean copies her body language and I can see he feels put on the spot. Nancy raises an eyebrow and Grace lies down, trying to make herself really small and pretend she's not there.

'No, really,' Sean says, failing to pull off a good lie. 'We were just talking about oyster pirates and tide times and . . .' he waves his hand around.

'And . . . ?' Nancy asks. I swallow hard, feeling Sean's predicament. Does he own up to them or does he keep them secret like he's just told me to do?

'And . . . the native oysters growing in the second bay,' he says very quickly, failing to skirt round the question any more.

'So you've got native oysters and you didn't tell me?' Nancy starts pacing up and down the living room.

'I'm going into town, anyone want anything?' I try and lighten the mood, but they ignore me.

'I wanted it to be a surprise.' Sean's trying to smooth things.

'A surprise! It's certainly that. Especially since I'm your oyster broker. When were you going to tell me?'

I slide out the front door and pull my hat down to avoid the midges. It's a Monday night and the committee will be meeting in the pub.

'Hey, when d'ya leave?' Margaret throws open her arms when she sees me and makes me smile.

'Change of plan,' I say, pulling off my coat. 'There was an accident at Sean's place last night.'

The committee's gathering, slowly trickling into the pub. Margaret grabs my arm and clutches it.

'What happened? Is Sean OK?'

'Oh, nothing like that, he's fine, well, not fine exactly. It wasn't that kind of accident, no one was hurt.' She finally releases my arm.

'You had me worried there,' she says, and visibly relaxes, taking a large slug of white wine. 'So what did happen?'

'It was stupid. Some oysters got . . .' I lower my voice, '. . . stolen.' I keep it low. 'And then some got damaged in seeing them off.'

'Oh God, so what's he going to do?' She puts a straw in her wine and sucks through it.

'Buy new stock,' I answer as simply as possible.

The pub is beginning to fill up; that is, Evelyn and John Joe have come in, along with the two barflies and Frank.

'I'll get the drinks,' I say, and squeeze out from the bench seat. I stand in between Frank and Padraig and Seamus.

'Evening,' they say in unison.

'Nice evening?' says Seamus. And then I remember that he saw Margaret and me on the bench.

'Oh, quiet.' I wave a hand.

'Really? I heard there was a bit of a commotion up at your

place?' Padraig says, putting his hand on his waist.

'Nothing we couldn't handle,' I say, but narrow my eyes, feeling like they're laughing at me. I grab the bottle of wine and two glasses and make my way back to the table. I'm about to tell Margaret, but at that moment Evelyn and John Joe followed by Frank come and join us.

'So, ideas! Anyone come up with anything?' Margaret asks. The barflies are looking at me and I try and concentrate on what she's saying. 'A film night, maybe?' she's suggesting.

'What about a fishing competition?' There's a murmur of approval from the men.

'Or a spa night?' says Rosie.

'What d'you think, Fi? Think holiday-makers would come for any of those?' Maire asks. I take a big sip of drink, then a deep breath, and am about to say what I need to say when the door opens and in comes a face I'd recognise anywhere.

'Ah, two pints of your finest please, barman,' says a broad American accent. I glance at him then look out of the window and notice the big black 4x4 parked out there. Just like the one at the farm the other night.

'Jesus Christ!' I splutter into my drink.

'I don't think he'll make it to the spa night, dear,' says Evelyn, who's got out her knitting and is showing Maire.

I duck down behind Margaret.

'Fi, what are you doing for feck's sake?'

'Dropped an earring,' I say stupidly, clutching my left ear. See, I just can't think on my feet.

'Wow, this is quite a place,' I hear the man at the bar saying.

'Fi, we'll find it in a minute. Now, will you get up off the bench,' Margaret says crossly, 'you're disrupting the meeting.

Now, what were you going to say? We need to decide on something. Come on!'

'I can't!' I hiss.

'Can't what?' Margaret bends down to meet my face.

'I can't let him see me.' I nod towards the man at the bar.

'So this is where it all happened? This is where my fore-fathers sat before me.' He's looking round the bar. He's tall, about six foot. He has neatly trimmed black hair around his ears and a baseball cap firmly on his head with sunglasses on the top. His teeth are bleached white. If I didn't dislike him so much for what he'd done I'd say he was, in fact, quite good-looking.

'I feel like the returning hero, coming home,' he gloats.

'Returning hero, my foot!' I sit up, but still with Margaret in front of me to shield me.

'Fi, what are you talking about?' Her face is up close to mine.

'He's the one who stole Sean's oysters. He's the oyster pirate!' I hiss and point. 'Him in the baseball cap.'

Margaret spins to look at him. She doesn't need telling twice.

'Hey!' she shouts. I cringe. 'You!' She points and comes out from behind the table. The American turns to face her in surprise. The young woman with him takes a step back. He looks left and right and then puts his hand to his chest, sticks out his chin a little and mouths, 'Me?' He looks surprised but not displeased. He turns to smile at his companion, who doesn't look so convinced.

'Yes, you!' Margaret starts to stalk over to him, still pointing her finger. I can't help but wish I had just a little of her chutzpah. Margaret's the sort of person you'd want in your corner. But I also realise I need to be in hers if we're to be friends. I jump up and stand by the table in support.

'What on earth do you think you're doing here?' Margaret accuses him. But strangely he smiles some more and then reaches into his inside pocket and pulls out a pen. He turns and picks up a cardboard mat from the bar. Margaret stares at him in disbelief as he holds the pen to the mat.

'What's your name, sweetie?' he smiles, showing some very white teeth. I'm now standing right behind Margaret and we're both looking at the beer mat.

'My name?' she fires back angrily. 'How about you tell me your name and I get the Garda up here to arrest you?'

'Arrest me?' he laughs, but his smile slips just a little. He looks at me and his smile slips a lot.

'Oh no, oh hang on!' He lets his hand fall with the beer mat still in it. 'That was a misunderstanding.' He waves the pen between the two of us. Margaret takes a small step forwards.

'So you admit you were at Sean Thornton's farm?'

I don't have the words to do what she's doing. My cheeks are bloody blushing again and my feet are starting to look for the black hole.

'Well, yes, but—' He shrugs and Margaret cuts him off.

'Patsy, call the Garda. This man stole Sean Thornton's oyster crop last night.' She could just as well have said '*J'accuse!*'

'Righto,' says Patsy, slinging his tea towel over his shoulder and making his way out of the bar to the back room.

'Hey now, hang on! I didn't steal no oysters! I was just looking, that's not a crime is it?'

'It is if you're looking to steal them!' Margaret, as self-appointed prosecutor, continues, and the crowd at the table by the fire all bang their glasses and mutter, 'feckin' right' instead of 'hear, hear'.

'I wasn't stealing any oysters!' There's a hint of desperation creeping into his voice, as though he's about to get lynched. His companion shakes her head, looking worried for him. 'Honestly, I'm no thief! Look, I'm Dan Murphy, from Boston. *Murphy's Seafood Suppers*? TV series?' He looks at Margaret for some recognition but gets none. 'Mary Jo, get her a copy of the book. Tell you what, I'll sign it for you,' he says, as if trying to soothe a frustrated toddler. Mary Jo nips out of the front door.

'I don't care if you're Michel Roux himself!' Margaret persists. 'You can't just come round here helping yourself to people's oysters. It's their livelihood. This place was built on oyster farming. We used to be known worldwide for our oysters and our oyster festival.'

'I know! That's why I came. My family is from here. I'm researching a new book about my family's ancestry, visiting some traditional Irish pubs, eating in oyster houses, following the food trail across the country.' Mary Jo comes back in and hands him a book. 'Look, it's me! Dan Murphy.' He shows her the smiling photo on the front cover. 'I did come to the farm the other night,' he says in a lower voice, and tempers seem to be calming a little. 'I thought it was a beautiful place and I wanted to take some photos for the new book. Then I saw,' he raises an arm in my direction, 'in the . . . buff.' Sniggers from the two barflies and Frank who gets an elbow in the ribs from Evelyn. Rosie and Lily both have their heads cocked adoringly to one side, staring at Dan. 'So I jumped in my car and scarpered. I'm sorry, really I am. I didn't mean to scare you. In fact, if anyone got scared half to death it was me when that dog went for me. But honestly, I wasn't planning to steal any oysters.'

There's silence.

'I've seen your programme, you're lovely . . . I mean, it's lovely,' says Rosie, and Lily nods in agreement. Dan's smile spreads across his face again. He looks to be back in his comfort zone. He offers the book to Rosie, who accepts it with a giggle, especially as he signs it: 'To Rosie, with love, Dan'.

'Garda's on his way,' Patsy announces, and I suddenly get that sinking feeling. What if I was mistaken? I didn't actually see his face. But if Dan Murphy didn't steal the oysters, who did?

'So you see, Officer, I didn't steal any oysters, I was just taking some shots for my new book. It's a great setting.' He pulls out his phone and starts showing the photos he took. 'And then I accidentally scared the living daylights out of this young woman here.' Dan is telling the story again, only this time he's sitting down at a small round table with a pint in front of him. Garda Eamon is taking down all the details in his black notebook.

'What makes you think it was this man?' the Garda looks at Margaret who's got one hand on her hip. She points at me with the other one.

'She told me,' says Margaret. 'She was there.'

Garda Eamon looks at me and rolls his eyes. 'You again?' he says, as though I'm the local troublemaker, and ridiculously I feel like it.

'Well, he was looking in through the window one night and then the oysters were gone. What else was I supposed to think?'

'Sorry about the trouble,' says Garda Eamon to Dan,

giving me another sideways look.

'No problem, have a book,' Dan says, giving him one from the pile Mary Jo has brought in from the car. 'Can I get you a drink?'

'Don't mind if I do, I'll have a pint.' Garda Eamon takes off his hat and lays it on the bar. 'So you're researching your ancestors, you say, what was their name?'

I'm furious with myself. Rosie and Lily are fawning over the photos in the book. And it's not the food they're looking at. Even Evelyn is a little excited about having a 'celebrity' in the town.

'Grandad would be the one to tell you. He knows everything there is to know about these parts.' Garda Eamon nods to a sleeping Grandad.

'All I know is they were oyster farmers here. Heard stories about the oyster festival.'

Margaret and I sit at the other end of the bar and pour two more glasses from the bottle. I knock it back, hoping it'll take away my embarrassment. I listen to Dan telling everyone how it was in his blood, oysters and restaurants, and how he's so proud to be back where it all began for his family. I find myself saying 'blah, blah, blah' in my head.

'I'm never going to fit in around here,' I say to Margaret. I feel even more of an outsider than ever. This Dan Murphy is suddenly being treated like a local because he's got a relative who once came from here. However hard I try I'm never going to fit in.

'Hey, maybe you could open our table top quiz – a celebrity guest!' says Rosie.

'Yes, or do a cookery demonstration for us,' shouts out Evelyn.

'Or a sponsored leg wax,' says Lily, and they all go quiet and look at her.

Margaret and I finish the bottle, deep in our own thoughts. All I know is I can't leave Dooleybridge yet. I have to find a way to help Sean get his business back on track before I can do that. He's given me a second chance and I have to try my best. I can't mess this up now. I need to find a way to pay off my debt, and I think the answer may just be staring me right in the face. I swing round to the group by the fire.

'You know, you were right, Maire.' I wave my glass in her direction.

'Was I, dear?'

'This town needs to forgive and forget. The past is the past. It needs its oyster festival back.' She stops doing Evelyn's knitting for her.

'I knew you'd do it.' Maire claps her hands.

'Do what?' says Margaret, turning round to join me.

'The oyster festival,' says Maire. 'Fi here is bringing back the oyster festival,' she beams. It's the best way I can think of to help Sean sell his oysters at a good price.

'There's not much time. You can't get a festival together in eight weeks,' says Evelyn.

'We can all help: ideas, volunteers . . .' Margaret is getting excited. 'See, I told you, born leader. I knew you could front up the festival.'

'Oh, I'm not going to front it up. What we need is that man there to be the face of the festival.' And all eyes turn to look at Dan Murphy.

Chapter Twenty-four

'You suggested doing what?' Sean's face drops. I've rushed through my morning jobs to tell him my news. He's leaning against the kitchen cupboard. Nancy is putting on her boots.

'I suggested we bring back the oyster festival. It's the obvious answer. You can sell oysters on the day and use it as a platform to get big buyers.'

'Forget it. It's a ridiculous idea. A village fête, that's all it is,' Nancy interrupts while pulling on her left boot.

'But this way the whole town will be involved and Sean's oysters will be the main talking point.'

'I don't know,' Sean shakes his head. 'There's a lot of history . . .'

'But it's the perfect way to put the past behind you. Prove to them all that your uncle was right all along. The waters here in Dooleybridge are clean.'

For a moment he says nothing.

'It's fine the way things are. Sean doesn't need to prove anything to anyone round here. I do the selling. Everyone's happy. I will be taking all native oysters for my restaurant. It's all sorted. They are exactly what I need to get the New Restaurant of the Year award.' Nancy stands up and pulls herself up to her full height. I turn to Sean, which means turning away from Nancy.

'And there's this American TV chef, Dan Murphy. We want to get him to be the face of the festival. He's over here researching his family history.'

'Did you say Murphy?' Sean visibly stiffens.

'Dan Murphy?' Nancy suddenly looks interested. 'He's going to launch this festival?'

'We'd like him to. He was the guy looking in the window the other night. He wanted to take photographs. He wasn't responsible for the oyster raid,' I tell Sean.

'Hang on a minute. If you have a TV chef involved, this might work. It could be a great opportunity to launch the restaurant. With a celeb on board and true native Galway oysters on the menu, it could make all the difference to The Pearl.' Nancy's eyes are dancing like she's on something.

Sean shakes his head. 'People won't come,' he says.

'Leave it to me,' Nancy says, and Sean puts his cup in the sink.

'This is why I didn't tell you,' he says quietly, and walks out.

Nancy turns to me. 'You can help me, but don't do anything unless you run it by me first. I need to meet this Dan Murphy and tell him what I need from him. In fact, you'd better come with me and introduce me. Set up a meeting for Thursday. Evening. I can't believe I didn't think of this before.'

You didn't, I think, but don't say so. In fact, Nancy's involvement suits me fine. I don't want to be in charge. I'm more than happy to let her be at the helm. If it helps Sean get his oysters sold then I'm all for it one way or another. So I smile and say, 'Of course.' Out of the window I can see Sean is gathering ropes and planning to tow the tractor from its watery grave. 'I have to get on,' I tell her.

'Fine. I have to meet the decorators at the restaurant. I'll pick you up Thursday, about eight,' she says bossily, then scoops up her big handbag, swings her hair and swoops out. She waves to Sean. I pull on my waterproofs and go down to meet him at the water's edge.

'Grab this rope. We'll pull this thing out before I go to work.'

The water seems darker than usual, the drizzle wetter and colder. There's no small talk as we finally pull the dripping tractor out of the deep, dark sand. I thought Sean was going to be thrilled with my plan for the oyster festival, but I get the impression he's not happy with the idea, not happy at all.

The next couple of days pass in the same way. Sean only speaks when he needs to; otherwise, when he's not at the sailing school, he's got his head stuck under the tractor bonnet.

By Thursday I can't stand the silence a moment longer. I make a coffee and open the back door. The wind and drizzle hit me in the face and I know the coffee's going to be cold by the time I get it down to the tractor. I pull my coat round me.

'I made you this,' I say to Sean, who barely acknowledges me. Right, that's it! 'Look, if you want me to cancel the oyster festival I will,' I say with all the boldness I can muster, which isn't a lot, and it comes out as a bit of a squeak if I'm honest. But I've said it. I can't live like this and if it means cancelling the festival then so be it.

He stands up, his hair flopping round his face. He uses his forearm to push it back but it keeps falling into his eyes. He spots the coffee.

'Thanks.' He takes a sip and pulls a face.

'Cold?'

He nods and gives a little laugh. It's the closest he's come to talking to me since the mention of the festival.

'Did you mean what you said?' He takes another sip of the cold coffee.

'Yes,' I say, my nerves subsiding. 'If you hate the idea of it, I'll tell Nancy we're cancelling it. Tell her it was a ridiculous idea.'

He raises his eyebrows and works at cleaning his dirty hands. 'I don't think Nancy would agree with you. In fact, I'd say she's pretty set on the idea now.'

The thought of trying to stop the force that is Nancy fills me with dread. 'Look, maybe I should've talked it over with you fir—'

'Yes,' he cuts across the end of my sentence, 'you should've.' He throws the rag onto the bonnet. 'Start her up, will you?' He nods to the tractor seat. 'You can remember how to start her up, can't you?'

'Yes,' I say, like a teenager back-chatting a parent. Why can't he just say he hates the idea and doesn't want anything to do with it? I climb into the tractor seat. God, he can be so irritating at times.

'I'm sorry I didn't talk to you first. I just thought it was a great way of getting the oysters sold and getting a really good platform for them. I thought I was helping.' I check the tractor's not in gear and that the accelerator isn't stuck down by pulling it towards me with the toe of my welly.

Sean is looking at me, deep in thought. 'There's a lot of history.' He throws the cloth down angrily.

For a moment I think about saying nothing else, but my mouth seems to be working independently from my brain. 'And this is the way to put it right, for your uncle. If you have native oysters here, your waters are clean. Everyone should know.' I want to put everything right, but Sean is just so bloody hard to help.

'Start her up,' he says, picking up the oily rag again. Frustration is building inside me; he may not like the idea but he doesn't need to sulk. The engine turns over, but only just.

Sean used the engine noise to block out the conversation. He was finding this really hard. The memories kept flooding back to him. His uncle had died thinking everything he cared about, everything he'd worked for, had been a failure. But it wasn't just that. It was all the other memories it had brought back, about his arrival here in Dooleybridge. He'd arrived a week after being released from prison, but only days after being released from hospital. He'd come back alone, and that was never how it was supposed to be. He and Emily had talked about coming back here together one day, once they'd seen the world. But they hadn't seen the world and he'd come back alone, arriving in the village just before the festival. The locals had put two and two together and come up with seventeen. It had all come flooding back to him and he didn't seem to be able to find the words to explain. Fi was doing her best. He wanted to tell her but he found it so hard. Nancy knew, of course, but never mentioned it.

'Try again,' he called to her.

Rrrrrr, Rrrrrrr, Rrrrrrr. The engine groaned.

'Ah, come on!' he shouted at the tractor, and banged at the bonnet with his fist. Without the tractor he couldn't even work with the few oyster bags he had left. He turned away and wiped his damp curls from his eyes with the crook of his elbow. He looked at the sea, grey and moody. The thing was, he realised, as painful as it was to remember, he needed Nancy's restaurant to take off in order to sell the oysters. If he didn't let this go ahead now, what the hell else was he going to do?

'Try once more,' I shout to him. I can see he's frustrated. The accelerator seems to be working much more freely now. I wiggle it up and down again with the toe of my welly. He turns back to me as if he's got the weight of the world on his shoulders.

'I don't think it's going to work,' he shakes his head as he turns to me.

'We can't just stop trying,' I say. 'We don't have any other choice.'

He looks at me for a moment and I wonder if he's going to explode, but his face suddenly changes expression, as if all the air has been let out of a balloon about to burst.

'OK,' he says, suddenly very calm. He turns back to the engine and pulls a face as he works away.

'Now!' he shouts, and I turn the key and stand on the accelerator.

Suddenly the tractor roars into life, sputtering and gasping as if it's been electrocuted. Sean takes a couple of steps back. He gives me a satisfied nod and the engine settles down into a rhythmic hum.

I stand up and jump down from the tractor.

'Good work, English,' he says. 'You're a trier, I'll give you that.'

I feel myself swell with pride. I turn to go back to the cottage. I may have been able to persuade him to keep going with the tractor, but it doesn't look as if I'll be able to do the same about the festival. I can't keep going with it if he hates the idea.

'English! About this oyster festival . . .' He stops me in my tracks. I turn round slowly. I have no idea how I'm going to tell Nancy and Margaret that we have to cancel it. I decide to make one last attempt to persuade him.

'It's a great opportunity to put your oysters back on the map, put Dooleybridge back on the map.' I try my best.

For a moment he says nothing. Then, slowly and quietly, he says, 'Providing we've got oysters to sell.' He raises an eyebrow. 'I'm just not happy with us setting this whole thing up and for there to be no oysters. It'll be like a public hanging.'

'You're the best oyster farmer around here. It has to be worth the risk, doesn't it?'

Again he says nothing, just slams down the lid of his toolbox and starts to make his way towards the barn. As he passes me he says, 'Looks like I don't have much choice.'

Is he saying what I think he's saying?

'So you think it's a good idea?' I suddenly feel very relieved.

'No, I'm not saying I think it's a good idea.'

My lifted spirits plummet like a bungee jump from a high building.

'I'm saying, just make sure it isn't a total fuck-up. I can't afford for anything to go wrong.'

He marches back to the shed and I follow. At least he's stopped sulking and is talking again.

Chapter Twenty-five

'So Sean likes the festival idea?' Margaret claps her hands together.

'I wouldn't go so far as to say "likes",' I say cautiously to Margaret the next day, as we pull up in the car park of one of Galway's smartest hotels.

'But he's in?'

'Well, let's just say he's coming round to the idea.'

'Hi, how can I help you?' says the tall blonde woman on the hotel reception.

Margaret takes charge. 'Hi, we're looking for Dan Murphy. I believe he's staying here?'

The receptionist doesn't smile. She turns to her computer screen while I look around the foyer. Modern and minimalist. Out of the hotel, across the busy road, is water, more water, no doubt leading to the harbour where I went with Sean the day I thought I was going to be getting on a plane and leaving Ireland. The day I finally accepted my marriage had been a fake.

'Who shall I say wants him?'

I spin back round. The receptionist is holding the phone and her hand is hovering over the dial buttons.

'We're . . .' Margaret misses a beat.

'Work colleagues. We have some news about the family

tree he's working on.' I smile. The receptionist doesn't, but dials the number. She speaks in such hushed tones that I can barely hear what she's saying.

Margaret is giving me a 'WTF?' look.

'Well, you probably know his relatives. You know everyone,' I whisper.

'He'll be down now. Take a seat,' the receptionist instructs.

We do as we're told and shuffle shoulder to shoulder over to the soft seats in the huge window and watch the traffic pass by. Margaret finds a magazine and turns straight to her horoscopes.

I watch the steps and see an old red Skoda pull into the drive. I recognise the driver and passenger. A large delivery truck is in their way and they honk the horn. I'm about to point them out to Margaret when I notice the large bag of oysters in a black mesh bag on the back seat. The truck moves on and the Skoda carries on round the back of the hotel. It couldn't be, could it? I could just be putting two and two together and coming up with seventeen, but it does seem odd. I don't even know if they are Sean's oysters, but my gut feeling is shouting at me that they are.

'It's him!' Margaret hisses from behind her magazine. I spin round quickly to see the receptionist pointing towards us.

'Hi, I'm Dan Murphy, you wanted to see me—' His smile drops as soon as he registers who we are. He looks from me to Margaret, peeping out from above her magazine.

'Hi again,' she says brightly.

'Hi,' I say with a little wave.

Now he's looking quite irritated. 'What is this, some kind of joke? Come to set the Garda on me again, have you?' He turns to leave. A couple in their sixties in matching Irish shirts, checking in at reception, turn to stare.

'No, nothing like that,' I try to say, but thankfully Margaret steps in. She jumps up, practically bouncing with enthusiasm.

'Actually, we've come to do you a favour. You're tracing your family tree, right?' she asks. I'm a bag of nerves. 'If you want to trace your family tree then you should come back and meet Grandad. I could introduce you. He knows everyone who's everyone.' Margaret's still beaming. I stand up and look out of the window as the old red Skoda reappears. Seamus and Padraig are smiling away like a pair of cats who have got the cream as they pull out into the traffic.

'Isn't that right, Fi? Fi?' I suddenly spin back to Margaret who is looking at me to back her up.

'Oh, right, yes . . .' but I'm not sure what she's said.

He's looking at us warily, like we're the last people he wants to see.

'You want me to come back to Dooleybridge with you?' he says slowly.

'Yes.' Margaret is beaming.

'Yes,' I add.

He looks sideways at us as if he's being lured into some kind of trap.

Dan looks round in disbelief as he steps into the café, pushing past the hanging dressing gown, now reduced to 50 cents. He takes in the umbrellas in the bucket by the door, all at 20 cents each, and then slowly looks at the other goods on sale: the bulging make-up bag, the worn slippers and the slow cooker. Gerald is creating steam with his new urn. Dolly Parton is playing on the stereo.

'Grandad, wake up!' Margaret nudges Grandad who shakes himself into life. Dan puts his man bag on the chair next to him.

'So, this is Dooleybridge's coffee house?' He's still looking like he's landed on Mars, and I remember that feeling. I push a nylon nightie off the table and onto the shelf beside us. Dan looks at it like it's going to bite him.

'It was his wife's,' Margaret whispers.

'Is she dead?' Dan looks as if he's going to run or be sick.

'No, she left him. Went off with a Father Dougal lookalike after Tedfest and never came back. So he's selling all her stuff.'

Dan's eyes practically pop out of his head. I'm pretty surprised too; I always wondered what all this stuff was.

'What's Tedfest?' he asks, getting out a notebook and pen.

'A festival on the Arran Islands, over there.' Margaret points in the general direction of the islands. 'They all dress up as Father Ted characters for a weekend. It's a great craic.' Then she sighs. 'See, even the Arran Islands have people going there.'

I touch her arm.

'So this is where my family is from then.' He looks around, still adjusting to his new surroundings. 'This is where the Murphys worked the oyster beds,' he says, warming to his theme. 'From poor and humble beginnings . . .'

Margaret smiles and nods at me. It might be working; he might just want to spend more time here and get involved with the festival. I'm beginning to feel a bit better about getting him out here on false pretences.

'I'd love to meet some of my family. It would make a great

end to the book. Travelling across Ireland, all the food I've tasted on the way, the meals I've had, to finally end up here, coming home to meet my family.' I swear his eyes have gone all misty. Margaret claps her hands together in glee. Dan has an eager expression on his face. 'It would be great to actually interview one of them, some old aunt or something?'

Grandad suddenly sits up and cuts across him. 'Oh, there hasn't been a Murphy round here for years.'

Margaret and I freeze. Gerald comes over to take the orders.

'Tea for me, please,' I say quickly.

'Coffee please, Gerald,' says Margaret.

'Macchiato,' Dan says, and Gerald gives him a wary look.

'That's two coffees, Gerald,' Margaret says helpfully. Gerald nods.

'Anything to eat . . . scones?' His pen is poised. Margaret and I shake our heads, but before we can warn him Dan says, 'Oh, a scone, lovely.'

Gerald hurries away, happy to have made a sale, and Grandad chuckles.

'So, about my relatives . . .' Dan holds up his phone to Grandad, obviously recording him. Grandad gives the phone a suspicious look and gently pushes Dan's hand away.

'There haven't been Murphys around here for years. Sold up, moved out. Their land went to developers. It used to be a great mussel farm but then developers tried to put in an executive estate looking out to sea. Those were the last Murphys I remember around here. Moved on after the last oyster festival.'

'Executive estate, you say?' Dan cuts into the scone and

both Margaret and I watch worriedly. It falls open, pale and dry. Dan looks disappointed.

'Ghost estate, more like. The houses were never finished. I think they got the plumbing in but after that they had to stop. Just by Sean Thornton's place.'

'Who's he? Perhaps I could interview him' Dan looks at us and we look at each other. I can't see Sean agreeing to that one.

'Just by the farm you were at the other day, where I work – where he set the dog on you,' I add helpfully, hoping to put him off.

'Oh,' says Dan. 'And the Murphys? Where did they go?'

'America I think.' Grandad reaches for his tea with unsteady hands. 'Or was it New Zealand . . . ?'

'Like most people round here. There's no work, nothing for them,' Margaret joins in.

'But you're still here,' Dan points out, putting butter on the scone.

'Let's just say I feel my destiny is here,' Margaret says with a smile.

Just then Sean walks in and Margaret's face lights up, proving to herself and everyone around her that she is right.

'Sean!' she says brightly. 'This is Dan, Dan Murphy. We were just talking about you.' She's smiling so much I wonder if it's making her face ache.

'Coffee, please,' he says to Gerald.

'Do you want to join us? We're just discussing . . . planning things,' I say.

'No, you're all right. Just on my way into town.' He takes the coffee, pays for it then turns back to us.

'A Murphy, is it?' he says to Dan.

'Yes, I understand our families were once neighbours. Look, sorry about that misunderstanding the other day . . .' Dan goes to stand up.

'Take my advice and stay away from my land,' Sean growls. I sigh. The pair hold each other's stare for a moment and then Sean stalks out and Dan sits down. This is going badly wrong. Very badly wrong.

'So, no family to speak of,' Dan says flatly.

'No, but I might be able to help you with some photos. Why not come up to the pub and we can see if there's any of your family pictures on the wall. They might've taken part in the oyster festival. Talking of the festival, I do have another idea for the end of your book . . .' Margaret hooks her arm through his and leads the way.

In the empty pub we look round the pictures on the wall. Grandad's bright as a button, as though the pictures have transported him back to happier times.

'So, are these all from past festivals?' Dan asks as we study them.

'That one was the year it went to sudden death,' Grandad says, remembering each picture as if it was yesterday.

'That's Sean's uncle, isn't that right, Grandad?' Margaret points out a picture of a short man with a white apron tied around his middle.

Grandad nods. 'Tom.' He tuts and shakes his head and I don't know if it's because he blames him for the trouble in Dooleybridge or because he misses a friend. Tom's standing in the middle of five other men in the photograph, holding a large silver cup.

'But none of Sean?' I ask absently.

'No, he was always busy entering competitions every-where but here,' Margaret says. 'All over Europe from what I've heard. Was quite a champion shucker, until he came back—'

'Hey, there's a Murphy!' Dan cuts across us and makes Grandad jump. Dan whips out his phone and takes a picture. 'Such a shame that this is all I've got for the end of my book,' he says out loud. 'I'll get Mary Jo to come in and photograph things properly.'

I nudge Margaret heavily. Suddenly there's an almighty ruckus outside, dogs are barking.

'Ah, feck it, the dogs are chasing the post van again.' She flings back the door and bellows at them.

'Well, thanks for your help. I'd better be going.' Dan puts his phone away and takes a final look around the walls for any he might have missed.

'Wait!' I say with a funny sort of squeak, looking for Margaret to come back and explain our idea. He stops and looks at me. He has bright blue eyes and I wonder whether they are natural, or whether they're contacts.

Margaret's trying to steer two wayward dogs back across the road through the cars.

'I'm sorry, but I really have to go.' Dan looks at his phone. 'We're leaving tomorrow and we have an early start. But thanks for the pictures. Shame, I'd hoped for something more.'

Frustrated that Margaret is missing and Grandad has fallen asleep, I blurt out, 'You could always stay.'

He looks at me and his smile widens.

'Well . . . wow! You're a fast worker. I mean, I wondered if there was some kind of connection between us after, y'know, the bathroom incident, but this has come as a bit of a shock. Give me a minute to think on it. I mean, I like you and all that, but we hardly know each other.'

My mouths gapes like a fish out of water.

'Have you told him?' Margaret is back and out of breath.

I shake my head, staring at her like a rabbit in the headlights, not knowing which way to run.

'Look, basically, this could be a great end to your book. We want to get the Dooleybridge oyster festival back up and running and we want you to be the face of it.'

'Me?' He swells and looks even more excited.

'You're from round here, you're returning to your home-land, it could make a great finish to your book. You, back in the bosom of your ancestors.' Margaret beams.

I could never have said it like that. It looks like she's pressed all the right buttons, too.

'Oh, I don't know . . . On the other hand, if I stay around here I could have some peace and quiet to actually write the damn thing.' He's nodding thoughtfully to himself. Margaret's holding her breath. Then he looks at me. 'And you're part of this festival revival, are you, um . . .'

'Fi,' Margaret says helpfully.

'Fi,' he says with a shiny white smile, staring right at me.

I clear my throat.

'Yes, I'm . . .'

'It was Fi's idea. She thought you'd be perfect,' Margaret says with gathering enthusiasm.

'Well, I . . .'

'In that case,' Dan clasps his hands together and gives me one of his very blue looks, 'I'd better get myself some accommodation sorted and you can tell me all about it, Fi.'

I try and smile but I get the funny feeling, thanks to Margaret, that someone's just got the wrong end of the stick.

Nancy sounds her horn loudly just before eight and I don't keep her waiting. I grab my waterproof and bid Grace goodbye. Sean is plucking away on his guitar by the fire.

'You can come if you like,' I offer before leaving.

He smiles back and shakes his head. 'Best one of us stays here. Just in case we get any returning visitors, coming back for the few bags they've missed.' He puts down the guitar, goes to the fridge and pulls out a can.

Not only do I have to work out how we're going to pull off this festival in eight weeks, but I also have to put right any misunderstanding between me and Dan. I'd hate to think he was going to miss his flight tomorrow because he thought I fancied him. I am strictly off romance of any description.

Nancy looks me up and down as I climb into the passenger seat of her clean car, and at the muddy footprints I make in the footwell.

'No Sean?' she says by way of a greeting.

I shake my head. 'He's watching out for the oyster pirates.' Although I suspect he's glad to have the excuse.

She sniffs and then starts up the engine and heads for town, just missing Freddie and Mercury who are standing by the white donkey's gate. I should get out and take them home but she's careering down the road, firing out instructions as we go.

'Marquee; it's got to be classy. Make sure you organise it from the city, not from some hill farmer out here. Tickets, promotions, newspapers . . .'

'I was thinking we should try and make it as close to how

the festival used to be as possible. Grandad was telling me all about it. The locals seemed to be a big part of it, and the whole town would turn out. I was thinking we could have a local band, activities for the children,' I offer up.

'Good God, no! We may be using local oysters but that's about as parochial as it's going to get. It's got to be classy. It's got to compete with the festival in Galway and over in Clarenbridge. It's got to be bigger and better.'

We obviously have totally different ideas about how the festival should be run.

'You do know we've only got eight weeks to get this together, don't you?' I tell her.

'I'm sure you'll manage it.' She turns to me and gives me a big smile. 'Anyone who can get Sean Thornton's cottage as sorted as you have is capable of rising to a challenge.'

I think she's giving me a compliment but there's a look in her brown eyes that just unnerves me.

'Besides, you don't want to let Sean down now, do you?' she adds much more quietly.

Chapter Twenty-six

'So it's official, we're bringing back the oyster festival. For real!' Margaret is telling anyone who'll listen from behind the bar. 'It's brilliant. I mean, that's exactly what we need. Fame, right here in Dooleybridge. I knew it would happen. It said so in my horoscope today.' She pulls out a well-thumbed copy of a magazine from under the bar. The paper's so thin it crackles as she turns to the page she knows off by heart. She starts reading with dramatic projection. 'Prepare for your world to take centre stage—'

'Margaret,' I interrupt her.

'Oh hi! Dan's on his way. He's moved into Rosie's chalet. Should be here any minute.' She looks like she's won the golden ticket. 'My horoscope is just brilliant.' She holds up the magazine again. Nancy gives an impatient little cough.

'Oh, Margaret, this is Nancy Dubois.' I swallow. 'Sean's—'

'Oyster broker,' Nancy finishes for me.

Margaret takes in Nancy in much the same way she did me when we first met. Her eyebrows arch.

'He'll be here any minute. I told him we wanted to talk,' Margaret says.

Bang on cue the door swings back with its usual crash. Dan smiles and marches in with Mary Jo behind him.

'Hey,' Margaret gives him a wave. Nancy's head spins round.

'Dan Murphy? I'm Nancy Dubois, festival organiser,' Nancy says with a smooth smile and flicks back her hair. Again Margaret's eyebrows lift. Nancy's hand shoots out to shake Dan's.

'Festival organiser? I hadn't realised. I thought these two ladies were behind all this.' Dan looks from me to Margaret and is probably wondering if we're a bunch of screwballs.

'I'm in charge of media,' Margaret quickly appoints herself. 'Unless you wanted to do that?' she turns to me.

'No, no, you go ahead. I'm happy doing the behind-the-scenes stuff.'

'This festival will be a huge affair. We're going to have restaurateurs and buyers from Dublin, Galway and France. It's going to be a very prestigious event and we'd love it if you'd open it. Your family are from here, I gather . . .' Nancy turns to me to confirm this and I nod quickly. 'You're the perfect choice.' She smiles a stunning smile again, tinged with a little flirtation.

'Happy to oblige,' Dan says. Nancy turns triumphantly to Margaret and me, as if she's just got him to agree to it herself, despite our hard work earlier. 'I feel drawn to here. It's in my blood. I'd be happy to help my homeland.'

I can see Margaret out of the corner of my eye. She's putting a finger down her throat, making a gagging gesture behind their backs. I look away quickly, fighting to suppress the giggles.

'We'll organise some media stuff straightaway, get the festival launched, won't we, Maureen?' Nancy turns to Margaret who quickly stops making the gagging motion and pretends to be scratching her nose instead.

'Yes, of course,' she smiles. 'And it's Margaret,' she corrects, but Nancy doesn't seem to notice or, if she does, doesn't care.

'And you can judge the Pearl Queen competition,' Margaret tells Dan. 'That should get even more coverage.'

'The what?' Nancy looks irritated at Margaret's interruption.

'You know, like a beauty queen. Someone to be the beautiful face of the festival – no offence like, Dan, not that you're not beautiful, but you need a glamorous girl on your arm,' Margaret explains, making me smile.

'If we must,' Nancy barely gives it a thought.

'Great,' he grins. 'And will you be entering, Fi?' He turns to me and my cheeks instantly burn bright red.

'Oh no, like I say, I'm strictly behind the scenes,' I manage to say.

'But I will,' Margaret butts in.

'Fi here will be organising the festival itself. If you have any questions, just ask her and she can ask me,' Nancy tells Dan, and Dan nods appreciatively in my direction.

'I'll be heading home like we planned, tomorrow,' Mary Jo says to me. 'Need to get back to the office, and the family,' she says with a slightly watery smile. 'Lovely as it's been, I can't wait to get home. My little boy will be missing me. I can leave my husband home alone only so long.'

'Yes, I need you to go and hold the fort. Tell the publishers I'm on to it, not to panic.' Dan pats Mary Jo on the shoulder. 'I'll have the book ready to tie in with the new TV series.' I'm staring at Mary Jo and realise I'm pushing down my feelings of envy. She's getting on a plane and going back to her home, family and friends. I wonder if I'll ever have half of what she's got. I know that's why I've got to stay and throw myself into this, until these feelings go away. A sharp nudge in the ribs brings me back to earth.

'So? It's going to be just like it used to be?' Rosie asks. 'Grandad can tell you everything you need to know.' She points her Bacardi Breezer at him. Grandad sits up straight in his wheelchair.

'When I was a boy you couldn't move for oysters here. Native oysters . . .' He's spreading out his fingers, seeing the beds in front of him.

'Not now, Grandad,' chorus the group that's gathered around us.

'Excuse me,' Nancy says over their chatter, 'this is supposed to be a private meeting.' For a moment no one says anything. Then Frank laughs, showing his missing front tooth. 'No such thing round here,' he says, and the others chuckle in agreement.

'This is going to be a professional affair. Obviously we'll need waiters and waitresses, cloakroom staff, that kind of thing. But it'll be a dinner and dance. I'll be bringing in a chef from my new restaurant and I'll be organising the oysters, obviously. A seafood extravaganza!' Nancy announces and stands up to leave. She smooths down her dress and puts out a strong hand for Dan to shake. 'Great to have you on board, Dan. Fi will sort you out from here. If you need anything, just call her.'

'I will,' he says with a wink.

Then Nancy flicks out any hair that has caught under her handbag strap on her shoulder and we watch as she sweeps out of the pub into the rain.

'How do you think it's going down with the rest of the locals?' I say quietly to Margaret.

Margaret looks around and rocks her hand from side to side. 'Excited, I think. Like you say, time to forgive and forget.'

I look around. I'm desperately trying to see any trace of excitement.

Seamus and Padraig are finishing their pints and Seamus pulls out a wad of notes from inside his jacket pocket. They're chuckling and then look straight at me.

'No Sean tonight?' Seamus asks.

'No, he's at the farm in case the oyster pirates come back,' I say, narrowing my eyes.

'Shame, would've liked to buy him a pint. Had a little windfall,' Seamus chuckles a tobacco-filled rattle and Padraig joins him. I feel my hackles rise.

'So, that's settled then, Fi,' Margaret interrupts my thoughts. 'You'll organise the venue, I'm doing marketing, and Dan, you'll do a publicity launch. Oh, it's going to be fabulous. I can't wait!' Her face is glowing like a child's on Christmas Eve.

'Only trouble is, I need to contact suppliers and things. There's no reception up at the farm. How are we going to organise a festival without internet access?' I look at Margaret.

'And I have emails I need to send,' Dan says.

'Gerald's café! Let's call it Festival HQ! Keep it local.' Margaret goes back behind the bar to serve Seamus and Padraig. I can't help but look at them. If they did take the oysters I can't let them get away with it. But what can I do?

'Sounds like there won't be anything local about it,' says Seamus gruffly.

'A bunch of blow-ins telling us locals how to do the festival,' Padraig sniffs. 'That Sean Thornton and his French partner and his English assistant. Nothing local there,' he says loudly to Seamus.

'Hey, I'm doing it and my family's lived here for . . . ever!' Margaret puts her hands on her hips and Grandad agrees angrily. 'And so's Dan. He's a Murphy. Murphys have always lived here.'

Seamus and Padraig shake their heads. They're not going to be persuaded.

'It'll be great to get the media back to Dooleybridge. Show them what we're made of,' Margaret gives out to them loudly.

I can't help but wonder exactly what it is that Margaret thinks Dooleybridge is made of. Seamus and Padraig are right; it's going to be a marquee on the GAA pitch. Customers will turn up, eat, maybe stay overnight and then leave again, with luck having ordered lots of Sean's oysters. But apart from that I can't really join in Margaret's enthusiasm and see how it will turn Dooleybridge into some kind of oyster lovers' Mecca. Not when they have County Clare on the other side of the bay. But one thing's for sure, I'm going to give it a damn good try; I owe Sean that at least. And what's more, I'm determined to prove Seamus and Padraig wrong.

'So, can I put you two down for car parking duties?' I hold up my pad and pen. They practically spit their beer out with laughter and I squirm with embarrassment.

'No you can't,' Padraig answers flatly.

'How about you, Seamus?' I persist, despite feeling a right fool.

'Not for me.' He shakes his head. 'Surprised you have time to do all this, what with your boss being away so much. Must be lonely up there on that farm on your own,' he says, as though I won't work out what he's implying. But I have. I just haven't worked out how to prove it yet.

'It's fine,' I reply quickly. I am so going to make them laugh on the other sides of their faces.

'What about you, Evelyn, John Joe? Could you help at the oyster festival?' I hold my pen over my pad. 'Cloakroom?'

Evelyn thinks for a minute. 'I could make some scones if you like,' she says with a sniff.

'Ah, OK, well, thanks for that, Evelyn. I'll get back to you once the chef has told us his menu,' I say, wondering how on earth I'm going to let her down gently. I don't dare turn to look at Margaret or I'd giggle again. But really it isn't funny. Unless I can rustle up some interest, this event will be dead in the water before we've even started.

Chapter Twenty-seven

There's an early morning mist across the water the next day. The sun is barely up, but the tide is out and I can hear the tractor. I jump out of bed and look out. Sean is driving the tractor up from the oyster beds. The heron is hopping from rock to rock, following him.

He pulls up the stony bank and reverses the trailer round to the sheds. The doors at the back of the van are open. I pull on some clothes and go out to join him. He doesn't ask about the festival meeting. On the one hand I'm irritated that he hasn't asked; he could take an interest, at least. On the other hand I'm grateful because without a bit of local support it will be just another one of my embarrassing failures.

'Where are you going with this lot?' I ask, looking into the back of the van. There are a few crates of oysters with dark, wet seaweed hanging from them, a garden table from the shed and four plastic chairs.

'Farmers' market.' He pulls the bags of oysters from the trailer. 'Switch on the washer,' he instructs, and I do. 'Had a word with a mate and managed to get a pitch in Galway this morning. I'll go on to the sailing school after lunch.'

'Right,' I say.

'Now I can't get the big orders out, thought I'd sell these direct to the customers. Six at a time and throw in a glass of

212

white wine,' he's telling me as he puts more oysters through the washer and I put them into crates the other side. 'Should bring in a bit of money. Won't be a fortune, but it'll all help. We'll load up and grab a coffee on the way.'

We load the crates and layer wet seaweed in between the oysters to keep them fresh.

'Always put them in with the cup down like this.' He holds one in his hand and it nestles into his palm. 'That way they stay in their own juices and don't dry up,' he says, and I swallow hard for some reason.

We finish loading and close the van doors, then head off into the city. Sean parks up and finds our pitch. It's early and still chilly, and stallholders are setting up all around us. Sean sets up the table and then hands me a knife. In front of me he puts down three oysters and a tea towel.

'Pick up your oyster,' he tells me as he does the same. 'Then put it on the tea towel and wrap the tea towel around it.'

I watch him and follow his lead.

'There's only two ways you can hurt yourself. You can miss and cut yourself, or, and I think this is the most painful, you can get shell under your nail. It feckin' hurts, I can tell you.' He wraps the towel around his oyster, although I know he's only doing it to show me. 'Then put the tip of the knife into the hinge, here.' He taps the pointed end.

I put the tip in. 'Grip the oyster hard and push the blade in, really hard,' he says encouragingly. I do but it won't go in. I push again and the tip disappears into the shell. 'Good, now push it in as far as it will go,' he tells me. His blade has disappeared. Mine won't budge.

'It won't go in,' I say, pushing but terrified it's going to slide out and slice my hand. I grip the tea towel tighter.

'Don't be scared of it,' he says.

That's easy for him to say. I am terrified of slicing my fingers off.

'Look, like this . . .' He comes round to my side of the table and is now standing behind me. He suddenly puts his large hand over mine, holding the knife. My heart starts to quicken, as does my breathing. His fingers wrap around mine and my heart and my breathing quicken again. There's a fizz of excitement in my stomach, like a passing crowd of butterflies have just done a Red Arrows fly-by in there, zooming in and out. I grip the oyster harder and push; his arms around me tense up and he pushes too and the shell starts to move. He wraps his other arm around me, his fingers cupping my other hand, and I can feel his warm breath on my neck. I think I may have stopped breathing altogether. Oh God, here comes the butterfly fly-by again.

Suddenly the knife slides into the oyster.

'Great,' he says, and his words dance on the skin of my neck. 'Now, twist it to and fro until it pops.' He loosens his grip on my hands but doesn't leave me. I twist, rocking it this way and that, and then it pops.

'As a champion shell-shucker once said, in order to open the oyster you have to first work out what's keeping it closed,' he says quietly. 'There's a muscle on the top and on the bottom. Slide the knife along the top edge of the oyster.' He guides me and I feel the oyster muscle. He pushes my hand forwards and I cut at it. Clear juice starts to dribble out all over our hands and onto the table but we don't move.

'There, pull away the top of the oyster shell,' he says, and I do. I've taken off the top shell and inside is the soft, fleshy, plump oyster.

'We're not finished yet,' he says. 'Now, slice under the oyster, there's another muscle that needs to be cut before it's free and can come out of the shell.'

I slice.

'Good, now flip the oyster over in its shell and it will start to produce brand new liquor.' I flip over the creamy oyster and it does just as he says. He lets go of my hands and I start to breathe again in short bursts, but my heart is still racing.

'Now, all you have to do,' he cups my right hand again and lifts it up, 'is eat it.' He holds it to my lips. The butterflies rush in and do a much more impressive fly-by, making my whole body shudder. I look at him then down at the oyster and bottle it. I shake my head. He gives a half-smile and puts the oyster to his own lips, tips it back, chews and swallows. I watch his throat muscles squeeze and move up and down, my own moving involuntarily at the same time. I'm staring at his throat and the oyster has gone. I'm breathing heavily again. My face is so close to his I can smell the salt on his skin. I can see his lips are wet. He bites at them, sucking in the last of the juice.

'Now you're on your own,' he says, suddenly stepping back and returning to his side of the table. I feel like I've been blindfolded, spun around and then told to walk in a straight line. I wonder if he's done it on purpose, if he knows the effect it's had on me. I pick up an oyster, flustered and cross. I hold it in the towel and force the knife in. I twist and pop. I slice, open, slice, flip, and the juice runs free again.

'Very good,' he smiles, and I'm blushing, possibly glowing. It must be the exertion, I tell myself as I stand back from the table to admire my first shucked oyster just as our first customers roll up. But I don't shuck. I spend the day seating customers, taking the money and serving them wine, leaving the actual shucking to Sean. It reminds me of being back in The Coffee House back home, which gives me an idea. That evening, with the radio playing and the fire dancing merrily, I set to work making lots and lots of chocolate brownies.

The next morning Freddie is halfway down the lane again. We'll have to rename him Romeo and the white one Juliet at this rate. They're obviously very much in love. I get him home and let out the hens, and they mingle around my legs as I put down the food. Then it's Brenda and her gang's turn. I outrun her easily now. I double-check Freddie's gate tie and then take Grace on the path around the bay to the rocky headland that leads to the second bay where the native oysters are nestling in their beds. You can't get any further on foot. But it looks quiet and undisturbed and that's the most I can hope for. A shiny black head pops up from the water. The seals! I sit down on a rock, pull my hood up against the drizzle and watch as two, four, six seals bob around, playing in the water in front of me.

Eventually I pull myself away from them and make the walk into town with Grace at my side and a large Tupperware box under my arm. I hesitate as I approach the café, but when I step inside it's empty and I breathe a sigh of relief.

'What can I get you?' Gerald smiles broadly and the urn gives an enthusiastic rumble behind him.

'Actually, Gerald,' I say, gathering confidence as I speak, 'I was wondering if I could do something for you.'

'Really?' He wipes his hands, shows me to a table and sits down opposite me. 'If it's about a job, I'm afraid I just haven't got anything.' He looks around at the empty café. I shake my head. I decide to let the brownies do the talking. I open the Tupperware box and the smell of warm chocolate wraps itself around me like a hug, filling the little café. Gerald's enjoying the same feeling by the look on his face.

'I'll get some tea,' he says.

When he's back with the mugs he hovers his hand over the Tupperware box. 'May I?'

I nod and he reaches in and pulls out a fat, gooey brownie. He looks at it like a jeweller studying a diamond. Then he bites. I watch his face. At first he doesn't react, but then his eyes close, his head rolls back, and finally he opens his eyes again and smiles the widest smile.

'My dear, they're marvellous, but I'm not sure I can afford to buy them from you. You can see how business is.' He looks around again. 'Thursdays are busy because it's court day in the local library, but other than that, this is the worst summer I've ever had. Between you and me, if things don't pick up this will be my last season.'

I feel for Gerald. It's a lovely café; well, it would be if he'd get rid of his ex-wife's belongings.

'Actually, Gerald, I was wondering if I could give you these to sell in exchange for me using the computer. I don't want any money, just a straight swap for computer time.'

'Really?'

'I can make more if you don't think there's enough . . .' I look at his gobsmacked face.

'No!'

'No?'

'No, I mean, no, there's plenty. That would be great. Let's see how these sell and I'll let you know if I need any more. And you work away. Use the computer as much as you like.

You're the only one round here who does, apart from Margaret, of course, but she's got her own hand-held thingy. Delighted to do business with you.' He stands up and takes the brownies. I go straight to the computer and start looking up local marquee companies and sending out emails about public liability insurance. It's lovely sitting in the corner of the café, watching Gerald and the occasional customer. I like it here.

Chapter Twenty-eight

It's early evening a week or so later when I hear a car coming up the lane. A little silver Fiesta with long eyelashes over its headlights is bouncing its way towards us.

Sean and I are hosing down the shed, getting the oysters ready for tomorrow's farmers' market after a full day of grading and washing.

'Ah no, I think you've got a visitor.' He sweeps all the more forcefully.

'Hi, Sean,' Margaret beams as she jumps out of the car, making me cover a smile.

'Did you not see the signs?' Sean says grumpily. 'No entry.'

'Ah, Sean, I thought that was just tourists and oyster pirates you wanted to keep out.'

'No, seriously, you could have an infection on your car that I don't want near my oysters,' he says, absolutely deadpan.

'Hey, Margaret,' I wave and go over to her. Margaret looks like the wind has been taken out of her sails. 'What's the matter?'

Just for a minute Margaret is able to ignore Sean and speaks to me as he walks off to the back of the shed.

'Dan's called a committee meeting at the pub, seven-thirty p.m.' She's looking worried. 'I just hope he isn't going to pull

219

out. We haven't had a single name for the shell-shucking contest or the Pearl Queen competition. I reckon he's going to call it off. He won't want to look a fool.'

'Oh, Margaret.' I put my arm around her. Sean turns back to me, frowning. The hosepipe is back on. Margaret pulls away and sniffs, holding her finger to her nose.

'Phew, what's that smell?'

I know. I put my fingers to my nose and sniff. There it is. The smell of the sea and oyster sacks.

'Right, look, you go and get ready and I'll meet you at the pub.' Margaret still has her finger under her nose like a pencil moustache and is shooing me towards the cottage while she gets back into her car. I sigh. This is my life: oversized waterproofs and wellies and the smell of oyster sacks.

'Actually,' Margaret sticks her head out of the car, 'come back with me. I'll give you a makeover if you like.' I'm ready to say no but she looks like the suggestion has cheered her up. How bad could it be?

'OK, give me ten minutes.' I run back into the shed to finish up. I ache and I can't wait to have a shower and get clean. Maybe a makeover is just what I need. Sean's still frowning.

'So, you're meeting up with Dan Murphy again, are you?' He wipes his hands on a towel.

'I don't know why you don't like him. At least he's trying to help,' I say before I can stop myself. I'm shocked. I don't do arguments. Brian and I never argued, we just sort of skirted the issue. Another attack is out before I can stop it. 'This festival is for you, y'know! To sell the oysters!'

'Shh!' He's looking at Margaret who's sitting in her car with the radio on.

'She can't hear anything,' I tut.

'I'm just being sensible.'

'You're being overdramatic,' I say, using the towel. 'These people want it to work as much as you do.'

'Overdramatic? Well, it might have escaped your memory but I just lost an entire crop and I'm not prepared to do it again. I want this place and those oysters kept secret.'

'But the point is to get people to see where they come from. You're selling the package – the sea, the beach, the view, the clean air,' I look around.

'Careful, you're beginning to sound as if you like the place.' He raises one eyebrow and a half smile.

'Oh you're just . . . so . . . so . . . so . . . I'm going to the pub.' I drop my broom loudly by the shed door in frustration. I can feel Sean's surprise as he watches me walk over to Margaret's car and get in.

'Aren't you going to bring any clothes?' Margaret is leaning against her window.

There's no way my pride is going to let me get back out of the car now. 'How about I borrow something of yours? Make it a proper makeover,' I say, hoping that Margaret might own some joggers and a sweatshirt I can borrow, or a pair of jeans and a T-shirt maybe.

'Oh brilliant!' Margaret perks up no end as she reverses the little car out on to the narrow track, just missing the gate post. And I suddenly realise that I have never seen Margaret in a pair of joggers or jeans, or anything that wasn't dayglo or covered in sequins and sparkles. It's like asking Lady Gaga for loungewear and I start to wonder what on earth I've let myself in for.

* * *

I feel like a sausage at a bar mitzvah; everyone's staring at me and giving me a wide berth. Margaret has spent well over an hour getting my look 'just right'. But 'just right' for whom? I'm not sure.

'You sit down, I'll get the drinks.' She's still admiring her handiwork. I get a glimpse of myself in the mirror behind the bar – at least I think it's me. I'm wearing a bright pink T-shirt with 'Poke me!' written on the front, denim shorts with pearls and diamantes, leopard skin leggings underneath and a fake leather jacket with more bling on the back. The shoes are red and add another foot to my height. Maybe finding somewhere to sit out of the way would be a very good idea. I head for the corner of the pub where I sat on my first day here.

'Over there,' Margaret points to the group by the fire. I turn the high heels in the other direction, slowly. Evelyn's glaring at me and it's not the false eyelashes or the purple lipstick that's offending her. I know exactly what the problem is. It's the brownies Gerald's selling in the café. I saw her come in while I was working on the computer. She didn't see me of course, tucked away, but she spotted the brownies straightaway.

'What are these?' she asked.

'Try one, they're delicious!' Gerald enthused. Evelyn regarded them like a child eyeing a Brussels sprout. She slowly picked one up and took a bite.

A small group of schoolchildren had come into the café and spotted the brownies, buying a couple each with delighted cries. 'Better than those scones yer have,' the tallest lad in the group shouted.

'Yeah, they're disgusting,' said a short girl with a fat tie.

Evelyn stormed out, taking the brownie with her.

'Sorry,' I mouthed to Gerald. He smiled and shrugged as a young mum came in and bought a tea and another brownie. I dipped further behind the computer and sent out an email asking about glass hire.

Now Evelyn is glaring at me across the pub. It doesn't help that I feel like I've got a neon sign above my head saying, 'Dog's dinner!'

I look down at the red high heels I'm wearing and wish I could click them and just go home.

'Hey!' Dan arrives just in time to help Margaret over with the drinks.

'Wow!' He stops right in front of me and stares, his mouth open and his eyes wide.

I shift around uncomfortably, pulling at the hem of my shorts. I think it's best Dan just gets this over and done with and we can have a few drinks to drown our sorrows.

'You should dress up more often. You look amazing,' he says enthusiastically in his usual loud voice. He puts the wine down in front of me and then comes and sits next to me on the bench seat, making Evelyn budge up with a tut. Margaret sits on the stool opposite. She's wearing a similar style outfit, with a tight-fitting top. I feel like a younger sister trying to imitate her older, cooler sibling.

'So, how's it all been going?' Dan pulls off his jacket and I shuffle up, trying to avoid the arm that's now resting along the back of the seat behind me. He pours the wine and I take a big sip to soothe my unease. A few more of these and I won't feel like a dressed-up clown at all.

'How's Grumpy Sean?' Dan leans into me and gives me a friendly nudge. I laugh, trying to swallow at the same time and nearly choking. A dark shadow falls over the table.

'He's just fine, thank you for asking,' says Sean, and at that point I do choke and Margaret has to pat me on the back.

'Sean!' Dan doesn't miss a beat. 'Come and join us.' He stands up. 'What are you drinking?' He pulls out his wallet but Sean shakes his head, lifting the pint he's already bought to show Dan.

'Sean? What are you doing here?' Margaret's face lights up.

'Wanted to hear all the festival news.' He looks straight at me. 'After all, I probably should show more of an interest,' he says, and takes a sip from his pint. And then he slowly frowns, looking at my top, the shorts and leggings and shoes. I find myself tugging at the tight T-shirt, feeling more ridiculous than ever.

'He practically insisted. I had a table booked at Bar Eight, but there was no budging him tonight.' Nancy appears behind Sean. My nostrils are filled with thick, spicy perfume. I rub my nose to make sure I don't sneeze.

'Hi, Nancy, good timing.' Dan smiles even wider, if that were possible. 'I didn't know you were in town.'

'No, well, trying to get himself away from this place isn't always easy.' She rolls her eyes at Sean, pointing her gin and slimline at him.

'We were just about to discuss the festival as it happens.' Dan picks up his pint.

Nancy turns to me and takes in my appearance, as if she hadn't recognised me to start with. She raises her eyebrows and then sips her drink to hide her smirk.

'Here, come and sit down. There's plenty of room,' Dan says, making us all budge up to make room for Nancy. His large thigh is now resting against mine and I can't move along any further. Dan picks up his drink and raises it to me before sipping. Sean is scowling. I take another big mouthful of my wine and feel the large flower clip in my hair slip and flop over. Margaret stands up next to Sean.

'So, how are things going with you girls?' Nancy asks, despite me being the same age as her. She pours the last of the tonic from its bottle into her drink.

Sean moves back to lean against the bar. Margaret follows him. Sean is staring at me. He's still frowning, but I suppose I should be grateful he's come and shown an interest, even if it is too late. If Dan pulls out, it will all be over.

'I have a marquee sorted,' I say, distracting myself from his stares. Maybe we could still make this happen without Dan, I think optimistically, but I know that's not really possible.

Nancy nods.

'What about seating, chairs, tables?'

'Actually, Sean has a load of them in the old barn.' I'd seen them when I was painting the window sills before the inspection. 'I thought we could give them a good wash down, and decorate them, like in the old festival pictures. We could cover the tables in white rolls of paper and put oyster shells out with salt and pepper in. And have large stones from the shore for table numbers. And put gorse in pots for flowers.'

Sean's face seems to soften a little.

'Too rustic. Forget the shells, gorse and stones. Keep it white and simple. I want it classy,' Nancy instructs. 'Tables and chairs?' she directs at Sean.

Sean puts down his pint and nods. 'From when the festival

used to be run by my uncle and the others round here. They're mostly long tables and benches.'

The locals turn to look at him but no one comments.

'Oh no, we'll need something better than that,' Nancy cuts in. 'Get the marquee company to lay them on.'

'But won't that be eating into profits?' I protest.

'If we manage to sell the tickets,' Margaret looks like a deflated balloon. I reach out to touch her hand. 'I can't raise much interest in the press and no one has signed up for the shell-shucking – and there are only three entrants for the Pearl Queen contest, including me!'

Everyone sighs.

'Shame,' says Rosie. 'I'll enter the Pearl Queen competition, Margaret, if it helps.' She pats Margaret's knee.

'Look, maybe it's best to cut your losses. It was a great idea but people don't associate Dooleybridge with oysters any more. They go round the other side of the bay for that, and anyone who wants to sell their oysters round here sends them to Dublin or France. That's the only way to make it pay these days,' Sean says flatly. 'That's what Nancy knows.' Sean waves his hand at Nancy who looks like she's silently seething.

'It's ridiculous,' she says with a Gallic shrug. 'How hard can it be to rustle up some media interest and deliver a classy meal for potential customers? I'm doing my bit. I have the customers and the contacts, but they'll want to know there's something worth coming for. Amateurs,' she tuts testily. 'I'm sorry about this, Dan. I really think I've been let down by certain individuals here.' She looks at me and then Margaret. 'You said you were great on back-room work,' she hisses to me.

Sean bristles. 'Now hang on,' he says, putting down his pint.

'What?' Nancy throws him a challenging look.

'I don't think you need to be so hard on everyone,' Sean says to my surprise. 'It just wasn't ever going to work like this. I think we,' he emphasises the 'we', 'need to go back to the drawing board, in private.' He nods his head in the direction of the door.

The rest of the group are staring at Sean and Nancy like an episode of *Coronation Street*. Sean picks up his jacket. Nancy doesn't move. Dan breaks the ice with a melodramatic cough. We all turn to him.

I would have liked to tell Nancy that I'd done everything she asked me to do, and that if only she'd done it my way then more of the locals would've been involved and interested. They don't want a 'classy' do where they're the hired help. They want a good old-fashioned oyster festival, like it used to be. But what would I know? I'm just the blow-in. I take another swig of wine. Dan coughs again. I wonder if he's going down with something. Must be the damp air. He looks slowly around.

'Well, I've had an email today. Mary Jo's leaving me. She's pregnant again. She's taking a career break.' He sucks in his lips.

'Oh that's lovely,' I say without thinking, pushing aside the twinge of envy again.

'I need the career before I can have the break,' says Margaret sulkily.

'I'd take the career any day,' says Nancy with a shiver, looking at Sean.

'Hmm, leaves me in the lurch a bit, however . . .' Dan says, enjoying the audience's attention.

'Oh no, that means you're going back and the festival will definitely be cancelled,' Margaret wails. 'You're the only thing we actually got confirmed.'

Nancy takes a sharp intake of breath. If Dan's leaving, Margaret's right – there definitely won't be a festival.

'Actually, on the contrary. Mary Jo has been working on a deal and has just got it in place before she leaves.' His eyes are bright. 'She's managed to secure a sponsorship deal. The TV company I work for want to come over and film the festival.' He beams. 'It'll be a great finish to my book and great publicity.'

'Bit hard if it's just three people in the shuck-off and a bottle of flat fizz. No offence, mate, but this is going to make you look a bit of a prat,' Sean says, fiddling with a bar mat.

Dan takes a deep breath and then says, 'Not with a €10,000 prize for the shell-shucking contest it isn't. And no offence taken,' he shoots back at Sean.

'What?' Margaret's hands shoot to her face and hold her cheeks.

'Say that again?' I ask in shock.

'The TV company is putting up a €10,000 prize for the winner of the Dooleybridge oyster festival shell-shucking contest,' he beams at me.

For a moment no one says a word and then Margaret screams and throws herself on Dan.

'Oh my God!' I shout and hug Margaret. The whole group is on its feet in excitement, chattering, shouting and hugging like we've won the Eurovision Song Contest. We haven't. But we have got ourselves an oyster festival. Margaret whips out a phone and the flash of a camera goes off. We all cheer and order more drinks. Sean even manages a smile in my direction and the butterflies perform a quick unscheduled fly-by in my stomach.

'Looks like this festival has got legs after all.' Dan raises his glass to Sean, who warily raises his pint back.

Chapter Twenty-nine

The walk home is dark and a bit wobbly. Probably all that white wine sloshing around inside me. Or maybe it's the heels. My feet are killing me. I shine the torch I've borrowed from the pub in front of me. I just hope Dan's plan works. This could be it! Nancy's restaurant will get all the publicity and I'll have helped Sean pay back the loan. All we have to do is keep the oysters safe. Dan has come through for us – well, Mary Jo has. Dan's a good man, his heart's in the right place.

As I think about Dan my mind immediately switches back to Sean's smile. Had I imagined it? Had that smile been just for me in the pub tonight? Or was he simply pleased the festival was going to work?

I look up at the stars, remembering the silly names we'd given them the night before the inspection.

'Hey, English!' I hear his voice and shake my head. Way too much wine, I think.

'English, wait up!' I turn to see a figure jogging towards me. My heart begins to race.

'Sean?' I shine the torch right at him and squint as the familiar outline comes into view. 'You nearly gave me a heart attack.'

'Sorry.' He's slightly out of breath. 'You nearly blinded me.' He's holding up an arm to cover his eyes.

'I thought you were staying in town with Nancy,' I say, shining the torch away from his face and back to the pavement. He drops his arm.

'Change of plan,' he says matter-of-factly. 'Early start.'

'For you or for her?'

'Both of us,' he says, and we fall into step beside each other. Sean is walking in the road and I'm on the thin pavement. The sound of our feet is the only noise against the backdrop of whispering waves from the sea. Crunch, crunch, crunch; Sean's boots march on. Clip, clip, clippety-clip; I try really hard not to trip up on the stony path but it isn't easy in Margaret's heels.

'So,' he finally breaks the silence. 'Whose idea was the new look?' I can't see his face but I can hear his smile. I bristle.

'Actually,' I begin, before catapulting into his side and making him break my fall. Suddenly I start to laugh too. 'Margaret's. Terrible, isn't it?' I say. He's still holding my arm.

'Take them off!' he instructs.

'What? I can't walk home barefooted!' I protest.

'You're not going to. Take them off and climb on.' He turns his back to me.

'A piggy back?'

'We'll be here all night otherwise,' he says.

I think about arguing but my feet are throbbing. I don't know that I can make it on my own. I slip off the shoes and quickly jump on to his back – not something I would ever have considered without the wine.

As he carries me up the lane, I can hear the noise of the waves as we get closer to the farm. The tide's in. I'm telling him about Evelyn and the brownies, which he finds very funny.

'Shh,' he says suddenly and stops. We hear it at the same time. He bends down and drops me with only a tiny oomph, then runs as fast as he can up the rest of the lane. I slip on the shoes and stumble towards the farm as best I can. Clip, clip, clippety-trip. Hop, stumble, clippety-clip. Sean is there way before me and as I come closer I see there's a light out on the water.

'Get Grace,' he hisses. He's over by the boat, undoing the ropes.

'Be careful,' I say in a low whisper. It's dark out there. How will he see where he's going?

I run to the cottage and let Grace out. She bounds out, nearly sending me head over heels in her excitement.

'Get them, Grace! Pirates. Pirates!' I grab my waterproof and wellies from inside the front door. I run down the stony bank to the shoreline, stumbling over loose stones as I go, but it's an improvement on the high heels. The ground gets wetter and my feet begin to sink in the soft mud, throwing up its familiar smell. The torch light snaps up and shines right at me. I hold up my hand to cover my eyes. I can hear laughter. It sounds like more than one voice. I try and make out them out.

'You feckin' bastards!' I hear a slap of sails and see a torch flashing around frantically. Sean's got the boat out and is heading for them. 'You bastards! You sons of bitches! Thieving shites!' He carries on his tirade, waving a hand in fury as the boat slaps through the water. There's a shout and another splash from near the pirate boat, like a bag of oysters being dropped and left behind. There are muffled argument-ative voices and then the other boat's engine changes from its annoying little hum to a high-pitched whine as it shoots off into the dark night, whooshing through the water.

'Bastards! I'll feckin' kill ya!' Sean's still roaring as the little boat phut, phut, phuts off into the night and suddenly it's all silent again.

Sean has stopped shouting his threats. Grace has stopped barking. There's just the sound of sails slapping in the slack wind.

'Sean?' Mine's a lone voice in the dark. I hold up my hand and strain to see.

There's a sloshing noise and the hooker appears in a streak of silver moonlight. Sean's shoulders are drooped with disappointment. I have a sudden urge to hug him, to tell him it's all right, but I don't know if everything will be all right and I certainly can't hug him. He looks up at me and tosses me a rope, which I catch and help tie up the boat.

'Good work, English,' he says casually, slinging his arm around my shoulder as we walk back to the cottage, 'let's get to bed.' My heart does a silly skip.

Inside the cottage we slip off our wet clothes and hang them up.

'Pass me your clothes, they're soaked,' he says in a low voice.

'What?'

'Your tights, leggings whatever you call them, take them off,' he says firmly. 'I'll put them by the fire.' He tuts at my reluctance. 'OK, I promise not to look, but just take them off,' he says firmly, and turns his back to me. He's still in his wet joggers too.

Feeling very self-conscious, I slip my leggings off and hand them to him. Then I shoot into the bathroom, grab a towel and wrap it round my waist. When I come out the fire's blazing and there are two glasses on the table, a bottle of whiskey beside them.

'Something to help you sleep.' He picks up a glass and hands it to me.

Sleep? I might just keel over at this rate!

'Who do you think it was?' I ask, watching the orange glow from the fire light up the little room and sipping at the whiskey. It still burns but it's nice. Sean sits by the fire on the settee. I pull up a chair from the table.

'Someone who wasn't expecting me to be here.' He sips his drink.

Whoever it was certainly didn't seem to be put off by me being here, but they're scared of Sean. I have a damn good idea who it is. But if I tell Sean he'll just charge into town, confirming what everyone already thinks of him. I just need to work out how to stop them.

The next morning I'm up early, baking. The radio's on quietly. I hear a car on the lane and run to look out of the window, just in case the cheeky buggers are coming back for more, by road this time. But it's Margaret's little Fiesta. Sean appears from outside, hair messed up from the wind.

'Oysters, great for a hangover!' He grins.

'I haven't got a hangover,' I smile back, but my headache says different. 'And you are never going to persuade me that eating them is a good idea!'

'Fi!' Margaret raps on the door and lets herself in. She's practically bubbling over with excitement. 'You wanna see the entrants we've had for the competition, they're coming from all over and ticket sales have gone mad! Grab your coat and come down to the café. You have to see the website. Oh.

Morning, Sean.' She stops to flirt as he heads to the kettle.

Sean does a good job of hiding how pleased he is at the news, but the fact he's not frowning means something.

'A big success then?' I say, loud enough for Sean to hear, and give him a smile of satisfaction. He tries not to smile back as he puts coffee into his mug.

'You were right, I think is the phrase you're looking for,' I tease.

'Well, if we'd left it to you it would've been a disaster.' The atmosphere in the cottage suddenly turns chilly. Nancy has followed Margaret into the cottage. This woman seems to have a habit of turning up without being heard. 'All that rustic nonsense. Thank God the TV company want to invest in something with some class.' Nancy looks around at the clothes drying on the chair in front of the fire and looks sideways at me, then out to sea. 'God, this place is hell.'

'It's feckin' busy,' Sean says, heading into his bedroom.

'So can you come and see the website?' Margaret's like Tigger, jumping up and down.

'If that's OK with Sean,' I shout in the direction of his room.

'Fine!' he shouts back.

'I have these to deliver too.' I pick up the box of brownies. 'Wait,' I tell Margaret as we head for the car. There's something I want to take with me, and I grab another cardboard box from the shed and fill it with oyster shells from the pile by the front gate.

'You see, they're coming from all over. This one's coming from Sweden,' Margaret points at the screen in Gerald's café.

'Fi, love, that last lot went in a flash,' Gerald grins as I hand over the batch of brownies. He gives me a steaming cup of tea and holds up a hand when I offer to pay for it. I thank him, take off my coat and join Margaret at the screen.

'It's great.' I sip the tea.

'Isn't it?' She's beaming, still looking at the screen and all the emails from people wanting to take part in the competition, the Pearl Queen night and buy tickets for the event. 'This is bigger than we ever expected!'

'Yes,' I agree, and she's right. But something is nagging at me. 'Just one thing, Margaret . . .' She turns to me and frowns. 'Where are they all going to stay?' I ask.

Her mouth drops open. 'Oh my God! What are we going to do? I never thought of that. We weren't expecting this amount of people in the town!'

'We'd better get some bed and breakfasts organised,' I say, putting down the tea. 'We'll print off flyers and deliver them to every house in the town suggesting they take in B&B guests for the oyster festival weekend, and contact us to make a list of accommodation in the area.'

'Right,' Margaret agrees, and we get to work fuelled by tea and brownies.

Before we leave the little row of shops I call in on Maire at the art shop.

'Wondered if these were any good to you, Maire?' I call to her in the back room and put down the box.

She's wearing a cloche hat with shiny buttons all over it. She peers into the box and looks back at me, grinning.

'Perfect!' she says. 'Oyster shells!'

'Well, there's plenty more where they came from,' I say, and swing out of the door with my flyers.

* * *

'That'll put presents under the tree from Santa this year.' Rosie holds the flyer tightly in her fat fingers and beams.

'Hope it does well for you, Rosie,' I say, and move on to the next house until all the flyers are gone.

I stop off to tell Dan the good news about the ever-growing number of contestants for the shell-shucking contest and discover that Nancy has already beaten me to it on her way back into town.

'Seriously, it's great,' says Dan, who's wearing joggers and a T-shirt and has obviously been working at his small computer on the coffee table.

'How's the book going?' I ask, making small talk and thinking I wouldn't have bothered to come if I'd known Nancy had already been.

'Great.' He's dipping a tea bag on a string up and down in a cup and spilling it everywhere.

'Say, I was thinking, how about we go out and celebrate, have dinner? There's a little restaurant near Galway in a place called Barna. Does great seafood. O'Grady's. I could book us a table for this evening?' He opens the little fridge and takes out a small carton of milk.

'Well, I don't know, I'll see if Margaret's about.' I suddenly feel put on the spot and look around for a distraction.

He laughs, twisting open the milk lid. 'I didn't mean you, me and Margaret. I meant you and me, a date.' He puts way too much milk in the tea and hands it to me. 'I've really enjoyed working with you, Fi.'

'A . . . date?' My mouth goes dry. My toes are curling upwards and I'm getting that chest rash again. I down the milky, weak tea. 'Um, that's really nice of you, Dan, but I'm afraid I'm not really . . . dating, just now.' I think that's how they say it in America.

'Not dating?' he says loudly. 'There's someone else, right?' He sits down by the coffee table with his own cup of coffee.

'No, there's no one else,' I shake my head. 'I'm single, and I plan to stay that way,' I say. There, I've said it. No tears, no panic attacks. I'm not a long-term girlfriend, fiancée, Mrs Goodchild (although I don't know if I ever officially was), I'm just single. I take a deep breath and smile.

'You and Sean, you're an item?'

'No. Definitely not.' I put the cup down firmly on the work top. 'He and Nancy are very much together.' I don't know who I'm trying to convince more, him or me. 'No, I'm just happy being single,' I say. Maybe it's true, maybe I am happier than I've been for a long time. Maybe I'm actually enjoying my independent life . . . as an oyster farmer's assistant.

'Well, if you change your mind, I'm here.'

I wonder if Kimberly, back home at The Coffee Shop, would think he was 'out of my league', too, just as she'd said about Brian. And as I step into the drizzle, I realise I don't care what Kimberly would think. It was nice to be asked.

Back at the farm Sean's packing up folded washing into a battered brown leather holdall.

'Something I said?' I joke, as I let myself into the cottage.

He looks up from pushing some T-shirts into the bag, which is on the pine table.

'No. I just need to go away for a few days, if you'll be OK?' he says, straightening up. 'Going to visit Nancy's parents in Arcachon. We haven't been for a while, and Nancy has some business contacts she wants to invite to the festival. It's just for a couple of days. Do you mind?'

'No, of course not. Why would I mind?' I feel myself blushing.

'Well, it's just with the oyster pirates . . .' He zips up the bag.

'The oyster pirates, yes, of course!' I'm blushing some more. Of course he meant the oyster pirates. What else? I put the kettle on.

'Make sure you don't tell anyone I'm away. But it's the spring tide and by the looks of it they're not that interested in coming when the tide's low, or I wouldn't feel comfortable going.'

'I'll be fine,' I say.

'Do you think you can turn the sacks on your own?' He goes to get his toothbrush.

'Yes, I'll give it a good go,' I say.

'And whatever you can bring up to wash and grade, we can get them ready for the next farmers' market,' he tells me as he puts his washbag in the holdall.

I'm nodding frantically, still feeling stupid at my own silly misunderstanding. Sean's looking this way and that. I hand him his wallet from the kitchen work surface.

'Thank you.'

'So, doing anything nice while you're there?' Oh, what a stupid question! He's going to France with his attractive partner, of course they'll be doing nice things!

'We're meeting some of Nancy's old contacts. She seems to think they'll be more interested in coming over if they meet the grower. I feel like a feckin' dancing leprechaun in a travelling circus,' he growls.

I try not to laugh and roll my lips in on each other.

'Great,' I enthuse. 'It'll be great for the festival. Staying somewhere nice?' Why can't I just stop? I don't want to hear about what a lovely place they'll be staying in!

'With her parents in Arcachon. Then with friends of Nancy's, just outside St Emilion.' He picks up the bag.

'Wow,' I say without thinking. It's another world. A far cry from walking holidays and pub grub. It's sounds quite exotic, but then Nancy is exotic. I, on the other hand, am probably more bargain bucket.

He raises a smile, grabs his phone and waves it at me.

'Got it! Call me if you want me. If you can. Look after Grace. And Grace? Look after Fi.' Then he turns to go, awkwardly.

'Have fun,' I say, waving Sean off with Grace by my side, grinning until my cheeks ache. But deep in my chest a huge well of disappointment is opening up.

Chapter Thirty

The next day and night pass uneventfully. The following day I wake with the feeling of disappointment still there. It's 21 August. My birthday. I feel older. I pull the covers over my head and hope the day will disappear. Grace nudges at me to be let out. At least when Brian and I had been together there had been a ritual to birthdays, just like there had been rituals for everything else in our lives. He'd hide all the cards that had arrived in the post and put them by my bed, with the individually wrapped presents. He'd bring me a cup of tea and then we'd start with the cards. There were never many: his mother, a friend of his mother's, the hairdresser's, and occasionally one from my mother, round about the date, but mostly there wasn't one from her. Then I'd have to open the one from him and put on the birthday badge, which I always slipped off by the time I got to work. Then it was presents, smallest first.

But this birthday is different. I'm in the middle of nowhere, on my own. There are no presents or cards or mid-week takeaway. Today, I'm thirty. At twenty-nine I thought I had it all: fiancé, flat, job. Today I don't even own the clothes I'm standing up in. Well, not all of them.

But it's no good lying in bed dwelling on it. That's the way to lunacy. Grace nudges my elbow again. I throw back the covers, pull on my clothes, and Grace and I go out to the shed. I can hear the hens clucking, desperate to get out and about and on with the day's work.

'Morning, ladies!' I put down their food and watch as they strut out of the hen house. Martha, Sarah Jane, Amelia Pond. I decided to name them after various Doctor Who assistants. Mind you, it's been that long since I've watched television there could be another six assistants by now. They peck away happily around my feet. I put down the goose feed and jog my way back to the gate with Brenda half-heartedly chasing me.

Freddie is pushing open his gate. 'Oh, no you don't.' I catch hold of his head collar just as he's trying to make a break for it. 'What you need is something to occupy you, a job,' I tell him firmly. I turn his head back towards the field and give him a push from behind. 'All that energy should be put to good use.' I start retying the rope and pat Mercury, who is looking away from Freddie, as if embarrassed.

Grace has her breakfast and I have mine: tea, soda bread and some of Frank's honey.

There's no way I'm going to spend the day moping, I decide, lifting my chin. I need to keep busy. I know, I'll tackle the old barn where the tables and chairs are kept, see if there's anything else that might be useful for the festival.

I make myself another cup of tea and then pick up the bunch of keys from the hook by the door. Slipping on my wellies and hat, I make my way down to the old barn. I use the rusty key and open the stiff door, pushing it open as wide as I can. My eyes have to adjust to the dark. There's piles of old benches and long wooden tables, a big old oil drum barbecue and boxes of junk. I push back my sleeves, take a slug of my tea, and decide to start by taking everything out and seeing what's there. Sean couldn't be cross with me for tidying up in here. And if he is, I don't care. I'm going to do it anyway. It's my birthday and this is how I'm choosing to spend it.

In France, Sean was feeling . . . unsettled. Which was a ridiculous way to be feeling. The sun was shining, he was in beautiful Arcachon with a beautiful woman, enjoying a wonderful lunch, sipping a red wine laid on by his good friend Jean François, Nancy's father. Sean had bought spat from Jean François when he was starting out, as his uncle had before him. Jean François had been more than happy to cut Sean some slack when it came to settling up, keen for him to get established and carry on his uncle's tradition. The two older men went way back.

'You deserve a break, *chéri*,' Nancy told Sean. Nancy's French accent always got stronger when she was actually in France. 'You have been working very hard, and now you have a new assistant we should be able to spend more time together.' She sat with one long leg crossed over the other and stroked his arm. She was right; he had needed to get away. He had been feeling . . . confused. He and Fi had spent a lot of time together and there was no denying how he'd felt the day he'd taught her to shuck oysters. He had come to care about Fi. She worked hard. But she was his employee. He had come close to wanting to step over that fine line the other morning, and he'd promised her that that would never happen, and it mustn't. Maybe it was a good thing he and Nancy were spending time together, with her family.

Jean François was topping up their glasses while his wife Monique laid out pâté, bread and *cornichons*.

'How are the oysters, Jean François?'

Nancy's father took some bread and bit into it, shaking his head. 'The spat is fine. No problem. I rear it from seed in the sheds, but as soon as we put it in the water,' he shook his head again, 'pah! They die. It is happening all over the place. No one knows why.' He cut off a corner of pâté.

'Papa, it's time you retired anyway. The business has been dead for years. Sit back, take it easy,' Nancy scolded him.

'Pah! An oyster farmer never retires,' he said, and laughed chestily.

'Isn't that right, Sean? Once oyster farming is in your heart, it's in your veins too.'

Sean nodded and they clinked glasses and ate their starter. Nancy sniffed.

Sean felt bad about leaving Fi on her own, especially with the oyster pirates around. He was hardly giving her any wages right now, and he couldn't give more until the native oysters were ready to sell to Nancy. To be honest he hadn't believed she would stay. But true to her word she was trying to help him put things right at the farm.

It had been a lucky day when she'd arrived in Dooleybridge. Admittedly, she'd been a bit of a disaster at first, what with her not telling him she was afraid of water, and then there was the cock-up with the stock going missing, but she really had proved herself as a worker. And the fact that she was prepared to work for next to nothing until the oysters were sold showed how honest she was. He'd take her back something from France, he decided. A small gift to show his appreciation. He'd look round the town after lunch.

'Sean?'

'What?' Sean realised Nancy was talking to him.

'Where is your head? I was talking about the festival. It'll be good for business.' She cut into her very rare steak, letting the blood run across her plate, colouring the *frites* she was never going to eat. Fi would have eaten them, he found himself thinking. What was wrong with him? They'd spent too long working with each other up at the farm. He needed to focus on selling his oysters.

After a glorious lunch with Nancy's parents, they said their goodbyes.

'Au revoir, Maman, Papa,' Nancy barely hugged them. Sean hugged them both warmly. Then they drove the small hire car back to St Emilion. Nancy went for her manicure and pedicure and Sean strolled up the little cobbled streets of the hilltop town. He sat down to enjoy a beer, watching the tourists move slowly up the steep hill, en masse, towards the church. He opened his wallet to pay the waiter and saw the tiny pearl he'd found the day he'd shown Fi the native oysters. It was misshapen and probably worthless, not perfect at all, but it meant something to him, and to Fi too, he hoped. Finishing his beer, he took a stroll to the jeweller's on the hill and went in.

With the pearl set into a silver setting and on a black leather cord, he tucked the little gold bag into his pocket. He held his face up to the sun out on the French street. In a nearby café where he'd arranged to meet Nancy he ordered '*un café*'. He slipped the necklace out of its bag and looked at it again. It was just right, he thought. Simple. Not too much that it gave the wrong idea, just enough of a memento of the work she'd done at the farm. It was August now. The festival was in four weeks and then Fi would move on, her debt paid. He just hoped he'd be able to pay his.

'What's this?' A red-manicured hand slipped round his neck and down his chest.

By the time they reached the drinks party that evening at the nearby chateau, Sean and Nancy were barely speaking. She'd seen the necklace and demanded to know who it was for. Sean had tried to explain, but there was no stopping her raging jealousy. At the party she flirted with each of the restaurateurs and vineyard owners who'd come together for the soirée, in particular the chateau owner and Nancy's childhood friend, Henri Chevalier. Sean failed to make polite conversation with the other guests and stood scowling out over the vineyards and sunflowers from the terrace. He was worried what would happen if the oyster pirates returned and he wasn't there. Nancy got increasingly annoyed at his inability to network and socialise.

'Just talk about oysters, for God's sake.' She took another gin and tonic from a passing waitress.

Nancy was describing the festival, using her charm on every male guest, making it sound like the event of the year. Sean couldn't help but think it didn't sound like anything he'd want to go to. She swished her hair, tilted her head, giggled and ate strawberries from Henri's champagne. Sean didn't mind that so much, but he did want to go home.

Chapter Thirty-one

My mouth feels like the dustpan I've just emptied, full of dust. It's tea time. I'm parched. It's mid-afternoon and I've emptied everything out of the barn and hosed it down. It's a massive space. I look around and up into the rafters. The exposed beams reach up to the tin roof. There are no internal walls, but at one end there's a small store room under a loft space. Other than that, it's just a big open room. Such a waste!

There's a fireplace at one end, and little windows to the front, made up of tiny squares of glass. It's stopped raining so I sit down on one of the old wooden benches outside and sip my tea. I push the boat out and have one of the brownies from the fresh batch I've baked for Gerald. I bite into the gooey chocolate centre. It feels well-deserved.

I'm halfway through my tea and brownie when I see Margaret's silver Fiesta bumping up the lane.

'Hey, this is where you're hiding.' She gets out of the car cheerfully. 'On your own?' She has a quick scout around for Sean as usual. She's nothing if not persistent.

'Yes, all alone, well, apart from Grace, that is.' I pat her head as she lies gently panting at my feet.

'Oh, OK. So, drinks in the pub tonight? Sevenish?' Margaret says cheerily. I smile but shake my head.

'Oh, and happy birthday!' She hands me a present wrapped in balloon-covered wrapping paper with curly ribbons. I'm absolutely gobsmacked; one, that she knew it was my birthday, and two, that she's gone to the trouble of bringing me a present.

'What?' I stare at the present. 'How did you know?' I feel my eyes prickle.

'It's just a little something, nothing major. I saw it in Maire's shop and thought of you.'

'But how did you know it was my birthday?'

'Leo, twenty-first of August, remember? Born leader.' Margaret reminds me of our first ever conversation in the café when she thought I was Sean's new love interest. That seems like an age ago now, when I'd been new to the area and everything had seemed so . . . odd. Now it all seemed strangely familiar.

'You shouldn't have,' I say with unexpected delight, unwrapping the present, making sure I do it carefully so the paper can be reused.

'Ah, go on, just rip it!'

I look up at Margaret. Why not? I think with a carefree grin. And I rip.

Inside is a lovely handbag, covered in sequins and buttons.

'She's fab with a sewing machine, is Maire.' Margaret pushes her hands into the back pockets of her leather-look hotpants.

'You shouldn't have!' I shake my head, feeling quite overwhelmed with her kindness.

'Of course I should've! It's your birthday! Oh, and I've finished with this. Thought you might like it.' She hands me a well-thumbed book. *Fifty Shades of Grey*. I take the book.

It's been ages since I've had time to read. I'd gone mad on Amazon and bought a whole pile of books for the honeymoon, but I left them all behind when I ran.

'So, drinks tonight, sevenish then?' she repeats. 'We'll have great craic!' She rubs her hands together with excitement. But I shake my head again.

'Sorry, Margaret, not tonight.' I think if I was to go out for a couple of glasses, I'd just get all maudlin and sorry for myself. 'I'm having a quiet night in.'

'But you can't! It's your birthday!' She flops her hands to her sides and looks gutted.

'Sorry, Margaret.' I stand up to hug her. 'Thank you for this.' I hug her again.

'OK, I've got to get back. Said I was popping out for coffee. Might still have time for one if I'm quick.' She jumps back into the little car and I'm relieved she doesn't pressure me any more into going out tonight. A shower and a good book sounds perfect. Besides, I really don't have that much money and I need to save what I have got.

'Oh, Margaret!' I run after her. She stops reversing and winds down the window. 'If you're going to Gerald's, would you take him the brownies I made?' That way I won't have to see the outside world at all today and tomorrow will be just another day again.

As Margaret and the latest batch of brownies bounce off down the lane, I get back to work with a smile on my lips and my spirits well and truly lifted. I go to the shed and get the old silver and rust radio and take it to the barn. I put on RTE 2, turn up the volume and sing along at the top of my voice. Why not? No one's going to hear me. I belt out the songs for the next couple of hours as I replace all the tables, chairs and boxes, which I'm putting up in the roof space at the far end of the barn. I keep back a large bell I've found, an old silver cup and a whole bunch of silver trays.

I'm still singing along to the radio when a voice cuts me off in mid-verse.

'Hello?' The radio goes silent and I stumble halfway up the little wooden ladder to the loft space, dropping a box of rosettes. Grace jumps up from her heavy sleep and barks in surprise at the man standing in the doorway. I recognise him straightaway, and the thug behind him. It's Jimmy Power and his 'lad'. My good mood evaporates immediately and I suddenly feel very nervous. I cling to the ladder.

He steps in and looks around the barn with a sniff. He's holding a cigar and the putrid smoke sticks in my throat. His earring catches the light, flashing a quick spectrum of colour across the barn. I grip the ladder tighter.

'Is Sean here?' he asks, still circling the barn floor, getting closer all the time. I can't think how to answer. My brain has frozen, my functioning brain cell obviously having decided to take the day off.

'He's, um . . .' I can't think. I don't want to say I'm on my own, but on the other hand I don't want him hanging around to speak to Sean. 'He's around . . . somewhere . . . maybe he's just popped out, but he'll be back, really soon.' Why couldn't I come up with a good lie? Or even tell the guy to get off Sean's land and that he's trespassing.

He laughs, making his belly wobble. His sidekick laughs too.

'Just thought we'd take a look around, being as I'm an investor . . .' His voice is dripping with sarcasm. 'Just let him know I'm looking forward to getting my money back. Four weeks' time. Tell him the clock is ticking. Tick, tock, tick, tock,' he laughs some more.

'I'll tell him,' I say curtly, not wanting to argue or prolong the conversation.

'And he's left you here on your own, you say?' He throws his cigar to the floor and stamps it out. The floor I spent all afternoon cleaning!

'Hey!' I shout and turn without thinking and slip on the ladder, missing a rung, stumbling to regain my footing and jumping to the floor. I'm at eye level with Jimmy Power. He steps right up to me and I lean against the ladder. He presses his belly against me, pushing me against the wood. Suddenly he thrusts one leg in between mine. I can smell his stale cigar breath and his body odour. I gag. I'm pinned there. I hear 'the lad' snort with excitement. I turn my face away, looking for something I can reach out and hit him with. I'm holding my breath. He laughs. The stench is disgusting.

'Get off me,' I try and push his heavy carcass away.

'Or what?' he says. 'I'm just being friendly, getting to know the staff. I'm sure Sean would want you to be friendly to his investor.'

I look around hopelessly. I can't even jerk my knee up to get him in the bollocks. I want to bite him. I can't scream. I can't do anything. I freeze.

Then I hear another car on the lane, and another. Oh my God! He's brought reinforcements!

He looks up, surprised at the sound of car doors slamming.

'Company?' He raises one eyebrow, suddenly releasing me. So they're not with him then. I take short gasps of breath and try to scramble back up the ladder, but he has me by the shoulder, hard. If they're not with him, who are they?

'Fi?'

I could cry with relief at hearing Margaret's voice.

'In here!' I manage a good loud shout. 'I think you should go.' I finally manage to say something sensible to Jimmy Power.

'Oh, really,' he laughs, as does his lad. 'Says who?'

'Says me.' Frank is standing in the doorway, carrying a barrel of beer. He shoves it towards the loan shark, knocking him backwards.

'And me.' It's Dan, standing behind Frank, carrying a box of lager. He doesn't actually do any shoving like Frank but he looks as if he might.

'And me.' It's Margaret, in short purple hotpants and tights, her hands on her hips. Rosie and Lily are behind her.

'I don't know who you are, but you better get going. This is private property.' Frank pushes some more with his barrel and eyeballs the loan shark. The atmosphere is practically crackling with tension. Jimmy holds Frank's stare before suddenly turning and nodding to his companion.

'I will be back,' he says with a wet smile to me. 'Oh, happy birthday by the way,' he says, pushing past Rosie who's holding a happy birthday balloon and a tray of sandwiches. I know all the colour has drained from my face.

There's a slamming of doors and the sound of a car leaving down the lane at speed. Not until I've heard the car engine disappear can I breathe or speak.

'Oh my God, thank you!' I fall on Frank and then Margaret and Dan, who puts his arm around my waist.

'Who was that?' Margaret asks.

'A low-life. Don't ask. Just some guy Sean's doing business with.' I roll my shaking hands together.

'Nice guys,' Dan says, and I slip out of his hold.

'Frank, you were amazing.' I hug him again.

'Bare-knuckle fighter in his day, weren't you, Frank? Local champion,' Margaret tells me.

'I remember his last fight,' Grandad says as Evelyn wheels him in carrying a cake on his lap.

'Hey, this is great.' Dan looks around the barn.

'What are you guys doing here?' I finally manage a flabbergasted laugh, part hysteria, part relief.

'If Muhammad won't come to the mountain, the mountain will come to Muhammad.' Margaret claps her hands together, seemingly forgetting about the guys she's just seen off.

'But what . . . what?' I stammer. 'Sean'll kill me if he finds out I've had people here.'

'But Sean isn't here,' says Margaret naughtily.

She's right, I think. And right now there's no way I want to be on my own. They've just saved me from . . . who knows what, and I'm not about to send them away. Sean should be grateful to them. Who knows what might have happened if they hadn't turned up.

'Can't have our festival organiser sitting on her own on her birthday.' Dan puts down the beers.

'Festival Girl Friday,' I correct him with a smile.

'Got any candles?' Grandad asks.

'I can't believe you've all turned up for me.' Now I am getting teary. Margaret hands me a small glass from her jacket pocket and pours a vodka into it.

'Thank you,' I say. The radio goes back on, sandwiches are put on a table, and candles in bottles come out of one of the boxes I was putting away. I down the vodka and then another. Must be the shock, I think, feeling a mixture of relief and gratitude. Besides, what harm can a few quiet drinks with some friends do?

Chapter Thirty-two

'So how did you end up in Dooleybridge?' Dan's shouting over the music.

'Ah, long story. Let's just say I was lost for a while.' I swig on the bottle of lager. I've never drunk lager from a bottle before. It tastes really nice.

'And now?' He looks very serious, making me giggle. I think that could be down to the large amount of vodka and lager I've drunk.

'And now, I'm not lost, just sort of stuck,' I splutter, finding my own joke really funny. Dan seems to find it fairly amusing too. And to think I always thought I couldn't find the right words. It's amazing how the lager has just got them flowing.

Evelyn and Maire are jiving. John Joe's sitting with Grandad, looking round the old barn. Evelyn still hasn't forgiven me, but she seems to have thawed a little ever since I put the flyers round for the festival bed and breakfast. She and John Joe are letting all three of their rooms and they're going to camp in the garden for the duration of the festival. Rosie is toasting marshmallows for her kids over an open fire and Patsy has arrived after shutting the pub with another carload of people I barely know – but what the heck, the more the merrier. It's a party! And I haven't had a birthday party in . . . ever, now I think about it. It was always meals out or takeaways with Brian. And my mum certainly wasn't one for cheese and pineapple on sticks and a bouncy castle.

I haven't had so much fun in ages. Rosie is now wheeling Grandad around the barn in time to the music. The people who arrived with Patsy have brought musical instruments. The radio goes off and a fiddle starts playing, then a squeeze box and a drum join in. This is fantastic! My feet are tapping away to the happy tune.

Dan pulls me up to dance and I find I want to join in, moving arms and legs around him as he dances in front of me. I don't care what people think – this is fun!

'Yip! Yip!' People are clapping and calling.

'Having fun?' Margaret shouts above the music and puts another bottle in my hand.

'Brilliant! Thank you!' I hug her. The memory of the loan shark is still playing on my mind. 'I'm so glad you were here tonight,' I say to Dan, thinking about what might've happened. He takes hold of my hand and pulls me closer. Grace is being fed sausages and Freddie's being led round with one of Rosie's children on his back.

'Tequila slammers!' someone shouts, and Margaret and a few others cheer, and then I realise it's me cheering. Patsy holds the tray and the little glasses are filled.

'One, two, three . . .' and I'm slinging another hot shot down my throat, making the dangers of the day disappear.

Suddenly there's a shout from outside. Margaret turns and the music stops. I follow Margaret and Dan, hoping the loan shark isn't back with reinforcements. But this time I'm ready for him. I grip my bottle. But it's Frank, wielding his beer barrel. He's standing in the shallows of the bay.

'Oh God, Frank's gone,' says Patsy. 'Stand back.' He puts an arm in front of me.

'What? What do you mean "gone"?' I say, but it comes out a bit slurred.

'Best leave him to it when he gets like this. He doesn't know what he's doing.'

I look at him as he throws his barrel effortlessly, high and far into the water with a huge splash, and then wades in deeper after it. I suddenly feel like someone's dropped a bucket of cold water over me.

'No, wait, he can't go in there!' I shout. He's wading out deeper and deeper. 'Frank, come back!'

'Feck off. I'm going to Africa,' he bellows, and surges forward.

I run down to the water's edge and grab his arms, which he swings back, and I fall into the water. The barrel bobs around in the shallows like a shipwrecked boat before it sinks.

'Frank, stop!' I stand up, dripping. 'Stop, stop! Get out of there! Dan, do something!' I shout.

'I'll call the Garda, shall I?' Dan reaches for his phone.

'Stop!'

'Let him to it. Best way. There's no stopping him when he's like this,' Margaret says.

'You can't be serious! The oysters! He mustn't go near the oysters!' I'm beside myself, hands on my head. 'Dan, do something!'

'I thought they'd all been trashed. Hardly anything left,' Margaret slurs.

'Not those oysters. The other oysters,' I cry desperately, then roll my lips together. I'm frowning so hard it hurts.

'What other oysters?' Margaret's confused. 'I wish Sean

was here, I'd've shown him what he's missing out on,' she mumbles.

I have to save the oysters. I can't let it happen again. I have to get help.

'His wild oysters! The native thingy-me-bobs,' I blurt out, the words tumbling out before I can stop them.

'Wild oysters? Here in Dooleybridge?' I hear someone say, and a ripple runs through the partygoers. 'There hasn't been wild oysters here in years.'

'Feckin' fantastic!' says another voice.

'Aye, brilliant news!'

'Yes! Now please, you have to stop him!' I point at Frank wading ever deeper.

'Africa!'

But no one moves. There's still an appreciation for the wild oysters in the air.

'Yes, wild oysters!' I confirm loudly. 'Now Frank, get out of the fucking water!' I shout.

I didn't hear the engine noise, the van pull up or the door slam. But suddenly there's a dark figure cutting through the crowd, running into the sea, creating a spray of water. Thank God for that.

'Dan?' I turn round. Dan is still trying to get reception for his phone.

There's a muffled cry, a splash, a slap and a shout.

It can only mean one thing: Sean's back.

Chapter Thirty-three

'Now get the hell off my land and don't come back! That goes for all of you!'

I've never seen Sean so angry. He's clutching his back. People are shuffling towards their cars and down the track. Frank is being helped into one of the cars. The engines start and, very quickly, there's just me left. It's gone very quiet.

'It was my birthday,' I say stupidly, standing in the kitchen.

'Fi?' It's Dan. He's outside.

'Happy birthday,' Sean says sarcastically and winces in pain.

'Are you OK?' I go to put out an arm.

'No, I'm not OK.' He's pouring himself a large whiskey. He winces as he turns towards a chair.

'Here, let me help you,' I try again. He brushes me away.

'I think you've done enough, don't you?' He holds on to the work surface. 'Sorry, Fi. I thought I could trust you. You know the one thing that's important to me. I didn't want anyone up here. I don't want anyone finding out about the oysters.'

There's a silence between us.

'I think it would be better if you went,' he says, sipping the drink. Pain is etched on his face.

'OK, I'll come back in the morning. Put everything straight.' I turn to leave.

'No, I think it would be best for both of us if you didn't,' he says angrily.

'What?'

'I'm sorry, but that's how it has to be. You're fired, Fi.' And I watch as he grabs the whiskey bottle and hobbles off to bed.

'Fi?' Dan calls from outside again.

'Sounds like your boyfriend's looking for you,' and Sean slams the bedroom door shut.

Outside, I let the cold rain hit my face. I couldn't feel more stupid and cross with myself if I tried. There's a beep of a car horn. I hold my hand up to cover my eyes against the headlights. A tall figure gets out of the driver's side.

'Designated driver for the night,' says Dan. 'I dropped the others in town. Just thought I'd come back and see how things are,' he says, and at that point I collapse into a heap of drunken tears against his broad chest.

I wake with a thumping headache, in a strange bed. It's light. It must be the morning. I look around, trying to work out where I am. It takes a while for me to take in the floral curtains, the velour headrest, the fringed lamps. Then I hear a voice on the phone.

Oh God, I'm in Rosie's chalet, in Dan's bed! I sit up and check to see what clothes I have or haven't got on. I seem to be wearing most of them. The door opens and Dan is standing there holding a mug.

'Tea?'

'Oh my God, we didn't, did we?' I say straightaway, not

giving him a chance to answer. 'I mean, not that it wouldn't have been lovely, but . . . y'know.'

'No, we didn't,' he laughs, putting the tea on the bedside table. 'I slept on the couch. And am still feeling it.' He rubs his neck and rolls his head from side to side with a wince. 'I'm hoping to trade you for a massage later,' he says with a smile, sitting on the bed.

'Oh, no,' I groan as it all comes flooding back in glorious Technicolor detail. I grab a pillow and hold it over my face.

'Oh thanks.' Dan stands up and I quickly drop the pillow.

'Oh no, not you, I mean, just . . . everything.' I fall back into the pillows and pull the other one over my face, but the unfamiliar smell makes me take it away again. 'Look, Dan, I said a lot of things that I—' I start.

'It's forgotten.' He gives a quick, bright smile. 'Now then, how about lunch?'

My stomach flips over and not in a good way.

'You OK?' He stands up quickly and backs away. I can't help but like Dan, he makes me smile, like a dopey older brother.

'You don't give up, do you?' My stomach settles and I fall on the tea.

'I like to get what I want in life,' he beams.

I'm beginning to think that this isn't a bad thing. At least he knows what he wants. But right now I have work out what I want.

'It's just that I was thinking. We work well together, you and I,' Dan says, as I blow and sip my tea, wondering how to let him down gently.

'Hey,' Margaret bursts in through the sliding patio doors and I'm relieved at the interruption. 'I've been looking for you. That was some night, eh? Hope Sean wasn't too mad at you.' She looks as fresh as a daisy.

Dan looks frustrated. I, on the other hand, don't want to have the 'friends' conversation with him again.

'Actually,' I tell Margaret as I finally manage to take a good swig of tea, 'he sacked me.'

'No way!' Margaret shrieks, making my head bang. 'For having a few birthday drinks?'

'In fairness, it was more than a few drinks, and he had specifically told me not to have people back to the farm.'

'Why not, for God's sake? And after you saw off those thugs, I hope you told him about that. Ah, tea, lovely.' She takes the tea Dan is holding and then looks at it doubtfully.

'Actually I didn't. Didn't get a chance. He sacked me last night so I stayed here with Dan.'

'Really?' Margaret's eyes light up over the cup she's holding in front of her.

'Not like that,' I tut and blush.

'On the couch,' Dan joins in.

'Nothing happened,' I say at the same time.

'Well, leave Sean Thornton to me. I'll go up and have a word,' Margaret says boldly.

'No, I don't think that's a good idea. I think Sean just needs to be given a wide berth right now.'

Once Margaret and Dan leave, I fall back into the pillows, pull the covers over my head and stay there for the rest of the day.

The following morning Margaret's back. I'm up and showered and feeling human again.

'So what are you going to do now?' she says, taking more tea from Dan who's been working away on his computer.

'Well, I'll hang around until the festival and then . . . go on to my mum's, I suppose.' I try and sound upbeat but I'm not sure it's coming across. Margaret looks crestfallen.

'Actually, that's what I wanted to talk to you about.' Dan puts down his mug but Margaret's in full flow.

'Ah no, don't leave.'

'I can't stay around here without a job, and besides, I don't think I'd be very welcome.' Sean's angry face comes flooding back to me.

'You would! I could ask if there are any shifts at the pub.' Margaret's on the edge of her seat.

'It's kind of you but you know that there's hardly enough for you. I'm amazed Patsy can keep going.' I put down the mug and stand up. I think it's best not to think about this too much right now. 'Look, I have to go and get my stuff from the farm. Sean will be at Galway market today.'

'Then let's go out for lunch,' Dan pipes up.

'Well, it's just . . .'

Dan's face becomes serious, he frowns, and it makes me want to laugh. 'Actually, there's something I want to talk to you about, Fi.'

I'm intrigued now, and to be fair he has been very kind letting me stay here.

'As long as it's not a date,' I say.

'Not a date,' he crosses his heart with his finger. Margaret's looking from me to Dan and back again with an incredulous look on her face.

Chapter Thirty-four

Sean will be out at the farmers' market by now, I think, as we bump and sway towards the gates. The lane is so familiar; it's odd that the place I disliked so much when I first got here feels strangely like home now.

'I'll just nip in and get my belongings. I'll be straight back out,' I say to Dan.

'Great, then I can take you for that lunch,' he beams a shiny white smile.

'Stop!' I suddenly put my hand on the gear stick. He slams on the brakes and shoves his sunglasses up on top of his baseball cap. He looks down at my hand and so do I. I whip it away but he's still looking at me with a wide smile on his face.

'The van's still there,' I quickly explain, looking through the sparse hedge. I scan the yard but there's no sign of Sean.

'Perhaps we should come back later, after lunch.' Dan shifts in his seat. He moves the 4x4 slowly into the drive and starts reversing into a three-point turn.

Sean's van is on the drive with the back doors open, but it's empty.

'He should be long gone by now,' I say out loud. I'm puzzled. Dan's now got the truck turned round and is pushing the gear stick into first. He tilts his head back towards the main road.

'Let's get out of here and come back when he's out.'

I wind down my window and can hear the hens making an almighty racket; they haven't been let out yet. There's no sign of Grace either. Now that is odd.

'Sorry, Dan.' I undo my seatbelt. 'I really think I should go and see what's going on.' I push open the truck door.

'Hey, now hang on. He was in no mood for chit-chat the other night. I don't think he'll be ready to make small talk just yet. Let's just go into town,' he says slowly and deliberately, as if telling me to 'back away from the gun'. 'Let's get some lunch and I can run my idea past you. Then I'll bring you back and we'll collect your stuff while he's out.' He pats the heated leather seat.

He's right. Sean isn't going to want to talk to me.

'Look, I wanted to save this and talk to you over lunch, but seeing as you're proving tricky to pin down I'll tell you now. Mary Jo is leaving, like I told you, and I'm going to need someone to run my office, deal with all the organisational stuff. I thought it might suit you.' He looks at me and cocks his head.

'What? Where?'

'Boston, of course. You run my office, organise the diary, make sure I get to events, that kind of thing. I can find you an apartment and the pay's pretty good.' He's looking straight ahead, like the poker player who knows he's holding the winning hand.

Oh my God, this was everything I could have hoped for! A new job, far away from here. A fresh start.

The hens let out another almighty squawk and I still can't

see Grace. I have to find out if everything's OK.

'Just give me an hour or so to get my stuff. I'll meet you back at the chalet.'

'Arr, for feck's sake!' Sean shouted as he looked in a cupboard for painkillers and ended up knocking packets of neatly stacked cereal boxes to the floor. Even Grace didn't jump forward to hoover up the bits, just stood patiently behind him. He clutched his back. He was cross, mostly with himself. He shouldn't have gone away. He shouldn't have trusted his business to someone else. He was cross for taking his hands off the reins. A drunken blowout, here, for feck's sake! So close to the oysters. He'd made it clear no one was to come to the farm.

If he was honest, though, he'd been so riled because he'd found the farm so different to how he'd been expecting it. He thought she'd be here on her own. He'd wanted to thank her for her hard work and loyalty, but she'd had plenty of company. In particular that Dan. He thought she'd have better taste. It was Margaret leading her astray; she was even starting to dress like her. But she wasn't Margaret, she was lovely-looking as she was, natural. He stopped and pulled himself up. What was wrong with him? Now he was talking as if he fancied her.

'Aww!' he cried out again, pain shooting up through his lower spine. He dropped to the floor and lay there until the pain stopped. Grace whimpered and lay down by his side.

But she'd caused him trouble too, he reminded himself, looking up at the plastered ceiling. If it wasn't for her, he wouldn't have lost all those oysters in the first place. And now she'd let the world and his wife up on the farm, anyone could have found out about the native oysters. And on top of that she'd organised his house, the sheds and his business to within an inch of its life and he couldn't find a feckin' thing! He needed to find the painkillers, and then get the oysters into the van and get to market before he lost his pitch to the olive guy. When he got back, he'd go and check the oysters.

He went to lift himself up.

'Aggghhh!'

He needed help, he thought resignedly. He needed Fi. He couldn't do this without her, but there was no way she'd come back now. He'd seen her leave with Dan, wrapped in his arms.

'Argggggghhh!' he yelled again, loudly, and collapsed back onto the floor.

The hens cluck round me like a returning friend. Even Brenda has second thoughts about chasing me and flaps around, delighted to be let out of her shed. I feed Freddie and Mercury. Down by the shore the oyster bags are in the shallows, waiting to be pulled out to go to market.

I take a deep breath and knock on the cottage door. There's no reply. I knock again.

'Go away!' comes the reply.

I steady myself. I'm not scared of Sean Thornton.

'I've come for my stuff,' I say crossly, and then Grace barks. 'Sean, I've come for my stuff.' But he doesn't reply. Well, it's still my home too until I get my things, and I push down the door handle and march in.

I catch my breath. Sean's lying on the floor. His face is pale, his eyes deep-set and dark.

'Don't go getting all panicky on me. I'm just doing some back exercises,' he says, grimacing.

'Wouldn't dream of it,' I say, and rub Grace's head, then she bolts outside. But I am worried. He's obviously in a lot of pain.

I go into my room to fetch my things, wondering what to do.

'I'm going then,' I say, with a carrier bag of belongings, mostly made up of a torn and trashed wedding dress.

'OK,' Sean says.

Oh, he was so annoying.

'Do you want a hand getting up?' I offer.

'Nope, just lying here, stretching out my back.' He goes to make a move and yells in pain. 'Just need to stretch out and then I'll get to market. Was looking for painkillers but some idiot's moved them.'

'Oh, for God's sake.' I drop the bag and go to him.

''S OK,' Sean says again. He's pale and there are beads of sweat on his forehead.

'Who did this?' I take hold of his upper arm and help him to sit up. 'Was it Jimmy Power and his lad?'

Sean screws up his face. 'What?'

'The loan shark? Jimmy Power? Did he come back?' Guilt is wrapping itself round me like a growing vine. I should have warned him.

'What d'you mean "come back"?' He's struggling to his feet with my help. His face contorts in pain again and I hold him up. He can't talk and walk.

'Really, I don't need any help,' he says, as I let him lean on me as we slowly make our way to his bedroom, him holding the backs of chairs all the way. He's short of breath. 'I just need a little lie down and then I'll be fine. Tell me about Jimmy Power.'

'He came here looking for you last night. Said he was checking up on his investment.' I take a deep breath. 'He . . . wanted to . . . he made a pass at me. And he wasn't offering oysters and champagne with it!'

Sean stops and holds the door handle. 'The bastard! I'm going to see him. Right after I've been to market!' he spits angrily.

'You can't go to market. You can't even stand up straight,' I say, guiding him to the bed and letting go of him. He falls onto it, wincing.

'Did he hurt you?'

I shake my head. 'Frank arrived just in time, and the others. They were brilliant, Frank, Margaret and Dan.'

He looks down. I can't tell if it's fury or pain on his face.

'Let me help you,' I say, going to lift his legs.

'I said I'll be fine. I don't need anyone's help!' he shouts, and then collapses down onto the pillows.

I storm into the kitchen and find the painkillers from the medicine box I've made on top of the kitchen cupboards. I fill a large glass with water and take it back into the bedroom. He hasn't moved. I put down the water and the tablets on the bedside table. He goes to roll over.

'I told you,' he says, the pain clear in his eyes.

'I know, you don't need any help! You never do! You're a stubborn fool, Sean Thornton!' I blurt out. I turn to march out.

'What's it got to do with you? You don't even work here any more!'

'Seeing as you weren't paying me anyway, it doesn't make

much of a difference.' I slam out of the cottage with Grace by my side. I'm furious with him. He's obviously in so much pain he can't even stand. I have never met anyone so determined not to ask for help. If only I knew how he'd hurt his back. Was it my fault? I march down to the water's edge, grab the oyster sacks and load them into the van. Then, with Grace in the passenger seat, I climb into the van and turn the key. At first she won't start. On the second attempt she coughs and splutters but still doesn't catch. I'm beginning to panic. The last thing I want is Sean lurching out of the house to find me taking his van.

'Come on!' I shout, putting all my frustrations into standing on the accelerator and willing the engine to life. I've never driven a van before but it can't be that different from a camper van. Oh God, stealing big vehicles is becoming a habit!

'Come on, old girl!' I shout as she roars into life, and in a funny way I feel I have too.

Chapter Thirty-five

I get to the farmers' market and discover someone is in my pitch. It's the snag man. He raises a set of long-handled tongs at me by way of a greeting. I'm silently seething. There's a small space in the shade on the other side of the lane. It's not as nice as the pitch we should've had, but it's the only space left. I'm pushed back practically into an alleyway, out of the way of passing footfall.

I carry the small table and two chairs from the van, which is parked in a nearby school. Then I bring over the crates of oysters. I lay out the plastic glasses, the box of wine and paper plates. All I have to do now is wait for customers. I pick up an oyster and try and remember how Sean taught me to open it. I don't have to wait too long to practise. The first of my customers sit themselves down at the table and I serve them wine. Then, with shaking hands, I start to open their half-dozen oysters. It's slow. At first I can't do it, can't get the knife in, but I remember Sean's arms around me and push the knife into the hinge firmly. Hey presto! I did it! After that the customers come in a steady stream all day, and with each six I shuck I become more and more relaxed. I even accept a hot dog from the snag man by way of apology. It's nearing the end of the day and my money bag is full. I'm serving oysters to a couple of American tourists from Seattle, when I hear a voice I recognise behind me and I freeze.

'Henri, it's all in hand. I have agreed to take all the native oysters and said they will only be sold in the restaurant. But I'll have plenty of surplus and that's what I'm offering you. You're to deal with me, not him. I'm the broker. He'll never know. Has some idea that he wants the oysters to stay local. Doesn't want them to travel. But I'll pay Sean a flat rate for them, tell him they're for my restaurant, and then I'll sell what I don't need on to you and your customers out there. The profit margin will be fantastic.' My stomach turns over.

I turn round quickly to see Nancy coming out of a low purple front door, off the main street. I look up at the sign. The Pearl. Of course, her new restaurant. She has no intention of putting Sean on the map as a supplier. She just wants the oysters and the profit for herself.

She spots me, quickly finishes her phone call and slams the phone shut. She stops, and by the look of it is gathering her thoughts. Then she comes towards me.

'Fi. Not Sean's usual pitch,' she smiles smoothly. 'Is he here?' she looks around. I shake my head. I'm so incensed I can't speak. 'Good oysters, aren't they?' She turns to the American couple, who agree. 'Come back when my restaurant opens, we'll have native Galway oysters then, they're really something special,' she says charmingly.

'So it seems. Sounds like you're going to have more oysters than you can handle.' The words are out of my mouth before I've even had a chance to think about how terrified of Nancy I am. But my blood is boiling. She's sending the oysters to France. It's just what Sean didn't want, and by the sounds of it, to add insult to injury, she's cutting him out of the deal as well.

Nancy pours herself a finger of white wine from the box, takes a sip and gives a grimace, letting me know my choice of wine is a joke.

'Whatever you think you may have heard, Sean will never believe the hired help over his partner. I'd think very carefully before blabbing about things you know nothing about. Without me, Sean doesn't have a hope of selling any oysters. He'll be doing market stalls for the rest of his life and that won't pay for his licence.' She knocks back the rest of the wine, turns and smiles at the American tourists. 'Don't forget to come back and visit me.' She points to the restaurant sign and disappears into the crowds, pulling out her phone and putting it to her ear again.

Chapter Thirty-six

As I pull into the farm, I switch off the engine and just sit, letting the peace wash over me. It wasn't that I didn't enjoy being back in the hustle and bustle of a city. In fact, I did. But now I have to face the music.

I push the door open sheepishly, hoping Sean isn't going to roar at me as soon as I get in. It's all quiet.

The cottage is freezing. I open up the fire and put a match to a firelighter and some kindling. Then I throw in some turf and slide the kettle onto it. I pull the money bag out of my big waterproof jacket. I can't put it off any longer. I push open Sean's bedroom door.

He's lying with his eyes shut. Peaceful. I step out of the room and go to pull the door to.

'English!' He stops me in my tracks. 'You came back.'

'Of course I came back. I wasn't stealing the van. I just went to do the market.' He still looks very pale and isn't moving. 'Here,' I set the bag of money down next to him. There's an untouched baguette by his bed and a bottle of Coke. He sees me looking at them.

'Nancy brought me lunch.'

'Right,' I say, backing out of the room again. Nancy was checking up on her investment.

'She wanted to agree the terms for the oysters,' he says weakly.

274

I have to tell him, tell him that she's stitching him up. I take a deep breath and wonder where to start.

'At least this way I can get Jimmy Power off my back, eh?' he says.

My courage runs out on me. How can I tell him what Nancy's up to now? He'll never believe me, I think hopelessly, and what good would it do? If Nancy pulls out, he'll lose the farm to Jimmy Power. Whatever I think of Nancy and her plan, I have to put up and shut up, for Sean's sake.

'I'll unload the van and then I'll make my way back to the town.'

'You can't do it on your own.' He looks up at me.

'Is there a choice?' I say, looking at him in bed. 'Unless Nancy's coming back to help?'

'I just feel so useless!' He slams his hands into the duvet. I don't know how to make this better. He leans over for his drink and I pick it up and hand it to him. 'Where are you staying?' he asks.

'In Rosie's chalet,' I say, wondering why I'm leaving out the important bit.

'With Dan,' he fills in.

I hear the kettle coming to the boil. I dip out of the room, go back into the kitchen and make tea and coffee and find some more painkillers.

'Here, take these. I'll finish up outside.' I hand him the tablets.

'Yes, Miss,' he says, struggling to prop himself up, and I can't stop myself stepping in and helping him. 'I couldn't find them,' he says with an attempt at a smile. 'Somebody keeps tidying up.' He takes the tablets.

'So how did it happen?' I need to know if I'm responsible

for this too. I put the glass of water back by his bed. He doesn't look anywhere near ready to get up, and I have to get back to Dan, find out about the job. But as I've already left him waiting for nearly an entire day, I guess a little longer won't hurt.

'An accident, car crash.'

'What, last night?' I sit on the edge of the bed. He shakes his head.

'Years ago. I'd just got out of prison. I was with my . . . fiancée.'

'Nancy?'

He shakes his head again. 'It was way before Nancy and I got together.'

'Oh.'

'I'd just got out of prison. We were out celebrating. Car hit us head on. I injured my back. It reoccurs every now and again.' He looks into his lap.

And although I don't really want to, I ask, 'And your fiancée?' He shakes his curls again. My eyes widen.

'Died.'

I take a sharp intake of breath.

'Of course, the gossip-mongers round here went to town. As if my uncle didn't have enough to worry about.'

I move further on to the bed so my feet aren't touching the ground. 'Like what?'

He looks at me as if a piece of him has been unlocked and he's right back there. 'The waters around here had been declared unclean. There was a building firm, bought the land down the lane and were building that estate on the Murphys' land. Their waste was going right into the waters.'

Finally I'm beginning to see. 'So the Murphys sold to these builders who were poisoning the waters?'

Sean nods. He's getting weary. The painkillers must be kicking in, maybe that's why he's finally talking so freely.

'When the builders stopped the work, the waters cleaned up again, but people wouldn't believe my uncle. The damage had been done. Local orders had been lost. A lot of people went out of business.'

'And that's why you sell yours abroad mostly?' I swing my legs up onto the bed.

'Means I don't have to worry about local gossip. And I had restaurant sales in Dublin.' His eyes begin to droop. 'But now the native oysters are back. That'll show them . . . Show them the waters are the cleanest possible.'

I want to make this work for him.

'Yup, it's different this time. They're staying on home turf.' His eyes shut for a moment. He looks peaceful. Grace is lying by the bed.

I want to tell him, but I can't. I mustn't. I go to stand up.

'Thank you,' he says sleepily, his eyes open again, 'for everything.'

'Sean, about the party. I'm sorry. I shouldn't have . . .'

'No, you shouldn't. But I shouldn't have left you here to face that thug. I'm sorry. Happy birthday, by the way.' He rummages around on his bedside table and hands me a little black and gold packet. I open it up and the little pearl necklace drops out. I hold it in my hand and take a sharp breath.

'It's beautiful.'

'Fi, this isn't easy, but will you come back and work for me? I can't do it without you. You're the only one who knows . . .'

'I know, about the oysters,' I nod, and realise that's not true any more.

'No, you're the only one who knows where everything is!' And I think that's the closest Sean Thornton has ever come to asking for help.

I go back outside to empty the van, feeling inexplicably happy. I look out to sea and think, I could be there, America, Dan is offering me a ticket out of here. Or I could stay. It's a no-brainer, but then I don't think it's my brain that's making the decision.

Chapter Thirty-seven

For the next week I rise early, feed the chickens, collect the eggs, retrieve Freddie from his early morning escape, make coffee and breakfast for Sean, and brownies for Gerald. Then I begin the work with the oysters. Every morning I drive the tractor a little further into the water so I have to jump in a little deeper. Then I load the van and drive to one of the farmers' markets in other nearby towns, setting up my pitch and serving up oysters. With Sean out of action and no hope of him working at the sailing school, it's the only way.

Come the evening, after doing the farm chores, I deliver the brownies to Gerald and go home to prepare supper for Sean and myself. As the week draws to an end I have blisters on my blisters, my nails are broken and torn, my once-sleek bobbed hair is wavy and long and only contained by the hat I seem to wear all the time. But strangely I feel more alive than I think I ever have. It feels so . . . real. It's just me, out in the fresh air, collecting the food that's to be sold on to keep the farm running. I have never been so tired, but never so content either.

Most evenings it's some kind of egg supper for Sean and I. The hens are laying every day, their days as battery hens before Sean rescued them a dim and distant past. It feels daft for me to sit in the living room eating alone while Sean eats in his bedroom, so I've taken to sitting on the end of his bed while he tells me about the oyster festivals he used to visit, the farms he's worked on and the restaurants he's shucked in.

For the first few days he can't sit up and I have to cut up his food and help him eat it. It's hard for both of us to start with. Our embarrassment's almost palpable, him having to rely on me and me having to be so intimate with my boss, a man I'm finding more and more attractive by the day.

'Nancy called up today,' he tells me as the week draws to a close. He's propped up on pillows and I've just got back from Moycullen market. There's another shop-bought baguette beside his bed.

'Oh, really?' I say, carrying a tray with mushroom soup and bread on it.

'She didn't stay long. You know Nancy. Can't wait to get away from here, especially when I'm no use to her.' He looks almost back to his old self.

'She must be dying to get her hands on you once you're well.' I bite my lip. 'I didn't mean that to come out like that. I meant you can really get together. I mean, she must miss you.' My tongue is tying itself in knots as I try hard not to tell him what I heard on the phone, how I think she's shutting him out of the deal.

Sean shrugs. 'It worked for us. Neither of us wanted anything more.' He looks at the tray. The word 'wanted', past tense, doesn't go unnoticed. Am I imagining it? He looks up at me and just for a moment we hold each other's gaze. I reach down and put his tray in front of him and the back of his hand touches mine, setting off explosions deep inside me.

'I put oysters in yours,' I nod at his soup.

'But not in yours?' He smiles at me and I shake my head.

'Let's not get carried away.' I smile back.

'No, let's not,' he says quietly, and my explosions fizzle out, hissing and spitting as they go. He picks up his spoon the wrong way up and goes to eat his soup, then rights it again quickly.

'So how's the festival shaping up?'

Now this is a surprise, Sean taking an interest in the festival.

'Good, thank you. Still won't change your mind about entering the shucking competition?' I sip at my soup.

Sean shakes his head. 'I just don't think I'd be welcome.'

I want to argue with him but think better of it.

'Margaret's been doing great work on the publicity,' I carry on brightly. 'We've got a website and everything. She's been out with me taking photographs of the customers eating oysters, and of the town. She wants to do a whole gallery of "then and now" pictures. In fact, she's left Dan's camera in the van. I'll have to get it back to her.'

He says nothing for a moment and then puts his spoon down next to the empty bowl.

'There's a box,' he says, 'with photos in it. Would you bring it to me?'

I know exactly the one he means: the one over the coat rack that I knocked down on my first day.

I sit next to him on the bed and we go through the black-and-white pictures of his uncle and the colour ones of him. Underneath the pictures Sean tugs at something.

'What is it?'

He pulls it out triumphantly.

'My old shucking knife. My uncle bought it for me when

I was eighteen.' He holds it in his hand, enjoying its feel, as if he were slipping on a pair of handmade shoes. I sigh.

'What's the matter?' He puts down the knife.

'It's just . . . our festival isn't going to be anything like this. This is what the locals want; they want it how it used to be.'

'Here, have these. Tell Margaret she can have them for her website as long as I get them back,' he hands me the pictures and puts the knife beside him on the table.

'I will,' I yawn, and clear away the bowls.

'You're shattered. Get some rest. Take the camera and photos in the morning,' he says.

I decide to do just that. Tomorrow will be the last day of this spring tide, which means tonight is high tide. It's calm and bright as I fetch the camera in from the van.

It's dark when I hear the familiar sound of the outboard motor. I jump up. The moon is clear and bright. I can see the boat from my window. Sean is fast asleep. I look around and grab the camera from beside my bed. This time I'll get them to stop.

I pick my way along the familiar path round the bay, skirting the deep mud and tackling the little stone steps with ease. I reach the end of the path where I watched the seals and from where I can see the boat all too clearly.

'Oi!' I shout, throwing a stone into the water. This time when they look up I press the button on the camera.

Flash! Its bright light bounces off the water and their two surprised faces.

Flash! It goes again and I hear their voices low and arguing.

Splash! The bag of oysters is dropped back into the water.

Flash! I hear the engine start up and the men swearing under their breath.

I can feel the huge grin on my face as I pick my way back over the rocks and along the path to the cottage and quietly slide back into my bed, the camera tucked safely into my wardrobe.

The following evening on my way back from Galway I stop off at the pub for a drink. Dan is there, propping up the bar and tapping on his laptop.

'Hey, let me get you a drink,' he says as soon as he sees me. He stands and goes to hug me but then takes a step back and pats my shoulder.

'Eau de oyster seller no doubt,' I laugh, pulling up a bar stool. I spot Padraig and Seamus straightaway, trying not to look in my direction. Padraig is actually pulling his hat down over his face with his finger.

'How did you do today?' Margaret asks.

'Great. Loads of customers and I got my pitch back.' I take the glass of wine she pours for me.

'And Sean?'

'Getting better every day. Up and about.' I take a sip of the wine. 'In fact he's nearly ready to be out and about and then I can really bring him up to speed with everything that's been going on while he's been ill,' I say loudly and take another sip. I can't swerve what needs to be said any more. I've spent my life taking the path of least resistance and look where it got me. I take a deep breath and plaster on a smile.

'Oh, just need to get your camera, it's in the van. Took some lovely shots of the bay last night. Maybe you could use them on the website,' I tell Margaret. I slide off the stool and walk close to Padraig and Seamus and say in a low whisper, 'And if you ever come near his oysters again, I'll show him the photos I took of you last night. And let's be honest, we've all heard about Sean Thornton's reputation . . .'

I bring back the camera and put it on the bar.

'Did you save any you wanted?' Margaret reaches over and takes the camera.

'I did.' I give the pair another look, but inside I'm shaking like a leaf. Then they nod back, which I take to mean we understand each other and the whole business is over and done with. I take another really big swig of wine and inside I'm doing a happy dance.

'All ready for the Pearl Queen party on Friday?' Margaret squeals and claps her hands together.

'Yes. Can't wait. Many entrants?' I start to relax.

'Uh huh,' she says. 'Ten so far, including me.'

'Are you allowed to enter?' I think out loud.

'Yes, of course. As long as I'm not judging it as well,' she assures me. 'Dan's a judge, so's Patsy, and the editor from the *Galway Gazette*.'

'You entering?' Dan shuts down his computer and turns to me.

'Oh yes, do!' Margaret says, putting glasses back on the shelf. 'It'll be great craic! I could do your make-up again!' She starts to get even more excited.

I hold up my hand. 'No, I won't be entering. But I'm happy to help out with anything that needs doing on the night,' I say, and wonder what on earth I'm going to wear. Not one of Margaret's creations again. They look great on Margaret, but not on me.

Evelyn, John Joe and Maire come into the pub. Seeing

Maire gives me an idea. Maybe I do know what to wear after all.

'OK, well maybe I'll get you to mop my brow or something like that,' Dan jokes. 'Say, how's Sean getting on up there?' he asks with genuine concern, which is good of him considering how I stood him up on that day I went to market and turned down his job offer.

'Good, thanks. On the mend. Maybe I could persuade him out next weekend.' I sip my drink.

'Yes,' he nods. 'And you're managing everything at the farm? No other oyster problems?' I presume he's talking about how I ran them over in those first few weeks; unless he means Seamus and Padraig.

'No, no problems at all,' I beam proudly.

'Good, good. Y'know, we'd still make a good team, you and me. I still haven't given up on us working together. But maybe there's a better way . . .' He gives me a smile and tips up his pint. His eyes are glinting.

'What do you mean?' I'm intrigued.

'Just saying that I'm working on a business plan and you might be just the person to help me with it. In fact it was you that gave me the idea.'

'Really?' I can't think that I could've come up with anything useful.

'I'll know by the festival. Could be just right for both of us,' he says, and I can't help feeling curious.

Chapter Thirty-eight

The next evening I pull into the drive and notice it straight-away. The hooker is missing. There's nothing there. My heart starts pounding. How will I tell Sean about this one? Then, just as I'm about to get back into the van and go and call the Garda, it comes into view round the corner of the bay. Its big red sails are full and fat. Sean is sitting with his hand on the rudder, but when he sees me he stands up and throws his hands in the air.

'They're ready!' he shouts at the top of his voice. 'They're feckin' ready!'

A huge surge of excitement bubbles up in me and I run down to the water's edge. I can see the sheer joy on his face. He's smiling like he's won the lottery. And his back looks to be holding up well too.

'Get a lifejacket, quick!' he shouts, and without giving it a second thought I run up to the shed and put the lifejacket over my head and do up the ties. I run back to the shore. Grace is bouncing up and down. Oystercatchers fly off and land again. The heron is there, flying slowly and steadily by the side of the boat. Sean pulls up at the little jetty and throws the rope to me.

'You have to come and see, they're perfect!' He grabs my

arms and I wonder if he's going to hug me, but instead he turns to help me into the boat. I'm shaking but take his hand and let him guide me.

'Sit up here beside me,' he says, and we sit either side of the rudder. Sean flicks and pulls at the ropes. But I'm still clinging to the side for dear life and I keep focused on the shoreline. He unhooks the rope and pushes us away from the jetty.

'OK?' he asks, still beaming, and I nod. We say nothing until we're out in the middle of the bay.

'Here, you take it,' he pushes the rudder towards me. At first I shake my head, but he does it again and so I quickly let go of the side of the boat and grab the rudder. It's harder than I was expecting. The wind is in Sean's hair, making the curls bounce this way and that. He looks alive and happy, really happy.

'There, now you're in control. You decide where you want to go.' He puts his hand over mine just for a second or two, helping to push me out round the headland from where I took the pictures of Seamus and Padraig. The seals are there to greet us, bobbing up and down playfully.

'Right,' Sean takes over the rudder and puts us in the middle of the second bay. Then he drops the anchor. 'Look,' he says, standing in front of me with one foot on the side of the boat. It's swaying to and fro and I'm feeling uneasy again. 'There's nothing to be scared of. Nothing will happen, and if it does, I'm here.' He gives a little shrug. He pulls off his raincoat with a slight wince. Underneath is his wetsuit. He pulls out his knife, the one from the box of photos, and puts it in his mouth.

I tentatively look over the edge. The water is as clear as can be and I can see all the way to the bottom. There are layers and layers of round shells.

'Splash!' The boat sways from side to side and I catch my breath and cling on. But like Sean says, he's there. He comes up from under the boat, his hands full of the oysters.

'Here,' he hands the round, wet shells to me and I let them tumble at my feet. Then he grabs the edge of the boat and swings himself in.

'You see the different shape,' he says, brushing away the water from his face. 'They're flatter, rounder.' He picks one up and so do I. 'Its shell is harder. It has to be to survive in the wild.' He looks straight at me and I look quickly at the oyster. The shell is ridged with a slight blue-green sheen. 'And they're harder to open, a lot harder.' He pushes in the knife with force and then slides it and twists it until it gives a really loud 'pop'. He looks up at me again and we smile together. He slides the knife along the top shell and opens it up. The flesh inside is plump and creamy. He flips it over and the juices run.

'Sunny side up,' he says. 'You try. Hold it in the palm of your hand. Put the frill into the base of your thumb.' I watch and follow. 'Now squeeze the knife into the hinge.'

He's right, they are hard to open. I grip the knife harder and suddenly the hinge breaks and I slide the knife along the inside of the top shell, cutting through the muscle.

'Did you ever think you'd be doing this when you came to Ireland?' He watches my hands.

'There's a lot of things I never thought I'd do before I came to Ireland.'

'Not all bad, I hope.' He looks up at me and it's 5 November in my stomach.

'No, not all bad.' I pull off the top shell and flip the oyster inside over with a proud smile. 'I thought I was safe, you see, with Brian. Life was mapped out. I thought that was what a good relationship was,' I find myself saying, and feel he understands.

'You don't need to feel safe,' he says as I move the oyster towards his lips. 'You need to love and be loved back.' He doesn't take the oyster from me; instead I put it to his lips and tip it up. Some of the juice trickles down the side of his mouth. I take away the shell and he chews and swallows. I open another oyster and hold it to his lips.

'Impressive,' he says, and catches hold of my hand and looks me straight in the eye. My breathing is heavy and slow. My whole body is aching with desire.

'You don't need to learn how to open oysters,' he says softly. 'You need to learn how to eat them.' He takes my hand and guides it to my mouth. He is up on his knees in front of me. I can smell the saltiness of the sea and the minerals. He moves it closer still, so the fringed edge of the shell is sitting on my bottom lip. Our eyes are locked together. I can taste the briny liquid. I lick the juice from my bottom lip and then suddenly he tips the shell up and I open my mouth just enough to let it in. It's soft and meaty. I bite down and suddenly there is a rush of the sea on my tongue, a blast of the Atlantic and a faint metallic taste.

I can feel his hot breath on my face, watching as I chew the oyster and swallow, and then smile widely. Slowly, I open my eyes to see his face up close to mine, smiling too. He looks into my eyes, his own sparkling with excitement. We hold each other's gaze, then, hesitant at first, our faces tip slightly to one side. My lips are aching to touch his and I lift my chin just a little more. My heart is thrumming to the same beat as the one between my legs. He looks into my eyes again and then, like magnets, unable to resist each other's draw, his mouth is on mine and a full-blown firework display like new year's eve at midnight takes place in my belly. The sun is beginning to set in the salmon pink sky.

The outside world melts away; there's only him and me. The wind sets my skin alive as we wrap our arms and bodies around each other, let our lips find each other's again, and there, nestled against the polished wood and lifejackets, the coils of rope concealed in the hull of the boat, lost in the moment, I let wave after wave of pleasure wash over me.

What in God's name just happened? I'm sitting in the boat, lifejacket and the rest of my clothes back on. I feel like my body's been woken from a 100-year sleep, jump-started after years of neglect. I mean, I know what happened. The most fantastic sex I've ever had just happened. I can't help but glance sideways at him to find he's doing the same to me. I'm smiling and it won't leave my lips. I'd forgotten what it was like to enjoy life, enjoy sex. To say that my sex life with Brian was boring is the understatement of the century.

'I didn't mean for that to happen,' Sean says.

'But I'm glad it did,' I say boldly.

'Me too,' he smiles back, and I feel relieved and emboldened some more.

'That was the loveliest time I think I've ever had. I won't forget this afternoon, ever.'

'It wasn't just about the sex, y'know, English. I've wanted to do that for a long time. I hope you don't think I pounce on all my employees.' He steers the boat round the bay.

I shake my head.

'I didn't plan to fall for you.' He looks from me out to sea again. 'It just happened. It was hard to resist. You're very beautiful, funny, and bloody gutsy. I just couldn't help myself.'

I'm not blushing, I feel like I'm blossoming. The empty feeling has gone. I feel happy. I want to make plans.

'And you are a dreadful patient, infuriating and unbelievably fanciable,' I shake my hair out in the wind. Who is this woman and where is the old Fi? I feel almost serene, but there's a nag at the back of my mind. I have to face facts. No matter how much I enjoyed my afternoon of lovemaking with Sean, he is in 'an arrangement' and this can't happen again. Oh, and of course Margaret must never find out about this either. It would break her heart and our friendship. But I've kept enough things locked away inside during my growing up and throughout my time with Brian; this can go in there with them and I'll just bring out the memory when I want to enjoy it. However, I wouldn't say no to a repeat performance, here and now, just to go in the memory box, and I wonder if he's feeling the same.

Sean couldn't deny the happiness he was feeling. It was like a new beginning, a fresh start. The heron was keeping pace with the boat and right now Sean felt he was flying with him, free from the thoughts that had kept him prisoner: the guilt about the crash; not being able to make it right. But now, he felt anything was possible. He had to speak to Nancy and explain. They were both adults. Theirs had been a relationship of convenience. Now he'd found love and he had to take a chance on it. But he mustn't let this happen again until he had finished with Nancy. It wasn't fair on either of them. He turned the boat round the headland and headed for shore.

There, in the distance on the driveway, was the black BMW. He had from here to there to work out what to say.

Chapter Thirty-nine

My happy bubble is burst. In its place, guilt is pouring in. But I remind myself that I'm not the only one with a secret around here now. And more than ever I need to tell Sean about Nancy's betrayal.

'Well, well. Out on the boat? I thought you didn't "do" water.' Nancy is tapping an envelope with her bright red acrylic nails as I walk up the bank towards the cottage.

'There are a lot of things I didn't used to "do",' I say, and I just don't recognise my own confident voice. I keep walking, my fingers holding the little pearl necklace round my neck. I leave her standing on the shore, partly because I feel so guilty and partly because I don't want to see them together. I go into the cottage, and although it's still quite warm outside, I put turf on the fire. I hear Nancy and Sean approaching. They appear to be having words. I tense up and decide to head straight for the shower. I don't want this lovely feeling that's still glowing away inside me to leave just yet.

'Ah, Fi,' Nancy catches me on the way to the bathroom. I don't want a confrontation but if it comes to it, I'll say here and now what I heard her saying on the phone; how she's cutting Sean out of the oyster deal.

'This came for you while you were having your . . . sailing lesson.' She smiles tightly and holds out a cream envelope.

That puts me on the back foot. I frown. I haven't received any post in nearly three months. No one knows I'm here.

'Well, I'm guessing it's for you.' She's still holding it out to me and I have no option but to take it from her, like the poisoned chalice or maybe even the black spot. I look down. I recognise the handwriting straightaway, and the humiliation and shame I felt when I first arrived here comes flooding back.

'It says "For Fiona Goodchild",' Sean's looking over my shoulder and I can feel his breath on my neck and want to melt into the same pool of passion I've just stepped out of. '"Dooleybridge Oyster Festival",' he reads aloud. 'Looks important.' Sean puts his arm around me to take the letter. I turn to look at him and he returns my look. It seems we're there for just a second or two longer than we should be and I find it hard to tear myself away, him with his arm around me and his hand on the letter, his breath on my neck. But I must and I do, furious with myself as I feel my cheeks starting to flush, giving me away.

Nancy tilts her head slightly and narrows her eyes. I know she's seen something in that look and she knows I know that.

'By the way, Fi,' she finally says. My stomach tightens. 'Dan was asking after you in the pub today. Says he hasn't seen you for a while. I said you'd be at the Pearl Queen selection party,' she smiles sweetly, too sweetly.

'Well, I'll be there helping out,' I bluster.

'I think he was hoping for a date. You haven't been stringing him along, have you?' Nancy says mischievously, and tuts. 'No one likes a tease,' and she snakes her arm around Sean's shoulders.

My throat goes dry. 'No.' This is too uncomfortable for

words. 'It'll be lovely, I'm sure,' I find myself saying, as if it's going to throw her off the scent.

'Good,' she claps her hands together, 'I love matchmaking.' Her eyes sparkle, but not with pixie dust, more like poison. She's marking my card. Sean pulls away from Nancy, suddenly looking thunderous. Nancy looks like a cat whose mouse has got away and is determined to get it back. Sean's obviously regretting what just happened. Maybe it was nothing more than a moment of madness, a wonderful moment of madness.

'I'll take that. I'll sort it out.' I take the envelope from Sean and shove it in my back pocket. Sean tuts and goes to put on his boots by the door.

'Someone you know?' Nancy is keeping her eyes on me.

'Someone I used to know, more like,' I say quietly. Nancy looks in Sean's direction. He opens the door and Grace rushes out.

'Looks like someone's keeping secrets,' she says loudly and cattily.

'Maybe I'm not the only one with a secret,' I say quietly back, out of Sean's earshot. 'Just when were you planning to tell Sean about your deal with Henri?' We hold each other's glare. I pull away and slip off to my room and push the letter into the drawer by my bed. There is no way I can face whatever it is that Brian has to say right now. I don't want to think about it. My cheeks burn with humiliation. I don't need to be reminded of what a fool I feel.

Even in such a small cottage it's amazing how Sean and I manage to avoid each other for the next week. Sean has taken over the farmers' markets again and is back giving lessons at the sailing school. He says it frees me up to get the Pearl

Queen night ready with Margaret, but I think he just doesn't want to be anywhere near me.

We're holding the competition in the library, where we can push back the bookshelves like they do on court days. Dan's hosting it from the podium used by the magistrate and the contestants will walk up the middle of the room. They'll use the space behind the bookshelves at the back as a green room. I'm baking up a storm in the cottage kitchen: sausage rolls, mini pasties, ham sandwiches, and tuna and cheese puffs.

A car horn beeps on the drive and I run to my bedroom and look out of the window. Margaret's getting out of the car, holding her coat around her against the wind. I can see her looking around for signs of Sean. Once again that guilt takes hold of me. How could I go from feeling so positive about life to feeling this low again?

I take down the dress that Maire's altered for me from my wardrobe door. In return I've made another delivery of oyster shells to the art shop. Then I go to the kitchen and pick up the trays of sausage rolls. I open the front door and Margaret sails in on a gust of wind and excitement.

'Oh, wow, you've done an amazing job here,' she says, slipping a sausage roll into her mouth. 'I can do your make-up again tonight, if you like.'

'D'you know, I think I might have a go at it myself tonight,' I say as we head to the door.

'Cool,' she says, still chewing on the sausage roll. 'Use my stuff, whatever you want.'

'Thank you.' I want to tell her what a good friend she's been and what a crap one I've been. But I can't.

'Are you OK, Fi?' she asks before we head to the car.

'Yes, fine,' I say, checking on Grace and keeping my blushes to myself.

'You seem . . . different,' says Margaret, helping herself to another sausage roll.

'No, don't be daft, I'm grand,' I say, realising I've slipped into local-speak.

'Hey, is there something you're not telling me?' She's expanding further with hot air and excitement by the minute.

'No, there's not, nothing, really . . . Now, come on,' I usher her out, our arms full of bite-sized morsels. 'And don't eat any more on the way!' I say bossily, deflecting attention from my guilty secret. Margaret keeps looking sideways at me all the way to the library.

I'm clearing down the last remaining books from the librarian's desk and arranging the sausage rolls and tuna puffs on it. Rosie and Lily are going to do teas and coffees.

'I've got it!' Margaret shouts.

'I wonder if we should've offered a bar,' I say, looking at the table of food. Margaret waves away my worries.

'They can have a drink afterwards. Otherwise they'll be up and down to the bar and we'll never get the important business done. The festival is only a week away and we need to crown a Pearl Queen. Anyway, are you listening? I said I'd got it!'

'Got what?' I look around her. Raffle tickets, money box, microphone. I can't think of anything we've missed.

'It's Dan!' she beams. I look round. I hadn't seen anyone come in.

'Where?'

'Not here. But it is, isn't it?' She's grinning and clutching a poster for the event to her chest, sellotape in each of the corners.

'Sorry, Margaret, what are you talking about?' The poster's stuck to her. I peel it away.

'You and him.' She rolls her eyes from side to side. 'You finally got it on!' she announces, and my mouth drops open, just as the door blows itself open, sending the poster up into my face.

'I knew it,' Margaret mouths as she grabs the poster back off me and slides off to put it up outside. I have no idea where to go with this. Do I keep denying it or do I let her think it's Dan? Maybe then that'll be an end to it.

As we head back to the pub to get changed, Margaret links her arm through mine, chuffed to bits that she thinks she's found out who's put the glint in my eye. Wickedly, I decide not to dissuade her. Not for the time being anyway.

'It was just a one-off,' I say, as she tries to quiz me some more, swallowing hard and trying to get rid of the bitter taste of lies from my mouth.

'I think it's lovely.' Margaret has a soft, dreamy look on her face as she takes down her dress from the back of her bedroom door. 'I just hope Sean decides to finally have a moment of madness with me.'

I am cringing inside.

'Just going to use the bathroom.' I stand up, grabbing my own dress and taking it with me.

I slide my altered wedding dress down over my hips and it hugs me in all the right places. It feels perfect, not like before. Before, this dress made me feel like someone I wasn't. Now it feels like me. Shorter, simpler, stripped of all the unnecessary trimmings. I love it.

I pull out the shaving mirror and put on some tinted moisturiser, then a dusting of eyeshadow, mascara and a light pink lipstick. I finish it off with a lick of lipgloss, smack my lips together and then look in the mirror. There is a smile tugging at the corners of my mouth. I feel happy with how I look. I wonder if Sean will turn up this evening. My whole body aches for him all over again. I want to tell him that there's nothing going on between Dan and me. But I know I've got to keep away from him. I can't let what happened on the boat happen again. I run my hands over my hips and go back into Margaret's room.

'Wow!' I say as Margaret turns to me.

'Wow yourself!' she beams back. Margaret is wearing a deep blue short dress with a long fish tail at the back. She's got pale shimmering tights on, blue high heels, several hairpieces, and matching diamanté earrings and tiara.

'You look fantastic,' she says, staring at me, her mouth open. 'Where did you get that dress from?'

I look down at it. My hand touches the little pearl around my neck.

'It was my wedding dress. Maire altered it for me.'

'It's so you! It's perfect!'

'The only thing I've realised is that I don't have any shoes to go with it.' I look at my feet. 'I threw away the matching shoes.'

'I've got just the thing,' Margaret says, and dives into the bottom of her wardrobe. 'Here!' she pulls out a pair of shoes and turns to me. She's holding a pair of light pink ballet-style pumps.

'Oh, Margaret, they're perfect!'

'They're yours. I've only worn them once. They're not me,

but they're definitely you,' she smiles. 'Right, let's go and get this party started,' she says, scooping up her little clutch bag. I slip on the shoes and she hangs on to my arm for dear life as she totters down the stairs and out into the bar.

There's a wolf whistle from Frank, and Patsy gives her a proud hug.

'We'll be over now. Good luck, love,' he shouts after us as we totter out into the drizzle. Margaret holds her clutch bag over her head and we clip-clop our way to the library.

Evelyn arrives and takes up her post by the door. Contestants from outside the area turn up and Evelyn directs them behind the screen of books. Even Rosie's sister, Lily, has decided to enter. I think it's the chance of dinner for two with Dan that has brought in a lot of the contestants.

'Not entering yourself?' says Frank as he sidles into the row of seats behind me. The library begins to fill up. Margaret slips out from behind the book screen to see me.

'All OK?' She bobs down as if trying to hide herself from the public. Evelyn and John Joe's family are here supporting their daughter and a daughter-in-law-to-be, who are both entering. Rosie and her parents and the kids are there supporting Lily. Joan the library's cleaner, who's six foot tall with an American football player's shoulders, is taking part along with the girls from the hairdresser's. All of them are short with matching hair colour, and Siobhan, the owner. There's Brid from the bank who's wearing a brooch in her suit lapel and has decorated her thick glasses with tinsel for the occasion. Deidre, one of the school teachers, who's heavily pregnant with her fifth child, but has brought a huge following from her class. Even the local vet and the Polish basket-maker from Galway market have come. Gerald brings in Grandad, and Evelyn negotiates him a place down the front after much chair moving.

'Brilliant turn-out,' I whisper to Margaret.

'Oh, I need another wee. It's the nerves.' She looks around. 'Is he here yet?' she whispers, not taking her eyes off the room.

I shake my head before realising she's not talking about the same person I am.

'Oh, no,' I shake my head again. Just then my heart gives a lurch as Sean appears in the doorway. His hands are shoved into his pockets. People turn to look at him. He spots me and I spot him. I raise my hand in a half wave and he starts to make his way towards me.

'Oh, look, there he is,' says Margaret, standing up straight. 'Dan, over here!' Dan's standing in the doorway behind Sean. He rubs his hands together and smiles round at the gathered audience.

'Excuse me,' he says, and pushes past Sean towards Margaret. Sean's face darkens as Dan passes him. Dan slides into the seat next to me, stretches out his long legs and rests his arm around the back of my chair.

'So, we all set?' he looks around at the makeshift venue. 'Would you do me a favour?' he hands me his camera. 'I need plenty of shots for this chapter in the book.'

'Sure,' I say. I'm much happier hiding behind the camera than I am in front of it.

'I'm going back there.' Margaret points to the makeshift green room but she's looking at Sean. 'Enjoy yourselves!' She winks and disappears.

'No, wait . . .' But she's gone, leaving me with Dan, his arm still around my chair.

'Actually, I've got to check on the um . . . food,' I point towards the desk where Frank is now tucking into the sausage rolls. I brush past Dan and he grins.

'You carry on, I'll just get a feel for things.' He stands up after me and walks towards the podium.

Sean's still standing at the back of the room. His face brightens a little when he sees me and the butterflies do the pogo in my stomach.

'Hey,' he says.

'Hey,' is all I can reply.

'Sean, you came!' Margaret appears from nowhere and throws an arm around him. He keeps his hands in his pockets but smiles affectionately.

'I see he's making himself at home,' Sean nods towards Dan who's adjusting the microphone to the right height. I stifle a smile but should really defend Dan. He's the one pulling in all the punters.

'He's doing a great job.'

'You would say that, now that you and he are . . .' Margaret does that head shaking thing again.

My mouth drops.

'What? Margaret!'

'Sorry, I know it's meant to be a secret but you can trust Sean. And I think it's so sweet!' She claps her hands together. 'Rather wish I'd bagged him for myself now.'

'No, it's just . . .' I'm lost for words. I look back at Sean's face, and it's as if the dark cloud has just rolled in again and is threatening a storm.

I can't say anything. I can't say that it was Sean, not Dan, in front of Margaret. But saying nothing means he believes I'm now actually with Dan. Oh, bugger it!

He turns to leave.

'Not going already, are you, Sean?' Margaret looks gutted.

'Just came in to see you had everything you need. And I see you have.' He looks straight at me. I am bursting with indignation. I have to say something.

'It's not like I was in a relationship or anything. I'm a free woman. I'm not hurting anyone . . .' I'm just digging myself a deeper hole.

He turns to leave, running straight into Nancy who arrives on a cloud of Coco Chanel.

'Oh, I thought I'd find you here.'

My bravado disappears.

'I never hid anything,' he whispers under his breath to me.

My heart is banging so loudly I think everyone else can hear it. Margaret is glaring daggers at Nancy.

'Good evening everybody,' Dan booms across the room, stopping everyone's conversations.

'I'm just leaving,' Sean says to Nancy.

'Oh no, not yet. All the press are here. Besides, I have a surprise later,' she smiles naughtily. Sean doesn't react.

'Any more entrants before we begin?' Dan continues. 'This is, as you all know, for the title of Pearl Queen and her Princess for the Dooleybridge oyster festival in just a week's time.'

'You can stay, I'm off,' says Sean.

'You can't go,' Nancy suddenly looks unusually flustered.

'Why not? You don't need me here. All you need is my oysters,' he says through gritted teeth.

'But I'd like you to stay,' she pouts. 'Besides, without me those oysters won't have homes to go to.' She smiles sweetly. I can't believe she just said that.

Sean takes a deep breath.

'Of course,' he says.

'Besides, I think I'd look rather good on the front page of the Galway Gazette as the Pearl Queen.' She throws off her coat and Sean catches it over his arm as she sashays her way towards Evelyn to give in her name. Margaret glowers. This looks like war.

The contestants gather on stage and then one by one Dan will talk to them. Once they've answered his questions they'll walk off the stage and down through the audience to the waiting area. There is a wall of ice between Sean and me as we stand at the back of the room watching. Dan approaches his first contestant and we all clap politely. Nancy is contestant number 7.

The competition has really livened up by the time Dan gets to Nancy. 'So, Nancy, as festival organiser, what does bringing back the Dooleybridge oyster festival mean to you?' Dan asks.

'Well, I think the business opportunities are obvious. It will open more doors when we take the oysters produced here overseas, it will help people recognise the name and make it a brand. That can only be good for local suppliers.' We all clap and Evelyn and John Joe nod their heads in agreement.

Sean leans over and whispers in my ear, 'I'm sorry. I'm sorry for everything.'

I wonder if I've heard him right. What does he mean? Sorry it's worked out like this or sorry it ever happened? My mind is buzzing.

Margaret is contestant number 8. She doesn't wait for Dan to ask the question. She grabs the mike out of his hand.

'This festival will put Dooleybridge back on the map.

People will come here and see what a fab town it is. It'll make us famous worldwide and everyone will want to visit. The festival will remind people what a great town this once was and can be again. Dooleybridge is gonna rock!' she shouts, and Frank, Seamus and Padraig, Evelyn and John Joe are up on their feet. Grandad is rolling backwards and forwards in his chair with glee.

There's a short interval where the rest of the sausage rolls and pasties are devoured and half the audience go outside for a fag break.

'You were great,' I tell Margaret. Sean hands Nancy her coat and says nothing.

'And our Pearl Queen is . . .' Everyone is back in their seats and the contestants are biting their nails on stage. Dan has obviously been watching *X Factor* and is keeping the audience waiting for ever.

I've got everything crossed for Margaret. She wants this so much and she deserves it. None of this would be happening if it wasn't for her.

I hold my breath.

'. . . Nancy Dubois!' Dan announces with a fake drum roll.

Some of the room claps, others mutter the word 'fixed' and a few just get up to leave.

Nancy steps forward to accept her diamanté crown, the one Margaret hand-picked and has been practising wearing for weeks. Margaret looks like she's been kicked in the guts.

'And the runner up is . . . Margaret!' And the whole place erupts with cheers and clapping. Those who had been leaving stop and join in. Margaret straightens herself and steps forward to where Dan is waiting to greet her. He gives her a small bouquet, much smaller than the Queen's, and then goes to kiss her on both cheeks. Margaret, all of a dither, goes the wrong way and they end up meeting in the middle, on the lips, while the photographer from the *Galway Gazette* clicks away.

Back at the pub, it's busier than it has been in ages.

'I need you to help,' Patsy calls to Margaret, who puts down her clutch bag and totters behind the bar. I sit on the stool at the end of the bar.

'I really hope you don't think I did that on purpose,' Margaret is still fretting about the kiss and is apologising to me. At least it's taking her mind off the many acts of violence she wants to commit on Nancy.

'Of course not,' I laugh and wave a hand, wishing I could tell her that there's no reason for her to feel bad. 'Honestly, it's fine.'

Nancy arrives, holding onto her tiara and carrying her bouquet. There are large daisies among the flowers, Margaret's favourites. Her posy is in a pint pot at the end of the bar. It's mostly chrysanthemums.

Margaret is serving drinks. Sean comes in behind Nancy, who is chatting with the *Gazette* owner and Dan.

'Let me get some drinks,' she says, smiling all the way to the bar.

'Prosecco, please, a few bottles, and hand them round,' she instructs Margaret, who turns away and bites her bottom lip in fury. Sean stands beside me but says nothing. I can smell his aftershave, soft yet spicy. I feel as though he's waiting for me to say something, but I can't think what. It's like we're back to where we started in the pub. Only this time there is so much stuff that I want to say. Like how I can't bear standing this close to him and not being able to touch him. Like how I love the way his hair is too long and falls round his face and drives him nuts. Like how I love how passionate he is about his oysters and how I loved the night we looked up at the stars together. There are many things about Sean Thornton that I have come to really love, I realise as I stand there.

'Now then, if we've all got a glass,' Nancy says, 'I'd like to thank everyone for coming, for making this a very special night. And to make this even more special,' she looks to me and then to Sean, 'I'd like to announce my engagement to my partner, Sean Thornton!'

She raises her glass and the photographer clicks away as she kisses Sean's surprised face. My hand flips over, sending my Prosecco all over the bar and me at the same time.

'You're engaged!' I blurt out, and Nancy looks at me and smiles.

Chapter Forty

I thought they were breaking up, not getting married! This must be what he'd meant when he said he was sorry.

'Hey, congratulations,' Dan comes over and kisses Nancy on the cheek and shakes Sean by the reluctant hand.

'Thank you,' Nancy poses for another picture.

'Hope you don't mind me taking your fiancée out for dinner as part of her prize,' Dan jokes. Sean doesn't move.

'It was the perfect time to do it, what with all the press here,' Nancy says under her breath. 'Great publicity. The Pearl Queen and her oyster catcher, did you get that?' she says loudly to the journalist.

'We should've discussed this,' Sean says under his breath, but I overhear.

'Sorry. I just saw the opportunity and went for it. It's great for business. Now, pose for a picture. Sorry, my shy fiancé,' she flirts with the journalist. 'And think how happy Maman and Papa will be.' Sean looks at her then excuses himself and goes for a cigarette.

'Congratulations,' I'm quick to say to Nancy, to show I'm not at all distressed.

'Thank you,' she says smugly and sips her drink. 'And once we're married, what's his is mine, right?' She arches an eyebrow at me. 'It's our business. So whatever you think you might have overheard, or whatever plans you might have had for you and Sean, he and I are engaged now. It's our business.'

The oysters. Of course, why else would she want to do this? She thinks I'm going to tell him about her plan. She thinks I'm going to get in between her and the native oysters.

I take the tea towel from Margaret and mop the spilt drink from my dress.

'They're getting married.' Margaret looks like she's had all the fight taken out of her. She picks up a glass of Prosecco from the bar and knocks it back in one. Her night couldn't get any worse.

I knock back another Prosecco too.

'I thought it was a casual thing, a relationship of convenience,' I say without thinking. Too late. Margaret is staring at me in horror.

'It wasn't Dan, was it? It was Sean!'

She bursts into tears and runs out of the bar. Nancy looks like a peacock showing off its colours, surrounded by the press. I feel like a bigger fool than I ever did when I first arrived here. It's happening all over again. I grab my waterproof and half run, half stumble all the way back to the cottage. In my room I pull out the letter that arrived at the farm. It's from Brian. But I can't read it. My eyes are full of tears. I put my face into Grace's fur and she keeps me company until dawn finally comes.

Sean drove back to the farm just before dawn and went straight out on the boat. What a fucking mess! He held his face to the wind and shut his eyes. His body ached from sleeping on Nancy's settee. They'd had an almighty row when they got back after Nancy's engagement announcement in the pub and he'd refused to join her in bed. He knew there was no way he could come home last night. Not until he'd worked this mess out.

He didn't love Nancy. They'd never talked about marriage. She'd never wanted anything like that. It was a relationship that had worked for both of them. And then he'd met Fi. Funny, sweet, kind, trustworthy, brave Fi. She was a lioness, protecting what she cared about. And he thought she had come to care about him. There'd been no mistaking the chemistry between them that day on the boat. He gave a little shiver of excitement at the memory.

The heron's wings beat rhythmically beside him.

He didn't want to marry Nancy, but without Nancy and the restaurant he wouldn't be able to pay the loan back. He'd lose the farm, but most worrying of all, he'd lose Fi – if he couldn't offer her a job she'd leave and he'd never see her again.

He let out the ropes, urged the boat to go faster. He stood up, feeling the full force of the wind against his body, shutting his eyes.

Nancy had organised an engagement party for the night before the oyster festival in The Pearl. All her friends and family were coming over from France and she hoped it would swell numbers even more and start the festival weekend with a bang.

There was nothing else for it. He had to go ahead with Nancy's plan or he'd lose Fi for good.

The final few days before the festival drag. The weather matches my mood: dark, grey and miserable. Margaret hasn't been anywhere near the farm and Sean has been staying in Galway, coming back early in the morning to harvest the oysters. He's out on the boat, dredging them, and I'm in the shed, washing, purifying and bagging them ready for festival day. We work silently from sun up to sun down. When the tide is too far out to get the boat close to shore we float the oysters in on a raft and then load them onto the tractor and I drive them to the shed. I am more alone than I have ever felt before, and not in the physical sense. I've quite enjoyed being here with Grace, Freddie and Mercury, Brenda and the hens. But I have lost Sean for good. And I have lost my best friend. I take a break and sit down on a rock, on the banks of the bay, and hug my knees to my chest. Oh God! I cringe, putting my head on my knees. I've ruined everything.

The day before the festival, I'm up early but we've run out of tea. I grab my bag, call Grace and walk into town, swatting away midges as I wander towards Rosie's in the early morning mist.

Outside the B&B there are lots of cars. I frown. One in particular I recognise. A black BMW. Nancy's BMW. The front door suddenly opens and there's Nancy. Her long dark hair is falling through the fingers of another as she kisses him farewell. She and Sean have obviously made up and decided not to stay at the farm. I scuttle on past, my head down.

'*Au revoir, à tout à l'heure,*' I hear her say. It's unusual to hear her speaking French. Then he replies, in French. Only it's not Sean, I realise, as I glance quickly round – just in time for Nancy to see me and for me to see Nancy sneaking out of another man's room at dawn. I need to find Sean and tell him exactly what's going on.

I march back to the farm and go straight to the sheds. Where is he? He's not back. I grab a broom and start sweeping while I work out what I'm going to say. I switch the radio on as I pass it. The odd tiny crab scuttles out at me and I scoop them up and plop them into a bucket. I try and run through a mental list while working out what to say to Sean. The marquee is up. The chef from Galway has been emailing his requirements constantly. The B&Bs are ready for their guests, the Galway bands are booked, and the bar is stocked. The oysters have finally been harvested, cleaned and bagged.

I hear tyres on the gravel and run out.

'Sean!' I shout.

But it's not Sean. Nancy is standing there wearing high black patent leather boots, and her hands are in the pockets of her black coat, like an iron fist in a velvet glove. She smiles at me but I don't attempt to smile back. I turn back to the shed. She follows me.

'So, we all ready?' she asks.

'The oysters are ready, yes.' I carry on sweeping furiously.

'Good. Our guests have started arriving and everything's ready for our engagement party tonight.'

I give an ironic laugh.

She looks around the shed, her boots clip, clipping on the stone floor. 'I'd invite you, but I know you have a lot on,' she says pointedly.

'Well . . . actually, everything is ready. All I have to do now is tell Sean about your cosy set-up with Henri.' I lean on the broom.

'Like I say, you'll be busy . . . packing for one thing,' Nancy glares at me. The smile is gone and her lip is curled. Her eyes are as dark as the sky outside.

'Oh, I'm not leaving . . . certainly not until I've told Sean what you're up to and who with.'

'Oh yes you are. I want you out of here. Those oysters are finally about to make me, and I don't want you . . . distracting Sean. We're engaged now. Those oysters are half mine and I don't want anything or anyone coming between us.' She's pointing a black-gloved finger at me. If I am going, I'm not going quietly, I decide there and then.

'You don't love Sean. You're tucking him up. You're not even letting him in on the deal. You're going to pay him a flat fee for the oysters and sell the ones you don't need on to lover boy, I presume. I heard it all.' I grip my broom.

'Like I say, I don't want you around causing trouble. I want you gone by the time those oysters leave here for the kitchen. By the time they're served up to the guests and the shucking competition, you will be on a plane out of here. I take it you heard that too?'

I lift my chin.

'Where to?'

'Anywhere!' she spits.

I have to ask and I do it with a shrug, 'And if I don't?'

'Without me and our contract Sean won't have a buyer. You'll put yourself out of a job and you'll ruin him. Jimmy Power will call in his debt and Sean will have to sell. That's not what you want, is it? Someone else taking over the farm? There's already been interest,' she says patronisingly.

Fury bubbles up inside me. 'Sean has to know! He'll find another buyer. You're not the only oyster broker or restaurateur who wants those oysters. In fact, the place will be heaving with new customers at the festival tomorrow. You've done him a favour!'

'Those oysters are staying with me. There will also be a lot of press coming tomorrow. I can think of a couple of tabloid magazines who would love to know the story of the woman jilted by her gay groom, who left her at the altar for the best man. And him a minor celebrity! Ex-rugby player turned radio presenter. That sounds like just the sort of story they'll love.' She's holding my envelope, the one from Brian. She's been in my bedroom!

'Give me that!' I shout, and snatch the letter from her hand, but it's too late; she knows more about what's written in it than I do.

'Brian knows where you are now, what you're doing,' she says, confirming more details of the letter. I hold it to my tightening chest.

'I want you gone,' she says, turning on her heel. 'Or else everyone will know about your wedding day fiasco and how you ended up an oyster farmer's assistant in the middle of nowhere. You'll turn this farm into a tabloid tourist destination. There'll be strangers crawling all over the place wanting to get a glimpse of the runaway bride.'

'And what about Sean, what about what he wants?'

'Sean doesn't want unwanted visitors! You've seen what happens when members of the public come up here. He wants his farm and the quiet life. He'll do anything to keep it. We both get what we want from this,' she shouts over her shoulder. 'Sean pays his licence, I get my oysters. We're both happy. Sean would never pick you over his farm,' she laughs hollowly and goes to get into her car.

Just at that moment Sean's van comes down the lane. He pulls up next to Nancy and gets out quickly.

'What's going on?' he asks, concerned, looking from

Nancy to me. I don't know what to do. Should I tell him? Or is she right? Would I ruin him if I say anything? Will I ruin him if I stay?

'Fi and I were just going over the arrangements for the weekend. Making sure we understand exactly what needs to happen.' She pulls down her dark glasses and walks towards her car.

Humiliation returns to hit me round the face like a wet fish. This time it's worse than before, with Brian. This time I'd had my eyes wide open; I knew he was taken. Only this time I actually fell in love. But he chose Nancy, not me. He chose his business, not me. I feel used, stupid and ashamed.

I look at the pair of them. 'You know what, you two deserve each other.' I throw down the broom with a clatter and walk towards them. I don't have anything to lose any more. 'I would rather spend one day with someone I love and who loves me back than a lifetime married to someone because it "worked" for me. I thank God my fiancé Brian didn't have the balls to go through with married life. At least I've finally managed to find out what it means to really love someone. And if I never feel that again, at least I will have known what it was like.' I take a deep breath to stop any tears falling and then turn and run off down the lane towards town.

'Fi, wait!' I hear Sean shout, but I just keep running, well, until I'm out of sight of the farm. My heart is pumping and so are my veins. I put my hands to my knees and take huge dragging breaths. Then slowly I stand up and walk the rest of the way into town. I am going to leave, like Nancy said, because I don't want to stay and watch Sean and Nancy get

married. I can't see him with someone else, someone he doesn't love. But I won't go to my mum's. I'm not going back to that. I need to keep moving forwards. Who knows, maybe one day I'll be able to stop running.

Chapter Forty-one

When I reach the chalet in Rosie's garden I knock loudly.

Dan opens the door looking surprised.

I dive straight in. 'Dan, hi, look, about the job, the one you were telling me about the other week. I know it's a long shot, but I was wondering if there was any chance it was still free?'

He stares at me blankly. I try to slow down a bit.

'Dan, I've come about the job. Have you found someone, in Boston? If not, I'm your woman. I can leave now,' I gabble. His face lights up.

'This could be perfect!' he exclaims. Then his face drops to a frown again. 'What about you and Sean? I thought you were still working with him.'

'I just think it's time I moved on.' I muster a smile from somewhere, but find I'm swinging my arms to and fro nervously and knock over a lamp which we both try and catch.

'You think we can work together?' Dan asks.

'Absolutely!' I say, neither of us letting go of the lamp. 'I think we'd make a great team . . .'

He looks at me. 'There's just one thing,' he says cautiously. 'I may have misled you, given you mixed signals. I may have suggested there was more on offer than a job.'

'Oh no, I . . .' The elephant in the room just got bigger.

'But the thing is, I'm sort of . . . involved with someone now,' he says slowly.

I hold my hands up. I've heard enough.

'Dan, I want a job. One as far away from here as possible. I want to work for you, I definitely don't want to sleep with you,' I say.

'That's what you said before, remember?' A voice cuts across us and then she appears from the bedroom wearing nothing but one of Dan's T-shirts.

'Oh my God! Margaret!'

She can't help but grin from ear to ear as Dan pulls her to him and kisses the top her head.

'Margaret, what I did was unforgivable. And if it's any consolation I am hurting now more than I ever thought possible. I was a fool to myself and to you.'

'Well, he was pretty fanciable.' Margaret looks up at Dan. 'But I think you did me a favour.' She breaks into a broad smile and I hug her and then him.

'So, about the job?' Dan breaks up the hug. 'It's yours if you want it. I still have more business here in Ireland,' he looks at Margaret, 'so I can't leave yet. But it would be great to know the office is in safe hands. You can leave straightaway?'

I nod, more than I need to.

'But what about the festival?' Margaret suddenly looks horrified. 'It's tomorrow!'

'It's all organised. I'd only be doing coat duty and I just don't think I can watch the happy couple any more.'

Margaret's eyes fill up and she hugs me.

'I have to go,' I say, but choke. I feel her nod as we hug again. She understands.

'You are the best friend I have ever had,' I tell her as the tears roll down my cheeks.

'Ditto,' she says.

Back at the farm, Sean is just closing up the shed. The oyster bags are all laid out on the mended trestle tables, which I destroyed all those months ago. They're ready for tomorrow. Further down the bay the dark clouds are rolling in. Even Grace looks like she's lost a chicken leg and found a wishbone. She's lying with her head between her paws, like she knows everything is about to change.

'High tide tonight,' Sean says.

'Hadn't you better go and get ready? Nancy'll be wondering where you are. It's your engagement party after all.'

'Fi, about that . . .' he says.

'I think we've said all that needs to be said. This place means the world to you. You have to hang on to it and Nancy's your best bet for that,' I say, and a few more tears roll down my cheeks. I swipe them away. 'I'm leaving, Sean. It's time for me to move on. I've paid my debt.' Still the tears roll.

He steps closer to me. 'You could stay. If this goes well tomorrow and we sell the oysters, there's plenty of work for you, you don't have to go.'

'I think we both know that I do.' I wipe away the tears and try not to sniff. 'Just . . . watch yourself. Look after you. Don't get hurt trying to hang on to something you love.' He frowns. He looks like he's going to say something, but I don't want to hear it.

'You have to go,' I hurry him along.

'Look, let's sleep on it. We can work it out. See you tomorrow, yeah?' he says.

319

'Yeah,' I say, knowing that I won't. There's nothing else to talk about. I'll be gone by dawn, it's all arranged. David, the postman who doubles up as the hackney driver, is picking me up. Soon I'll be taking 'cabs', not 'taxis' or 'hackneys'. My flight's booked. This time tomorrow, while the oysters are being served, I'll be on my way to my new life in the States.

'Are you going to the festival? The shucking competition?' I ask.

'No, I don't feel part of this place. Maybe I never will. But at least now I can show them my uncle was right, these waters are clean. The cleanest. We have the oysters to show for it.' He breathes in. Nancy was right. This place means everything to him and he'd never risk that.

'Right, see you tomorrow.'

The rain hits my window and slides down it like tears. I pull out a large black bag. This takes me right back to when I was growing up. My mum would come home, produce a roll of value bin bags, and I'd know we were on the move again. At least this time I know where I'm going, well, on paper anyway. Dan has organised an apartment for me. Mary Jo is meeting me at the airport and taking me out to dinner. Then there's a week's handover and my new life will begin. It's everything I could want, an office job dealing with all Dan's engagements, his public appearances, his book publications, and all his media work. I'll be doing what I do best, working behind the scenes. It's what I did for Brian and I know I can do it for Dan. I fold the work clothes I've lived in: the cut-off jeans that became shorts, the joggers Sean found for me and the rest of the eclectic mix of clothes I've gathered since I've been here. I fold away the wedding dress that Maire altered. I doubt I'll wear it again.

Once I get to Boston, Dan's going to give me an advance to help get me settled. I'll go shopping and buy some work clothes. I wonder what kind of shops there will be? Big department stores, all bright lights and fragrance in the air. I try and smile to myself; it's a long way from Dooleybridge, Gerald's café and Rosie's petrol station. Back to being in a city again where everything is to hand: shops, theatres, cinemas and cafés.

The wind is picking up outside. I hope it doesn't rain too much and make the lane difficult to get down. I'll walk to the end of it to get the hackney, I decide. He's due at six tomorrow morning. I doubt I'll sleep at all tonight.

The wind outside is picking up and I go to the front door to check how bad it is. Grace comes with me as she usually does. I'm going to miss her so much. Maybe one day, when I'm settled, I'll be able to have a house and a dog of my own. I rub her head as I look at the waves starting to roll in.

I go back into the cottage, stoke the pot-bellied stove with turf. There have been so many things I've done that I never thought I'd do: the sailing, the market stalls, the oyster eating. The butterflies rush in and do their crazy dance in my stomach again. I touch the pearl around my neck and undo the necklace. I put it on the table and head to bed.

I'm woken by a crash and a whoosh. I think someone's breaking into the house. Grace is howling. My mouth goes dry. Coming round, I realise it's not the plane crash I was dreaming about; there's a storm outside, doing its worst. The one that was due to miss us, no doubt! I don't know what the time is; there's been a power cut. I grab a torch and grapple for my clothes.

'Shh, Grace, it's OK,' I tell her, although my heart's still racing. I pull on the hat and waterproofs that I hadn't planned on wearing again. I open the door a little and it flies open. I look at my mobile phone hopelessly. Why should I think there's going to be any signal here tonight? But it does tell me the time: ten past twelve. I shove it back in my pocket. Sean and Nancy's party will be in full swing. Then there's a huge gust and I clutch my hands over my mouth as I watch a mesh bag full of the oysters, Sean's native oysters, get ripped from its trestle table; the elasticated ropes must have given up. It flies across the bay and lands some way away on the rocks.

I shake my head and then watch the next and then the next bag fly off its mooring. 'No, no, no!' I scream out loud. 'Noooooooo!' My face is screwed up. My stomach is in knots. 'Please, no more . . .'

What if the storm hasn't even reached Galway and Sean is blissfully unaware of what's going on? Everything he cares about is being trashed right in front of my eyes. I turn back to the cottage. I'd like to think this isn't my problem any more, that I could just walk away. I get as far as the house when I hear more bags ripping away from their tables and splashing through the water.

Oh God! All that work, for nothing. I can't let this happen again. I've run away from everything that has gone wrong in my life, just like my mum, but I don't want to be like her. I can't do it this time. I run round to the sheds, pull back the big doors and grab a lifejacket. I put it on, take a huge breath and head towards the jetty where the boat is moored.

But it's no use, the storm's too rough. I'll be tossed out of the boat as soon as I sit in it. I wait and watch for the next two hours, my fingers in my mouth, as each bag flies in a different direction, making a mental note of where they've gone. When the storm begins to recede I run back down to the boat. It's still rough but I untie the first rope and then the second. The boat sways violently in the wind. I can't get in. I jump down into the chest-high water. I bounce and jump but can't make it into the boat. My arms don't have the strength. I bounce and jump again. The boat begins to move. Oh God, I'll lose the boat as well at this rate. I give an almighty jump this time and tumble head first into it, rolling onto my back.

I've done it before, I can do it again, I tell myself, as the Greek holiday comes flooding back. I push it to one side. I have let my fear of 'what if' hold me back for too long. What if I don't do anything! Now that will be a regret.

I grab hold of the rudder. Grace is watching from the shore. I can see the green glints in her eyes as I swing the torch round and suddenly the boat takes off at a lick.

'Argh!' I scream and I tumble backwards. I can see the corner of an oyster bag in my torch light, poking up in the water. I steer the boat towards it and scoop it up, dripping with water and seaweed.

'One!' I shout at Grace who barks back. A wave crashes against the boat, knocking me sideways. I quickly put the bag in the boat and grab the rudder. I guide the boat around the bay. Slowly it's starting to get light. At one point I have to put down the anchor and, summoning all my courage, jump out of the boat again. The water is up to my chest and I climb up the rocks and grab another two bags. I can see some other bags have blown into the bay next door. I get back in the boat and head further out. The wind fills the sail and it takes all my strength to guide the boat round the bay.

In the restaurant the party was in full swing. It was late, well into the early hours of the morning, but no one seemed to care. Sean sighed. A long buffet table was being constantly reloaded and glasses of champagne topped up. There were purple and silver helium balloons on the tables and soft jazz music filled the air, taking the edge off the forced laughter. Waitresses walked around offering bottles or trays of bite-sized delights. But none of it tasted of anything to Sean. The only good thing was that Jean François and Monique, Nancy's parents, were there. In fact they were about the only people Sean recognised – apart from Henri, that is. Sean had never liked Henri and had given him a wide berth all night. As had Nancy, surprisingly, until now.

Jean François, Monique and Sean had been sitting at a table all night, trying to discuss the worries of the French oyster farmers and the good news about the native oysters.

'Your uncle would be so proud of you,' Jean François told him, putting his hand over Sean's. 'We are proud of you.'

Monique nodded in agreement. 'You are like family to us.'

The band had slowed things down and people were getting up to dance together, some propping each other up. Henri and Nancy seemed to gravitate towards each other, Sean noticed, as did Jean François and Monique.

'Nancy is a very determined lady,' Jean François said. 'She is driven and knows what she wants. She can't bear the thought of being poor again, like she was growing up. We did our best, but oyster farmers like us, we weren't rich. But I was in here,' he banged his fist to his heart. Monique nodded in agreement. 'My heart was full because I loved what I did and I loved my family.' He put his arm around Monique, who blushed and smiled. 'It is your heart that matters in life. Make sure it is always full.'

Every single one of Jean François's words made sense to Sean. He looked at Nancy.

Henri and Nancy's heads seemed to be getting closer and closer as they held one hand and wrapped the other around each other's waists. Sean wondered if Nancy remembered he was there at all. Jean François and Monique seemed embarrassed and Sean felt for them. They were such good people. Strangely, he didn't feel much himself, just an overwhelming desire for it to be over.

Without Nancy, Sean would lose his farm, but without Fi his heart would be empty. He remembered her words: 'Watch yourself, don't get hurt.' He looked at Nancy again.

'I think I may have to lose something I love,' he said out loud to Jean François. 'Nancy is a wonderful woman,' he said, 'but I can't marry her.' Sean was dying inside, thinking about the pain he must be causing this dear couple.

But suddenly Jean François was smiling. 'You will always be family to us, whether you and Nancy are married or not. Let me give you some words of advice. If you find someone you love, hold on to her very tight. Nothing is more important than love,' he said and Monique nodded, looking back at Nancy and Henri.

'They have been in love since they were eight. They're just too scared to admit it yet. Both too in love with business to have room for love in their lives. Don't be scared of love,

Sean. It's a gift.' Monique held her husband's hand.

Sean watched Nancy and Henri for a moment more and then put down his untouched champagne, kissed Jean François and Monique on both cheeks and walked out, just as the singer announced a toast 'to the happy couple' and everyone cheered.

As the sun starts to creep up over the horizon, the wind has all but gone and I can see the final few bags that have blown up the shore and onto the bog land beside and behind the sheds. I moor the boat and put the bags in the shed.

When I reach the cottage I find I'm absolutely shattered. Every bone in my body is aching and I'm soaked. My stomach turns over and I find myself rushing to the toilet where I'm sick. I turn on the shower and let hot water pour over me, grateful that it hasn't chosen this morning to play silly buggers. My knees are like jelly. The sun is creeping up into the sky and it looks like it's going to be a nice day. Once I'm dry, I dress, and give Grace a final pat on the head.

'Your master'll be back soon,' I assure her, and then I pick up my passport and my bag and head for the door. I can't look back at her. I feel like I'm abandoning her. And it's so hard, but it's for all the right reasons.

I can hear a car coming down the lane, which has saved me a walk, as I'm struggling to put one foot in front of the other. I take a final look at the bay. I know I'm leaving having done my best for it and Sean. I turn back to see Sean's red van pulling into the gates. Behind it is the hackney.

Sean jumps out of the van.

'I just heard it on the news, about the storm.' He looks around worried. 'Are you OK?'

'They're all in the shed. They're all safe,' I say wearily, and walk to the hackney that's turning round. I get in, watching Sean pull back the shed doors. I don't think he's realised I'm leaving and I think quite possibly that's for the best.

'Galway coach station, please. I'm catching the bus to Shannon airport.' Then I sit back and close my eyes so I can't see the town as I leave.

Chapter Forty-two

'Fallen tree in the storm last night. Whopper, wasn't it?' says David the driver as we stop and start our way into Galway. I open my eyes, agree with him, then stare out to sea. But the more I stare the more I keep thinking I can see a red sail in the distance. Probably tiredness.

I feel wretched. I've let it happen all over again. I'm humiliated and hurt, only this time it's much worse. I feel angry with Sean for settling for his loveless marriage, but more than anything I'm angry with myself for letting myself fall in love. The one thing I said I didn't want to do. I shut my eyes again all the way to the coach station.

Sean watched as the red hackney drove over the bridge and up into Galway city centre. There was no way he could get to her now. Even if he moored here in the harbour, he'd never make it up to the coach station on foot. He'd tried everything to catch up with the hackney and stop her from going. He sat down in the boat and it bobbed to and fro, almost as if it was panting from the exertion of the wild run into the city.

'Hey, nice boat, mister,' some young boy called from his jostling group of friends who were eating sausage rolls from paper bags and throwing crumbs to the waiting swans.

'Give us a ride,' another shouted and pushed his mates playfully.

Sean gathered the ropes together and prepared to turn the boat about. She'd chosen to go and he hadn't had the chance to tell her how he felt. He'd been wrong about Nancy and he'd been wrong to try and run away and hide from his feelings for Fi. She'd saved his oysters but stolen his heart, and now she'd gone it hurt like hell. He pulled at the ropes and the hooker began to come round, heading for home. The heron landed on the brow of the boat. Even he'd struggled to keep pace with Sean, but he'd kept going, never doubting he'd find him. Sean set off again as did the heron. The heron knew his way home. Sean just hoped that Fi did too.

Chapter Forty-three

I'm on autopilot as I go through security and visa inspection. I've bought a bag from one of the airport shops and packed the contents of my black bin liner into it.

I'm checked in and my bag is on its way to the plane. I go into the departures lounge and look up at the screen. My plane's delayed. I sigh, and then see a computer offering internet access. I decide to have one last peek at the festival website, just to kill the time. The live feed should be up and running now, organised by Dan's TV company. I type in the oyster festival and a message flashes across the screen: 'Venue flooded. Festival postponed until further notice.'

I'm in shock. All that work, all that effort and the oysters won't even get their moment of glory. I log out and head for a seat. I wonder if they've noticed I've gone. Was anyone trying to contact me? Of course they've noticed. Gerald will be wondering where his brownies are, Patsy will be wondering why I'm not there to help set up the bar, Chef will be shouting for his oysters, Margaret will be running round like a headless chicken now the venue's been ruined. I suddenly feel very weepy.

I go to pull out some loo roll from my pocket and find Brian's letter. I'm holding the letter and before I know it I'm ripping apart the thick cream envelope. I pull it out and can see the creases where it's been handled, traces that show it's been read by Nancy. There's even a faint trace of her perfume. It makes me feel sick. Nancy knows what she wants and she goes out there to get it. Maybe now I finally know what I want, but it's too late.

Dear Fiona,

I hope this letter finds you and finds you well. If you're wondering how I knew where to send it I've been trying to track you down for ages but had no luck, and then by chance I came across an article online about a new oyster festival in Galway. It was in a newsletter I subscribed to when I was researching the honeymoon. And there you were. It took me a while to recognise you, your name didn't fit, but it was definitely you, celebrating the launch of the festival.

Shit! It must've been taken on the night Dan got the prize money for the shuck-off. I should've been more careful.

You looked so different, you looked happy. And I hope you are. I hope you can be as happy as I am with Adrian. Who'd've thought you'd be part of the oyster-farming community, what with your fear of water? But then you were always able to take on whatever life threw at you. It was one of the things I admired about you.

I don't know whether to laugh or cry some more. Brian admired something about me. I never knew. I suppose that's why we were able to live side by side for so long, hiding behind each other.

I'm so sorry I didn't have the guts to end things sooner and that I let things go as far as they did. Believe me, I never meant to hurt you. It must have looked like a really cowardly thing to do, but it was the hardest thing I have ever done. I could've carried on being your husband but neither of us would ever have really been happy. One of us had to be brave, for us both to find happiness. I want you to be happy, Fi.

We were just kidding ourselves because we were too scared to go out and start living. You only get one life, go out and live it.

I've enclosed the marriage annulment. This gives you a fresh start, one where you can be yourself and not just be there for me to hide behind. You have so much to offer the world, but you need to be you. Just like in Dirty Dancing, *'No one puts Baby in the corner', well, no one should put Fiona in the corner; go and dance your own tune.*

My love, gratitude, and friendship, always, Brian. xx

Tears are rolling down my face, but I don't feel distraught. My husband finally tells me our life together is over and I'm elated. I mean, his timing was crap. Shame he couldn't have actually realised this before we got to the altar, but then Brian never was one for being impetuous. And as a first attempt, it was better late than never. He did it for both of us.

I smile. I feel I can do anything I want to. Sean may have decided to stay with Nancy, choosing his head over his heart, but this isn't just about Sean. This is about me and the people and the place I've come to love.

I pull out the paperwork Brian has sent me and sign my name where he's marked with a cross. Fiona Clutterbuck, I write with a flourish. Not Fiona Goodchild, not Fiona English, but Fiona Clutterbuck. It feels good to be me at last.

Nothing to forgive. Thank you, x, I write at the bottom and push the paperwork into the pre-paid envelope and seal it.

Brian's right. I have to be my own person; not one that runs every time the going gets tough. I can't be scared any more. I have to find my own place in the world and right now . . . that's back in Dooleybridge, with or without Sean.

Now all I have to do is find a post box on my way out of here. I march up to the desk just as they're announcing that my flight has been cancelled due to bad weather. I'm Fiona Clutterbuck, I can do what the hell I want, and right now, I have a festival to rescue.

Chapter Forty-four

It's a scene of utter devastation as I stand at the entrance to the marquee. Outside the sun may be starting to shine, but inside it's like a paddy field. You can't see the coir matting that Nancy wanted, and the chairs have been knocked over, their big purple chiffon ribbons soaked in dirty water. I feel totally wretched.

'You came back!' Margaret shrieks.

I swing round and beam too, opening my arms to hug her.

'I knew you would,' she says, and she puts down her bucket and mop and hugs me tightly.

'How could I not?' I say, pulling away and looking round at the mess.

'Came out of nowhere.' Dan's standing behind Margaret. 'So how come you're not in Boston?' He looks a bit peeved, and I can't really blame him; that's twice I've let him down about this job.

'Slight change of plan. Thought I might be needed here,' I say truthfully.

'What are we going to do?' Margaret wails and puts her head into Dan's chest.

'Well . . .' I do have one idea but I'm not sure I can make it happen. Dan and Margaret are looking at me but the words won't come out, and at that moment Sean comes in carrying

334

a tool kit. My stomach flips over and back again, like a gymnast doing flick-flacks across the floor.

'Well, that's the drain unblocked but I'm not sure what we're going to do about this . . .' He stops in his tracks. 'Fi!' I could be mistaken but I'm sure his face suddenly brightens. Even my eyeballs are hot from blushing. But being around Sean is something I'm going to have to get used to if I'm staying here.

'Hello, Sean. How was the party?' No point dancing round the subject.

'Illuminating,' he says. There's an uncomfortable silence. Dan and Margaret look at each other. I don't want to hear any more; I don't need a blow-by-blow account of how spectacular it was.

'What are you doing here?' I ask, but I know Nancy must've sent him. Why else would he be helping out?

'Let's just say, someone made me realise that I needed to get a bit more involved with . . . all of this.'

'In that case,' I cut Sean off before I lose my nerve, 'you could do worse than getting really involved.'

He frowns and gives me a look that says he might not like what I'm about to say.

'Go on,' he tilts his head like he always does when he's listening, and stares right at me as if he can read my thoughts.

'I mean, if we're to have an oyster festival, here, today, we need to ditch this idea.' I look around.

'What?' Margaret shrieks, her hands fly to her face. 'Cancel it? Everyone wants to celebrate, what with the native oysters being back. Everyone's so delighted. Ah, shite!'

'No,' I say slowly, 'not cancel it, relocate it. Take it back to the farm. The tide'll be out. If this festival is going to happen at all, it needs to be a festival the local people want.' I look straight back at Sean. He stares at me hard, narrowing his eyes, but I stand my ground and stare back at him.

Suddenly he nods his head briskly. 'Let's do it,' he says quickly and firmly, and Margaret shrieks and jumps up and down with delight.

Sean and I drive back to the farm in silence and at speed. Margaret and Dan follow in Margaret's Fiesta, as do others in various different vehicles. Freddie and Mercury are missing from their field and there's no sign of them on the lane up to the farm. Maybe the storm scared them.

'Margaret, you get online and announce the venue change on Facebook, Twitter, and on our website. Oh, and stick a note on the door of the hotel too, just in case! Tell them the festival's moved. Tell people to bring their wellies and come ready for a good old-fashioned oyster festival, the way it used to be. A tenner on the door and there'll be music and food. Let's see if we can get Dooleybridge oyster festival trending!'

'Music? But the band's cancelled,' Sean says.

'Sean, it may not be Wembley, but dust down your guitar and see who else you can rustle up to play with you.' Surprisingly Sean doesn't argue.

'Oh, and can you organise for people to go out in the boat to collect some oysters or pick some up from the raft. It's the best spring tide of the summer, according to the weather website. We should make the most of it.'

'Who's going to take them if I'm busy on stage?' Sean protests.

I grin. 'I can handle it.'

'How are we going to feed everyone? The chef from Galway has refused to come out.' Margaret looks worried.

'Dan, follow me.' I lead him and Margaret down to the old barn and fling open the doors. 'We'll put up the tables and chairs, and Dan, can you drag that out and fire it up?' I point to the oil drum barbecue.

'No problem, boss!' he jokes, but I notice Sean is glowering at him.

'Sean? Van keys?' I hold up my hands in a cup shape.

He pulls away his stare from Dan and tosses them to me without question.

'You boys, play nicely while I'm away,' I joke, pointing to Sean and Dan, buoyed up by my turn-around decision.

Happy that everyone is organised and we've got a plan, I drive back down the flooded lane, the pot holes filled with water. There's a massive rainbow right across the town showing every colour. I reach the small bungalow at the end of a short drive on the other side of town. There's washing on the line already, slightly greying, but blowing gaily in the wind regardless.

I knock on the white plastic front door.

'Hello, Evelyn.' She looks at me suspiciously but then we both speak at the same time.

'I'm sorry to hear about the festival . . .' she says.

'About the festival . . .' I say. We both stop.

'You go first,' I say politely.

'Sorry about the festival, love. Hear it's cancelled. I may not have said this before, but you put a lot of hard work into it.'

I smile.

'Actually, Evelyn, it's back on. Up at Sean's farm. We're

going to have an old-fashioned oyster festival, music, pick your own oysters, and the shell-shucking contest. Everyone's welcome.'

'Really?' Her face lights up. 'Well, that's grand! Just grand! Hear that, John Joe?' she calls over her shoulder. 'Ring the kids. Tell them the festival is on, just like the old days, up at Tom's place. I mean Sean Thornton's farm,' she corrects herself. Accepted at last, I think happily.

'Now, what can I do to help? Want any scones made?' she rubs her hands together.

'Actually, Evelyn, it wasn't scones I needed,' I say, hoping that this isn't going to blow our new-found friendship. 'I was thinking . . . how about fishcakes?'

'Fishcakes?' She screws up her nose.

'Yes, they'd be great on the barbecue with the oysters and, well, I just thought you might be the woman for the job.'

'I suppose I could give them a try. I've got quite a lot of fish in the freezer, of course, what with John Joe having the boat.' She's thinking. 'Maybe we could do them in a bun, like a burger . . .'

'Perfect!' I clap my hands together.

'Well, I'm happy to give them a try. I'll bring them up to the farm as soon as they're done.'

We say goodbye and I turn to leave. The sun is shining and my cheeks are warm. I strip off my coat and jump back in the van. I know exactly where I'm going next.

In the pub there's a smell of cleaning fluids and stale beer. The fire's lit despite the sunshine outside. Just like when I first arrived in town, I push open the door and it crashes back. I walk in, stand and stare. Propping up the bar are

Seamus and Padraig. They pull their hats down and turn towards their pints.

No one says anything. I march over to them.

'Right, you two!' To say they're shocked is an understatement. Seamus clings on to his pint with both hands. Padraig pulls down his baseball cap further. 'Get yourselves up to Sean's farm and start putting out the tables and chairs for the festival.'

They stare at me in surprise.

'You paying us?'

'You must be joking. Shift yourselves, unless you want me to show Sean those photos I took of the pair of you. Or the Garda for that matter. This is payback time.' I put my hands on my hips. They nod a lot and push their pints away. 'Oh, and while you're at it, seeing as you know the lay of the land so well, you can show the punters across the oyster beds to collect oysters for the barbecue. Clear?'

'Clear,' they say, and push and hustle each other out of the pub.

'Hey lads, not finishing your pints?' Patsy laughs, watching them go, and takes their pints off the bar. 'I guess I'll save them for later.'

'Patsy, are you still OK to run a bar today?'

'Got the drink still, it's just the marquee that's down.'

'Great, bring it up to Sean's farm, say at about two? I'll have a table laid out for you. Now then, Grandad.'

Patsy nods to him dozing by the fire.

'Bring him up to the farm too. I've got just the job for him.'

'Righto,' says Patsy. 'Grandad, get yourself moving. It's oyster festival day,' he calls over as I leave. I feel the excitement too.

Next I check on Margaret who's working hard on the internet in Gerald's café. The café looks different.

'Gerald, you've had a clean out!' All his ex-wife's clothes and belongings are gone.

'Time for a fresh start,' he says, handing me a takeaway tea.

'It looks twice the size in here,' I say, impressed.

'Let's hope after today I have twice the number of customers,' he smiles.

Tea in hand, I head back to the van via Frank's place.

'Frank, what are you like at tracking down donkeys?'

'Leave it to me, Fi.' He touches his forehead. Looks like everyone is happy to help.

Chapter Forty-five

It's a hive of activity back at the farm. Sean has opened up the field opposite as a car park, and there are plenty of cars there already, all in neat rows. Rosie's kids are doing a great job as car park attendants by the look of it. I park the van where I'm directed with big arm movements like windmills, and smiles to match.

Seamus and Padraig are putting tables and long benches out in the sunshine. Sean is making an old raft into a makeshift stage.

Rosie and her sister are hanging out bunting.

'That's lovely. Who made it?'

'Maire,' they say in unison.

'Gerald gave her all his ex-wife's clothes. She's been running it up into bunting all morning,' Rosie says from the ladder as she hangs it on the outside of the barn. The sun is pushing further up the sky. It sparkles off the water like thousands of tiny fairy lights. The heron is watching from his position on the jetty. On the rocks further out I can see movement.

'The seals.' Sean's beside me.

'The seals!' I say excitedly, before remembering that he and I may be working together for the festival but we're not really speaking, despite my insides doing a bongo dance at his very presence. The tide is beginning to slip back down the shore, leaving patterns in the sand. I hope today is the start of a new pattern that will keep coming back year after year.

'Hey, Fi!' I turn to see Frank leading Freddie who is whining in sheer joy. Mercury is following, as is a little white donkey.

'Frank! We only lost two donkeys.'

'Freddie wouldn't come without her. Besides, the owner wanted shot of her. Can't afford to keep her on. She can pull a cart and everything. I thought we could use her to bring in the oysters,' he says. Freddie is standing beside his true love, happier than I've seen him in weeks. I look at Sean.

'Room for another waif?'

He shrugs and smiles.

'Maybe Freddie could give rides too?' I say, as Frank rubs his long ears.

'Great idea.' He gives me the thumbs up.

The farm is looking fantastic. I walk over to the old barn and Sean follows me. Inside there are tables covered with white paper from a big roll we've found. At one end is a long table on its own where I've organised for the shell-shucking competition to take place.

'The judges are on their way from Galway and Margaret's got the list of entrants. The oysters are all ready in the shed.' I'm going through my list out loud.

Inside the barn Maire is stepping back from a huge mirror she's put on top of the stone fireplace. The surround is made from hundreds of oyster shells.

'Maire, it's wonderful!' I'm stunned.

'Thought this was just the place for it,' she says with a smile. 'Who knows, maybe someone will want to buy it. I've got a few other small ones if it's OK to put them up?'

'It's the perfect place to show them, Maire. Let's hope you get lots of buyers.'

Tea lights are being placed on all the tables by Patsy's wife, and there's a pile of plastic plates and cutlery.

I help move the blackboard over from the shed to write up the contestants' names and their scores.

'And can we get a table set up over there for the bar?' I instruct Seamus and Padraig, who do as I ask without question. There are more tables and chairs round the outside of the big room.

'Actually, English, I need to talk to you,' Sean says, as I'm laying out the big bell and clipboards.

'Not now, Sean. We'll talk later, eh? Let's just have today,' I say. He says nothing then gives a tiny nod.

'Where d'you want it?' Patsy comes in carrying a huge barrel of beer on his chest. 'Oh, and this is Grainne, a freelance journalist from Galway. Found her down at the marquee site. Nancy organised for her to come, she wants to cover the day.'

'Great,' I say to the young woman. 'It's Margaret you need to speak to. She'll be here soon. Make yourself at home. Or better still, make yourself useful,' I say, giving her a paint-brush and pointing towards a sheet that needs a sign painting on it.

'Sure. And you're . . .'

'Fi, just Fi,' I say.

'Not from round here then,' she says, holding a pen over her notebook.

'No,' I say, 'I'm a blow-in.' She gives me a look that says she'd like to know more, but I make a quick sidestep and leave her to paint while I go and find Dan who's setting up the barbecue.

'Hey!' There's smoke billowing out from the oil drum. Dan is waving his hands around. 'You're just in time.' He pulls out a bottle of what looks like champagne from a cooler box under the barbecue.

'Well, I'm not sure about celebrating. Dan, about the job . . .'

'We're celebrating because I've just about finished the book. I've written up all the notes and recipes from my travels. Just the last chapter to go.' He peels off the foil and strains as he twists the cork.

'The one where you write about finding your true spiritual home.' I accept the sparkling, fizzing drink he hands me in a plastic glass.

'Well, seeing as how there isn't going to be any happy reunion with a long-lost relative, I've had another idea that put my roots very clearly on the map, very clearly indeed.' He finishes pouring himself a glass and holds it high in a toast. 'So here's to our future working relationship,' he says, and suddenly the music has changed to heavy rock before I can tell Dan I'm not taking the job.

Sean is looking over at me, scowling. I'm going to have to tell him that I won't be his bit on the side. He's engaged to Nancy and I can drink champagne with whoever I like. I lift my chin and clink glasses with Dan.

'To new beginnings,' Dan shouts. I look out at the bay. You'd never believe it was the same place I arrived in four months ago. I take a sip. Who needs Boston when you could be here, drinking champagne and looking out at that sparkling sea. Everything looks just perfect.

'So, how?' I ask, enjoying the heady rush the champagne is giving me. 'How have you found yourself some real Irish roots?' I shout, just as the music stops suddenly.

'I'm going to buy some!' He beams at me.

'Buy some? How can you buy some ancestral roots?' I take another sip.

'Well, if I can't actually find any real ancestors to put in the book, I can buy me a bit of Ireland.'

That makes me laugh.

'OK, which bit?'

'This bit!' he says, knocking back his glass. 'I'm buying this farm.' And I choke on the bubbles that catch in the back of my mouth and I wonder if it's going to come back up.

'But you can't buy this bit. This is Sean's bit.'

'I have it on good authority that he's not going to be able to pay his debts and this place will go up for sale. I'm ready with the cash.'

'That's rubbish. Of course he'll be able to pay. The oysters are fine. Nancy has a load of buyers lined up. He'll get the cash he needs.' I put down the glass.

Dan raises his eyebrows. 'Looks like things have changed while you were away.'

'A lot has changed since I've been away.' I narrow my eyes at him and begin to feel a steely determination growing inside me.

Margaret appears round the corner of the old barn.

'Ah, there you two are! Thought you'd be up to no good.'

I can't bear to tell her how much no good. She picks up the glass of champagne.

'Good to see so many people here. Even Seamus and Padraig.' She has her Pearl Princess sash over her arm.

'Oh, did that journalist arrive?' She looks around.

'I got her painting a sign,' I say, looking sideways at Dan. 'Now let me show you the barn,' I suggest. 'Where's Grandad?' I ask as we walk into the old barn together.

'I'm going back for him now. Oh my feckin' God!' Margaret stops and stares from the doorway. 'It's feckin' perfect!'

'Let's just hope the public come,' I say nervously. Whatever Dan means, this festival still matters to Sean by the looks of it. I watch him as he goes to inspect the oysters.

A crowd of women turn up clutching bowls of salad. I recognise them from the Pearl Queen selection night: the school teacher, some of the mums, the librarian and the cleaner. Then Evelyn turns up, grinning.

'Fishcakes!' she announces, proudly peeling off the lid of a large plastic box.

Chapter Forty-six

There's a queue of cars as far as the eye can see, stretching down the lane. The sun is shining and I swear the rainbow ends right over Sean's farm. It could be perfect if I wasn't worried about Dan wanting to buy Sean's farm. But it's not for sale. Nancy and Sean won't sell it.

Frank is leading the donkeys across the wet sand with children riding on their backs. He has a cart that Juliet, as we've decided to call the white one, is pulling, and it's loaded with oysters. Dan is cooking oysters on the barbecue and people are standing around with drinks and plates of brown rolls, oysters, salad, and hot and tasty fishcakes served with sweet chilli sauce.

Grandad is sitting outside the old barn. I can hear him speaking: 'When I was a boy, all of this was oyster farms. This was our playground,' he's telling children sitting at his feet and grown-ups standing behind them. He'll be able to tell them story after story all afternoon. I smile to myself. This is just how it should be.

'Hello again,' says a deep voice, and the smell of cigar smoke makes me retch. I turn to see Jimmy Power and his lad. 'Looks like it's all going very well,' he says, licking his lips before sucking on his cigar.

He smiles a yellow-toothed smile at me and smoke oozes out from between them, like a dragon smiling on his prey. Grace barks at him. I put my hands on my hips.

'What are you doing here? You'll have your money when the festival is over.'

'Just come to check on my investment. Lovely spot. Would be great for a house, looking down the bay here.' He looks around, sizing things up.

'You're not going to build any houses,' I say, clenching my fists.

'That's not what I heard,' he says with a chesty chuckle.

'Hey!' Sean runs over to me. 'I'll take over here, English,' he says.

'But . . .'

'I'll deal with it. Thank you,' he says firmly.

I walk towards the barn but keep looking back over my shoulder. Margaret is putting up the list of names for the shell-shucking contest on the blackboard.

'We're short a contestant for the last of the first rounds. Only got three,' she's looking at her list.

'Why is Sean's name on the list?' I'm suddenly confused.

'Because he's entering.' Margaret puts down her chalk, brushes off her hands and looks around.

Out of the little paned window I can see a film crew has arrived and they're following Dan. He's showing them around like prospective buyers. I grit my teeth. I turn back to Margaret, still not sure what's going on.

'So? Sean? Entering the shell-shucking? He always said no way . . .'

'Well, looks like there's a way now.'

I have to know what's going on.

'I've been trying to get you on your own,' Margaret explains. 'I had a text while I was at Gerald's. A friend of mine was a waitress at The Pearl last night. She says that halfway through the party Sean stormed out. She says the engagement's off.'

'What, she called it off?' I'm outraged.

'No, he did! Said he realised he shouldn't be marrying for any other reason than love. We should grab it with both hands when it comes our way.'

My jaw is now waggling up and down like a ventriloquist's dummy.

'And he walked out.' Margaret's eyes sparkle.

That must have been when he got back here. After I'd rescued the oysters.

'So now what?'

'Well, looks like the only way he can pay off his debts, without Nancy, is the shell-shucking prize money,' she gestures to the board.

'What, you mean if Sean doesn't win this he'll lose the farm to that scumbag out there?' I'm not sure if I mean Jimmy Power or Dan.

Margaret nods and picks up the big brass bell.

'Ready?' she nods to the two judges who are enjoying oysters and bread, and then to me. I take a deep breath and nod back. 'Let's get this competition started!' Margaret slips on her sash and tiara and rings the bell with gusto.

Sean is standing a little way from the other competitors, one foot up against the wall. He's rolling his shucking knife round and round in his hand, staring at it as if his life depends on it. And it does. I want to go over and ask him about last night, but I can see it's not a good time. If what Margaret says is true, could this mean there might just be a chance for us?

'So this is the first round of Dooleybridge's resurrected oyster-shucking competition,' Patsy shouts into the microphone.

'Yay!' There's a huge cheer, the loudest from Margaret. She has a pen in one hand and a stopwatch in the other. Next to her is Grandad, beaming from ear to ear.

'So, round one,' Patsy reads out the list of four contestants as they make their way on to the stand. One is Swedish, two from Clifden, and Frank. Patsy blows his whistle and Margaret pushes down on her stopwatch. The crowd noise begins to swell as the contestants quickly and methodically push their knives into the oyster hinge then prise off the top shell. They work skilfully, their blades catching in the sunlight. When each shucker has shucked all thirty oysters, they step back from the table, signal to Margaret and their time is noted.

The judges, one French, one a restaurant owner from Galway, and another a big seafood seller in the city, all step up to the table to inspect the boards. They move along the line, pointing out the oysters, looking for stray bits of shell and tidy presentation. The four men leave the stand.

"Scuse me, Fi? Fiona?' Grainne, the journalist, interrupts my thoughts.

'Sorry, miles away,' I say.

'I wonder if I could just ask you a few questions, about how you came to be in Dooleybridge. You were on your honeymoon, weren't you?' She's holding her mobile phone out to record what I say.

My heart suddenly starts pounding like the noise of an

impatient crowd. Nancy's gone through with it! She's told the journalist about me. I look around in panic and see Nancy in the doorway. She's whispering to Dan, who nods and then makes his way to where the other competitors are waiting.

So, hell hath no fury, I think. Sean's finished with Nancy and now she wants to bring me and him down. Looks like that's where Dan's got his information from too.

'Fi?' the journalist pushes.

The judges nod in agreement.

'Sorry, I have to go.' I dash up to help Margaret clear away the boards of oysters and set up for the next round.

This time it's Nancy's French friend Henri, who gives Sean a smile as he rolls up his sleeves. There's also a Galway shucker and one from Clarenbridge, the winner of the world shucking competition three years in a row, and a Londoner.

'Some of them seem to be slower than usual, not used to shucking the native oysters, it seems,' Patsy says, like he's commentating on Formula One motor racing. 'And these oysters are from right here in Dooleybridge!' A cheer goes up from the crowd.

But this round ends in disaster for the world title holder when he catches the corner of his board just as he's finishing in front and the whole lot flips over and hits the ground. There's a groan and at the back of the room little betting slips are ripped up like confetti around Seamus and Padraig, who are rubbing their hands. Grace dashes in to help clean up the tipped oysters while I run and get a mop.

'Look, you might as well know,' the journalist is waiting for me as I come out of the house, 'I'm going to write about you and how you came to be here anyway. So help me get it right,' she shrugs. I look at the phone she's holding out and then give my mop bucket a nudge, slopping soapy water over her high-heeled boots.

'Urgh!' she jumps back and I rush back to the barn. I clean it up and then get up on the stand with Margaret to set up again.

'Nancy's told the journalist,' I whisper to Margaret as we put the oysters onto platters ready to hand round to spectators.

'Told her what?'

'About me!'

The crowd are getting drinks from the bar at the back of the barn. Nancy is standing at the back too, next to Jimmy Power and his son. She nods to Dan and then looks at me and smiles, revenge written all over her face.

'What about you?' Margaret looks puzzled as she wipes down the table.

'About how I came to be here. About how I was jilted and my husband ran off with the best man,' I hiss again.

'Oh my God!' She stands up suddenly and it looks like the penny has dropped and smacked her over the head. Dan is making his way to the stand and everyone is watching him. Margaret straightens the last couple of oysters.

'How do you know?'

'That journalist has just told me. I'm going to have to get out of here—'

'Everything all right?'

I jump and turn. It's Sean. I feel lightheaded for a second or two.

'English? You OK?' His face is full of concern. If Margaret's right and Sean has walked out of his engagement party, this competition really is his only chance now to pay off the loan and keep his farm.

Dan is smiling as he takes to the stand. The sharks are circling and I feel as if someone has walked over my grave.

'Fine, fine,' I say. 'The oysters look great,' trying to cheer him along. 'Everyone's loving them.'

'Tasted one?' He half smiles and all my fury melts.

I shake my head and say, 'Good luck.' There's so, so much more I want to say, but for now 'good luck' will have to do. He stares at me and I can't stop looking back into his eyes.

'Look, I really need—' he starts to say and touches the tips of my fingers. Sparks of electricity run through me.

'Fiona? It's Fiona Goodchild, isn't it?' The journalist is beside me again. I snatch my hand away and turn to her. Sean gives her a dark look. I go to walk away and Sean grabs my wrist.

'You're sure you're OK?' I nod and look at Nancy whose face is frozen. Sean lets go of my arm. 'We need to talk, as soon as I'm done here,' he says firmly.

'OK,' I say as he takes off his jacket. He's wearing a white T-shirt, the top of his arm rippling with tension as he rolls the knife in his hand. He takes his place on the stand. I don't want anything to distract him. He has to win this. I can't watch.

I try to edge away from the journalist and into the growing crowd. She follows me.

'I'm sorry. I can't talk now, I'm busy . . . festival to run and all that . . . busy, busy, busy,' I try to sound light-hearted. Patsy is counting down. A hush falls over the barn and all eyes are focused on the stand.

'Three, two, one . . .'

* * *

It was hot in there. He ran the back of hand across his forehead. Beads of sweat were making him blink. He rubbed his face again with the back of his hand. If ever he needed to concentrate, it was now. He wasn't bothered that Nancy was there. She and he were history. His only regret was taking his eye off the ball as far as his sales were concerned. He'd trusted her, when all the time his trust had been misplaced, he realised. He looked to his left. It was a Finnish competitor. They nodded to each other and the Finn smiled. Then he looked to his right. It was Dan. He felt himself tense up. Were he and Fi an item now? Was she leaving with him, going to America? He was taking away the woman he realised he loved. Who else would go out in a storm to save the oysters and delay her move to a new country to help at a local festival? Who else could make him laugh when they were grading oysters in the pouring rain, work by hand when the generator broke down and keep him from giving up, even now. He dared a quick glance up. The journalist was still talking to her and she looked like she was trying to get away. He glanced to his right again. Dan looked wolfish. He had his baseball cap on backwards and Sean felt an overwhelming urge to flick it off and wipe the smile off his face. But he took a deep breath. 'Come on. Focus,' he told himself.

He had to beat Dan. There was no way he could let him take his farm and Fi. Sean had wanted to throw him off his land when he'd turned up with his pathetic offer to buy the farm that morning. He and Nancy were in it together, he was sure. Winning this was a far better way to show Dan what he could do with his offer.

He felt his jaw twitch. His eyes came into focus as he picked up the first oyster. His oysters, round and ridged. It sat in the palm of his hand. He just had to win the prize money, pay off the loan, and he was back in business.

'Three,' he heard Patsy shout. The noise of the crowd began to disappear as he entered his own tunnel of concentration.

'Two!' His determination deepened. He gripped the oyster tighter. His knife was poised for war. He needed to win this, but he realised he needed Fi more and he couldn't bear the thought of losing her again. He'd already thought he'd lost her once.

'One!' He focused on the hinge of the muscle and pushed the knife towards it. Everything had gone silent. He prised open the first oyster and slid the knife across the top shell. It felt good, just like old times. He would win this and then he would ask Fi to stay. His eyes flicked up momentarily towards the door where Fi was exchanging cross words with the journalist. She was about to run out. The journalist followed. He couldn't lose her again.

'Hey, English!' he shouted as he saw her trying to leave and the journalist following her. 'No! Don't go!' And his knife clattered to the floor.

Chapter Forty-seven

'No, no way!' I hear him shout. The front door of the cottage slams shut.

I'm grabbing my belongings.

'You can't do this, not again.' Sean is standing in the doorway.

'Sean! Get back in there! You're on, for God's sake!' I can hear myself but my voice is choked with tears.

'I'm not going back in there until I can be sure you're not going to do another moonlight flit.' He's angry and his face is etched with pain.

'Sean, you don't understand. I have to go. I came back and got the festival up and running. I came back to give you your chance at making this happen. Now I have to go or . . . or . . .'

'Or what?' he demands, leaning against the door and holding one hand inside the other as if cradling it.

I sigh, throwing my bag on the bed.

'There's a journalist here who's going to report my story, sensationalise it, and then you'll be plagued by uninvited gawpers, people wanting to stare, on top of what Nancy's done.'

He wraps his arms around me and I fall into his chest. It feels like I'm home, but I can't stay here.

'You have to get back in there.' I push him away.

'Otherwise Dan will win and then he'll buy this place.'

'I'm not going back in there. I would give up all of this if it meant knowing that you were beside me for the rest of my life. I don't care about any of this if it means I can't have you.' He nods towards the crowds milling around the barn.

'But Nancy?' I hug myself.

'It's over.' He emphasises each word. 'Nancy didn't want me. She just wanted the oysters and she was using whatever methods she could to get them. And I didn't really want her. I just didn't want to risk falling in love again.' He takes hold of my elbows. 'But it's too late for that.'

I fall back into his chest. There is a slow hand clap and appearing behind Sean in the doorway are Nancy and her journalist. They're both smiling.

'Touching,' she says, and I want to wipe the smile off her face.

She gestures to her journalist friend.

'Get back on the stand, Sean. There's still a chance,' I say.

'His round is finished. Dan won,' Nancy tells me.

'Get out, Nancy. You've got what you wanted. Have the oysters. I have something more important than you'll ever know,' Sean says calmly. 'Get out of my house.'

She gives me a considered look then turns to leave.

'Tell them to put you in the next round,' I say through gritted teeth. 'Tell them . . . You can't give all this up for me,' I'm begging him.

Sean looks at me and shakes his head.

'Why? Why not?' I'm frustrated.

'Because blood in the oysters is an automatic disqualification.' He holds up the hand he has been cupping. There is a cut right through his palm and it's dripping on the floor.

I run outside to where Nancy is swapping notes with her journalist friend.

'So that's it. I get the oysters and the story . . .' Nancy smiles, swishing her hand as Grace sniffs around her. 'Don't unpack. Dan'll be buying the farm from Jimmy. It'll be business as usual in no time. The only thing missing will be you and your boyfriend.'

'Oh no it won't,' I say, and before I can think about what I'm doing, I march back towards the barn, knocking Jimmy Power and his lad sideways as I push my way into the crowded room and march up to the stand.

Chapter Forty-eight

I take a deep breath and do something I should have done a long time ago. I step up on to the stand behind the white-covered tables and the crowd quietens in expectation.

'My name is Fiona Clutterbuck,' I say, like an alcoholic at the end of one road and the start of another. 'I was jilted on my wedding day. I stole the camper van we were due to go on honeymoon in and ended up here.' There's a sharp intake of breath. The loudest from Margaret.

'What are you doing?' she hisses.

'And do you know what?' I look at Margaret. 'It was the best thing that ever happened to me. Because here is where I learnt to be myself and not someone I'm not. And if I had my time again, I wouldn't change a thing,' I say, and see Rosie sniffing into a tissue. 'Someone once told me that when you get old, it's the memories that matter, so make sure they're good ones.' I smile at Grandad, who's clapping, his eyes watering like mad.

'I was once scared of being found. But what I realised was that I hadn't found myself until now. So Patsy, I'll be the final contestant in this round.'

Margaret rushes around getting a knife. 'Are you sure you know what you're doing?' She is laying out a board and oysters. Her tiara has slipped to the left.

'Never more so.' I clear my throat.

'Well, that prize money could really set you up.' She straightens.

'This isn't about the money, this is about standing up for what's right.'

I think the fact that I'm up against Seamus and a couple of others who have spent too much time at the bar helps me make it through to the final. More luck and too much Guinness on their part, I think. But now it's for real. It's the final.

'Excellent, excellent.' Dan is beside me, whispering in my ear. 'So, make this look good, open a few oysters and then I'll win and your job is still safe with me, baby!' He grins and holds his hand up to high five me. I tap it gently and swallow hard. Yes, I could just do what he says. Leave this mess behind. Open a few oysters then get back on that plane to Boston and start all over again.

Dan is picking up the oysters and inspecting them.

'And these are the native oysters you told me about?' He's tapping one. I groan, remembering how I let the cat out of the bag on my birthday. He said I'd given him the idea. It was me who'd told him there was gold in these waters! Margaret is laying up the boards. I have to tell her.

'Dan's in this with Nancy. He wants to win and then buy the farm out from under Sean. He's going to pay off Sean's debt collector and take the farm for himself.' Margaret stops laying out the oysters. 'I don't want to hurt you again, but you have to know. You know I wouldn't lie to you. I'm sorry.'

She looks up at me like a kicked puppy.

'Contestants ready?' Patsy is sounding more and more like the commentator from *Gladiators*.

I glance up and see Sean has slid in at the back of the barn. He's looking worried. I look at Dan, who winks at me. To his left, Frank is swaying slightly. To the right is the Swede.

'This is the final of the Dooleybridge shell-shucking contest. Contestant number one is Al Sterky from Sweden.' He raises both hands above his ruddy red face and there's a small cheer from one corner of the barn. 'Then, erm,' he consults the clipboard Margaret is showing him, 'Fiona Clutterbuck from the UK.' There's a huge cheer. I look up to see Rosie, Lily, the kids, Seamus, Padraig, Patsy, Margaret and Grandad all rooting for me. Tears prick my eyes. I can just make out Sean shouting his support through his cupped hands, even though one of them is bandaged up.

I wipe away the blurriness with the back of my hand. What Brian did might have felt cruel at the time, but he did it for both our sakes. Now it's my turn to do something I believe in. I pick up my first oyster.

'Go, Fiona!' I hear a Cardiff accent and look up again.

'Betty?' It can't be! 'Betty? Who's minding the café?' I ask in astonishment.

'Thought it was time Kimberly had a try. Whatever mess-up she makes, it's time she had a go at proving herself. Now, I've come all this way to see you win! Brian had that Googley alert telling him about the oyster festival.' Garda Eamon is standing beside Betty. 'He's been ever so helpful,' she tips her head at him and says in a loud whisper with her hand to her mouth, 'Gay network, Brian says. I caught the first flight over once he'd confirmed it was you. We miss you, love.'

'Dan Murphy, all the way from Boston,' Patsy shouts, and the cameraman moves in on Dan. I'm still in shock. It's all so surreal. Dan stands up and raises his hands above his head too, then turns his baseball cap back to front, ready for battle.

'Remember, make it look good,' Dan smiles at me. 'Let me win and you get a whole new life in Boston.'

'Oh, I will, Dan, I will.' I grip the knife.

'There's all to play for,' Patsy is bigging it up for the cameras and Margaret is deep in thought when Patsy shouts, 'GO!'

I hold the first oyster, frill to the base of my thumb, but my hand is shaking so much I can't get the knife into the hinge. I tighten my grip, take a deep breath, hold it steady and finally I'm in. Then I push the knife in all the way, closely missing cutting the palm of my own hand. I look across to either side of me. Al the Swede is sweating profusely. He's working so hard to get into the oysters that he's getting shell fragments in them. Dan is working methodically. There's a crash and Frank falls into the table where Patsy and Margaret are sitting, sending clipboards and stopwatches flying. Margaret straightens her tiara and steps away from the flailing Frank with dignity.

I look back at the oysters and focus. I can open them but I'm nowhere near as quick as Dan. He's opening them like a knife going through butter. I put the knife in again and push and twist, and then I imagine Sean has his arms around me, just like he did that first time he taught me.

'Understand what's keeping it closed,' I hear his voice say, and my knife goes straight to the upper muscle and slices through it in a clean cut, releasing it from its shell and the same for the bottom muscle. I flip it and start the next.

Suddenly I'm in a rhythm and the oysters are opening in clean, quick movements, like I've suddenly got a magic key. Aim at the hinge, push, twist, pop, slide, slice and flip. I'm so into my rhythm I don't notice I've run out of oysters. I quickly stand back at the same time as Dan. Al the Swede still has two left and throws down his knife, beaten. So it's between me and Dan. He looks at me with a confused frown. He's panting and grabs at his water bottle.

'Good work,' he says in between sips. 'Who knew, eh?' He's frowning and confused. I'm just numb, hoping it was enough, but it may not have been.

'Contestants, leave the stand, please,' Patsy instructs, throwing out his arm. Al the Swede is bright red in the face and is handed a pint of lager. He downs it in one and holds it high to the applause of the audience. I step down and am immediately scooped up in Sean's arms. He hugs me so my feet are off the ground and I want to stay there for ever.

'I'm sorry, I don't think it was enough,' I say.

Dan stands down and looks over at Margaret. She folds her arms and turns away from him with a sniff.

'What the . . . ? What is going on here today?' His arms are open, his shoulders high. Margaret decides that's enough of the silent treatment and stomps over to him. The judges are looking at the two boards, pointing with their pens and looking at their clipboards.

'I can't believe you're going to do this,' she says, none too quietly. 'How could you? You can't just buy up a farm and put another farmer out of business.'

'But, honey, I thought you wanted the world to know about Dooleybridge oysters again?'

'I do, but not like this!'

'I'm sorry,' I say quietly into the crook of Sean's neck. I breathe in the smell of turf and sea air.

'Hey, nothing to be sorry about. You did it. You came out of your shell. It doesn't matter now if you've won the money. You found you. Feel good?'

'Bloody brilliant!' I say, and beam and then kiss him, long and deep, and he kisses me back, like he means it.

'And the winner is . . .' Patsy announces and regretfully we pull apart.

'Finding you was all that mattered,' says Sean, and tweaks my nose.

'On presentation . . . our very own *Fi English*! Or should that be,' he consults the clipboard, '*Fiona Clutterbuck*!' he shouts again so the microphone crackles and pops and whines. The crowd cheer and suddenly I'm swamped by people patting me on the head, hugging me and shaking my hands.

I can't believe it! I actually won! I'm being pulled out of the crowd and then I'm on the stand again, being handed a silver cup and a fat envelope of cash. Cameras are flashing and the TV crew are right in my face, only this time I don't mind. In fact, I think I quite like it. I look at the cup then hold it above my head; actually, I love it! The crowd in the barn cheers even louder.

'I am Fiona Clutterbuck, Champion Shell-Shucker!' I grin until my cheeks ache. Everyone I care about is here and they're cheering and clapping.

I grab hold of the envelope and rip it open. Ten thousand euros.

'What are you going to do with the money?' the cameraman asks. 'Go travelling?'

'No,' I smile, 'I'm going to stay right here,' and I march over to Jimmy Power.

'Fi, wait!' Sean catches my arm. 'You don't have to do this. This is your money. You can start over wherever you want now.'

'I want to be right here. This is my debt, remember.' I turn back to Jimmy.

'Five thousand, right?' I say.

Jimmy smiles. 'The debt just went up. Overdue payment, tut, tut,' he grins, again just as Sean's fist hits him in the jaw, knocking him sideways and stumbling out of the door.

'Everything all right, Sean?' says Garda Eamon.

'Just about perfect now, thank you, Garda.' Sean stretches out his hand. I pull out a bunch of notes, count them and toss them on top of Jimmy Power, who is being helped to his feet. Frank, Seamus and Padraig, Patsy, and even Al the Swede are standing behind Sean, backing up a member of their oyster family.

'Get out and don't come back,' Rosie shouts from behind them.

'Never did like oysters anyway,' Jimmy mutters as he hurries away with his lad in tow.

Sean is beside me. He picks up one of the oysters and holds it to my mouth by way of celebration. I hesitate and then shake my head. He frowns and I feed it to him with a smile.

'Let's get this party started!' I shout, and another cheer goes up.

Outside the sun is beating down. Seamus and Padraig are leading donkey rides across the sand, where the sea is starting to come back in. Grandad is sitting by the barn, drink in hand.

'And you could see for miles. Oyster beds all over, there were,' he's telling a group of Swedish tourists here with Al.

Margaret and Dan are making up by the barbecue, where Rosie is serving up the grilled oysters.

'So, you two make up?' I ask.

Margaret gasps and hugs me. 'So, you're staying?' She holds my hands.

'I am,' I smile, squeezing her back.

She looks coyly up at Dan. 'Dan's asked me to go to the States with him, now that he's not buying an oyster farm here.' She suddenly looks crestfallen. 'That's if you don't mind. But if you're staying and don't want the job, well, I would.'

I'm thrilled for her. 'Oh, Margaret, that's brilliant. You should go. You need to let the world see Margaret from Dooleybridge.'

'Well, now I can see that Grandad is right. Life is made up of memories, so make them good ones. It's no good sitting and waiting for life to come to me any more.' We both look to where Grandad is sitting with Betty beside him, pointing out the sights and telling her about Dooleybridge in its heyday.

'And I'd like to say I'm sorry.' Dan holds out his hand to Sean, who eyes it suspiciously. 'I just got carried away. I'm going back to the States now, but I'd be really interested in talking to you about supplying me with oysters. I'm going to open up a new restaurant paying homage to my Irish roots, an oyster bar. I'll pay top whack.' Sean looks at the hand again and then smiles and shakes it.

'I'll send you over all the Pacific oysters you like, but as for the native ones . . .' He looks over at the barn where the drinkers are enjoying Guinness and eating the barbecued oysters hot from the foil, 'they're going to stay right here.'

I don't get a chance to find out what Sean means. Betty is on her way to the bar. 'Just getting me and Grandad a top-up. Oh, Fiona, love, you were amazing. Who'd've ever thought it, little Fiona Clutterbuck from my kitchens, a champion shell-shucker. And now you'll be travelling all over the world entering shucking competitions.'

'Yes, yes I will, won't I?' I can't stop smiling.

'You know there's always a job for you back with me. You could move out front now if you like, Kimberly won't mind,' she says.

'Oh, thanks, Betty, but you know, this is home now. But give everyone my love, Brian and Adrian too. Tell them I send them all the luck in the world.'

'Will do, lovely,' she beams back and rolls off to the bar.

'How about some music?' Patsy comes out with his mandolin. Padraig follows with a fiddle. Lily's got a squeeze box.

'Sean, you up for it?' Patsy calls.

Sean checks to see I'm OK then goes off to get his guitar. I sit down at one of the tables outside the barn.

'What you need is a nice cup of tea,' says Rosie, and puts one down in front of me.

'Thanks, Rosie.'

'No, thank you. This is all down to you. You've given my kids their community back, something to bring their kids back to.'

I look out again at the children playing, the families

walking across the bay. Freddie, Mercury and our newest arrival are enjoying their jobs, no longer redundant, and Grandad is feeling much the same, I'd say. If only there was a way to keep this going. The band strikes up and Sean is on stage playing with them.

Maybe there is—

'So, looks like you're staying,' Nancy interrupts my thoughts.

'Looks that way,' I say, and sip the tea.

She sniffs.

'Y'know what, Nancy? You need to learn that oysters are more than just a way to make money. They're food and they're fun.' I grab a tray of oysters from one of the tables and thrust it at her. 'Try one. And chew, don't just swallow!' I instruct.

Just then Seamus and Padraig appear with Freddie.

'Nancy's just leaving. Perhaps you could see her off. But I think she wants to see the oyster beds before she goes.' I find myself smiling.

'Righto,' they say with a tip of the hat, not listening to any of her protestations and instructing her to roll up her trouser legs before lifting her onto Freddie's back and trekking her across the wet, soft, grey sand to show her where the oysters are grown. I don't think the sight of an ashen-faced Nancy being led along on a donkey, clinging on for dear life, will ever leave me.

'So what do you think about Connemara lamb, see a market for it abroad?' I hear Seamus and Padraig asking her as they lead her back up the shore, past a laughing audience to her car. She has a face like thunder.

'I hear Scotland has some very good oyster farms,' I call

after her as the BMW flies down the lane for what we hope is the last time.

Perfect. Everything is perfect, I think, as I stand and look out at the sight of the busy festival, just as my head starts to swim, spots appear before my eyes, I feel myself reeling, and then darkness descends.

Chapter Forty-nine

Bang, bang, bang.

I have no idea what's going on but it's making the whole barn shake. I stand up from bending over the red-and-white-check-covered tables that are spread out across the barn like a chessboard. I rub my big round pregnancy bump and retie my apron strings above it. I look out of the window. The sun always shines in April, according to Rosie. April and September apparently. And she's right. It shone for our September festival and it's shining again now through the windows of the barn. The light bounces off the newly whitewashed walls. At one end the big fire is crackling and spitting; despite the sunshine outside, it brings light and warmth inside.

'Right, you, time to put your feet up,' Sean comes in carrying a hammer.

'But there's so much to do before tonight,' I say, but can't resist sitting on the nearest bench.

'It's an end-of-season party, not a chance for you to have another fainting fit,' says Sean. He's right of course.

When I came round from the last one, I was in Sean's bed.

Seven months earlier

'I thought you'd be more comfortable in here. I can take the other room if you like.' Sean's holding my hand and right next to him is Grace. He strokes my head.

'Fiona, I'm the doctor,' says the man by the door. 'Look, I'm not sure why you fainted, but I need to ask, is there any chance you could be pregnant?'

Sean and I look at each other wide-eyed. I've been so busy, I just haven't thought . . .

The doctor hands me a sealed packet and withdraws diplomatically to the kitchen.

'Look, I don't want you to feel sorry for me or feel I'm trapping you. If I am, that is. You're one of life's free spirits. I'll be fine on my own. I'll stay in Rosie's chalet once Dan and Margaret have left.' My mouth's dry. I gabble, 'I didn't think I could . . .' I'm welling up. 'I was trapped because I was too scared just to be me. But I'm not any more,' I smile, and even laugh a bit. He puts a finger to my lips.

'No, neither am I.' His face breaks into a smile and tears fill the corners of his eyes. 'You taught me to love again, to trust again, to not be afraid. And now I've never wanted anything more,' he says, and kisses my forehead. 'So just do the test.' He helps me towards the bathroom.

'You need to rest,' says the doctor, once I'm back in bed, 'take things easy for a while. Women in the early stages of pregnancy need to look after themselves.' He smiles, picking up his bag. 'But I can see you're in good hands.' He smiles again and nods at Sean and then turns to leave.

'Thank you, doctor.'

'No, thank you. It's been a wonderful day. Lovely to have the community spirit back again,' he says. 'Now everything is fine, but just take it easy. Rest,' he instructs, and leaves.

'I will.' And frankly I can't do anything else. Sean climbs into the bed beside me and wraps his arms around me and finally I know I've stopped running for good.

Epilogue

I pick up the cup of tea Lily has made me and go outside to sit in the sun. I look up at the sign above the door: 'The Wild Oyster Shack'.

'Look, we have plenty of help getting ready for tonight,' Sean reassures me. 'Lily's laying up the restaurant. Seamus and Padraig are going to help me bring in the last of the native oysters. Grandad's coming up later to do some story-telling and man the visitors' centre. The donkeys are ready to do some rides. Evelyn's sending up more fishcakes and going to work the kitchen. Maire is going to decorate and put up some new paintings. It's all sorted. So . . . come with me, I have something to show you.' He leads me to the edge of the green grass in front of the barn and then turns me round. I'm looking at the barn. It looks the same, red front door, whitewashed walls and window frames, flowers in the window boxes, and it takes me a while to spot the blue plaque beside the door frame.

'Huh!' I take a sharp intake of breath and my hand shoots up to cover my nose and mouth in surprise.

'We got it!' I shout, and hug Sean.

'You did, you mean. All of this is down to you, Fi. It was you who saved the oysters and it was you who thought we could bring the customers to the farm. You're the face of The Wild Oyster Shack. It's you they've awarded New Restaurant of the Year to. It arrived this morning.' He beams at me and I hear myself letting out a little squeal and jumping up and down, which isn't a good idea, so I stop and just hold my hand over my face with excitement.

'Now, tonight we're going to have a party. It's going to be great. But then the oysters will be out of season and it'll be time to put your feet up. Promise?'

I nod. 'Promise. Good job Betty's finally retiring and coming out to spend some time with Grandad. She'll be so useful for babysitting come September.'

'What, when the restaurant reopens?'

'When I compete to hold on to my shell-shucking title!'

Sean takes me in his arms and kisses me and then he takes something out of his pocket. It's a small black box. He opens the box and takes out a pearl ring. He holds it out to me.

'It's the one from your necklace. I had it made into a ring.'

The tears are rolling steadily down my face, as they often do these days.

'I wanted you to have it to remind you of the day we made our own little pearl.' He puts his hand on my big bump. 'If you like,' he clears his throat, 'we could make it an engagement ring . . .'

I take the ring.

'Y'know what? I don't need to marry you to know that we'll always be together. I don't need a big dress or a piece of paper. I love you.'

Sean's eyes wrinkle at the edges as he smiles. I take one more look out over the bay. Seamus and Padraig are out in the boat, arguing about who's steering.

'And I've only just found Fiona Clutterbuck. Would you mind very much if I stayed being me? I don't need to change my name to know where I belong any more.' Grace nudges my legs and the donkeys start braying with all their might. 'But I wouldn't say no to a christening party once baby Pearl is born.' I've come out of my shell and I'm not going back in. Sean slides the ring up my finger and kisses me long and slow—

'Oh no! Who the feck let the donkeys out?' he shouts as he pulls away from me. 'Oh, don't tell me there's another one.' Sean marches off to the donkey field and I can't help laughing. I'm not so much at the end of the earth any more, but at the centre of the universe, my universe, Fiona Clutterbuck's.

Acknowledgements

It is because of the faith and friendship I have found through the Romantic Novelists Association that I finally wrote my book.

Thank you to Hazel and the team at Accent Press for first breathing life into *The Oyster Catcher*. Hannah Ferguson, thank you for listening to your 'gut instincts', taking me on and being a fab agent. And thank you Emily Griffin at Headline for loving the book and coming to find me – and to the Headline team for making me so welcome.

I have had so many words of support and encouragement on the way to finishing this book, from Anita Burgh who told me I could do it in the first place and suggested I join the RNA. Thank you, Annie. Thanks to Veronica Henry and Jane Wenham-Jones for pushing me towards the finish line. But biggest thanks of all to Katie Fforde for her constant faith in me and for the fabulous road trips.

Thank you too to Janie and Mike, for the times I've stayed at Chez Castillon on writers' retreats and courses. Thank you for the fun and the head space.

I couldn't have written a book about oysters without learning about them, so thank you, David, for your time and for showing me how it's done. I will never forget my oyster research . . . or the rain!

And finally to the Thomas family at home. For the tea, the gin, the cuddles and for coming on the journey with me. Thank you all for making it happen.

Now read on for an extract from Jo Thomas's brand-new romantic novel

The Olive Branch

Available in ebook from February 2015
and in paperback from May 2015.

Go to www.headline.co.uk
to find out more

Prologue

My hand hovers over the mouse. My heart is pumping and I'm not sure if it's the Prosecco we've drunk or pure madness racing through my veins.

I take in the bare room around me. It's soulless, empty of furniture and feelings. I look at my friend, Morag, her eyes bright with excitement. The clock is ticking and, with every passing second, my heart beats louder.

'Ten, nine . . .' the timer clicks down. My mouth is dry.

'Eight, seven . . .' I feel sick, again not sure if it's due to Prosecco or tension. This is insane.

'Six, five . . .' but then again, so are my surroundings. I look around the place I once called home – now an empty shell, like me.

'Four, three . . .' I consider my options. There's only one as far as I'm concerned. 'Two...' And it's utterly reckless.

'One.' I glance at Morag who looks as though she might burst and I don't know if I do it intentionally or if my finger just twitches involuntary. But I press the button and we fall, giggling, into a Prosecco-fuelled slumber on the lumpy settees.

The next morning, after Paracetamol and gallons of water have started to take effect, a slow realisation creeps over me like cold custard. I rush to the computer and check my emails.

There it is in black and white, bringing back my moment of madness and reminding me of why it should be compulsory to take a breathalyzer test before using the Internet late at night. *'Congratulations! You were the successful bidder!'* My heart jumps into my mouth and bangs noisily against my ears.

Now what am I going to do?!

My panicked thoughts are interrupted by a knock at the door and, as I stumble across the room to open it, my heart thunders some more.

'Hi, we've come for the sofas,' says a bright, well-spoken young woman with her eager boyfriend. I look at the couch where Morag is still sleeping.

'We'll just be a moment. I'm nearly done here,' I say as the young, eager couple start lifting the sofa that had been my bed just a few minutes ago.

There's only one thing I can do, says the mad, impetuous voice in my head again. And I realise it's mine.

Chapter One

As I watch the goat marching up and down the courtyard like a foot guard at Buckingham Palace, I wonder if I've bitten off more than I can chew.

'Recalculating! Recalculating!' My sole companion for the entire journey shouts, her voice cutting through me like a dentist's drill. I switch her off firmly, with pleasure, before turning off the engine of my little Ford Ka. The windscreen wipers let out an exhausted whine and the screen is a whiteout of water in seconds, like fake rain in a low-budget film. Only this is not fake. It's very real, I remind myself, as the water drums noisily on the car roof.

I take a deep breath. It's been like this ever since I left Bari, the sprawling port at the top of Italy's 'heel' where I'd stopped off to do a quick shop in Ikea for essentials and lunch. This is another thing I wasn't expecting aside from the goat: torrential rain during summer in Southern Italy.

I gaze out of the car window and pull my light-weight hoodie closer around me. A collection of silver bangles jangle on my wrist and I look down at my Rolling Stones T-shirt, which I'd cut into a crop top, and my paint-splattered ripped-off Levi's. I'm definitely underdressed. Grabbing my favourite vintage leather jacket from the seat beside me, I pull it on and shiver. I should be in waterproofs and wellies.

Taking another deep breath I pull the handle and push the car door open against the driving rain. I straighten myself up, holding one hand over my eyes, and shiver again as I look down at the envelope in my hand. The rain lashes against the paper, making the ink run, and I have to keep shutting my eyes against the deluge. The goat looks in my direction and I'm sure I hear it snort.

I use one hand to shield my eyes and strain to look at the house in front of me, then I turn back and try to focus on the long, pot-holed drive I've just driven down. I can hardly see the big stone pillars and red metal gates at the entrance. I pull out a printed picture of the house and shove the envelope back in my pocket. The image turns to papier-mâché in seconds, disintegrating and landing on the wet, worn stones at my feet. If I'm not quick, my canvas slip-ons will go the same way. This has to be the right place; there's nowhere similar nearby.

I'd passed a couple of small houses on the way as the narrow road had led me up and down and round and round like a fairground ride, with occasional pot holes for added fear factor. Some of the houses had had curved roofs, while others had been modern and flat-roofed. I had also spotted the occasional collection of dilapidated trulli – small circular houses with cone-shaped roofs, like clusters of field mushrooms, held behind crumbling walls. But I'm not looking for a trullo. The house before me now is like something from a film set. It's old, weather-worn, faded pink and big – much bigger than I'd imagined. There's nothing else like it on the lane. This must be it.

I hold my hand up against the punishing rain, and half wonder whether a plague of locusts is going to follow next.

Perhaps this is a sign . . . I push the silly thought away, along with the memory of my mum's despairing phone messages and Ed's disapproving emails.

My T-shirt is stuck to my skin and the rain is dripping down my short hair and on to my face, running off round my nose stud like a little waterfall. There's no point rummaging in the boot for my rain coat now, so I sling on my lavender leather satchel and wonder what I've let myself in for. I could get back in the car, drive away from here as quickly as possible and email Ed to tell him he was right all along: I am daft, impetuous and irresponsible.

But at least I'm not boring and stuck in my ways. There's only one way to go: forwards! I bow my head, pull my bag tighter towards me and I run towards the listing veranda groaning with an unruly and neglected bougainvillea.

With my chin tucked into my chest, I spot a large pot hole just before the front door and side step it, slipping and skidding on the cobbles. I'm now startlingly close to the cross-looking goat standing across the front door. I shudder, like I've just arrived into the middle of my worst nightmare.

'Maah,' the goat bleats, making me jump. God, that was loud. I stare at the goat and it stares straight back at me. Its eyes are different colours: one scarily yellow, and the other blue. For the first time in weeks, I have no idea what to do. Guarding goats was not on my list of essential information. I wonder whether 'shoo' has the same meaning in Italian as it does in English. It's not something I can remember covering in my evening classes. But I need to do something – I'm freezing out here.

'Shoo, shoo!' I say, waving my hands in its direction and backing away at the same time. I don't want it to run at me with its horns, which look pointy and sharp. You don't get goats standing in the way of your front door back in Tooting. The odd drunk camping out for the night, maybe, but somehow they seem easier to overcome than this.

'Shoo, shoo!' I try again, this time with more hand-waving. The goat flinches, as do the terrified butterflies in my stomach, but still it doesn't move from its position in front of the big, dark, wooden door. Even the long, three-day drive down through France and Italy, with stop-offs in laybys to catch forty winks and only an irritating Sat Nav for company, is nothing compared to this.

I've spent the past six weeks dealing with estate agents, house viewings and solicitors, packing up and dividing the belongings Ed and I had shared. I'd separated everything out and had even given over custody of our record collection and the player I found on eBay. I'd sold off redundant furniture, overseen its collection and moved myself out of our flat. I'd planned it all to a tee without a hitch; nothing had fazed me. But territorial goats? No idea! I throw my hands up and turn my back to it.

Opening up my satchel, I search around for some kind of magic bean that will help me out. Then I spot it: a half-eaten Kit Kat I'd bought in a service station somewhere outside Rome. I'd thought the sugar boost might get me round the greater ring road – that and Dolly Parton on the CD player. It had sort-of worked. I'd got round on a wing and a prayer, nerves jangling, heart in mouth, high on energy drinks and with a lot of hand gestures and horn honking – not necessarily mine. I pull out the Kit Kat and wave it at the goat. It steadfastly ignores me, looking the other way from its sheltered position. I quickly pull back the wrapper.

'Come on. It's chocolate.' I wave the Kit Kat, immediately feeling like The Child Catcher in *Chitty Chitty Bang Bang*, and break off a piece to toss in front of the goat. As it backs away I think I'm going to have to give up and find somewhere else to stay until I can find the bloomin' owner. Then it sniffs at the taster, snaffles it up with appreciative noises and starts walking towards me, no doubt hoping for more.

'See, it's good,' I break off another bit, tossing it in front of the goat which is now moving faster and faster while I walk backwards, getting quicker all the time. I feel I'm in a scene from *You've Been Framed*. I'm miles away from home in the heaviest rain I've ever seen, with my worldly possessions in a Ford Ka, trying to tempt a goat away from a front door with half a Kit Kat. I'm beginning to know how Noah felt, and I'm debating whether there would be room for goats on my arc. *This is all Ed's fault!* I think irrationally.

The goat keeps hoovering up the Kit Kat and I'm nearly at the end of the slippery stone forecourt. I step back and my heel hits a low stone wall, giving me a reality check. There's nothing for it: it's now or never. I throw the last piece of Kit Kat as far as I can, beyond the uneven cobbles. The goat turns and nearly topples over in its excitement to reach it, slipping, sliding and clattering across the stones before leaping on the tasty treat.

I throw myself towards the front door, pulling out the key. My hands shake as I push the big, rusting key into the lock whilst trying to keep one eye on the goat. I drop the envelope onto the wet floor, pick it up and then push really hard against the door. It doesn't budge. The goat is trotting towards me. I pull back, dip my shoulder and give the door an almighty shove. It flies open just as there is a huge crash of thunder and a silver sliver of lightening cracks across the sky. Desperate to escape the elements, I fall in through the front door into a big cavernous room, and the goat follows.

'Maah' it bleats loudly, dripping all over the floor. A great wave of despair washes over me. What on earth have I let myself in for?

The Olive Branch

JO THOMAS

It's amazing what you can buy online: memorabilia, fashion accessories, a crumbling Italian farmhouse . . .

After a Prosecco-fuelled girls' night in gets out of hand, Ruthie Collins awakes to discover that she has bid for her dream Italian home online – and won. Just out of a relationship, a new start is just what Ruthie needs. Anything is better than sleeping on her mum's settee.

But arriving in Southern Italy, she realises she doesn't know the first thing about running an olive farm. And with her new neighbours, the tempestuous Marco Bellanouvo and his fiery family, to contend with, all Ruthie wants is to go back home.

Life can change with the touch of a button. But all good things – friendship, romance, and even the olice harvest – take time to grow. Can Ruthie finally put the past to rest, and find her own piece of the Dolce Vita along the way?

Ebook: 978 1 4722 3692 1
Paperback: 978 1 4722 2370 8

The Chestnut Tree

JO THOMAS

A wonderfully funny and romantic short story by Jo Thomas, kindle bestselling author of *The Oyster Catcher*, available exclusively in ebook.

When Ellie Russet leaves home and her restaurant in the wake of disaster to housesit in the Kent countryside, the last thing she wants to do is cook for a living – ever again.

Ellie's new neighbour, Daniel Fender, is struggling to make ends meet as a furniture maker. Could the answer to his problems lie in the chestnut orchard at the bottom of the garden?

Only Ellie can help Daniel unlock the delicious secret that will bring them the fresh start they need. And as autumn approaches, romance will blossom amid the glowing embers of the chestnut fire . . .

ISBN: 978 1 4722 2375 3